HUNTER AND THE SKY-TOPS

It is not a time for slow thinking and Jason is not the sort to be wishy-washy about anything, especially with a sawtooth about to drop out of the sky and slaughter them. He takes no time to think, in his dreams and his games of pretend he has faced dragons and demons of every sort and he knows what to do. He is a trained archer. He is a master marks-man, even though he is only fourteen years old. Age has little to do with slaying dragons or flying dinosaurs for that matter. Courage and skill are what count at this moment—far more than age. Jason is going to kill the sawtooth and there is no back up in him.

Grabbing the bow from his back he shouts, "Hunter, run, get down under the ledge. Hurry! Go as deep as you can and stay there."

Topper takes Hunter by the back of his pants and lifts him over the rough ground and pokes him under the ledge before turning to defend him. Race is frantic in his cries and wants to jump into the air, but is reluctant to leave Jason alone on the cliff. He takes great bouncing leaps, his screams enough to terrify even the bravest of souls.

"Race, stop! You have to wait—let me get some arrows in him first. Then you can have him." Setting an arrow he draws the bow, "I have to stop him. Don't get in my way,"

Published by
Gwyder Studio
4710 Kannah Creek Road
Whitewater, Colorado 81527
gwyderstudios@gmail.com

All rights reserved
Printed in the United States of America
Library of Congress Control Number: 2011941964
ISBN 978-0-9827666-1-3

Cover Design and Painting by CaMary Wynne

HUNTER
AND THE SKY-TOPS

Merry Christmas
Mother!

Camary :)

CAMARY WYNNE

For Our Grandsons

HUNTER
AND THE SKY-TOPS

Chapter 1

THE SKY-TOP

The sun is high over the ragged canyon and there are no longer deep shadows in the valley below. A small herd of mountain sheep graze contentedly beside the busy stream, now swollen with spring run-off, and a graceful hawk circles looking for his next meal. All is peaceful and quiet except for the pleasant sounds of nature. Then a hollow strange sound comes from the mouth of a cave hidden in the pocked marked canyon wall. The sound comes again just as an adventurous field mouse scurries across the oversized opening. He stops to peer into the depths of the dark interior before hurrying on. The sounds are louder now and he quickly darts into a well used crevasse and follows a tiny trail leading toward the rim of the cliff above. Once on top he leans over the edge and watches, and is just in time to see a sky-top emerge from the mouth of the cave beneath him. For a moment the mammoth bird hesitates, then turns back and stops. Turning around several times, he seems to be confused for some reason. Perhaps he's worried, although for a creature the size of a small elephant to be worried or frightened seems rather preposterous.

Standing on his hind legs, the field mouse continues to watch the sky-top. He squeaks his encouragement, trying to help the monstrous bird make up his mind and quit turning in circles. *Why doesn't he leap from the shelf and fly away?* the field mouse wonders. Seconds later he is rewarded as the sky-top spreads his great wings and leaps from the cliff. There is a sudden thrust of air as the huge bird rises, his powerful wings whipping with wide sweeping strokes. Slowly he begins to climb higher and higher. Then a swift air current lifts him and he levels out with his wings stretched to their full extent—he's motionless. He seems to glide and rest on nothing. Then his wings begin to sweep the air once again and very soon he is only a small speck on the far horizon. With a little jump of excitement, the field mouse squeaks his delight and watches until the gigantic bird is out of sight, then with a satisfied sigh he hurries on his way.

While the field mouse is quite content, this is not the case with the young sky-top that has just left the safety of his cave. He has a very tight feeling deep inside and has chosen to ignore the feeling. This is not the first time he's flown off without out telling his parents where he's going. No, he's been flying into forbidden territory for several months now. He wanted to see what people looked like, and had let his curiosity get the best of him. He'd flown many miles beyond what he knew to be safe boundaries and discovered a lovely valley with people. There are two little boys who live in this valley and he loves to watch them play. They know how to have a good time and it is such fun to hear them laugh. Somehow the young sky-top is sure the boys would like to fly and he wants very much to carry them through the clouds and hear their laughter. Many times he's watched them play and nothing has ever gone wrong, so why the strange scary feeling today?

The sky-top shakes his long ugly head side-to-side trying to rid himself of the creepy feeling. He flies faster hoping to leave the heavy sick tightness behind, but it doesn't work. Right now he doesn't want to think about all the things his parents have told him about being safe, and careful, and staying out of trouble. He argues, *They never have any fun—they don't know what they are missing. People are so cool, I don't see why we are to stay away from them.* A wave of tight, horrible fear causes him to search the skies around him and hear again his father's warning. More than once, he's been told whenever he feels a wave of fear or worry he'd better pay attention. He's been taught that these feelings are warnings and are vital to his safety. Looking back he wonders, *Maybe something really is wrong—but it's always been safe before,* he argues with his feelings and chooses not to turn back.

Some call these feelings intuition, or conscience, or perhaps promptings. While these promptings are rather difficult to explain or understand, one thing is most certain, these feelings are real and the sky-top has chosen to ignore them. Instead of turning back he flies faster and faster and in time he lands on the edge of a sun baked cliff overlooking a rich green valley. There is a forest of ancient timber crowded against the base of the cliff with a swift moving stream running over the rough rock surface up on top not too far from where the sky-top stands as he studies the valley below. The rushing water roars and complains as it plummets over the cliff edge and crashes into a cold clear pool near the dense forest, before hurrying on through the meadows and farmland surrounding what is known as Lynn Farm. The mist from the falls makes this place on the cliff cool and comfortable even on the hottest of summer days.

Looking down on the Lynn home, and farm buildings, the sky-top sighs, still wondering over the fear he feels. His confused mind argues, *It is so beautiful here and it is such fun to watch the humans.* It's still and quiet today. Not one human is in sight. *Where is everybody—surely the boys will come out today,* his thoughts wander as he settles himself down on the warm stone rim to wait. He doesn't know the Lynns have all gone into the little town of Glendale to spend the day and won't be home until late this night.

Searching the skies the sky-top finds them empty and wonders, *So why do I feel something is really wrong?* Foolishly he chooses to ignore the warnings and stretches out on the warm sandstone making himself as invisible as is possible for a bird the size of a tall hippopotamus. Here he waits and watches. An hour passes, two hours, he sleeps and sleeps, the sun is low and cool when he raises his head and yawns. Pushing himself to his feet he stands his very tallest, and stretches his wings, and sighs—it's time for him to go home, he doesn't want his parents to worry. As he gives a final glance down at the farm, an immense shadow passes over him and jerking his head up and around he sees a sawtooth, his one and only real enemy. The sawtooth has seen him and turns back, already its claws are extended and he rips the air with his savage teeth, screaming his challenge.

How careless the sky-top had been to move before checking the skies. He knew better. How stupid he'd been to ignore the warning feelings. Now it's too late and with a mighty thrust he leaps into the air. Height and speed are his only defense and he whips the air with great thrusts gaining speed with every stroke. Higher and higher he climbs, every second counts. The sawtooth screams again and the young sky-top glances back knowing his chances are slim. He's seen several sawtooth battles and knows a single sky-top has one chance, and that is to run. His heart pounds as he wishes he was armed with claws and teeth like the dreaded sawtooths. Run, he knows he must get away. Frantically he strains against the air, while razor sharp teeth snap at his feet and he rolls out of the way, loosing precious altitude. It is a wild scramble of dodging, and twisting, all while fighting for speed and height. Up and down the peaceful valley the young sky-top darts, in a zigzag course hoping for a miracle. Then for a brief moment the sawtooth seems to back off. Glancing back the sky-top sees the sawtooth climbing over him and he fights for more speed. When the sawtooth dives, he misses as the young sky-top rolls toward the cliff, in a desperate effort to dodge the deadly talons. One of the sky-top's wings scraps against the jagged rock and he falters. Pinned as he is against the cliff wall, he has no room to maneuver. He is fast, very fast, and the sawtooth can't quite overtake him and snaps at his feet just missing again and again. With a terrific lunge the sawtooth grabs one of the sky-top's feet and yanks him back. As the sky-top feels himself being hurled backwards he twists in the air and their immense wings tangle. For a sickening second the sawtooth's wicked talons sink into the sky-top's back, and with a terrible cry of pain and fury, he breaks away and falls into the heavy timber beneath the base of the cliff, near the waterfall and pool above Lynn Farm.

For a moment the sawtooth fights with the air, his enormous wings pounding in the attempt to avoid crashing into the timber after the wounded sky-top. Recovering from the tumbled fall he slowly circles up—all is still as he watches for the sky-top to come out of the trees. He doesn't know the young bird is caught and hangs suspended in a tangle of limbs and vines within the heavy timber. Great vines and creepers loop up and around through the tops of the trees, tying them together in an unbroken web. It is into these the sky-top has fallen and is now a hopeless prisoner.

Puzzled as to where the sky-top might be, the sawtooth lands on the edge of the cliff and stares down into the dense foliage, looking for his prey. It is as if the trees had swallowed his victim. The only hint of the sky-top's fall is a slight hole in the midst of the mass of green. Nothing moves, not even a sound. Only the steady roar of the waterfall and the wind playing in the leaves beneath him can be heard.

Down in the maze of tangled limbs and branches the sky-top hangs in a net of twisted vines. His vast wings are held fast in a literal snarl of green. A fleeting moment of joy in his deliverance gives him hope for his future existence as he peers through his leafy refuge and sees the sawtooth on the cliff above. He knows he hasn't a chance of survival if the sawtooth decides to come down and tear him apart. He knows what sawtooths do to sky-tops when they catch one, and the thought isn't pretty.

Holding very still he hopes the sawtooth will choose to fly on—if he doesn't, all chances of escape are gone. After a few minutes he watches through the mass of green and sees the sawtooth glide from the cliff, then hears him land with a light "plop" somewhere not too far away. The sawtooth's ugly voice growls and screeches as he tries to force his way through the dense growth of trees and brush. Finding the wall of timber and tangled growth to be similar to a giant wall of rose bushes, he bellows in cursing anger. Bushes shake, and the trees shudder as he batters the wall of vegetation, and the sky-top feels himself slipping, and the vines growing tighter and tighter. One wing feels as if it will surely break.

Minutes pass and the sawtooth paces the outer edge of the tangled timber while the vines and branches holding the sky-top dig painfully into his wings and body. He can't hold still much longer, his back is numb with throbbing pain and he feels as if he will be pulled apart with his body pulling against his suspended wings. Little by little the sky-top moves and tries to ease the tension on the vines and branches, but nothing seems to help. When he feels sure his wings will break at any moment, he hears the sawtooth screech as he takes to the air. The sky-top watches through the leafy canopy and sees the sawtooth circle and disappear. Heaving a sigh of relief he begins to fight against the vines and branches holding him. It is a terrible battle and as he fights and snaps at the vines, he only tangles himself worse. The large branches begin to break, first one here, then another there, and he drops down and down, each time rather than falling free, the vines become tighter. Rolling and twisting he falls the last few feet and his long head and part of his neck and body hit the ground giving slight relief.

As night closes over the forest of old trees, the sky-top calls loud with great trumpeting sounds which echo round the valley, but the Lynns aren't home to hear. The sky-top hopes his father will hear and come, although he knows the distance is too far, and his father has no idea where he is. How foolish he had been to think he could watch the humans without being seen by the fearsome sawtooths. He'd gotten away with his adventure over the western mountains for weeks, *Why today?* he wonders. Giving the vines holding him another violent thrashing, several more branches break and his body rests a little more easily on the ground, but his wings are still snarled amid the vines and branches. Blood drips from one of his legs and runs in oozing rivulets from the wounds in his back.

He stops, gasping for air, his heart pounding, his immense beak open, his mouth dry. The sound of the waterfall reminds him of how long it has been since he's had any water. He can smell the moisture and feel its coolness in the evening air, and a tragic wave of hopelessness makes him whine a soft cry. He wonders if the little boys would help if they knew he needed them. Then he remembers humans shoot sky-tops with sharp pointed sticks they call arrows.

Why, oh why, hadn't he been obedient to the sky-top rules and stayed away from the valley of humans? He'd been told so many times to stay away, not only because of the human's fear of sky-tops, but also because the deadly sawtooths were always prowling around wherever humans lived.

Too late he decides he will never ever again break another sky-top rule. It's with these thoughts he fades off into exhausted, almost unconscious sleep.

Chapter 2

TOPPER

The following morning, as the sun raises high over the valley, ten year old, bright eyed Hunter Lynn sits near the stream not too far from the base of the cliff and the noisy waterfall. It is a beautiful day and the mid-day sun shines through the waterfall mist and makes rainbows of color. But Hunter doesn't notice; he is too busy digging. He's spent hours creating a big sand castle, a stick-and-mud village with miniature roads, canals, and a tiny lake where his carefully made little wooden boats wait to navigate the winding canal. Dexter, his big yellow dog, is asleep for the moment, but from time to time his big furry tail "thump, thump, thumps," in the rich smelling sand.

Dexter probably needs the sleep, he'd spent most of the night barking. There had been strange sounds wailing in the night making echoes off the canyon wall. The sounds had about driven Dexter crazy. What with Dexter's barking, and the weird moaning sounds drifting over the valley, Hunter's father had been up most of the night. He'd been a bit upset because he never found where the sounds came from. Things are okay now though, the strange sounds are gone and the warm sun and perfect digging sand makes everything feel just right to Hunter.

This sandy beach is one of his favorite places. He likes to pretend he is his father, Ruston Lynn, who builds things like houses, barns, roads, and canals. Hunter can build just about anything here in the damp, earthy smelling sand. Here, his creative imagination knows no limit. While big powerful horses harnessed to all kinds of equipment move his father's dirt and huge wagons and things, Hunter moves the dirt with his hands and a few crude tools. Someday, he knows he will be old enough to drive his father's big teams of horses and then he will be able to help with the building projects, or the plowing and planting. Right now he is a bit too small for big heavy work—but that's okay, he knows he will grow and his mother says he shouldn't hurry growing up.

A few careful scoops of sand and gravel, and a waterway opens from the rushing stream and begins to fill the little canals. With smiling satisfaction, Hunter watches the water reach his lake and his tiny fleet of ships begin to bob in the rising water. Hunter is a builder, a creator at heart, just like his father. He knows if he has designed his canals right, the water will flow all the way through his labyrinth right back into the stream. Will it flow the way he planned today? When the water reaches the big stream and flows back from where it came, Hunter gives a gleeful shout and Dexter looks up at his young master. With a lazy stretch, he yawns and trots to Hunter's side smashing roads and waterways every step of his way.

"AHHHHH! Dexter, you awful dog!" Water now spills through a smashed dam and floods his tiny village. Dexter sits on the edge of Hunter's building site and scratches a spot behind an itching ear. "Now see what you've done. What am I ever going to do with you? Mom says you do some of these things on purpose. Do you like to have me yell at you?" Turning, Hunter glares with clenched fists at Dexter who is not in the least concerned with his small master's anger. "Go on now, go some place else. This is off limits." Dexter lowers his head, cocking it first one way then the other. "Do I have to throw rocks at you to make you go away?" Hunter tries to look mean and angry, but falls rather short of it, his face a mixture of comical anger, a bit of laughter, and more than a little love. With a sigh, Dexter stretches out on the warm sand and closes his eyes. A breeze shifts a swirl of misty spray from the waterfall and fills the air with cool moisture. "Thump, thump, thump," goes Dexter's tail.

"That's better," Hunter mutters half to himself. "Now if you will just stay asleep maybe I can fix the mess you've made." Scratching the top of his dusty brown hair with a sand-covered hand, Hunter returns to his knees and begins pushing sand and easing the wayward water back into the neat channels while the little boats bob on the tiny lake, waiting to set sail on the damaged waterways.

A big bumble bee buzzes overhead and Hunter swats at it, his eyes never leaving the progress of his water—no problems. Making the dam a little stronger, he widens a narrow cut and places a, now muddy, hand on his cheek. An eagle calls from far overhead, its shadow circles the beach and the cry comes again. Dexter blinks a sleepy eye open and lifts his big head. For a moment he studies Hunter and decides, *Better not bother him,* as he stretches to his feet and wanders closer to the stream. "Sniff, sniff," an interesting smell from the sand has his attention. Placing his nose into the wet sand, the smell is most fascinating. A big paw scrapes the sand and a new hole begins. Digging just happens to be one of Dexter's favorite pastimes. He huffs and puffs as his front paws send great stinging showers of sand out from between his hind legs. Soon his head and shoulders are out of sight and only his rear end pokes out of his hole. Sand flies in every direction and Hunter is peppered with the stinging missiles. Then a large clod of wet smelly sand smashes Hunter right in the face. "Ahhh, if you don't quit throwing dirt all over me I'll send you home!" But Dexter doesn't seem concerned about the suggested consequence and digs with even more enthusiasm.

Spitting out a mouthful of sand, Hunter gathers up a wad of mud and smacks Dexter right in the backside—no reaction. The big dog doesn't seem to care that he now has a blob of mud on his rump, "Silly dog," Hunter comments to no one in particular. In an impish moment of play, he turns his backside toward his busy dog and likewise begins to dig and paw with his hands sending an explosion of soft sand between his legs, all over Dexter.

Now this is a new situation—digging and throwing sand Dexter understands. To a dog's way of thinking there must be something quite special about the place Hunter has chosen to dig or Hunter wouldn't be digging there, and Hunter always knows what's best. So with two huge bounds Dexter lands at Hunter's side, shoves him out of the way, and proceeds to make the hole bigger.

"Dexter!" Laughing and shouting, Hunter gives his dog a playful shove. With a mighty leap in the air, Dexter begins racing in frantic circles. "Go, Dexter! Faster! Faster, big boy," Hunter's voice echoes off the towering cliff and over the roar of the falls. Rocking back on his small heels he watches Dexter run with his pink tongue hanging out of the side of his mouth, almost seeming to smile. In and out of the water he runs. Making a last splashing run through the water he races up the bank, right to Hunter's side. There he stops and shakes his big hairy body.

Water splatters in every direction, especially all over Hunter. "Dexter! Mother is right, you do some of these yucky things on purpose." A big lick across his faces shuts Hunter's mouth, "Yuck!" he sputters, as he wipes his face on a dirty sleeve. Looking up at the sun for a moment, he squints his bright blue eyes turning them into narrow slits. "It's past noon and I'm hungry. I wonder what Mom packed for me to eat?" Hunter mumbles more to himself than to Dexter as he wanders over to where he'd left his back pack. Making a feeble attempt to shake the sand from his clothes he doesn't worry over the fact his hands and face are still smeared with dirt and grime. Since no one is around to remind him, he searches with his grimy hands through the goodies his mother had packed for him, and seems very pleased.

"Ummmm, sausage and rolls, this one has jam inside. Thank you, thank you Mom." Dexter moves in closer, hoping for a handout. "I'll give you a bite; only one little bite." Hunter hands Dexter a small corner of one of his rolls and the big dog pushes closer. "Dexter—back off!" Hunter growls and Dexter puts his head down and sulks away. Watching Dexter out of the corner of his eye, Hunter enjoys his lunch and eats every crumb. After licking his fingers he stretches out on the sand and closes his eyes. His rest is rather short because a large trout jumps out of the water after a tasty fly—SPLASH—Dexter lands with a flying leap in the water, right in front of Hunter who is now very wet. Hunter's eyes sting and he blinks as the water runs down his forehead. With a dirty hand, he wipes his face and leaves a smear of sandy mud. For a moment he stares at his ridiculous dog, who runs and leaps in great circles around his canals and castles. Rubbing the top of his head, Hunter makes his hair stand on end, then with a little giggle he shakes all over, just like Dexter, only it doesn't work—he is still quite wet. "Oh, well," he laughs a little laugh and reaches to pick up the biggest of his ships and ties a long string to its mast. Setting the ship in the edge of the stream he watches it work its way out into the rushing water. As he pulls his reluctant little craft back upstream, Dexter crosses the stream and sniffs around the edge of the massive thicket that encompasses the forest of ancient trees along the base of the cliff.

On Hunter's side it's sandy as a beach should be. The pasture grass with beautiful green clover grows right down to the bank of sand where Hunter likes to play. The far side of the stream is very different; it's a jumble of huge trees and tangled brush, vines, and branches. Playing over there isn't any fun; it's impossible to even walk through the trees because they are so close together and the bushes are so stickery. There are hundreds of wild roses climbing all over everything. They may be beautiful to look at, but they are terrible to climb through.

Dexter's hair stands up on end as he sniffs around and smells something very unusual. He doesn't seem to mind the sharp thorns and prowls and sniffs around in the prickly bushes, seemingly totally unaware of the sharp barbs. Hunter watches him and decides maybe Dexter's coat is a nice thing because he doesn't seem to feel the pricks. Then, while Hunter watches, Dexter stops and becomes very still— every hair on his entire body sticks straight up. He looks pretty funny with his pale yellow hair standing out in every direction, his tail rigid and poked straight out behind him—he looks stiff as a board. Hunter makes a little laugh at his silly dog and starts to pick up his boat when, all of a sudden, Dexter barks a wild frantic bark. Hunter jumps at the sound and splashes into the water almost falling on his face. Trying to see what Dexter's problem is, he loses his balance and almost falls again. Bracing himself in the icy water with the current tugging and pushing against him, Hunter manages to look up in time to see Dexter wiggle his way into the prickly undergrowth and disappear.

Now Hunter is not a very big boy and his parents and older brother are all the way across the fields beyond the pens in the valley below. He is alone, so when a great big noise explodes out of the dense forest, it's more than he can stand. Forgetting all about his boat, he scrambles out of the water and sprints into the field just as fast as his legs will carry him. After traveling a good distance he stops. The noise sounds like nothing he's ever heard before. It's bigger and meaner than his father's biggest bull; it's a scratchy trumpet sound like the loud noises his mother's geese make when they are mad and chasing him; it might even be a little bit like a growl, a very huge growl. This is the noise they'd heard last night, only up close!

"Garragg-eeeeeeek," wails and echoes over the valley. Could there be a huge lion or monster in the thicket under the trees? "Hoooowl," Dexter's voice is a frightened panicky sound that cries as he explodes out of the bushes at a dead run with his tail between his legs. This is a bad sign. Dexter is a very big dog, and he doesn't need to be afraid of anything. Running to Hunter's side he keeps barking big ferocious barks. With his hair still standing straight up he stops, looks up at Hunter and races right back toward the mass of trees and stickery bushes.

A wild thrashing and screeching sound comes from somewhere deep in the timber and it seems as if something might be having a fight with the trees and bushes. The tall trees jerk twist and thrash about. Then, everything is still except for a soft whining, almost crying sound, "Eeek-grag, sniff, sniff," and then another soft whine. Dexter stands with his head and shoulders thrust into the edge of the bushes with his tail rigid. He barks and whines and then barks again. Hunter wants to see what's in there, but he is too afraid to take one step closer.

Another very soft "Grragg" comes from somewhere in the trees and Dexter takes a careful step forward before creeping back into the dense undergrowth.

For a long, long time Hunter is still and listens for the strange sounds. He can't see Dexter. His dog, his very best friend, is in there with something! Seconds pass and he hears a tiny whine. Hunter steps forward. It's Dexter and he didn't bark, he whined a sorrowful whine. Hunter knows when Dexter sounds like that it means he is sad, not afraid. The whine comes again. It's the kind of whine Dexter always makes when he wants something. The bushes rustle and Dexter's big head pops out of the rich green leaves and stickery roses. He makes a funny whimpering sound and nods his head at Hunter and then turns around and disappears back into the heavy foliage. Hunter's fear is gone, he trusts Dexter, and Dexter wants him to follow and see what he's found. So with his heart pounding in suspense, Hunter hops from stone to stone across the stream and follows Dexter into the dark scary forest.

Dexter's little whimpering sounds keep Hunter moving and crawling through the awful tangle of limbs that scratch and scrape every inch of the way. After many seconds of crawling on his hands and knees, he finds he can stand. When he does, there hanging right in front of him, half-tangled in the branches and vines is a huge, redish-brown sky-top. Its head is on the ground in front of him; its eyes are closed and it is very still. Its giant wings are all bloody and wrapped up and tangled in the branches and vines. His body hangs half up in the air.

Fear, excitement, wonder, and curiosity all bump around in Hunter's mind. He's seen the giant sky-tops flying around on several occasions, but never ever up close. In one of Hunter's animal books there is a picture of a sky-top and the book says sky-tops are as tall as a giraffe, with skin like a leathery lizard, wings like a bat, legs like a chicken, and a head like a stork. *Yup, this is a sky-top all right.* Hunter decides as he studies the huge bird and realizes it is big enough to fly away with a full sized sheep or even a full sized person. While he watches a branch overhead strains under the extreme weight and snaps and the bird's body jerks and falls a few inches closer to the ground. *That must be very uncomfortable,* Hunter thinks as he twists his neck around trying to imagine what hanging like that must feel like.

Hunter is both excited at his discovery and afraid. The sky-top's head is as big as he is tall, even when standing his very tallest. Right now Hunter has a big knot in his stomach and his heart is about to jump right out of his chest. His legs are like rubber and he can't quite move. Why, for heaven's sake, does he want to touch the giant bird? Hunter can't remember anyone who has ever been this close to a sky-top before and lived to tell about it. Yet here he is—right this minute—not ten feet away from one that looks as if it's in serious trouble.

"I wonder what happened and how he got hung up like this?" Hunter whispers. "What a problem."

"Sniff, sniff; whineeee" Dexter's tail hangs limp, and that means he is worried.

"You know what, Dext, I think the big fellow is dying. He can't move all tied up like he is." Hunter gives the top of his head a good rub the way he always does when he thinks. It's why his hair always stands on end, he thinks a lot.

With a sudden little yipping bark, Dexter demands his young master's attention and Hunter jumps with a sharp jerk. Dexter pushes his big loveable head into Hunter's chest and wags his tail. Hunter pats him, his thoughts drifting again. "If we don't do something pretty quick it may be too late. Look at him—his eyes are all sunken in. You know what Dad says, 'Creatures look like that when they die.'" Creeping forward he touches the huge head—nothing happens. What should he do? "He may be dead already," he whispers. Studying the creature's body he sees very shallow breathing and smiles to himself. "No, he's not dead yet, and I'm going to see if we can save him." Pausing a moment he considers, "Dad may not like this. And if Dad isn't mad, Mom surely will be. She will about croak." This is not good. Hunter sighs and puts his little clenched fists on his hips and studies the injured sky-top. Dexter trots around and pushes against Hunter making another soft whine. "Be still Dext, I've got to think this all out. Dad says when I don't, it gets me into all kinds of trouble."

Soft whining sounds continue to come from Dexter, but Hunter ignores him. He needs to think this problem out. Dexter whines again and still he is ignored. So he gives Hunter a big shove toward the bird. It's quite clear, Dexter wants Hunter to quit standing around and do something. Hunter can't quite decide, he must be sure he's right before he does anything, and he knows this could be a dangerous situation. *But this sky-top isn't about to hurt anybody,* Hunter's mind argues. A sudden spasm shakes the monstrous bird, his beak opens and a sad cry of pain comes from the huge mouth and Dexter answers with a deep throaty cry and pushes his young master again toward the bird.

"You're right Dext, he needs help and Dad has taught Jase (which is short for Jason), and me to never-ever, let anything suffer. We are to give any kind of help we can, and that's just what we are going to do. We'll just hope that helping sky-tops is included on the things-to-help list Dad and Mom might make." He stops, and grins, a grin only Hunter can achieve, and says, "Somehow I don't think sky-tops will ever be on their list. But we can't be sure, so, let's get him untangled." Looking up into the towering branches, he wonders if he will be able to climb high enough to untangle the huge wings. If they could be cut lose it would let the sky-top down on the ground. That would be a nice place to start.

"It looks as though the sky-top might have fought to get away and made things worse. Look, Dexter, there are broken limbs and branches way up there. He pulled all those vines down with him and hung himself." Hunter glances back at the still sky-top and asks, "What did you want to come crashing down here for? You're too big—dumb bird—not too smart a thing to do if you ask me."

If Dexter could have spoken he'd have answered, *But nobody asked you.* However, Hunter is focused on what needs to be done and without another thought or much planning about what he might need to free the sky-top, such as his father for instance, he begins to break the branches and cut away the vines with his old and rather dull knife. With great care he climbs around the sky-top's huge wings and up into the branches that hold them. The branches hurt Hunter's hands as he twists, hacks, and cuts them off. The vines tangled around the sky-top's wings are almost too big and tough for Hunter's old knife and cutting the sky-top free is a long project. Hunter is tired, sweaty, and covered with small nicks and scrapes long before the bird's body is free.

When the sky-top's body drops to the ground, Hunter wants to shout for joy and hopes the wings will pull loose, but they don't and now the wings are pulled even tighter in the vines above and look as though they might break. Hunter knows it must be painful for the creature and hacks away even faster at the last vines. When the remaining vines are cut, the large leathery wings slip in slow motion to the ground and make a funny "flop" sound. The wings, an inch or two at a time, fold up next to the sky-top's body which causes Dexter to get excited and bark. The sky-top jerks with a frightened jump and blinks its eyes open.

Hunter races for the bushes then turns for a look and the sky-top looks right back at him. For a long minute they stare at each other. *He's free now, why doesn't he get up?* Hunter wonders. Standing there staring, it seems to Hunter that he can see pain in the creature's eyes—deep, terrible pain. "Do you hurt? Your wings are pretty bloody in places and your back is a mess. I wish I could help you."

Moving his head ever so slightly, the sky-top makes a feeble cry and as it opens its big mouth, Hunter sees it is very dry. Taking care of his family's chickens is one of Hunter's chores, so he knows what a thirsty chicken looks like. As he studies the sky-top he feels this sky-top must be very thirsty. With a little shrug he turns to go, "I've got water across the creek, just wait, I'll bring you some." As he speaks, he turns and hurries back through the bramble of bushes as fast as he can to where he had left his water skin. Grabbing it, he hurries back to the sky-top and squirts a stream of water on its long beak. Shudders go through the big head and neck, and the mouth gapes open. "Atta boy, this will help. You need water. How long have you been hanging like that? Too long," he chatters while he sends a stream of water into the gaping mouth. When the sky-top swallows, Hunter laughs. Again and again he squirts the water into the bird's mouth and when the water skin is empty he hurries to the creek for more. When the sky-top is satisfied, he looks a little better. While Hunter stands watching and wondering what to do next, the bird lifts its head and shifts its position to get more comfortable. Hunter steps back a good safe distance and looks with excited wonder, because when the bird raises its head it's very high in the air and is much taller than he had imagined. With a little laugh, he tells the creature, "You look sort of funny sitting there like a huge stork sitting on a nest." But the bird doesn't answer; he sighs a huge sigh and blinks several blinks while looking down at him.

A distant clanging comes floating through the afternoon air, "That's Mom's bell. I have to go," Hunter explains to the huge bird just as if it can understand him. "She rings when it is time for evening chores. You will be all right and when you feel a little better you can fly away. Remember I'm your friend and will help you if I can, but you can't carry off our sheep or pigs or anything like that." Hunter pauses as he considers the possibilities and looking up into the bird's eyes, he asks, "You don't do things like that do you?" The sky-top blinks and moves its head from side to side and Hunter laughs a startled laugh, "You don't understand me! What a joke!"

15

Turning around to go, he calls Dexter and steps farther away, "Remember if you need me I will help, only don't bother our animals. I'd like to keep you for a pet—if Dad will let me." This thought makes Hunter stop a moment to consider the possibilities, and then he shakes his head. "I'm crazy just like Jason says I'm crazy sometimes. I have too many funny ideas."

"Would you like to be my pet? No, I guess it is a pretty stupid idea. Nobody has ever had a sky-top for a pet." Hunter pauses, then continues, "Still, I'd like it a lot if you could be my pet, I'd call you Topper and take such good care of you. I'd like that." Then with a little shake of his head he considers the absurdity of his thoughts. It would be impossible to keep a sky-top for a pet, absolutely impossible. Taking a deep breath he reaches toward the battered sky-top, as if in a gesture of farewell and adds, "But you're free now, and when you are rested you can fly away. I'll watch from the house." He pauses considering the possibilities, then adds, "I'd like to see you fly."

The bell's clang sounds again and interrupts Hunter's thoughts. As he turns for home he shouts over his shoulder, "I'll come back tomorrow."

The sky-top watches as Hunter and Dexter wiggle their way back out of the dense undergrowth, and then listens as they splash across the creek. "Click–clickitty-click," comes from somewhere deep in his throat, the Hunter boy had come and he and his dog had saved him. He sighs a sad sigh, it was so nice to have the little Hunter boy close to him and to hear him talk. *The Hunter boy will come back—I know he will come back.* Gently he moves a wing, *Ouch, oh my goodness that hurts.*

Slowly he stretches out one wing as much as is possible on the cramped forest floor and cranes his long neck for a look at it, when satisfied there is no permanent damage, he tries to stretch out the other wing. He whines a soft whine and the wing trembles as it moves a little bit. This one doesn't look so good, then arching his head over his back he studies the wounds made by the sawtooth's claws. It's not a pretty sight. Giving a little shrug, he tries to feel how deep the wounds might be and pain runs down his back and shoulders.

I think I may be in bad shape, he says to himself as his eyes search for a way out of the snarl of trees. *If I can't get out, then the sawtooth can't get in—there's no way I can fight him and hope to live—I don't think I can even fly.* His thoughts are a bit disturbing.

16

With a great long sigh he stretches out to sleep remembering Hunter's touch, his nice cheerful words and his name.

Topper! The boy gave me a name, I'm Topper. His eyes close and he breaths deep and knows he's not going to die, his wings are not broken, he will fly again and see his family, and he knows the Hunter boy will come back.

Chapter 3

RUSTON RETURNS

This turns out to be a very difficult night for Hunter. His Uncle Watt, his Aunt Mandy, and their five daughters have come for a visit. To make matters even worse, they are to stay for an extended visit. His uncle has a bridge to build in a far away village and his aunt doesn't want to stay home alone. Hunter doesn't blame her, he wouldn't want to stay home with all those girls either—but, this is a fine pickle! Hunter has the most important discovery of his life, or of any of their lives, and his father is too busy to listen. "Sorry Hunt, not now. Your cousins are here and we all need to help your mother," Ruston says to him more than once.

Hunter feels like shouting, "But Dad!" He almost does, but a look from his father makes him very quiet. Hunter's father, Ruston Lynn, is a very blond and handsome man, with a strong square face, a short scratchy beard, sparkling gray eyes, powerful broad shoulders, and a wonderful sense of humor. He is always happy and loves to laugh and sing. Most of all he loves his family, his wife Lettie, and his boys, Hunter and Jason. Usually he has time for them, but not tonight. For a long time Hunter stays very close hoping for a chance to tell him about the sky-top, but no one ever gives him one second to say anything. It is a bad night for Hunter.

The next day Hunter feels like screaming when his father and his uncle harness their teams of big draft horses and drive away. His father is going to build the bridge with his uncle and they will be gone for a long time. Now what is Hunter to do? As things work out, not too long after his father leaves, Hunter manages to get Jason alone long enough to ask him to come with him to see what he'd found. Hunter is careful to warn Jason it has to be a secret and that their cousins can't know where they are going. So it is, that Jason and Hunter, dragging a big bucket of pig feed, start back to the tangle of trees beneath the cliff. Hunter hasn't told Jason what to expect. He's afraid Jason won't believe him, and if the sky-top happens to be gone he would surely be teased and laughed at, and Hunter doesn't like to be teased or laughed at. However, Jason does tease him as he half carries, and half drags the huge bucket of pig feed toward cliff pasture, and is very glad when Jason feels sorry for him and helps carry the heavy bucket. Hunter doesn't mind in the least Jason's belief that nothing he can think of would need a whole huge bucket of feed.

But it's worth all the teasing; Jason's shock is even better than Hunter had hoped. He is delighted at Jason's reaction. If the truth is to be known, Jason is very upset to see a sky-top up close, and Hunter makes him feel even worse when he walks right up to the big bird. Jason gives Hunter a real scolding, but Hunter doesn't mind too much—he's so glad Topper hadn't flown away. He'd been pretty worried he would be gone. It's nice to have Jason be there and see the sky-top too, even if he is upset and says a lot of loud things about sky-tops being dangerous. Hunter pats Topper and waits for Jason to finish stomping around and yelling. For a moment Hunter studies his brother and decides he looks just like their dad when he is really angry. *Yup, just shrink Dad a bit and that's Jason.* With a frowny squint he tries to imagine Jason with a beard and the thought tickles his fully bone.

"This isn't funny!" Jason raises his voice while he paces back and fourth along the edge of the clearing. "Sometimes you do the stupidest things. I can't believe the chance you've taken."

Hunter ignores the abuse and busies himself squirting water into Topper's big mouth. It takes a minute or two for Jason to adjust to the fact that the bird is not the least upset. Nothing dangerous has happened. No, the bird just sits there in front of him gulping water from Hunter's water skin. It takes Jason's fear and anger at Hunter's foolishness a little time to adjust, but within a few minutes he takes a step or two closer, "He really is thirsty." Pausing as he watches, "He wants more water and your skin is empty; here take mine." He hands Hunter his water-skin and watches. As he begins to relax, his horror soon turns to delight at the discovery—the sky-top wants even more water! He can see it in the bird's expression, it even looks glad to see them.

Jason pours water into Topper's mouth and has a million questions. He and Hunter laugh and joke over the possibilities of having such a pet and agree the name Topper is perfect. They wonder, "Wow, what will our friends think?"

For a moment Jason's imagination gets the better of him as he imagines himself riding Topper down Glendale's main street, "Chat Dixon wouldn't bother us if we rode a sky-top to school." He looks at his brother with a devilish grin.

"Man, oh man, how cool would that be?" Hunter catches the vision. "He wouldn't dare take my lunch away from me ever again if I had Topper with me." Giving Topper a respectful glance he adds, "He could pick Chat up and shake him around, then maybe I'd take his lunch from him. It'd be fun to show him just how it feels to have everyone laugh at you." Liking the idea Hunter pauses before adding, "If Topper went to school with us he could protect us and our friends from Chat's gang." The thought brings delighted images of Chat Dixon's discomfort into Hunter's vivid mind. With a little sigh he pats Topper's leathery neck and asks, "Would you protect us?"

Topper nods his big head and makes a funny little clicking sound as the boys dump some pig feed on the ground in front of him. It doesn't take very long for the boys to understand how pleased Topper is with the pig feed. Topper listens, but isn't interested in the problems Chat and his gang inflict upon the younger population around Glendale. He's too busy gobbling and slurping the feed and is rather funny to watch. Nodding his great head he makes strange clicking sounds while pecking and gulping up the feed. All along he'd known there was a reason sky-tops needed to get acquainted with humans and now he's positive.

Tasty, tasty, this is..., his sky-top mind delights in the glories of pig feed. *The Hunter boy saved me and now he brings me food—the best food I've ever had. Wait'll I tell Mom and Dad what I've discovered.* He purrs with his funny clicking sounds. Topper is very happy, despite his nasty cuts and bruises.

"He eats just like a chicken, doesn't he?" Hunter giggles a little sound as he watches Topper's enthusiastic eating manners. "I'm so glad he's still here. I was afraid no one would believe me. That's why I didn't tell you about him first."

Jason shakes his very blond head, and says, "You are right, I wouldn't have believed you. No one would have believed you. What a fine mess this is! Dad won't be back for weeks, and Mom won't know what to do." He pauses and gives Hunter a serious look, "You know if our cousins find us up here, there's no telling what will happen. Those girls don't have a single brain in all five of their heads put together. We have to keep this a secret." For a moment he smiles and tips his head to

20

one side the way he always does when he is deep in thought, "I'm so glad he didn't fly away, this is the coolest thing ever! I can't believe you found him and cut him down all by yourself."

As Jason looks up into the trees then around the small clearing he sees the broken branches Topper had fallen through and wonders, "You know Hunt, he doesn't look like he's very hurt, so why didn't he leave?" After studying the cramped clearing at the base of the tangled trees for a moment he points at the branches that arch like claws high over their heads and nods with a glimmer of understanding. "Look, this place is like a big cage." Circling the area he can see where Topper smashed down many of the smaller shrubs and bushes in his struggle for freedom. "He can't get out. He's too big. These trees and their branches make a cage for him. Something must have happened to make him fall in here. Hunt, if you hadn't found him, he might have died in here."

"He was almost dead yesterday." Hunter answers, and is glad Jason is pleased with him. "He was caught up in those branches. See where I broke them off?" Hunter points and Jason stares, impressed with his little brother's work. "Dexter found him. His head was on the ground and his body and wings were up off the ground all tangled in the branches and vines."

Jason can see where Topper had been, and is surprised at his little brother's handy work in freeing the giant bird. Slowly he walks a circle around the small clearing and decides the space is too small for such a big bird. "We need to clear some of the branches and little trees so he has more room, then when Dad gets home he'll know what to do. Come on lets make his cage as big as we can. I'd go crazy trapped in this spot if I was as big as he is."

For the next hour or so the boys work hard at hacking down little trees and undergrowth, clearing the area around Topper. From time to time they stop and with huffs and puffs admire their work. Topper's cage is now much more comfortable and he seems to appreciate their efforts as he struggles in a weak effort to stand. He wobbles a bit before making it to his feet—and oh my goodness, Jason and Hunter run, looking for a good safe place to hide. Unbelieveable! Topper is almost as tall as their two-story house. This is too much for Dexter who has been sound asleep under a shady tree. He is most upset and barks his biggest and most ferocious barks. Topper doesn't seem to mind the racket in the least, and stands looking down at Dexter with his head twisted a little to one side.

This is only a beginning and as the days pass the boys gradually clear more space in Topper's cramped pen. Every spare minute of every single day finds Jason and Hunter enjoying Topper's company. As the summer days pass, Jason and Hunter feel it must be time for their dad to come home. It seems to them like forever, but they know how to be patient, well, sort of patient. Their aunt and their cousins make lots of confusion, and laughter, and noise—but this is not all bad. In fact, if you asked them, they would both agree their cousins are a lot of help. The chores go so fast with everyone working and there are always funny things happening. Like when Cousin Amanda fell in the pig slop—that was pretty cool. Except, Hunter had laughed out loud and his consequence had been to wash Amanda's dress—that wasn't so great. Hunter is now careful not to laugh when his cousins get into unpleasant fixes. He just smiles inside and is glad his cousins are so much help, even if they are silly girls. The best part of having their cousins living with them is their mother is so happy. Their mother, loves her sister, their Aunt Mandy, and they enjoy doing all kinds of girl things together, which makes them forget to keep track of Hunter and Jason. You might think this should hurt the boy's feelings, sometimes it might, but not this time with Topper needing so much company and care. At the moment they are very glad the girls like to do their girl things, because it leaves them free to do boy things, and right now that is to be with Topper.

Some days are easier than others. Sometimes the girls try to spy on the boys. This gives Jason and Hunter fits. The rule is when chores are finished everyone may spend the day as they please. Hoeing Mom's big kitchen garden, feeding and watering the livestock, milking, and cleaning pens all take time, but if they work really fast and finish before the girls finish their chores they can slip away without a problem. The trick is to finish first, and that isn't always easy. It means Jason and Hunter are learning to work very fast. Lettie has noticed the difference and has wondered over the definite change. They are even doing their work quite well and she hasn't had to scold them or make them go back and do something over again. She's quite pleased. However, if she'd go have a look where the pig feed is stored she'd know something was up. The huge feed bin is almost half gone and the Lynns don't have that many pigs—but she hasn't looked, so no one has noticed. The day the girls went to town, no one was the wiser when two whole donkey cart loads of pig feed left for the cliff pasture.

At mid-summer, Topper is still a well kept secret and only a few little scrape marks and scars are left where there had been bloody sores and tears. Now that the sores are gone, he feels much better. Hunter and Jason have worked and worked clearing more space for Topper; they know he must exercise and keep his wings limber or he will not be able to fly. Now with more room in the dense thicket, Topper stretches his wings flapping them in quick whipping motions. This makes Hunter and Jason laugh and laugh, while Dexter barks and races about in silly circles. They enjoy this time together and are quite glad their cousins and their aunt are there to keep their mother company.

One hot afternoon, Topper is sound asleep and the boys find something upon which to disagree. Jason, in a spurt of anger or perhaps mischief, tells Hunter he's going to knock some sense into him. "Oh, no you won't," Hunter shouts and the race is on. Jason is far too close for Hunter's comfort and in desperation he runs straight to Topper and scampers up his wing and onto his back. If Topper hadn't been stretched out on the ground sleeping, Hunter could never have jumped so high.

This makes a sudden change in things. Jason forgets about wanting to pound his little brother and yells for him to get off quick.

"Promise, you won't chase me anymore? I don't like being chased," Hunter is quick to see his advantage.

Jason isn't given a chance to answer because Topper is now awake and very interested in the new situation. He snaps his huge beak a few times and stands up, then turns his giant head back to look at his small passenger. He blinks his big eyes and turns his head, first this way and then he tips it the other. Then a funny thing happens, he opens his big mouth and smiles. Gently he reaches his long beak toward Hunter's little foot and strokes it while making a funny little clicking sound down in his throat.

"He makes that sound when he's happy," Hunter shouts in excitement. Jason still isn't sure, but Hunter is, and tenderly strokes Topper's neck just the way his father taught him to stroke a horse's neck if it became upset about something. Topper's clucking sound is almost like a nice purr, only much bigger. This is the beginning of more excitement and possibilities than you or I might ever imagine and by the time Ruston Lynn and Uncle Watt are headed down the main road approaching Lynn Farm many things have happened. As they trot their big horses down the valley road, their heavy wagons making clouds of dust, Jason sees them. He's up in the very top of one of Topper's tallest trees and what a scramble. Never has Jason climbed down from anywhere so fast and shouting all the way. "It's Dad! It's Dad! He's home, he's home. Hurry Hunter, hurry. He's on the valley road." Soon their father will know their secret and they will have help getting Topper out of his pen in the trees.

What a secret to have kept all this time. It is an unbelievable thing to have captured a live sky-top, more unbelievable for a sky-top to be gentle, and impossible to believe a sky-top can be ridden. This is what they've been waiting for. They have talked of this moment all summer and both boys are well aware they need to be a bit cautions in how they tell their father. Knowing how upset their parents might be, they have decided to wait until after their cousins are gone before they say one word about Topper. After all, no telling what Topper might do with a bunch of silly screaming girls running around. So the next morning, just as soon as his cousins are rounding the bend in the valley road headed for their home, Hunter takes his father by the hand, and while looking up into his smiling face, he says with a degree of urgency, "Dad, Jason and I have something very important to show you, and it won't wait much longer. We've really needed you."

Although Ruston has many pressing things on his mind and a great deal of catching up to do, he recognizes something of the restrained pressure in his youngest son's request and asks, "What's the problem, son?"

"Dad, everything will be just fine if you will come with me and Jason right now," Hunter pauses not real sure how to continue. "...er we... don't want you to be mad."

"What have you done that might make me mad?" Ruston squeezes Hunter's hand in a reassuring way.

"...'cause Dad, we have a new pet an' he's kinda big. Well, no, he's really big an' we're afraid you won't like him," Hunter looks up into his father's face hoping to see a kind smile.

"So your new pet is really big and you're afraid I might not like him?"

"Right," Hunter nods his head and adds, "And we know he's too big for a pet, but we want to keep him anyway, and we want you to like him, and Dad, we've worried about it a lot." Then in a rush he tries to explain, "Dad, Dexter found him and he was almost dead, and we made him get well, and he's wonderful. Come, come on with us now. His name is Topper and we want to keep him forever." Hunter pulls his father forward and Jason hurries to join them. Both boys talk at once and

24

Ruston is glad to be home and able again to enjoy his children's excited expectations.

So it is that Ruston doesn't wait for a convenient moment to let Hunter and Jason show him their new pet and heads up the track toward the cliff pasture with pleasant expectation.

As Ruston and the boys start through the prickly tunnel leading into Topper's clearing, Hunter races ahead and asks Topper to sit. When Topper is down he is his very smallest and right now Hunter feels Topper needs to be as small as possible. He knows it will be a miracle if he and Jason can get through the next few minutes without upsetting their father. As Ruston and Jason step out of the thick undergrowth into the clearing, Hunter stands at Topper's side with his arms around the huge bird's neck. One look at Ruston's face tells Hunter all is not well and he shouts, "It's all right Dad, Topper is gentle."

"Hunter, I want you to be very slow and careful. Just step away and come back to us," Ruston commands in a carefully controlled voice. "You cannot be too careful. Come on now, ease away." Ruston takes a cautions step forward not wanting to excite the huge bird.

Dexter bounces around in front of Ruston and barks, and Topper tips his big head and clacks, then Dexter runs and plants his big feet right up on Topper's neck and Topper strokes him with his big beak.

"Here Top, I brought you an apple!" Hunter holds out a juicy red apple for his pet.

"Slurp – smack," the apple is gone and Topper thinks he'd like to have another one.

"Hunter, I told you to step away from the sky-top. Do it now!" Ruston demands.

"But Dad, you don't understand, this is Topper ..." Hunter speaks as he obediently steps away toward his father's outstretched hand.

"Dad, it's okay," Jason interrupts and darts between Hunter and his father, giving his little brother a gentle shove back toward Topper he whispers, "Get up on him quick."

Dexter recognizes the stress in everyone's voices and leaps toward Ruston and plants his big dog feet in Ruston's chest just at the right moment to stop him before he can pull Hunter away from Topper. By the time Dexter is out of the way, Topper is on his feet and Jason has a gentle but firm hand on his dad's chest hoping to help him relax. It is not a good moment for Ruston as he steps back, appalled at Topper's size.

"Dad, I tried to tell you how big Topper is..." Hunter doesn't get to finish; his dad is not listening.

"Hunter, be very careful and slide off. Just ease down. I'm right here and you'll be fine," Ruston doesn't even feel Jason's restraining hand.

"I will Dad, but I'm gonna show you how I can ride Topper first. Just watch," Hunter speaks as he guides Topper around the small clearing first at a swinging walk, then at a little bouncy trot.

There aren't words to describe Ruston's feeling as he watches his little son and the immense bird. If Ruston had carried his bow with him to the cliff pasture, things would be very different than they are at this moment. However, as it is Ruston stands in shocked wonder staring up at Topper while Hunter shouts and laughs and Dexter barks and runs in circles. Jason watches his father for a second then runs to Topper shouting, "Up." Obediently, Topper swoops his huge head and neck down to Jason who jumps aboard and as Topper raises his head, Jason slides down the neck in front of Hunter, just the way the boys do to get on their big horses.

"Watch Dad, we'll show you what we can do." Without waiting for Ruston to move farther out of the way, Topper begins making a tight figure eight round his small pen, his large swinging steps covering the ground many times easier than Ruston's big horses. Excitement fills the air with shouts and Topper joins in the racket with swan like trumpeting sounds. Ruston stumbles as he backs out of the way. He is speechless. When the boys bring Topper to a stop and command, "Down," Topper drops to the ground and Dexter makes a flying leap into the middle of the boys. Jason grabs the enthusiastic dog and both roll to the ground with Hunter right behind them.

"Dexter wants to ride too, only we can't figure out how to keep him from sliding off." Jason explains.

"What do you think, Dad? Isn't Topper great?" Hunter can't wait to know his father's thoughts. Ruston still stands in the edge of the trees, his face a little pale and both fists clenched so tight they must hurt.

Noticing their father's expression, the boys lead Topper to Ruston with the promise, "he is quite safe." With numb hesitation Ruston reaches toward Topper and lays his hand on the leathery neck. It is a tense silent second or two before Ruston finds his voice, "How did this happen. How is it possible?" is all he manages to say.

"Topper, this is our father, Ruston Lynn. And Dad meet Topper, the best pet we've ever had." Hunter pats Topper with enthusiasm and continues, "Topper say hello to Dad, he's not real sure he likes you yet and we've got to convince him you are safe." What happens next, Ruston nor the boys will ever forget, Topper opens his huge mouth or beak nodding his head as if to say, *nice to meet you*, all the while looking Ruston right in the eye and clicking in his funny happy way.

"He likes you Dad. He does!" Hunter shouts. "He only makes that sound when he is very happy and having a good time."

What a morning to remember—the questions, oh, so many questions to be answered. Every argument imaginable, every sane reaction is ready and waiting on the tip of Ruston's tongue, but they aren't surfacing. He's not saying a thing. It seems to Ruston the huge bird enjoys the boys, their noise, and their excitement. In silence he watches as the boys climb again onto Topper's broad back. Relaxation and acceptance are a bit slow in coming. After all, sky-tops have always been one of the village's greatest dangers. Sky-tops carry away farm animals and some carried away people, yet here his children are riding one and having a wonderful time. With a sigh he notices Topper smile a funny sort of smile. The three of them, no, the four of them, his boys, the sky-top, and Dexter make four, certainly are noisy, and the racket they make is wonderful—even if it is a bit deafening. Ruston laughs to himself as he realizes their racket drowns out the steady roar of the falls. Shaking his head, he wonders how they ever managed to keep this a secret from Lettie, anyone would think there was no possibility. Yet there is one thing Ruston is very sure of and that is his wife, beautiful spirited Lettie, hasn't the foggiest clue as to what the boys had been up to. A chuckle begins deep within Ruston's heart and it just won't go away, it keeps getting bigger and bigger. Soon a smile appears then the chuckle comes and Ruston shakes his head in speechless disbelief and laughter, real tension-easing laughter, soon follows.

Topper notices Ruston's laughter and stops, then steps to him nodding his ugly head—almost laughing with him. Jason and Hunter shout and cheer; their dad is laughing and that means things are going to be all right. When they tumble down Topper's wing to the ground, hugs and shouts of joy fill the air—and if you want the truth, Ruston has a tear or two in his eyes. This has been a very difficult time for him.

It is a very good thing Hunter and Jason took their father to Topper before he looked into the feed crib. This could have been an uncomfortable circumstance. As it is, he is now well informed as to how they had cared for Topper and how they had waited with great impatience for his return. In spite of all the explaining, Ruston is still startled right down to the bottom of his boots when he looks into the feed crib and realizes just exactly how much the sky-top had eaten in only a matter of weeks.

Keeping Topper creates a very difficult question for Ruston. No one has ever kept a sky-top before. In truth he wonders how many could afford to feed such a creature. Yet Ruston is a creative thinker and already his mind wanders into new areas, even so far as wondering what it would be like to fly. Was it possible? How long would it take to travel to the next village, or better yet, to the great ocean over the mountains if you could fly? He decides he wants to know. So it is agreed Topper may stay and, beginning in the next few days, the thicket will be trimmed and an opening cut to free Topper from his forest cage. The question is whether or not Topper will stay at Lynn Farm once the thicket is open. It is something they have to find out.

Chapter 4

TOPPER FLIES

Several days later, Ruston, with his heavy ax and team of work horses move a big tree and a mammoth pile of brush out of the way. With the tree and bushes gone there should be room for Topper to make it out of his small pen. Yet, even with the big tree gone, Topper has to put his head and neck very low and scoot out through the opening in the timber. Branches scrape his sides and Hunter is sure the stickers must hurt, but Topper doesn't seem to mind. Stepping out into the bright sunshine at the edge of the shimmering stream, he stretches very tall and lifts his beak toward the heavens and makes a huge trumpeting sound. He really is a great deal like a gigantic goose.

Hunter is right in front of him, both hands resting on one of Topper's legs. He's rather worried about turning Topper loose. He's afraid Topper will leave and never come back. The thing none of them realize, except for Topper, is that sky-tops need to drop off of a very high place to get into the air with any degree of ease. Taking off from the ground takes great strength, and Topper is still weak and not strong enough to leap into the air from the ground. Topper can't leave and as the days pass he is content to stay in the cliff pasture. He hides from the sawtooths in his forest cage and he's never lonely because the boys come and ride him everyday. All this while, Topper grows stronger and stronger. Day after day he runs up and down the cliff pasture beating his huge wings and managing to lift a little farther from the ground—one day at a time.

Skipping and whistling merry tunes, Hunter is headed for the cliff pasture to spend part of another morning with Topper. Only this morning Topper isn't there, and it takes Hunter a minute or so to realize what has happened. When he does, he sits down in the grass and fights back his tears, but they won't stop and keep rolling down his cheeks. His father had warned him this would happen, but still it hurts. Hunter wants to hit something, and to scream and yell. Then a secret something reminds him, *This means Topper can fly again and this is a good thing.*

It was sad to have Topper be too weak to fly. Hunter's tears stop and he begins giving flying some serious thought. He wants to see Topper fly. Looking up he studies the sky in every direction while calling Topper's name at the top of his voice. His voice rings and echoes off the shimmering cliff, it's a pleasant and strange sound, but it worries Jason who is in one of the upper pastures mending a fence. He hears his brother's wailing voice and wonders what could be wrong. Shutting the gate behind the calves, he hurries to Topper's pasture just in time to see their pet sky-top swoop low over where Hunter is bouncing up and down shouting for him to stop. Somehow Jason knows what is about to happen and screams, "No!" too late. He runs and watches in horror as Hunter jumps and grabs one of Topper's big feet and is jerked from the ground as Topper lifts in a huge swoop high in the air carrying Hunter with him, and Jason screams for Hunter to turn loose.

By the time Hunter realizes what he has done it is much too late to turn loose. In his wild jump to stop his oversized pet, he hadn't given much thought about what he was about to do. No, he had merely grabbed and hung on. Now, realizing what he has done, turning loose is the last thing he wants to do. You might describe Hunter's feelings at this moment as being those of panic. At this point he wishes he had thought before he'd acted. His father always tells him it's wise to think things out before you do them. Hunter knows he should have thought out the possible consequences before he grabbed Topper's foot, but he hadn't thought and hanging onto a sky-top's foot while flying high in the air is a pretty heavy consequence. He understands only too well he has made another, what his mother calls a "Hunter Mistake" and has a deep sick feeling in the pit of his stomach as his brother and their home both grow smaller and smaller beneath him.

Topper makes one circle, rising on the air currents up over the cliff and drops down on the very high and dangerous edge. Hunter is so glad to feel the solid warm rocks under his feet. He's a little weak, his knees wobble, and he's pretty shaky—real fear can do that. And so Hunter sits down and hangs his head between his knees taking deep breaths, while Topper strokes him with his beak. Hunter thinks he might be sick. After a few minutes he feels a little better and looks up and out over the edge of the cliff. *Boy, will Mom be mad.* Many worried thoughts crowd his mind, such as, *Now what am I going to do and how will I ever get down from here?* Looking down into Topper's pasture he can see his father and mother running up the cart track toward the cliff. He knows his mother will be crying. She still hasn't accepted Topper. She'd been quite mad at his father when she'd learned he'd told the boys they could keep him. Now he had blown it. Giving his mother some careful thought, he can see her in his mind. She's so pretty with her fluffy, curly reddish-brown hair. She's skinny and quick as quick can be. She can almost outrun Hunter and it's such fun to race with her and then laugh and run all over again. Hunter can almost see her face right now. She has big expressive eyes and he can always tell what kind of a mood she's in. They can look really sad and really happy, usually they are laughing eyes, only they are probably mad eyes right now. *Is it possible to be mad and cry at the same time?* Hunter wonders and isn't very happy with the thought.

"I need to go home Topper, I don't want Mother to cry. Will you let me guide you the way I do when we are in the pasture?" Pulling the small rope he always uses for reins out of his pocket he slips it through Topper's mouth. Topper clucks and clicks as Hunter climbs up his rubbery wing, and settles himself for a ride that makes him scared and sick to think about. For the next few minutes he sits very still on Topper's back trying to find the courage to move closer to the edge of the cliff. Topper wonders what the problem is and keeps looking back at him as if to say, *Let's be going.* But he can tell something is not quite right and waits for Hunter to tell him he may go.

Hunter doesn't want to look over the edge; it's such a long way down. Nothing is right about this and he wishes he hadn't acted so foolishly. Gently he strokes Topper's neck and says, "Take me back down, Top, only please don't bounce me off." A tear slips down his cheek and he wipes it away while gathering his courage. "Fly real still, this isn't like riding you around at home. Oh, be careful, I don't want to be afraid." Topper takes a step toward the edge and Hunter jumps, "Wait, I have to think this out and not do anything silly, but I've already done something silly, so I'd better do something really smart." Hunter reasons with himself as he strokes Topper's neck.

"Click-clack-click," Topper tries to comfort Hunter as he looks back and strokes his master's small leg with his beak.

Hunter thumps Topper's back with little pats and sniffs, "I have to go back down to my family. I don't want them to worry ... So lets go ..."

With a gentle, half felt nudge, he urges Topper toward the cliff and takes a deep breath and breathes a little prayer. As he leans forward and wraps his arms around Topper's neck, he closes his eyes, "Take me home, Topper." A little hop and a jump, then a huge swoosh of cold air rushes up into his face and his stomach is almost left somewhere far above him. Then a dizzy falling feeling makes Hunter open his eyes, and oh, my goodness, wonder of wonders, they are flying! The thrill of the wind in his face with the great wings stretched out on either side is more than Hunter can stand. He wants to shout for joy. Topper is big enough on land, but with his wings spread and the air pulling them tight, he is huge, bigger than Hunter could ever imagine. Hunter feels pretty small, but he is no longer afraid. The strength he feels beneath him is wonderful. It's much smoother than trotting around on the ground, there are no bumps at all, only wind, blue sky, and a feeling too exciting to explain.

Looking down he can see their shadow like a big X floating across the fields below. The shadow is going fast, racing fast. Everything on the ground looks so small, like little toys. They are almost over their farm and he can see Jason and Dexter jumping about. Yes, there are his parents not too far ahead, they are shouting and waving about in a rather wild manner. Forgetting why they might have reason to be upset, Hunter waves as he flies by. He is so happy. They are watching him fly! Then a swift air current sweeps them up and he leaves them behind.

Affectionately he strokes Topper's neck, and Topper clucks his happy cluck and Hunter laughs. Then Hunter tries a dangerous thing, he pulls his little rope and asks Topper to turn and they tip and it's scary as the world beneath them turns and everything feels all crazy. It's a dizzy thrilling thing to have the ground turn around. Now they are going back toward the towering cliffs. Only the cliffs aren't towering anymore, at least not to Topper or Hunter, because they are above the cliffs. The waterfall looks like a small silver ribbon, and the air is misty wet right over the falls. It's cold and he can hear the roar of the water as it falls over the edge. Then his mother's high pitched scream reminds him of his rather serious situation. He knows he has to figure out how to make Topper land. Swoosh! They are gliding right by his parents again and he knows how upset they are. This time he knows what to expect and braces himself as he asks Topper to turn and again they tip a big deep tip in the air and make a beautiful curve aimed right back toward his family.

It is very difficult for Hunter to want to come down. After all, men since the beginning of time have dreamed of flying. So it isn't very surprising that Hunter and Topper make several figure eight's high in the air over his screaming family before Hunter decides to come down. Yet, coming down isn't an easy thing to do, especially when you've never come down from the air on a sky-top before. How do you tell a sky-top to land? So Hunter and Topper circle and circle on the air currents for some minutes while Hunter wrestles with the problem before he thinks of using the word, "down." Topper understands the word "down," it means he is to sit so Hunter and Jason can get on or off.

With thoughts of the possible solution, Hunter guides Topper toward his family and says, "down," and with a sickening swoosh they drop out of the sky. Hunter almost falls off and yanks on his rope and Topper levels out missing Lettie and Ruston by only a few feet. The wind is terrific in Hunter's face, and his eyes fill with stinging tears and he can't see very well. Down the cart track toward the barns and house they fly. Passing the big main barn that stands across the paved courtyard from their house, barely over the trees near the valley road they glide before Topper drops the last few feet and touches the ground.

This part is quite gentle as Topper only takes a few quick steps to catch his balance. Hunter can hear his family, his mother's voice is quite clear, and he turns Topper back toward them. For the first time he asks Topper to go really fast on the ground. Seconds later his family is all around him. Lettie cries and looks all upset and teary as she grabs her little son and pulls him to her. It's nice to be loved, but Hunter doesn't like it when his mother cries. It's best when she is happy, laughing and ready to run races with him. Ruston stands off to one side with Topper rather absently stroking the bird's strong neck. He is deep in thought.

When the commotion settles a bit, he comments in his quiet way, "That was pretty close, son."

"It was an accident Dad. I didn't think. I just grabbed, and then it was too late." Hunter pauses, "Are you mad? Will you give me a terrible consequence?" Hunter's face is a mixture of excitement and worry. "It was pretty dumb wasn't it? I just wanted him to stop—I didn't want him to get away."

"Did it scare you?" Ruston asks with a curious smile.

"It scared me bad, Dad."

"Are you going to do it again?"

"Not like that! Ever! But Dad, riding him is fun and it's easy. Is it really bad of me to want to fly him again?"

"No, Hunter, I could see how well you sat him. You even made flying look easy, and now I'm thinking I'd like to fly him too. But I think we need some kind of a saddle so you won't fall off. I want you safe! Does that sound good to you?"

"You mean it? You will let me fly again?"

It's best not to look at Lettie right at the moment. Riding sky-tops around in the air is not a girl thing and her tears are rapidly turning into serious anger. Let us miss this and say Hunter is given no serious punishment for his dangerous mistake, after all it was an accident. But he does have to promise not to fly again until his father has made a saddle complete with a safety harness and plenty of straps to hang on to.

***

Summer is almost gone and thus far the Lynns have managed to keep Topper a secret. Ruston has worried about what the village people might do if someone happened to see him. He knows they have every reason to be frightened and to do their best to kill him, even though killing a sky-top is something few men have ever done. He remembers he would have shot Topper that first day if he'd been carrying his bow and arrows, and Hunter and Jason hadn't been there to stop him. Ruston knows they must do something because Topper can fly again and hiding a sky-top in the air is all but impossible. Sooner or later someone will see him, and then what?

There is also the question of whether or not Topper will stay at Lynn Farm now that he is well and able to fly. If he chooses to stay it will be because he wants to and not because he is forced. As the days pass it rather tickles Ruston's fancy to discover keeping a sky-top close is not a problem once they develop a taste for pig feed.

When the saddle is finished, it looks very different from other saddles. Hunter wanted a big pad to lean on in front so he wouldn't be thrown when Topper made dives and swoops. He also wanted stirrups like a horse's saddle. Lettie insisted on a shoulder harness or straps to keep Hunter down in the saddle, just in case things got rough, and he lost his balance. Remembering the rather sick feeling he'd had as Topper jumped off the cliff, Hunter asked that the saddle have a very high back, he didn't like the idea of being left floating out in space. Because Topper's wings are in the way there couldn't be a girth of any kind and this created a bit of a problem. So Ruston made a soft fleece-covered loop to encircle Topper's neck. This is to hold the saddle forward, and a strap to go around each of Topper's legs to keep the saddle back in a comfortable place. Nothing on the saddle is tight and every part is padded with wonderful soft sheepskin. Ruston wants

34

Topper to be very comfortable and for Hunter to be both comfortable and safe.

Now, it is time for Hunter to fly again and Ruston, Lettie, Jason, and Dexter are all with Hunter and Topper in the cliff pasture. Topper has become very good at running very fast and leaping into the air with his great wings beating with violent thrusts. Ruston reminds Hunter one last time to stay well away from where people might see them, and not to go too far away. With mild apprehension and excitement, Ruston helps Hunter buckle himself in and steps back with a fatherly knot in the pit of his stomach and waves him away.

Hunter's heart pounds as he tells Topper to go. This time Hunter knows what to expect and is not frightened, but he's very glad his father had taught him how to stand up in his stirrups to take out the jolts of the bumpy ride. When the bumps are over and the huge wings are pulsating beneath him, Hunter knows Topper's legs are no longer on the ground and they are flying. Topper makes a sweeping circle as he climbs higher in the sky and then Hunter feels a curious thing, a current of air comes up under them and Topper's wings stop and they rise. The air is taking them up. They rise motionless in the warm sunshine while they circle higher and higher. Hunter can see his parents and waves and yells, but they can't hear him. The saddle is perfect, and he wiggles around feeling the soft leather and sheep skin. His father makes beautiful things. The harness feels good, he's glad his mother had suggested it. The straps hold him tight in place. Releasing his grip on the front of his saddle he spreads his arms out wide. "I'm flying. Topper, I'm flying." Topper answers with a nod of his head and a different sounding variety of clucks as he reminds Hunter, *No, we are flying! Without me you wouldn't be up here.* The thought of Hunter flying without him gives him a chuckle that comes out with a very strange sound. *Preposterous, absolutely preposterous!*

***

In the days following, Jason learns to fly, and both boys explore in ever-widening circles around their home. The rule they are to follow is to never go beyond where they can see their home. Lynn Farm is many miles south of the nearest town, which is Glendale, and they have almost no neighbors, so keeping their interesting secret hasn't been very difficult, but Ruston knows sooner or later Topper and the boys will be seen. They have waited far too long to let their friends and neighbors know about Topper. He decides the best thing to do is to invite

35

Glendale's mayor, Mayor Daily, and the town council out to see his latest "project." He will not tell them what they will be coming to see. So it is planned and on an appointed day, Mayor Daily and a number of very important men will come to see Topper.

The Lynn home and farm buildings are built around a very large stone-paved area they call the "courtyard." It's a bit of a joke, because courtyards are usually for castles and the Lynn's don't have a castle or anything like it, but the area is like a small castle courtyard with the buildings and walls made of soft gray stone all grouped around the large paved area. The huge, main-barn towers a good three stories tall over and along the south side of the courtyard. It's the largest barn anyone in their area has ever seen—it makes everything look small. Some people call it Lynn's castle. The Lynn house is on the north side of the courtyard and faces the huge barn. The milk house, chicken house, and loafing sheds are placed on the west side, while the east opens into the orchard and the farm road that leads up to the cliff pasture. All the buildings and most of the fences are made of the same pale gray stone. A wild variety of vines and climbing roses cover parts of the buildings and stone fences and a big circular stone well, complete with a pump, is in the center of the courtyard offering cool water to all the people and livestock that come and go at Lynn Farm. It is a very pretty setting for the occasion. Topper is to land right in the center of the courtyard in front of their prestigious guests. It will be a grand entrance.

Hunter and Topper have practiced and practiced landing until Hunter can tell Topper exactly where to set down. The first time Hunter brought Topper into the courtyard and the other animals had a glimpse of him, things were a bit exciting. You could say it caused panic in every direction. The sheep jumped their fences and ran away, and it took almost a whole day to find them and get them home again. The pigs were too short to see over their stone wall, and missed all the fun. The horses were frightened, and left for the far south pasture and would not let anyone anywhere near them for hours and hours. Topper was at their barn and they wanted to be somewhere else—just about anywhere else. The donkey was the only one of all the animals that hadn't caused major alarm. All she did was stop a good distance away and watch with great caution. When she was sure Topper wasn't a threat she came for a closer look. It took the horses days to adjust, and when Ruston suggested Hunter put Topper in the big barn one of the young colts jumped out of his stall that had a half door, and ran all the way to Glendale. At least there hadn't been any injuries to speak of, only a few broken fences and gates, and in time all the animals adjusted. They accepted the fact Topper was there to stay and even when he dropped in rather suddenly from the sky, they no longer even so much as blinked.

***

Now, many days after all this excitement, it is the day of the mayor's visit. He and his guests are instructed to tie their horses on the valley road—they will understand soon enough. When the guests are all in place and everything is set, Ruston will wave a big red blanket, the signal for Hunter and Topper, who will wait on the edge of the cliff. On the appointed day, Mayor Daily is a bit peevish at having to walk all the way from the valley road, and Ruston smiles to himself knowing in a few minutes he will forget all about his fatiguing walk. With a few words about the necessity to remain calm, and not to move until he tells them it is safe, Ruston waves the blanket. Hunter shouts in his excitement as they drop over the side of the cliff and glide toward their target.

"Ruston, I certainly hope you haven't called us out on a wild goose chase. You know as mayor, I haven't the time to spend on silly inventions." He pauses as Ruston reaches out and turns him around and points up in the air. For a moment Ruston is afraid his honored guests will bolt and run. In horror they watch as the sky-top slips out of the sky and lands right in front of them—it's too much. Several make a run for the house while another is frozen in place, too frightened to even scream. Hunter thinks it's pretty cool, but is very careful not to laugh.

In disbelief they stare as Hunter strokes and speaks to his giant pet while Ruston steps forward and rubs Topper's neck while feeding him apples. Apples are even better than pig feed. "Son, now do some figure eights for us, we'd like to see you and Topper take off and fly."

In utter amazement the men watch, with their jaws gaping as Topper races away and leaps into the air. It's a thrilling thing to see a small boy perched up on a huge sky-top. While Hunter circles high above them, the mayor and his council begin to come out of their shock and ask questions. They all talk at once and as their excitement grows they get quite loud. Each wants to know how taming a sky-top was possible, and to hear the story first from Ruston and Jason, and then later from Hunter. When Hunter lands Topper the second time the men cheer and want to know if he is gentle enough for them to touch. Ruston hands them each some apples and tells them to be careful. Hunter is still seated on top and strokes and clucks, hoping to help keep Topper calm

37

as the excited men step closer. Their agitation and jerky manner make Hunter wonder if his cousins might have been more self composed Then again, he decides, *probably not.*

Topper wants to laugh just as much as Hunter does, but manages to control himself. What he really wants to do is wait until the men are very close, then jump at them or make a terrible noise. It would be such fun to see them run screaming away, but that wouldn't be nice and he is sure it would spoil whatever it is Hunter's father expects to accomplish with the demonstration. So Topper is a very good boy and is quite patient with the excited men.

The day is a huge success and Mayor Daily insists upon a great celebration. Needless to say, the Lynns are relieved to know Topper will soon be a celebrity rather than a community menace.

Overnight Topper becomes the town's main topic for discussion and debate. Gossip is amazing in how fast it can spread and what people choose to do with it. In this instance the traffic on Lynn's lonely valley road triples several times over with people walking, riding, and leaning out of carriages. Some people are so bold as to come right to Lynn's door and demand to see the sky-top. Dexter is given permission to bark and be quite rude in his welcome. Ruston is about fed up with some of their nosey visitors. Yet, he understands some people don't know how to wait very well. Being patient is something some adults don't do any better than small children. Someday, maybe they will learn. So the Lynns laugh and keep Topper hidden while people continue to nag and pester. And who can blame them?

***

The celebration day finally arrives and Hunter and Topper are flying high above Glendale waiting for Ruston to wave the red blanket. Hunter can hear the band playing and see the people hurrying about and pointing up at him. Banners and flags are everywhere and Hunter knows there will be food, lots of food, and he is so hungry. Just thinking about all the pies and cakes and sweets he loves to eat makes his mouth water and his tummy growl. A big circle is roped off in the middle of the square's grassy playing field. The church, school, bank, and shops are all built around a large park area called the town square. The trees are big and beautiful and crowd close to where Topper is to land. Leaning over to one side as they glide past the square, Hunter takes a better look. "Top, that little rope circle looks pretty small to me. Will you fit in that

38

little spot?" Topper looks back at his small passenger and nods his head. Oh, how he loves this little boy.

Hunter looks down at Topper wondering, *This crazy bird acts like he knows just what I said.* Hunter laughs and gives him a pat on his powerful neck. "Silly bird."

"Still, Top. It looks too small. Guess we'll just have to wait and see. Your body may fit in the circle, but your wings sure won't. They just don't understand do they? Well, they will see soon enough just how big a sky-top really is. You're going to be a sensation." Hunter's comments are lost as he sets himself for what some people would call a "roll-back." On a horse, riding one is one thing, but on a sky-top a roll-back takes on a whole new depth, like a hundred feet or so. So, banking with a very steep angle, Topper's wings tip to near vertical and they slide down through the sky at a frightening speed, then when Topper rights himself he is going in the opposite direction. You need to be very high in the air before you try a roll back on a sky-top.

Shrieks of every sort come up to Hunter and he can see people pointing and waving. "Guess, that did look pretty cool. They sure are excited." Topper clacks and almost seems to laugh. "You think they're funny don't you?" He pats Topper, who nods his head and smiles with his big mouth gaping.

They glide over the square, their shadow racing beneath them; the air is cool and sweet and the band plays a lively polka that makes Hunter want to dance. Everything is so different when you are gliding on nothing but air. You get a whole new perspective on everything. Making a slow graceful turn and heading back toward the village, Hunter can see people are still arriving. The roads are crowded with wagons, buggies, and people everywhere. "Would you look at all those people. There must be hundreds of 'em down there." Leaning off to one side for a better look he comments, "People must be coming from all around, cuz I don't think there are that many people for more than a hundred miles around here." He pauses giving the situation some thought and decides, "I guess a sky-top is pretty exciting, even a mean one. I think I'd go a hundred miles to see somebody fly on one." He considers further, Topper's wings beat a few powerful strokes and they climb and catch a rising current and glide on. "Yup, Top, I'd walk or even crawl a hundred miles if I had to, to save you all over again. Some of those people down there probably didn't believe you were real. Some people told Dad he was lying. It made him mad.

"Well, they are about to see up close that you are real and that not all sky-tops are bad. No, they just have a bad reputation, just like Dad says."

A flash of red catches Hunter's eye, "That's the blanket Top, it's time for us to go down." Topper seems to rest on the air, there isn't the slightest flick of a giant wing. He tips his great head looking at the colorful confusion beneath him. Hunter is sure Topper knows what he is to do. He hovers a second, then drops almost straight down. His big wings beat a gentle back wave to balance and slow them. As they near the ground, people scream and Topper doesn't like it one little bit. There is a moment of indecision and Hunter is afraid Topper will pull up and fly away. After all, Topper has never been to town before, he's never heard a band play, and he's never-ever seen so many people. Hunter pats him and clucks and clicks just the way Topper does when he is happy and strange as it might seem, Topper answers and clicks and clucks right back.

Down they come into the center of the circle and Topper stretches out his wings to their greatest length and whips them over the top of the crowd. He seems to want the people to stand farther back. In an effort to get away from the whip like wings there is a stampede in the way of retreat. People shriek in horror and do their best to run, but the crowd is so squashed together there is no way to run and not hurt someone. Some people are quite rude. Topper watches the confusion with a strange look on his face. Eyeing the people with a certain amount of devilry in his expression he opens his huge mouth and snaps at the people he feels are too close. The crowd is, at this point, in the road circling the square. Some are even back against the buildings, while others have ducked down the alleyways or gone inside wherever possible.

Standing his very tallest, which is very tall, Topper points his beak toward the heavens and trumpets and ear shattering sound then he stretches his long rubbery neck out and hisses at the people just like an angry swan—a giant angry swan. Everyone is terrified; it is a wonderfully scary thing to see.

Without doubt, Topper's entry is every bit the sensation Mayor Daily hoped it would be. Now the trick is to put order back into the situation. It's rather difficult to have a village celebration and picnic with a flying dinosaur standing near the refreshments and all the people in hiding. Ruston hands out apples to the town council who are to feed Topper and start the celebration. However there is a problem, the council members have just seen the Lynn's gentle pet rout the whole community in a few brief seconds—things aren't going well. Topper has a funny smirk on his face and Hunter is wise enough not to laugh. Jason steps up and tosses Topper an apple which he deftly catches. It's a little bit like you or me taking a pill, gulp and it's gone. Two more apples disappear, and Jason commands, "Down, Top." Topper sighs a sigh that only a sky-top can manage, and down he goes and up scrambles Jason. Topper looks smaller when he sits and folds up his wings.

Would you look at this—the mayor has an apple! You can see he's not real happy with himself. Yet, here he comes walking right up to Topper who raises his head cocking it to one side then bringing it down again, he gently takes the mayor's apple. He holds the apple a moment in his beak then crushes it. "Slurp, splat!" apple juice explodes and poor Mayor Daily gets it right in the face! Oh, did Topper do that on purpose? We will never know, but Hunter has about lost it. Thankfully, Jason is there and gives him a punch in the ribs, but it's too late, Hunter laughs. Two of the council step forward and offer apples. The now very messy splattered mayor, offers a couple more apples. It almost looks as though they are making peace offerings.

Topper seems quite happy with the situation and the gifts the brave community people bring to him in the form of apples, melons, and even a whole loaf of bread seem to have appeased the whole situation. Remember Topper likes pig food. Oh, my goodness, lets hope no one gives him a pie. It's best he never know about pies.

Chat Dixon and his gang of followers are there in the crowd and watch at a little distance. Then with a swagger Chat brings a melon to Topper who eyes the boy with suspicion. Jason and Hunter still sit on his back and he can feel their tension. *Could this be someone they don't like?* he wonders. Looking back over his shoulder he sees Jason make a fist with an expression of definite dislike. For a moment he wrestles with the problem then with a little clicking growl he takes the melon from Chat's hands and holds it in his huge beak for a second or two before raising it quickly over they boy's head and squashing it. Melons are juicy messy things and Topper was very careful to be as messy as possible. Exactly as planned, Chat's swagger is gone as he retreats with laughter all around him. Hunter loses it this time and Jason doesn't even bother to give him a good one in the ribs.

For the next hour Topper is petted, fed, gawked at and admired by every person at the celebration. Everyone wants to hear the whole story from Hunter and Jason and then again from Ruston. They wonder how it is possible for such a little boy to ride and control such a huge, ferocious beast. It is a miracle, and Hunter is a little hero. Mayor Daily finishes the festivities with an impressive speech and asks Hunter if he and Topper would be interested in carrying the mail. He thinks the sky-top should take important messages back and forth between villages and even over the mountains. This is a bit too much for Hunter and he's not sure what to say. Somehow the idea is too big to even think about.

So this is a beginning of something very new and thrilling in the little village of Glendale. Hunter is still very young, and there is plenty of time before he needs to think about grown-up things like carrying messages and mail. Ruston tells the mayor before the celebration is over they must give the idea of carrying the mail some thought before they make definite plans for the future.

That night when Ruston steps into Hunter's and Jason's room to say good night, Jason asks, "Dad, are there other sky-tops around close?"

"There might be. Why, son?" Ruston tries to keep his face very serious as he watches Jason's expression in the candlelight. Jason tips his head and grins as he asks, "Do you think it might be possible to train another sky-top the way we have Topper?" He's afraid his father might say, "no."

"You, know I've been wondering the same thing. We might see if we can find one, or even two, or three more. What do you think, Jason, would you like to have one of your own?"

"Dad, you know I would, and I think I'm old enough to carry the mail. Maybe?"

"Let's see if we can find another sky-top or two; then we will think about carrying the mail." Both Ruston and Jason are having trouble keeping quiet so Hunter can sleep. Ruston tries to be serious as he comments, "You know, there is something we really have to build before we can even consider another sky-top."

"What's that?" Jason is serious, he hopes his father doesn't have to be gone and build another bridge. He wrinkles up his face and tries to think of what his dad might be talking about.

"Think, Jason," Ruston laughs.

"I know! I know!" Jason shouts with laughter, "A bigger feed crib—we'll have to build a much bigger feed crib!"

By this time both of them are laughing so loud they wake up Hunter who is too sleepy to enjoy their joke. He isn't sure what's so funny about a bigger feed crib, but he is glad they are having such a good time. When his family laughs he doesn't have to understand, it just makes him happy.

Chapter 5

A PROMISE IS A PROMISE

The wind howls with a heavy late summer rain around the snug Lynn home. Deep thunder rumbles a distant sigh and Dexter raises his sleepy head. For a moment he studies his family gathered in a cheery group around their big keeping room table. He smacks his big mouth and wishes he could have some of what they have on their plates, it smells so good.

"Yum, Mom, you make gooood pies," Hunter rubs his tummy and holds up his plate for another slice. "May I have another piece, pleeeeese!"

Lettie looks especially pretty as she cuts Hunter another piece of pie and sets it on his plate. The lantern light makes her soft auburn hair a golden red and her big gold circle earrings sparkle and dance as she moves. "Jason, take smaller bites! You look like some animal wolfing down your food," Lettie corrects.

"Oink, oink, snort," Hunter teases and as he snorts again, chokes and ends in a spasm of coughing with occasional snorts and oinks.

Jason chooses to ignore his little brother and politely straightens his posture, "I know, elbows in and off the table, sit tall, bring your food to your mouth and not your mouth to your food, chew with you mouth shut, and never talk with food in your mouth." He relaxes and grins, "Your pie is just so good, Mom. I couldn't help myself."

Ruston finishes his pie and pushes his plate to one side and asks, "You spent a lot of time today up by the waterfall, what were you and Hunter doing?"

"I shot hundreds of arrows and I swear that blasted target moves every time I turn an arrow lose. Hunter had a better day than I did—he made quite a city with canals and everything by the pool at the falls."

"Yah, and Dexter kept sitting in the middle of my roads and thought it was funny," Hunter comments to no one in particular.

"How is it that the target moves around?" Ruston asks with an amused smile, his deep gray eyes sparkling with humor.

"Dad, my arrows always wind up in the upper left hand corner of the target. If I aim low and right they still go up and left."

"It sounds as though you are twisting the string or rolling it off your fingers when you release. It would make your arrows arc one way or the other. Your release must be straight and clean. Simply, open your fingers and set the arrow free. And you can't move either hand on the release." Ruston pauses and considers, "What does your finger guard look like?"

"I've almost worn it out."

"When you twist the string it whirls back to straight as it leaves your hand and that burns, and wears out finger guards. I'll make you another finger guard and tomorrow as soon as the rain clears, I'll go up with you and we'll see if we can get your arrows in a group closer to the target center."

"That'd be great ….."

"Jason," Lettie interrupts. "I can't figure out why this sudden passion for shooting arrows and why you wanted your dad's old bow rather than one more suited to your size. You could hardly draw the silly thing when you first started and your shoulders hurt until I was sure you'd give up."

Jason stares at his mother in obvious disbelief, "If you and Dad won't let me take Topper and go hunting for a sky-top of my own until I can shoot like a man, then I'd better practice. I'm in a hurry because school will start right after fall harvest and I won't have much time, so I'm practicing all I can now. And Mom, I just don't have time to be bothered with a kid's bow if I'm to shoot like a man." Jason takes a last big bite of his pie and looks up at his father as if he'd explained all that needed explaining.

There is a rather dramatic and sudden stillness around the Lynn family table. Hunter's eyes are about as big as his empty plate. *Jason must have rocks in his head if he thinks Mom or Dad will ever let him do that!* Taking a glance at his dad he notices he looks as though he might be sick. With a little wrinkle between his brows, he decides his dad is in shock and glances at his mom.

It's best we don't look at Lettie at all. She has turned very pale and her knuckles are white as she grips the side of the table. Jason has no idea what a bomb shell he has dropped on his good parents. Sky-top hunting is the last thing any sane parent would permit their thirteen year old son to do, or their sixteen, or eighteen year old either for that matter. How can Jason possibly think his parents will let him go off on such a venture? Things are suddenly clear to them. Now they understand the reasons behind the hours and hours he has spent suffering with aching muscles, fatigue, and frustration while fighting to force his father's powerful bow into submission.

Right at the moment Jason wonders what his father must be thinking to make him look as though someone had just hit him in the stomach and upset his pie.

For a moment Ruston stares off into space, then giving himself a mental shake he sits a little taller, "Son, I can't turn you lose to go hunting for sky-tops. You are only thirteen years old and no father in his right mind would permit such a plan."

"I'll be fourteen next month." Jason seems to feel this might make a difference. When Ruston's look doesn't soften, Jason explodes, "Then why are we building the new huge feed crib? I thought it was for the sky-tops I was going to catch for us?"

"I have told you that you may have a sky-top of your own, but I have never suggested you go and catch them. It was my intention to do that myself."

"But you can't," Jason almost raises his voice, "Topper can't carry you."

Ruston reaches out with a gentle hand and covers one of Jason's clenched fists and asks, "Have you stopped to consider how much you and Hunter weigh together and how much all the things you take up with you weigh?"

"No."

"Well, you and Hunter together weigh about what I weigh, and Topper is growing. Hunter asked me to let out Topper's harness straps only a couple of days ago and I was surprised at how much he's grown." Ruston studies Jason a moment and feels his son's frustration and understands his desire. "By spring I think our young giant rooster will carry me with considerable ease; and then I will go and find the sky-tops we both want."

"But you said when I could shoot like a man, you'd let me fly out beyond the valley—you said I could go and find where the sky-tops live.

That's why I've spent every last minute up there doing my best to shoot your huge bow." He takes a deep breath and sputters, "You can't go back on what you said."

"All right," Ruston pauses and takes a deep breath, "Jason, I'll give you some perimeters. When you can put six arrows in a six inch center of the target where it sits now with the shooting line at the edge of the irrigation ditch ...."

"Oooooh," Jason rears back in his chair with a terrible outburst, "Noooo, that will take forever!"

Ruston doesn't appear to have heard, "and you must shoot the six arrows within fifteen or less seconds."

"But, Dad! No one can do that."

Lettie sits very still watching and listening, "Your father can," she almost whispers.

Jason looks at her in disbelief, "No, way!"

"Your father was the finest archer in the king's palace guard. No one could beat him, and I've seen him, and he really can do what he has just said you must do."

Ruston appreciates Lettie's support and leans toward Jason, "Tomorrow we will work together, and son, when you can shoot the six arrows in fifteen seconds or less into the target I will let you fly beyond the cliffs. But, you are to stay away from any sky-tops you see and you are to return straight home before you are seen. Then together we will plan as to how we will catch the sky-tops. Is that understood?"

"Yes, sir," Jason sighs, "Dad, do you promise to let me go when I pass your test?"

With a little frown Ruston agrees, "Yes son, I promise." Then turning to Hunter he asks, "Hunter, do you understand?"

"Yes, sir," he frowns and mutters, "Does that mean I have to shoot like Jason before I can go. If it does, I'll be stuck here in this old valley for the rest of my life. I'll never ever be able to draw that big bow."

"In time you will. Right now it's time for Jason to learn. But you need to practice—shooting well takes time."

Lettie starts gathering up the dishes, "I hope it takes you years and years. You are way too young to go sky-top hunting, and Ruston, I don't even want you chasing after those big birds. Other sky-tops may not be like Topper. I can't believe what this family is considering. Each of you must be crazy."

Jason gives his father a worried glance, "Mom, when I can hit the target fast enough every time, just like Dad said, you'll let me go, won't you?"

For a moment Lettie looks fierce and mad, then she relaxes and is sad. Looking down, she studies the dirty dishes in her hands and gives her head an uncomfortable little shake. She loves her boys and wants to please them, but she also wants them safe. A few seconds pass before she takes a deep breath and looks at Ruston as if for help, then answers, "I'll have to let you go, I guess. Your father has promised."

***

Some promises are more difficult to keep than others and Ruston's promise proves to be one of questionable wisdom because a promise should be binding, and both boys have taken their father quite seriously.

For weeks now Jason and Hunter have spent as many hours every day as possible shooting arrows into what is left of their target. The fall harvest has begun and both boys are busy every waking minute. The winter feed must be put up, and all the vegetables and fruit stored so there will be food to eat all winter. Winter is the time for school and snow, and summer is to get ready for winter. Despite the heavy work schedule, the boys have managed to find time to practice, and the dedicated hours of practice have made a difference. Hunter now manages to hit the target most of the time with a certain degree of accuracy using his small bow, and Jason can hit dead center more often than not.

One afternoon they manage to finish work quite early and Hunter grabs his father's hand and gives it a good tug. "Say, Dad, when are you gonna come and watch us shoot?"

"How about right now?" Ruston laughs at Hunter's excitement.

A little later Ruston watches as arrows fly toward the old target, and is surprised to see Hunter draw his bow and hit well within the target with almost every shot. He is even more surprised to see Jason group his arrows in a space less than a foot across. Later that night Jason hears his father tell his mother, "Lettie, we'd better brace ourselves, Jason is going to be very good with his arrows much sooner than either of us expected. He has a special gift for accuracy and a swift easy way that will make him fast. I think very fast, perhaps the fastest I've ever seen. I don't know—it's just a feeling."

"I'm surprised you thought he might not shoot very well for a long time." Lettie gives her husband a funny look, "He's carried a bow around with him since he was old enough to walk. He's shot at everything including the cloths on my wash line, and my chickens and he's hit where he's aimed. I knew he was good, way beyond his years. And Ruston, you've helped him and thought he was cute with his little bows—well, you've taught him to shoot. All he has to do now is to have the strength to draw the heavy bow and learn to be fast."

Jason is a little embarrassed because he has overheard his parents talking and tiptoes away. Yet, he can't help feeling the thrill that goes with hearing their praise and confidence in him. He knows they are pleased as well as concerned.

***

Several days later, Hunter and Topper are flying back and forth over Jason while he practices with his arrows and Jason wonders if he could hit the target from the air. He stops and stares after Hunter and Topper as they grow smaller in the distance. When they circle back he waves and persuades them to land.

Hunter is quite sure Jason's idea is even crazier than some of his ideas. "You've got to be kidding—man I can barely hit the thing from the ground and you want to try from the air?" He gives the top of his head a serious rub and stares in disbelief at his brother. We must remember, both boys love to fly and between them they only have one sky-top. This makes things a bit difficult at times. It seems sharing is not always easy for brothers. Topper has no difficulty flying with both boys aboard at the same time so this is not the problem. It's the saddle, it has only one front seat. It's good they have two safety harnesses or one of the boys might have fallen off on numerous occasions.

Hunter listens to Jason's idea and is suspicious. Jason isn't asking to sit in front and do the guiding—no, he wants him to ride in front and take Topper back and forth in front of the target so he can practice shooting from the air. This sounds pretty cool. So it is with gleeful giggles that Hunter pulls Jason up behind him and helps him adjust his safety harness.

"You'll never hit it, Jace," he teases as he turns Topper toward the open field. With leaping strides Topper covers the ground and Hunter shakes his head in mild disbelief commenting, "Man, I can't hit the

49

thing standing still very well. It'll be a waste of arrows." But Jason isn't paying any attention, he's too busy getting his arrows all set. This is a bit difficult to do while Topper makes his racing strides before jumping into the air. Bump, bounce, scramble, Jason had better hang on. Topper runs in great racing bounds down the cliff pasture. The giant wings pound the air and then they are air borne. Now is a much easier time to adjust things.

Hunter's right—Jason can't hit the target anywhere near where he aims and this tickles Hunter's funny bone. He shouts gleeful laughter at every miss until he glances back and sees his brother's serious face, then he is very quiet. Sometimes laughing isn't nice, and he decides this is one of them. Finally, Jason manages to get his last arrow on the outer edge of the target. After gathering up his scattered arrows and trying again and again he's learned four things. First, he needs to take off with more than a handful of arrows; second, he must allow for much more wind resistance; third, to allow for Topper's forward movement; and fourth, that it is darned tough to aim down.

"Well you managed to hit the target a couple of times," Hunter comforts Jason as they fill Topper's feed bin. "I didn't think you'd do it, but you did, so don't be all put out."

Topper clicks a soft rolling sound and circles his long neck round Jason's shoulders and looks as though he wants to give advice and encouragement. Strangely Jason understands Topper's meaning and gives him an affectionate hug.

"Yah, I hit it, but it's going to take even more practice than I thought," Jason looks discouraged and Hunter watches his brother, not knowing quite what to say. Topper studies both boys a moment and places his great head next to Jason's and purrs soft sounds, it's amazing how tender such a huge bird can be.

"It's okay we'll do it again tomorrow and the next day and before you know it you will hit it every time," Hunter is positive and Topper is thoughtful.

The afternoon's shooting practice has given Topper some rather encouraging ideas. He knows it's only a matter of time before the sawtooth comes back. Before this time comes he must have a plan. As he considers Jason's arrows he wonders if one of those little barbed sticks could stop a sawtooth. *Not likely,* he decides. The best plan is retreat into the Lynn barn, the sawtooth might not follow and the thought gives him comfort. There is hope. He munches his feed peacefully while considering his options. It will be dark soon and he will go home and see his father, he must tell him about Jason's arrows.

***

The days are colder now and the hills and mountains around Lynn Farm are covered in the brilliant colors of fall. The baby lambs, calves, and colts are weaned, and the barns are filled with winter feed. Lettie's summer garden is all put away in lines of jars and crocks in her deep root cellar. Everything is ready for winter and Ruston has time to check on Jason's progress. He's watched the boys flying all over the valley and has been concerned about the hours wasted. As he and Dexter walk the cart track up to the cliff pasture he can't help but notice the once grassy lane is now a well beaten road. He also notices the cliff pasture's usual lush grass has been trampled in a definite pattern. Studying the condition of his pasture grass he wonders just how many times Topper must have taken off and landed to create such a bare stretch. Dexter gives an excited bark as a swift shadow passes over them and Ruston waves, signaling for the boys to come down.

While the boys land and trot toward him from across the field, Ruston unrolls a new target. Lettie has painted a mountain cat on a piece of cloth. It's a pretty mean looking cat and Ruston looks at Lettie's art work and thinks, *She's a pretty good artist.* He also hopes the fun of shooting at a cat will prove more exciting than at a bunch of circles.

"Gee Dad, it's great you've come to see us. We thought you'd never come," Hunter shouts as he bounces along with Topper's painful trot.

"We were about to come get you," Jason is so pleased, then adds, "We've been afraid you were too busy." Then both boys see the new target, "Wow, that's really cool. Did you paint it?"

"No, your mother did." But the words are lost in a moment of confusion as Jason and Hunter slide down Topper's wing and race to help set the new target in place.

Hunter runs as fast as his legs will carry him and rips the old target from the frame. He's glad, so very glad, the target is in such shredded shape his father didn't see the figure they'd been shooting at. He'd painted a figure on the target and they'd enjoyed shooting holes all over Chat Dixon's imaginary body. While Jason had humored him and even enjoyed shooting holes into Chat, Hunter knows his father would not approve and there would be an uncomfortable discussion about being good and kind, no matter how others treated you. At times such as this

Hunter would like to explode, *Phooey, you be nice and polite to Chat Dixon if you want, but someday I'm gonna smash his face in.* But first, Hunter has some serious growing to do and he doesn't want to talk about Chat Dixon right now with his father, so he wads up the old target face and crams it in under the hay target then looks around to see if his father had noticed. With a little sigh he smiles at Jason, who gives him a quick wink—their father had been too busy with Topper and the cat to pay any attention to Hunter's hurried repentance. *Sometimes older brothers are rather nice to have around,* Hunter decides as he grins and gives a little wink back.

Topper looks over Ruston's shoulder at the cat and is impressed. He nods his big head expressing himself with a variety of clucks and clicks and growls. He seems to be giving instructions of some sort—it would be nice if we could understand his strange noises. Regardless, his body towers over the activity and he does his best to help, when in reality his big body is usually in the way.

Giving Topper an affectionate pat, Ruston looks toward Jason and with a shake of his head asks if he can hit the target from a new line a little farther back. Jason answers with a nod and wonders why his dad looks so concerned. Ruston's next words answer his question, "Jason, you and Hunter have spent so much time flying all about, I'm wondering if you can still hit the target. Time is precious and shouldn't be wasted."

Hunter about chokes and he starts with a sputter to explain, but his words get all mixed up and Jason places a restraining hand on his shoulder, then he can't help himself and laughs.

"Boys, this isn't funny, I'm quite serious. You shouldn't be wasting your time flying all the time, there are other things that need to be done, you need worthwhile goals or a purpose....." Ruston's voice fades as he looks at his boys and wonders over their peculiar expressions.

Hunter looks up into his brother's face and gives an impish grin and they struggle to keep from giggling. Jason does his best to quiet the laughter that keeps bubbling around inside. He knows his father is serious, but he also knows he's been practicing and he's a little sad his dad hasn't understood what they'd been doing while they were flying back and forth over the farm and fields. Yet, how was his dad to know what they were doing? He was always working out in the fields or off somewhere building something for someone and has had no way of knowing what they were doing in the far cliff pasture.

With a funny little smile Jason walks back to the new line, "Where do you want me to group my arrows, Dad?" Ruston turns back toward his son and looks a little startled with the question as well as the confidences he senses. He wants to say, *don't worry about grouping your arrows, just hit the target,* but he doesn't. Instead he makes a small circle with his fingers around where the cat's heart would be, if he had one, and then joins his boys at the shooting line.

"Count for me, Dad."

Even more surprised, Ruston counts, "One, Two, Three," seconds while the arrows make incredible little zipping sounds as they whip through the air and smack into a small area over the cat's heart—all six arrows in less than fifteen seconds. Hunter jumps about and cheers and Dexter gets excited and races round and round leaping in the air and barking, but none of them notice. Ruston is too shocked to make a sound, but Jason doesn't give him time to recover as he asks, "Do you want to see me hit the cat from the air?" All Ruston manages is a little nod and says, "I'd love to."

Next thing you know Topper is in the air gliding along not too far from the ground with Hunter holding the reins and Jason ready with his arrow. As Topper's huge wing drops out of Jason's way he lets an arrow fly and the arrow actually hits the cat, only not exactly where Jason had intended. The arrow hits the cat's rear end and this makes Hunter laugh, but Jason doesn't seem to mind. After several passes every arrow is a hit, although not perfectly grouped. Ruston is so impressed that Jason couldn't care less about being teased about the arrows in the cat's tail.

Later Lettie has to see Jason shoot, and even she is impressed. She has to admit Jason is a superb marksman and with reluctance she agrees, Jason has passed the shooting test. This is a very difficult situation. Ruston wants to go with his boys, but can't. Topper isn't big enough to carry him and one of the boys at the same time. With a fearful tightness in his heart he knows Jason and Hunter are much too young for such adventure, but a promise is a promise. He knows he should have been stricter with his requirements, but how was he to know Jason would apply himself with such dedication or that he would have such an incredible talent with his bow and arrows? Jason's skill has now proved to be equal to the challenge, and Ruston realizes he must relent. He must keep his promise and let his boys fly beyond their valley in search of other sky-tops.

One thing is of great comfort to both parents. Jason is now one of the finest archers in their valley and equal to competing with any of the men Ruston has ever watched or competed against at the contests both near and far. Such knowledge makes a father's heart swell with fatherly pride. So it is that Ruston keeps his promise, and with a new set of rules the boys are given permission to fly beyond the cliffs.

Chapter 6

RACE AND QUEENIE

One crisp cool day, several weeks later, Topper and the boys are floating in the air many miles east of the cliff rim and Jason notices Hunter's safety harness has come lose. The buckle is broken and Jason can't figure out how to get Hunter strapped back into place. They decide to land and make some emergency adjustments, and Hunter aims Topper down toward a nice clear space on the top of a ridge and they drop out of the sky. While Jason does his best to fix the broken harness, Hunter slides to the ground and begins looking around. Flying beyond the cliff has been a great disappointment to them. Both had imagined what it would be like east of the cliff and had found their imagination to be quite wrong. It is a desolate place. It is no wonder the people of the valley never bother to hunt or explore beyond the cliffs to the east. The cliff top is all rock, with rocks and more rocks for miles and miles in every direction. Huge sandstone boulders are scattered about as though some giant might have dumped them out of his pockets. There are a few scrubby trees and shrubs that look abused and mistreated. Hunter studies the massive piles of sun baked stone wondering just how they got there and why there isn't any dirt. Muttering to himself he pulls a sack of apples out of their saddlebag and shows them to Topper. Taking a big bite out of an extra big apple he hands the rest to Topper and both seem quite pleased with the arrangement.

"Is all the cliff like this Topper, I mean just bare rock and scrubby trees?" Hunter asks with childlike sincerity and Topper shakes his big head. "We're looking for sky-tops like you, do you know where there might be more sky-tops?" Topper gobbles another apple and nods his head. Hunter laughs, "Silly, bird. I wish you could really understand me." Topper puts his huge head down, right next to Hunter's small face, and gives him a little push with a low sounding growl. "Hey, what's that for?" For an uneasy moment, Hunter wonders if Topper might be trying to tell him something. "Top, are ....,"

Jason interrupts with a command, "Hurry and get up, I've got your harness fixed with a very ugly knot, but it will work for now." He pauses to give Hunter a pull up into the saddle, and taking the bag of apples he shoves it deep into their saddle bag and continues, "We aren't supposed to land so let's get going. Mom and Dad will understand, but still...." Topper dives off of the edge of the ridge and Jason is unable to finish his thought for a moment. Diving from ridges has a way of taking your breath away.

Hunter finds his voice first, "Jace, I want to try something. Let's ask Topper to show us where the sky-tops are. He could take us to them if we could make him understand. Let's try ..."

No sooner are the words out of Hunter's mouth than Topper does an incredible roll back, slicing the sky with his giant wings, and levels out in the opposite direction. Hunter is very glad Jason had insisted they stop to fix his strap; there would have been no way he could have stayed seated in the saddle and ride such a dive without the harness. Catching his breath, Hunter pulls and yanks on Topper's reins, but Topper ignores every effort to turn him. Jason joins the tug of war and with their combined strength it is no use. Faster and faster they fly. Never has Topper flown so fast. The speed is beyond anything the boys might imagine. The thrill of the speed makes them want to shout and at the same time it frightens them. Topper is not taking them home, no, he is headed north and a little east and already they are farther from home than they've ever been before.

After some minutes of struggle, Jason encourages Hunter to release his death grip on the reins, and looking down at their pet sky-top he comments, "Hunter, he's taking us somewhere."

Hunter nods his agreement and adds, "Let's hope it's someplace nice. I have a very bad feeling about this."

"I don't think Topper would hurt us, but he certainly isn't taking care of us right now." Jason pauses as he watches a neat "V" of wild geese flying below them. Despite the many hours they've spent flying, the sheer majesty or perhaps the magic of it still leaves them in silent wonder and appreciation for their experiences with Topper. The boys watch the geese, enjoying their now distant cries then turn their eyes back to their captor. "It's like some unseen force is pulling him," Jason almost whispers in Hunter's ear.

The barren terrain of the cliff near Glendale is now far behind, and the farther they travel the richer the landscape is below them. There are trees and meadows with small streams wandering through the hills and rich valleys. The fall foliage is glorious in color as they soar over a low mountain where the air is much cooler and the floor beneath them heavy with timber. It is a literal patchwork of fall colors. Reds, yellows, oranges and greens all mixed together in a splendor of fall vegetation. Skimming the top of a craggy peak, Topper drops to a lower level, just missing the tree tops. This is heavenly fertile country. As the boys study the dense forest beneath them the ground vanishes as they glide over the edge of a sheer cliff. Their surprise is complete and Hunter gasps with a scream strangled in his throat. Topper swoops down into the deep curved valley, acting as though he might intend to land.

"Oh, no you don't, Top," Hunter yells while yanking up on his reins. But his feeble little pulls are a wasted effort, and Topper lands and trots across the valley floor in huge strides calling with a strange sound. His voice reverberates round them, echoing off the forest walls. Stopping at the edge of the timber, Topper throws his long neck high in the air and trumpets a horrible wonderful sound, then stands waiting.

Out of the forest comes an answering cry. Topper bobs his head and does a funny bounce dance in his excitement, his immense body jerking the boys in every direction. "That's it," Hunter has had enough, "no more being nice." He yanks on the reins shouting full volume his desire to get out of there quick. Pulling, kicking, and screeching his displeasure does no good, Topper isn't paying the least attention. Jason, however, does not follow Hunter's example, he's the total opposite— he's quiet and still. He waits and watches with an arrow set and ready.

The trees before them seem to shudder and several sky-tops step out of the dark towering forest and give a clucking greeting to Topper. Then, seeing Topper's passengers, they stop. Topper clicks and clacks nodding his head seeming to have an in-depth conversation with his friends. The largest of the sky-tops moves closer, his deep black body is about the size of their milk house, and makes Topper seem small. A dark brown sky-top that looks to be only a little smaller than the black monster, hesitates and seems a little nervous and bounces in little jumps back and forth a little distance away. The third sky-top is quite small in comparison and a pretty sky blue color. Jason wonders if this might be a female. It, she, or whatever, definitely has a feminine look. If sky-tops weren't so ugly, this one could be called pretty.

Jason and Hunter sit in fascinated wonder. It is quite obvious the huge birds are curious about them and are a little worried about coming closer. The big sky-top seems to be checking them out. Topper and the big black fellow make peculiar noises while nodding and wagging their huge heads. "They are talking," Hunter whispers back to Jason. "Yes, I know." Jason wishes his bow was bigger and meaner. He had the strange feeling his arrows were all but useless. "He could swallow us in one bite. We're the size of a nice frog to one of our geese."

"Jason, don't talk like that. Look at him—look at his eyes. He's only curious. Watch him."

Jason has to admit the big fellow is definitely interested in them; he acts as though he's never seen a person before. He doesn't look hungry or dangerous. An eternity seems to pass before he nods his big head and clacks with almost a smile. The tension seems to melt away and the other sky-tops click and clack too. The big brown one steps up close and looks Jason right in the eye. Jason keeps his bow ready, but nothing happens. After much head bobbing and tipping with endless clicking and clacking, Hunter manages to persuade Topper to turn and go. Topper doesn't want to leave and calls to his friends and they answer. With a little more urging Topper starts his run for take off and leaps into the air. He calls again with a wild screeching sound and Jason and Hunter watch with a rush of excitement as the three sky-tops make running leaps into the air and follow after them.

Jason and Hunter feel like shouting! What a thrill. Topper circles the valley gaining altitude and the boys look down and see the huge birds beneath them. They are so grand with their wings all stretched out. Topper calls again and they answer like mountainous swans. Jason and Hunter lose all caution and shout and cheer with sheer joy and excitement—three sky-tops!

Steadily they gain speed, each bird seeming to want to surpass the others. The boys marvel that the little sky-top can keep up. Wing tip to wing tip they move through the air. The boys glory in their speed and marvel at the four shadows skimming over the trees. The clucking never stops. All of a sudden the sky-tops make a steep turn and fly west, then a few seconds later they make a steeper turn back to the south. "I wonder what that was for," Hunter mutters, appreciating his safety harness and the fact they are headed toward home again.

The big sky-top is a little too close for comfort; he's looking at Jason and Hunter as if he might be deciding whether or not they are to be his lunch or dinner.

If they could understand the sky-top conversation they would know the big sky-top is most interested in how the boys are able to stay on. He had asked Topper if his passengers could stay on if they made a sudden turn. Then when the boys rode the turn he wanted to know why they hadn't fallen off. Topper then tried to tell him how the saddle and harness work, but the big sky-top didn't understand. So now in desperation Topper dives straight down then rolls back, his great wings beating the air in furious strokes. It happens so fast, Jason and Hunter pull leather and feel their hearts and stomachs have been left far above them. Topper's momentum is marvelous and he banks a beautiful turn and glides back in among his comrades almost laughing and clacking. Hunter and Jason have the funny feeling the birds are impressed. They look at the boys with a strange look of respect in their large soft eyes. The big black flies in close once again and this time, gliding right over Topper, he pulls on Hunter's harness and then nudges the saddle bags. Jason wonders if he can smell the apples and reaches toward him and clucks the way Hunter does when he's petting Topper.

The sky-top raises his head and cocks it to one side and clicks back in some kind of an answer. Taking a closer look, bringing his huge beak right up against Jason's back, he clucks and makes several guttural sounds from somewhere deep in his throat before dipping back to a wings length away.

The edge of the cliff overlooking Lynn farm is just ahead and the big birds circle back and start to fly away. Seeing their retreat, Topper banks a sharp turn and calls after them. Hunter is frantic and pulls and yanks as he tries to turn Topper back around toward home. The three sky-tops land on the edge of the cliff and refuse to follow. Topper calls and calls. If the truth is to be known, Jason is very glad the sky-tops have stopped. He knows his dad isn't ready for three more sky-tops. They need to make plans. What kind of a pen did they need? How do you catch a sky-top?

Topper circles over where the sky-tops stand and calls again and again, he clacks and makes all kinds of strange sounds. Hunter pats Topper's shoulder, hoping to give him a little comfort. He knows Topper is upset and wonders what he can do to help him relax so he will take him and Jason home. In a little burst of inspiration he gives Topper another firm pat and says, "Topper tell them we'll bring them some food tomorrow. We'll bring lots of food and put it right where they are now. Can you tell them that?" Hunter is quite serious in his desire, but doesn't know how to make the birds understand. Topper makes a huge trumpeting sound and heads back over his friends where he screeches and makes all kinds of funny sounds. The other sky-tops listen, their great necks stretched up following Topper as he circles. The boys watch

59

as the birds begin to bob their heads and the little one gets excited and jumps up and down and flaps her beautiful blue wings. Then with a little coaxing from Hunter, Topper tips in a deep turn and heads for Lynn Farm and the secure big barn.

***

Now Jason has every reason to be very excited about his and Hunter's afternoon. After all, how many young boys fly around hunting for sky-tops? You have to admit everything about Jason's and Hunter's day has been more than a little out of the ordinary. That evening while Jason tells his parents for, what must be, the tenth time all about the sky-tops, no one seems to notice Hunter hasn't said much and sits listening to Jason's elaborate retelling of their rather fantastic afternoon. Being quiet is not normal for Hunter. No, not normal at all. Usually Hunter tries to shout over his brother and always wants to tell the story himself. So what is Hunter's problem?

Hunter is a little bit worried about what to do. He knows something that no one else knows, and he can't quite decide whether or not he is being a "silly boy," as he is sometimes called, or whether he has hit upon something of great importance. Hunter doesn't like it when no one believes him, and he's a little afraid this will be the case if he tells what he thinks he knows. He puzzles in his mind over the times when he has been scolded for making things up. Those times aren't fun to remember. His heart is a little heavy as he considers how much he wants to be as important as his big brother. He had thought telling better stories would help him be more important. But, it hadn't worked. He'd told several made-up stories and each time the stories had turned out very bad for him. He wasn't going to tell made-up stories anymore.

As Hunter sits beside the keeping room fire stroking his mother's big cat, he watches Jason tell all about the three sky-tops and he keeps remembering his father's words the last time he had gotten into trouble for one of his stories. Ruston had told him, *Hunter, we deal only in truth around here.* His father had told him more than just that, but those are the only words Hunter can remember right at the moment. *We deal only in truth.* Hunter has the feeling when he doesn't tell the truth he is not a good part of their family, and he wants to be an important part of his family and to have them be pleased with him.

Hunter knows that if he tells them what he thinks he knows, it will be more important than Jason's story. Stories are important and he'd been working hard to learn to enjoy other people's stories and not to want to tell a better one. He must always remember that it isn't good to have to be the best all the time. Was his story important enough to stop Jason's story? Would they believe him or think he was just making it up? His small mind really wants to know.

Jason is in the middle of a sentence about how scary the huge sky-top had been when he looked him right in the eye, "I really thought he might try to eat ...."

Jason's words trail off as Hunter speaks in a very soft whispered voice. "There's something else that happened that Jason doesn't know." He hopes if it is really important they will know and let him share what he knows.

Ruston looks at his smallest son and smiles. Hunter is quite small to be as smart and as independent as he is. The fact that this little boy had captured and trained a huge sky-top is still difficult for him to believe. Unlike many ten year old boys, Hunter isn't silly very often. Ruston frequently is surprised at the depth of his youngest son's understanding. "What is it that Jason doesn't know, that you feel is important?"

Hunter gets to his feet, his back-side toasty warm from the big fire. It is obvious to Ruston and Lettie that Hunter is deep in thought and this makes them very interested in what he has to say.

"Dad, one of the buckles on my safety harness broke and we landed on top of one of the ridges east of here so we could fix it. While Jason was fixing the buckle I fed Topper some of my apples and I talked to him. I was just sort of wondering where the other Sky-tops were. I told Topper we were looking for more sky-tops and asked if he knew where to look." Hunter pauses and takes a deep breath. "I know this is dumb, but I was just sort of talking to myself. You know, out loud, but not really asking Topper because he's a dumb bird." Hunter stops again and leans toward his father and places his hand on Ruston's knee and looks up into his eyes. "Dad, Topper nodded his head and I thought it was funny and I laughed. It really was funny because I knew he couldn't understand me. I told Topper he was a dumb bird and he put his head right up to mine and looked as if he was mad at me. It was pretty strange. Topper's never done anything like that before."

Stepping away, Hunter wanders back toward the fireplace with his hands buried deep in his pockets. "Dad, I think Topper did understand me. I really think he did, because when we took off again I told Jason I wanted to ask Topper if he could take us to where the other sky-tops were and then I couldn't guide Topper at all. He just ran away with us."

Moving closer, Jason looks down at his little brother studying him with a puzzled expression. "He's right, Dad, Hunter did say that. Only he never had a chance to ask Topper anything. Topper just took off. It was sort of scary. He flew so fast, faster than he's ever gone before and he flew straight to where the three sky-tops were, and called them out of the forest. I was glad I had my bow and arrows, although I think they'd have been rather useless. The birds are huge. Topper is small beside the really big ones. Hunter's right, it wasn't an accident. Topper took us to the other sky-tops."

At this point Hunter forgets all his good intentions to say very little and while giving his dad's knee a violent shake back and forth, "That's not all, it's not all. Topper didn't want to leave his friends and I was afraid he wouldn't bring us home. I was really pulling and yanking on his reins and it wasn't working. Then I told Topper to tell his friends we'd come back tomorrow and bring them some food. He went right back and the sky-tops made the most awful noise clacking and squawking."

"Yes, yes, they were so loud and they jumped about like excited turkeys," Jason interrupts and everyone laughs because both boys are jumping up and down acting like the ridiculous sky-tops. Jason tries to continue above his families' noise then stops and stares at his little brother for a moment while Ruston and Lettie laugh at Hunter's imitations of the strange sounds made by the sky-tops. Hunter prances and jumps up and down and clicks, clacks and screeches just like the dancing sky-tops. It's all so funny, and Hunter loves it.

"Dad, Hunter is not making this up. He's right, the birds acted like they were having a conversation." Jason pauses then adds, "We'd better be there with food for the sky-tops tomorrow. Hunter said we would, and we have to be there."

***

It is now quite late that night and Topper is sound asleep in the Lynn's huge stone barn. Topper likes living in the big clean barn. The hay smells so good and Hunter keeps his bed piled high with wonderful clean straw, but the best part of living at Lynn farm is the feed. Topper loves pig feed. He is very happy on this night and sleeping quite well when he hears footsteps crossing the stone courtyard. He is not aware of the excitement the other sky-tops have caused or of the fact Hunter has told his family that he, Topper, might understand what is said. So he is surprised when he blinks open his big black eyes and finds three of the Lynns standing in front of him with a lantern shining in his face. He is even more surprised when Ruston asks very simply, "Topper, the boys think you understand what we are saying; is it true, can you understand me?"

Topper blinks again and stretches his long neck out in the soft straw on the floor where he had been sleeping and then curls his neck and body up into an upright sitting position. He looks down upon his family and wonders where Hunter is, then nods his head up and down. The situation interests him and he cocks his head to one side and looks down at Ruston, who has backed up a step or two with his lantern.

"Topper, did you take the boys to the other sky-tops?" Ruston asks and Topper bobs his head up and down with serious enthusiasm. "This is absurd!" Ruston comments, and is startled to hear a scratching growl come from deep in Topper's throat followed by a firm shake of Topper's head. Ruston can feel Topper's resentment at his words. "This isn't possible," Ruston mutters as Jason steps forward and pats Topper's long leathery neck.

"Do you like living with us, Topper?" Jason's small voice sounds lost in the massive barn. Topper nods and Jason goes on. "Would you like to bring your friends here to live with us?" The answer startles them because Topper not only bobs his head he squawks and clicks and clacks and makes it very clear, this would make him very happy. Apples and pig feed are the only other things in his life that cause this much excitement. "Do you think it will be difficult to get them to come and live here?" Topper answers with a negative shake of his long head.

Meanwhile, Hunter awakes from a very comfortable sleep and with one eye only half open, he glances over at his brother's bed, only his brother isn't there. The clear moonlight spilling into the room and across Jason's bed leaves no room for doubt. Sleepily, Hunter sits up to think this over. The house is too quiet. *Where is Jason?* Hunter slips out of bed and finds his fuzzy sheepskin slippers. They are warm and the floor is cold. He tiptoes out into the hall to find his mother or father, only they aren't in their room. He continues his search and learns he is alone in the house. Now Hunter is not the type of little boy who frightens easily. It is okay to wake up and find everyone gone. He knows there will be a good reason, but where could they be?

One thing is certain, if he is home all alone he intends to find some company. After very little thought he decides he will go and sleep in the barn with Topper and Dexter. Topper will take care of him and he is far too sleepy to play hide-and-seek with his family. For a moment or two he thinks about sleeping in the straw with Topper and goes back to his room for his pillow and his blankets, then half dragging, half carrying his huge pile of bedding he trudges across to the dark barn.

The door is part open. *'That's odd'*, he thinks as he drags his blankets along the stone floor. Boy, are those blankets going to be dirty.'

"What's everybody out here for?" Hunter almost shouts as soon as he finds his family gathered around Topper. He has managed to slip up behind them and the shock of his loud voice causes them to almost jump out of their skins. Dexter barks and Topper opens his huge beak and bounces little tiny bounces up and down. It is his way of laughing. "What's the big idea, everybody coming out here and leaving me all by myself?" Hunter plods forward, half tripping over his blankets. "My bed's all mussed up now, I'm going to sleep right here." While speaking he spreads his blankets and pillow under one of Topper's huge wings. It makes a nice tent.

"Topper, may I sleep with you? I think it's a good idea." Hunter crawls under his blankets and Topper nods in approval, and with his long frightening beak he gently picks up the edge of Hunter's blankets and covers the small boy.

Lettie is the first to gather her wits, "He really does understand; would you look at that. He understood every word." Topper nods his head and tips it to one side and looks closer at Lettie. If they could have read his thoughts they would have learned he had decided in that moment, Lettie actually has some brains. *She isn't half bad.* He will pay closer attention to her after this. *She's alright.*

"Topper, do you think the sky-tops will be on the cliff when we take them the food tomorrow?" Ruston asks and Topper's enthusiasm is apparent as he nods and clacks with sincere vigor. Lettie worries about Topper jumping up and doing the dance the boys had imitated and step all over Hunter. "I think Topper likes the idea," Ruston comments to Lettie and Jason.

"It's amazing, absolutely amazing. He really understands. No wonder Hunter and Jason have been able to do so much with him so easily. He understands." Lettie's words are spoken as she reaches forward and strokes Topper's leathery hide. "Take good care of Hunter tonight, please, and Topper, thank you for taking care of my boys. They are very important to me. It helps me to know you understand. I won't worry nearly so much."

Ruston watches this little exchange with relief in his heart. He has known how upset Lettie has been over the frightening sky-top living in their barn and sharing every spare moment of her boy's time. It will be easier now. Topper is more than just a big exciting pet—he has become one of the family.

The following day Jason takes a very large sack of feed up to the top of the cliff with Topper and waits for the sky-tops to come. Jason is about to give up and return home when he sees them winging their way high in the air toward him. It takes a little coaxing before they come near and try the feed. The big black sky-top takes a small nibble. Then a bite, then a gulp and the brown sky-top tastes and the little sky-top pushes her way forward and begins gobbling. It's obvious the feed is a success. Sky-tops like pig feed.

Each day for a week Jason makes the trip up to the cliff with more feed for Topper's friends. Soon he doesn't have to wait, because they are there waiting for him. Everyday he asks Topper to tell them they may have much more if they will come down to the farm. Then one day, the little sky-top, the one Jason has named Queenie, follows them home. The other sky-tops watch from the cliff as Topper and Queenie land near a very big feed trough. They watch as Jason carries several large buckets of feed and dumps them in the trough.

Jason calls for them to come. Topper screeches his loud trumpet sound and before Topper and Queenie finish too much of the feed the two remaining sky-tops take to the air and land some distance back from where Jason stands watching. Queenie follows Topper into the big barn that night and makes herself at home. She likes Topper's bed, and Jason is alarmed at the temper displayed by the two birds. Whoever thought of such a silly thing as fighting over a bed?

It takes more than two weeks before the middle sized sky-top, Jason has named Race, decides to come into the barn. He eyes Queenie's and Topper's beds and Jason points to the bed he has made for him. Queenie almost purrs from her cozy spot in the straw. Race answers with gentle clicks and soon walks several circles in his straw bed and sits down with a pleasant sigh. The largest sky-top they call Black Bert, because he reminds them of Bert, the big strong work horse that always wins the horse pulling contest each year at their valley farm show.

Bert comes to the trough to eat, but will not let Jason touch him and will not go near the other farm buildings. So at night he is shut out to sleep in the cold. It makes Jason feel bad to close the doors on the warm and comfortable barn and watch Bert fly off over the rim of the cliffs all alone. *Where does he go?* Jason wonders.

The first night Race spent shut in the big barn was a little worrisome. Jason ran to find his father and both stood together watching Race pace back and forth. Queenie kept a steady clacking going, trying to comfort him. Queenie likes the big barn, she even likes the pack saddle Ruston made for her. It is decorated with pretty red fringe on the soft blanket and looks quite festive. She enjoys flying with Topper and the boys and didn't mind when Ruston asked her to carry a small load of chickens to town with Jason and Hunter. They were to be delivered to the village market and had made a terrible racket. Queenie seems to love everything about Lynn farm and her new life.

***

By the time Jason feels Race is ready to fly with him it is winter and snow lies in drifts all around the farm buildings. On the day of their first flight together it would be difficult to decide who is the most excited Jason, Race, Topper, Hunter, Ruston, Lettie, or Queenie, not to mention Dexter who is excited over anything the least unusual.

It's a beautiful snowy day with the sun so bright it almost hurts their eyes. Jason squints as he watches Hunter and Topper take their galloping run for take off. Riding Race in the tiny space inside their barn hasn't prepared Jason for what it might be like to fly on this huge bird. In all honesty Jason is startled through and through as he feels Race's monstrous steps as he runs to catch up with Topper.

Ruston and Lettie cling to each other as they watch their boys speed down the farm lane toward the valley road and leap into the air. Sky-tops are supposed to be dangerous—they carry away sheep, pigs, and even people. They can't be trained—it has never been done before. And man certainly was not meant to fly, regardless of how large the bird happened to be. These are the traditional feelings of any sane human being, but Topper has proved so many things wrong.

Jason and Hunter circle in the cold, cold air; they laugh and shout, their voices making strange echoing sounds off the cliffs. Queenie flies round them and circles back to the Lynn farm, and dips down right over where Ruston and Lettie stand. She trumpets loud musical calls while Dexter barks and leaps into the air saying he wants to fly with them.

Jason and Hunter fly with Topper and Race every day Lettie feels is warm enough. Jason found a very ugly old fur rug and made himself a cape-like tent to put over and around himself. It has proved to be so much warmer than their winter coats that Lettie has been busy making elegant fur capes with big soft hoods for each of them. Only their eyes peek out into the cold. Jason is sure they could fly anywhere and be warm with their new fur capes.

The village people in Glendale have grown accustomed to seeing the Lynn boys flying all over their big valley. It is a thrill for all who see them. Sky-tops have become an important part of the village daily gossip, and everyone in Glendale is just a little bit jealous. Some of the older boys are especially jealous and pester constantly for sky-top rides. Chat Dixon hasn't been a threat because Hunter has told him Topper will carry him off and dump him in the mountains if he so much as touches him. The fact that Topper stood behind Hunter while he told Chat a thing or two and nodded his big head with deep guttural growls made a rather convincing argument.

While some people are busy talking and gossiping about the Lynn boys and their sky-tops, there are a few who recognize how valuable these incredible birds could be to their entire community. The mayor still presses Ruston to consider carrying the mail and Ruston is still firm that his boys are too young. Yet even Ruston knows sooner or later their sky-tops will be needed for something more than just flying around playing delightful games.

Chapter 7

NORTH PASS

It is a cold wintery day and Jason and Hunter are home alone, their parents have gone into Glendale and the boys are enjoying reading by the fire in their comfortable keeping room. Hunter looks up for a moment with a puzzled look on his face. "Listen Jace, there's a horse headed this way, and he's running?"

Jason closes the book he's reading on his finger, and looks at his brother. His face intent as he listens. "You're right and…" he pauses while the hoof-beats grow louder. "Only an idiot would run a horse with it so cold and the roads covered in ice—you can damage a horse's lungs … Unless…. Unless something is wrong."

Both boys are on their feet running for their heavy coats. Something has to be wrong. Jason steps out in the terrible cold and recognizes the ill kept, burly Mel Splading and his work horse pounding down the lane and into their icy courtyard.

"Master Jason, please take yr' sky-top and go to Keering Place and bring back the doctor. Master Tobson has taken a bad fall and we fear he'll die. There has been an avalanche in the pass and we can't get through to fetch him. Please go and bring the good doctor back!" He yells as his horse comes to a trembling stop.

Hunter steps close to Jason and whispers, "Race is the only sky-top at home right now, Top and Queen flew off with Bert hours ago. What can we do?"

"Go get him ready to fly, I'll get my things and you see if you can get Race to call for Topper to come back. Maybe he will hear and come home." Jason speaks as he heads back in the house to get his cape and gloves while mumbling to himself something about breaking every rule in the book. Then remembering their guest, he turns, calling over his shoulder for him go into the barn where he can take care of his tired and overheated horse.

Race is ready and Topper isn't back yet. Jason hesitates, not knowing what he should do. They were never to fly alone, they had been told to stay at home until their parents returned. His parents should have been back by now. He tries to imagine what his father would have him do. In his mind he keeps hearing the words in his mind, *A man may be dying. The pass is closed. You are the only hope.*

The anxious Mel Spalding, Jason, Hunter, Dexter and the magnificent Race all stand in the cold afternoon sun wondering what is best to do. With a worried sigh, Jason explains, "Hunter, I have to go. If Master Tobson were to die I could never live with myself. Dad will understand. He would have me go, there is no other way. I'm sure I'm right."

Moments later Jason and Race are headed toward the North Pass that will lead them to Keering Place, where there is a tiny village on the upper mountain slopes just beyond the narrow pass. Jason pulls his heavy fur cape tighter around him and tucks in all the loose edges. Race is able to understand just enough to know something is wrong or they would not be flying out alone in the intense cold. He can sense Jason's worry and flies faster. The wind whips past them and stings Jason's eyes, freezing the tears on his cheeks.

As Jason and Race disappeared over the far horizon Ruston and Lettie turn into the Lynn Farm lane and drive their big team into the courtyard. There they find Hunter, Old Mel, and Dexter in the yard staring after Race's vanishing shape. Confusion takes over for a moment while everyone talks at once, and Hunter knows how upset his father is. *Oh, boy is Jason going to get it!* But Hunter doesn't understand.

Lettie is very quiet, her big eyes look a little teary, and Old Mel wishes he was someplace else. Ruston is upset—very upset, but holding himself together with calm deliberation. Things change in the blink of an eye when Dexter whines and barks with excitement, and Hunter shouts, "They're coming, they're coming."

Ruston glances at the sky and sees the three missing sky-tops winging their way through the cold afternoon air. "Lettie get my things together I'm going after Jason. Hurry now."

Lettie looks a little puzzled and starts to ask, *How? Topper can't carry you that far.* But she doesn't. She knows Ruston far too well and realizes he is not in a mood to listen.

Ruston disappears into the barn as the sky-tops land in the farm yard. Hunter runs past Bert to Topper explaining in fast confusing words that they must go after Jason and just as they start toward the barn a rope comes from out of nowhere and settles over Bert's head and neck.

Now Bert has been at Lynn Farm everyday for several months and he knows his way around. He also understands most of what is said. He has become a part of the Lynn family although he doesn't like to be touched and refuses to go in the barn. As the rope circles his long neck he rears backward and feels the fearsome grip. His angry trumpeting voice is ear splitting. In one instant the area around him is empty. Bert stands fighting the rope with violent efforts and roars with indignation. Ruston has snubbed him to the heavy hitching post at the barn door and Bert can't get away.

Ruston steps out of the barn and sets a saddle over the hitching rail. Bert stands braced at the end of the rope with his eyes wild, and his beak wide open. Topper, Queenie, and Hunter cower near the barn, hoping they will not be noticed but too fascinated to retreat any further.

"Bert, you have been a part of this family for months now and yet you refuse to do your part. I've not wanted to push you. You are free, but you eat the food I work to provide and now I need you. My son is too young to fly alone. He is a mere boy," Ruston pauses as emotion shakes his voice. Then he continues, "Jason's life and the life of a dear friend is at stake—you will fly me to Keering Place after Jason, and you will help me bring the doctor and my son home. Do you understand?"

Topper gulps, sniffs, then creeps forward to tell Bert what Ruston has said, but before he is noticed Bert bobs his great head. "I know you don't understand family, Bert, but nothing else matters when a part of my family is not safe. You cannot understand ..."

Bert doesn't let Ruston finish his sentence, his mammoth wing span covers the yard area and he shrieks and snaps his giant beak just over Ruston's head. A volley of deep disturbed and angry sounds come from his great throat as he thrusts his head down into Ruston's face. Bert is mad and if we could understand his words we would have been given a whole new light on the situation. Only, no one can understand him. Then a strange thing happens, Queenie rushes forward and ducks under Bert's wings. The atmosphere changes in an instant. Bert holds little Queenie with tenderness and almost seems to caress her with his beak. Clicks and clacks are exchanged before he looks back down at Ruston.

"Bert, is Queenie yours?" Ruston almost whispers. Both Bert and Queenie nod and clack. Topper creeps forward and slips under Bert's other wing and the three sky-tops look with fixed eyes at Ruston. "Is Topper yours too?" They nod their answer and click and clack.

"Well I'll be! Maybe you do understand. Then you know how I feel about needing to be with Jason?" Bert nods and reaches out with his beak and snaps at the rope.

Ruston loosens the rope, "Bert, I didn't want to use the rope, I hate using any kind of force, but I didn't know how to be sure I could talk you into taking me. I couldn't risk your leaving." The rope slips loose and Bert relaxes and clicks what seems to almost sound like, "Thank you."

"Bert, will you please take me to Jason?" Relief and joy flood through Ruston and all those who watch as Bert lowers his head level with Ruston and nods.

In a matter of minutes a saddle and halter are adjusted and in place. As Ruston climbs into the saddle, Lettie runs toward him with a pile of extra blankets, a hamper of food, and a wonderful fur cape. These are swiftly tucked into place. Hunter hurries to get Topper ready and is disappointed to learn he is to stay home and take care of his mother.

"Hunter, we don't know what we are getting into. I want you to stay here and take good care of your mother. She shouldn't be left alone, and between you, Dexter, and Topper, I won't worry." Ruston looks at his son, hoping he will understand.

"It's okay Dad, I just need to know I get a turn with you and Bert soon."

"You bet, Hunter. If Bert is ready to be a real part of this family I will fly with you anytime!" Bert nods and clacks a weird sounding answer, and Dexter whines trying to tell everyone he wants to go too, only no one listens.

Moments later Ruston and Bert climb through the air over Lynn Farm. The power Ruston feels beneath him is unbelievable. He likes a big powerful horse and he loves speed and agility, so he is more than ready to appreciate these qualities in a giant sky-top. Bert presses himself forward through the air and Ruston is shocked at the speed at which they fly. The air rips at his cape and it is difficult for him to keep his eyes open against the wind.

How fast are we going? he wonders as he looks down at the north road and aims toward the distant pass. A sleigh gallops along the road beneath them and the bells make a beautiful sound in the clear still air. Bert overtakes the sleigh and passes it before Ruston can count to ten. How many times faster than a horse he wonders as his mind begins to mentally imagine the speed. "Am I too heavy Bert?" Ruston asks with honest curiosity.

Bert answers with a snort and a shake of his head.

***

While Ruston and Bert are setting an all time record for distance covered by man under any means of transport on their primitive planet, Jason is approaching the North Pass. Jason's first thought is to go higher and not venture into the narrow cut between the massive walls, but the cold has to be considered. If breathing cold air is bad for a horse, or man, then a sky-top should be no different. Peering out through the narrow slit in the fur covering his face, he can see Race's long neck and head in the gathering darkness. Icicles hang from his huge beak. He feels the sting of the cold air as he breaths and hopes Race is all right. Yet the bird seems confident, there is no hesitation in him.

"Is it too cold Race, should we go back?" Jason shouts down hoping Race will understand and is pleased to see Race look back and give a definite shake to his dark head.

As they enter the lower pass the shadows are eerie and Jason is tense with respectful fear. While Jason can see Race has ample room for his tremendous wing span there is little room for error. And no room to turn around, should they decide they needed to go back. Looking down, he can see the canyon floor and appreciates the risks the mail carriers endure to travel such a road. All is deep in drifts. It is a world of ice. Jason shivers and pulls his fur robes tighter around himself.

Ever since Jason can remember he's heard stories of the pass; it has always been a dangerous place. During summer, robbers haunt the crevice filled canyon, making no one safe without some sort of protection. People had died here. As a matter of fact, more people had died in this pass than any other place Jason can think of. In the winter there are avalanches and deep horrible snow. Many years ago a whole caravan had been buried. People still talk about it to this day. The pass is also where sky-tops are sometimes seen. People speak of them carrying off their farm animals and flying into the North Pass. Right now, Jason wishes he wasn't alone. The canyon is so dark and gloomy it's difficult to see anything of the road beneath him. All is in heavy shadow. The walls on either side are mere shapes that Race tips and turns between. The eerie shadows, the steady pulsating motions of Race's body, the cracking of Jason's ears as they climb through the numbing cold, and the fearsome mountain itself, all help Jason better understand his father's reluctance to turn him and Hunter loose to fly wherever they chose. For a moment he wonders if he has made the right decision. Should he have waited for his father?

A sudden gust of wind causes Race to stagger in mid air. "Are you okay?" Jason shouts down giving him a pat on his shoulder and is surprised when Race gives a definite nod and glances back with almost a smile on his massive face. For a moment Jason wonders if Race could be enjoying himself. Impossible!

Rounding a very tight spot between the walls Race tips and slides and somehow manages not to lose precious elevation. For a moment or two Jason's heart almost stops beating. When they level out again he wonders if his parents are home and if his father will try to follow on Topper. With a little shake of his head he wishes his father could fly with Bert. Flying Bert would be awesome. Thoughts of the big black bird make Jason wish he was next to him right now. Bert is so nice to have around. He can't imagine anything bothering Bert.

A sudden jerk and Race lifts his head, tension surges through his huge body and Jason knows something has upset him. It's something like when a horse spooks, yet doesn't turn and run. Race is tense and watches up ahead as if something might jump out at them. Yet what could possibly bother anything as big as Race? The narrow walls close in around them and Race increases his efforts. The air currents are unsteady within the narrow walls and Race has kept his long wings in steady motion ever since they entered the pass. Up and down they move in great sweeps through the sky. They are climbing. It is late and the sun is already low in the sky. Jason doesn't like the idea of flying back in the dark. There is a hint of smoke in the air and the thought of a warm cozy fire brings comfort. The smell of pine smoke increases and Jason can feel Race relax. "Was it the smell of smoke that bothered you?" he calls down to Race and smiles as Race answers with a reassuring nod. "I think it smells kinda nice."

On the top of the pass is a small valley where two roads cross and Jason can see a few houses and barns. There are a couple of stores and a big roadside inn all huddled together. This is Keering Place. It boasts a '*huge*' population of fifty, year round people. As Jason and Race come out of the canyon and see the little village, Jason remembers these people have never seen a tame sky-top, and considers what they might do when Race lands? He hadn't thought of this. Surely they've heard from people down in the valley about Topper and Race. Surely they have.

With a growing concern he circles and shouts, hoping someone will hear. A very fat lady with a basket comes out of one of the little sheds beneath him. She looks like a walking tent with her heavy robes and long cape flapping. Jason shouts cupping his hands hoping the sound will carry. He shouts again and Race dips down closer. The woman looks up, drops her basket, and taking a step backwards loses her footing and goes end over end down a little slope in the snow. Eggs roll in every direction and Jason knows better than to laugh. The woman is quite upset as she runs shrieking toward the house. Jason shouts again and moments later a man steps out of the house with a bow in his hands, and Jason turns Race up the valley and away. He shouts at the top of his voice, asking permission to land. His words echo in the icy mountain air. By the time Jason makes a second sweep overhead at least a dozen people are gathered in the snow packed road. They shout and point and Jason waves.

Jason hears the encouraging words, "There's a boy on top, don't shoot. It's a boy!"

"It must be one of the Lynn boys," another shouts.

With grim determination Jason circles back and dips low while waving, "I've come for Doc Hanlin. There's been an accident down in the valley. May I come down?" He sweeps past and circles again. "Where's Doc?" he shouts as he is momentarily overhead and sees the doctor separate himself from the crowd and wave motioning for him to come down.

Jason sets Race down a good distance from the people and slides to the ground, and places himself in front of his sky-top. There are several men with powerful bows who look as though they would shoot, they might even decide to shoot without a good reason. Some people are like that. They just want to shoot regardless of who or what is hurt. "Please put your bows down. He won't hurt you—he's a pet and perfectly gentle. May we come closer?"

Thank heavens for good Doc Hanlin. He has seen Topper and Race many times and understands Jason's concern. With some fast words and a slightly raised voice he persuades the men to set aside their bows, and Jason and Race walk up the street toward the people gathered in front of the village inn. Jason can see people peeking around corners, peering out of doors, and staring through windows. After a few seconds some of the brave move closer. They come out into the street and gape at the magnificent sight before them. They've heard of the Lynn brothers and their sky-tops, but none have ever seen them. Little by little a crowd gathers and the excitement grows.

While the Keering Place people recover from their shock, Jason takes a few minutes to take care of Race, all while explaining to the good doctor what has happened in the valley and why he must fly back with him just as soon as he can get ready.

Doc Hanlin doesn't seem pleased with the fact he will be the first guest or passenger ever to ride on one of the Lynn sky-tops. No, he stands looking somewhat numb, while Jason covers Race's back with the warm blankets he remembered to bring. Jason doesn't notice the doctor's stunned silence and pulls a partially filled feed sack from his saddle panniers and dumps a generous portion of pig feed on the icy ground. Race raises his head and smiles, then with a sincere click or two, he begins to gobble the feed. Between bites he lets everyone know how pleased he is with the generous treat. He certainly hasn't lost his appetite.

The children giggle and press closer while the more cautious spectators watch in spellbound wonder from a much safer distance. Jason is pleased to see Race hasn't overheated and seems quite content with the situation. Running his hands over Race's big body he feels for possible problems. *Nope, he's not overly warm, no steam that might cause a chill.* The flight must not have been as difficult for Race as Jason had feared. He had assumed that a two day trip on horseback would be tiring even for a sky-top. Yet they'd made the distance in less than two hours and Race seems ready for the return flight.

When the sensation of Jason's arrival eases and the children gather around to touch Race, Jason does his best to protect his sky-top from the confusion. During all this, Doc Hanlin still hasn't moved. He's standing in stupefied bewilderment; if you look a little closer you can see he's turned a little pale. Now, Doctor Hanlin is a man of great knowledge and compassion. He is a man of medium build with a large stomach and a round red face. His hair is completely white and covers only the outer circle of his shining head. He is the type of man that is always jolly and if he had a great white beard and a red suit we might mistake him for Santa Claus. However, at this moment Doc Hanlin doesn't look the least bit jolly. He has no idea, the well meaning Mistress Odwyer is in his room in the inn putting his things together. It hasn't occurred to her the doctor might refuse—and right now the doctor is about to come up with an excuse for staying at Keering Place. If the truth is to be known, he is afraid of flying on Jason's sky-top. He has spoken many words of praise and has even told everyone how safe they are. He has great experience and knowledge because he has known the Lynn family for years and years and had been in attendance at the birth of both boys. But all these words of confidence had been to ease the crowd and now it turns out he is required to fly back with Jason and this he doesn't want to do.

Yet he considers, *Do I want to stay here at Keering Place until the spring thaw?*

In a whirl of emotion he hurries to his room where the good Mistress Odwyer hands him his satchel and garment bag. In a moment's panic he takes the bags and begins going through them thinking, surely they are not packed just right. Closing his room door, he wishes he could simply vanish. A boy has flown all the way from Glendale after him, how can he tell him he is desperately afraid? Will his old heart stand the stress? But, a man's life is in danger. The doctor wants to scream, *but what about my life? Aren't my feelings important? Calm yourself—panic never does anyone one ounce of good.* Pacing the floor he is very glad to be inside away from the crowd. No one should see his suffering.

The shadows are long and soon the sun will disappear behind the western wall of mountains, and Jason wishes the doctor would hurry. Every minute they waste means a colder flight back to the lower valley. Gathering up the sacking he had brought with Race's ration of feed, he ties it back to the saddle then glances toward the inn wondering why it was taking the doctor so long. A screeching yell from one of the women shatters the pleasant early evening atmosphere. Two sky-tops are bearing down on them. The Keering Place's warning bell is sounded and men grab their bows and set themselves, while the women and children vanish behind closed doors. Jason rushes forward to stop the men with bows. "It's Bert, it's Bert. He's one of our sky-tops. The little blue one is Queenie." Jason rushes to one man and shakes his arm wanting to strike him. The man holds a steady aim waiting for Bert to come into range. "No!" Jason screams.

Ruston can see the confusion and Jason's efforts and circles up and away. As Bert makes a steep graceful turn the villagers see the small rider resting between the great wings of the huge black sky-top. The stubborn man with the drawn bow relaxes and watches the majesty of

Bert's graceful flight with the wondrous man aboard him. Women and children pour back out of the buildings to watch Bert and Queenie land. Never in all of Keering Place's history has there been such a spectacle.

As Bert and Queenie trot into the village street, Jason rushes to his father with a thousand questions all at once. Bert, his father is riding Bert! How is it possible? Bert doesn't even like to be touched.

While the village people crowd a little too close, Bert raises his huge head and neck to his very tallest. The village inn isn't even as tall as Bert's head. The people step back in awestruck amazement. Ruston slides to the ground and gives Jason a relieved hug along with hurried questions. Queenie doesn't want to be left out and pushes forward. Jason laughs at her excitement and affectionately gives her beak a hug, which pleases her very much. Everyone laughs and several children push forward and ask if they may touch her. Queenie is in her element. The children love her pretty pack saddle and Queenie purrs her pleasant clicking sounds. She loves attention.

Doc Hanlin realizes he can only stall so long and with white faced courage he steps back out into the cold street. Ruston sees the anxiety in his old friend's face, and understands his feelings. Anyone with brains would hesitate to climb up on a sky-top. It is insane to expect to fly anywhere, much less to be safe and have any degree of control. The whole situation still is a bit impossible, even in Ruston's way of understanding.

Gently Ruston guides the doctor toward Bert and does his best to comfort and distract his thoughts. While Ruston straps the doctor into place, a handsome young man touches his arm. "Master Lynn, could I ask you to take me back to Glendale, my mother will be worried about me. I have money and can pay you."

Ruston turns and sees a tall lean young man with rather shaggy brown hair and deep gray eyes, "You're Samuel Rickard aren't you?"

"Yes, Sir."

"You were expected home over two weeks ago, yes we've all been worried."

"Sir, the avalanche has the pass blocked and the snow is too deep. There is no way I can get the horses through. The mail will have to wait. My horses are safe here and I need to get back to my mother. She's alone, you know."

"Jason, make room for Master Rickard," Ruston shouts toward his son. Then turning back toward Samuel, "Get you things, and whatever mail that needs to be delivered—we need to leave as soon as possible. You may ride behind Jason. He'll take good care of you." Jason looks up at his father and appreciates his confidence, then breaks into a huge smile when Ruston gives him a quick wink.

So it is that Doctor Hanlin and Samuel Rickard are the first passengers on the Lynn sky-tops. Young Rickard isn't worried about his heart. He's not worried about safety. He just wants to fly. It probably wouldn't matter where the Lynns decided to take him, he'd be happy to go. His excitement can scarcely be contained. He has questions and more questions all while they are strapping things down, as well as him into place. He wants to know how best to sit and be comfortable and warm. Was it going to be bumpy or smooth—questions, so many questions. Jason turns in his saddle and looks back at his passenger, grinning. *This is going to be fun*, then aloud he explains, "You'd better tie your hood tighter. We'll be going so fast it will just rip right off unless you tie it tight. You only want your eyes to peek out; it's cold up there." Jason enjoys the wide eyed look on Samuel's face. Gathering his reins he asks Race to stand. "We're going up Dad. We'll circle till you're ready. Come on, Queenie, we'll race you into the air." As they begin their run for take off, they can hear the villagers shout and cheer. Both Queenie and Race seem to be enjoying every part of this adventure.

Jason is very glad his passenger is strapped into place because he's sure bouncing. "Stand in your stirrups and hang onto the straps behind my legs, it'll take the bounce out." Seconds later they are climbing in a great circle over Keering Place.

Bert only needs a few big leaps before he is in the air, but a few leaps are far too many as far as Doc is concerned. Rather than hang onto the saddle he's taken hold of Ruston, who'll have bruises for the next week from Doc's neck hold.

The people on the ground cheer and shout, and Samuel can't help himself and shouts back with his own cheers. Jason leads the way back through the pass and this time it isn't scary, even if it is almost dark. Having his dad and Bert along makes a big difference in how things look in the shadowy dark canyon. Now the shadows are beautiful in their dusty purples and blues with the light rimming the cliffs in pink and gold above them.

"This is incredible!" shouts Samuel back to Ruston as he shakes Jason's shoulders in his glee. "Do you realize it takes me on my fastest horses about half a day to be where we are already. Four of my horses for one sky-top Jason—what do you say?" When there is no answer, "O.K.? All my horses, everyone of them." He pulls his heavy hood back and takes a deep breath of the icy air while the wind whips his handsome face.

Jason glances back at his passenger, "You shouldn't do that. You want to stay as warm as you can, because we will be cold before we get back. You just wait and see."

"I want to be able to see. I want to see everything. It's all so different up here. It even smells different. And Race ... What can I say? Race is magnificent. He scarcely knows we are up here. Look his wings are barely moving," Samuel pauses then sighs with deep appreciation.

"We're going down into the valley and we're riding on a current of air. You can feel it lift us at times. Going up the pass was very different. Race had to climb up the air and had to work the whole way."

Ruston can hear fleeting bits of Jason's and Samuel's conversation and reaches back and feels the doctor's heavy robes. He can tell the doctor is rigid. "Doc, are you all right?" he questions the silent man.

"I'm recovering..... yes, I do believe I'm recovering. I don't know what I expected, but it certainly wasn't anything like this."

Ruston chuckles, "Just what had you expected?"

"I'm not real fond of riding horses. They seem to beat me to death with their infernal bouncing and plunging—they seem to hate me. I'll take a good wagon or coach any day." Taking a deep breath, he pauses, "I'm not sure how to answer. This is most comfortable. I don't feel as though I might fall off. The straps hold me good and tight. Everything is well padded. I have secure stirrups beneath my feet and heavy blankets and robes to keep out the wind and cold. The huge wings out on either side make me feel as though I'm seated on a huge moving carpet. A very comfortable carpet, if I do say so, and if I don't look down this is most pleasant."

"Then I suggest you not look down."

Bert, Race, and Queenie seem to slide through the air, slipping effortlessly through the narrow canyon walls. At times they tip and swerve through the winding corridor. What little light there had been fades as night gathers. All that can be seen are the wall's huge dark shapes. Jason looks up into the sky overhead hoping to see the stars and finds only darkness and a dizzy sense makes his head spin. In the dark there is almost no sense of up or down. Race's motion, the constant tipping along with the rise and fall of the air currents, all combined with not being able to see anything but huge moving shapes of stone along the walls give the ride a very strange feeling. Everything seems all sort of crazy, yet the sky-tops must be able to see just fine. Instinct seems to guide them and never once do they waver, or touch a wall.

A warm air wave greets Race and his passengers as they glide out of the canyon over the wide valley floor. Soon Queenie and Bert are on either side and the huge birds enjoy an exchange of clicks and clacks. Lights up ahead tell them they are approaching the Coe Farm. The lights look warm and inviting. "Master Lynn," Samuel shouts, "I have mail and a package for the Coes. It might be important, should I just drop it?"

Jason and Samuel land near the edge of the dark wood next to the Coe home and Samuel runs with the letters and the small package up to their door. Soon they are flying again and the miles melt with each stroke of the birds' wings. Doctor Hanlin is set down to care for Master Tobson, and Samuel is taken home. Jason, Ruston, and the sky-tops stand watching as Samuel's mother hugs her son with grateful silent tears. He had been gone too long and the passes with their deep snow, wolves, and so many dangers made it easy for her to lose hope.

***

Later that night in their cozy home with a big fire burning, Dexter and the big cat are asleep on the hearth rug, while the Lynns are celebrating the day's adventures. Lettie has made a feast and as she carries another basket of hot rolls to the table she asks, "Then Bert didn't stay—he left again?"

"That's right, but he did come into the barn and we fed him and took care of his tack and Hunter had a bed all ready for him. But when we closed the big doors it upset him," Ruston answers.

"Yes," Jason interrupts, "he went back to the door and banged on it trying to get it open."

"That's right, but Jason you mustn't interrupt," Ruston is firm as he passes a steaming kettle of stew for Jason to refill his bowl. "He wants the door left unlocked. He ate and enjoyed being there and seemed to be most happy. It almost looked as though he was putting Topper and little Queenie into bed. He was so tender.

80

"Then he picked up a big empty feed sack, and brought it to me and wanted me to fill it. I was curious and filled it up and he grabbed it and went to the door, pushed it open, and left."

"You know Dad, if Queenie and Topper are his, then he might have a family somewhere else. I'll bet they can't come and that's why Bert doesn't stay. He is needed in two places" Taking a big bite of buttery roll, Jason continues with his mouth full, "I'll bet you anything he's back tomorrow and wants another sack of feed."

Jason is right on several counts. Bert does come back every day, and everyday he asks for a sack to be filled with feed before he leaves. While Ruston is pleased with the new situation, he is at the same time alarmed at the amount the sky-tops are eating. He wonders if his once large feed storage is going to last the winter. These birds are very expensive to feed.

Another interesting situation has developed. Samuel Rickard has time on his hands with the pass closed. He has little to do so he spends his days at Lynn Farm following Jason and Hunter around, hoping for another ride on one of the sky-tops. At first Ruston is a little miffed at the intrusion, then he begins to notice the help Samuel contributes. Every stall is clean and comfortable. The stone floors are swept and the water buckets washed every day. Young Samuel is a worker. Ruston decides to leave the situation alone for the time being. He understands Samuel wants to do something, winter can be a frustrating time if there's nothing to do. The mail run up and down the valley is little to no work and the winter hours are long when shut up inside.

***

So the days pass and Samuel is an ever present part of Lynn Farm—while at the same time the feed disappears with nothing to replace it. One evening we find Ruston and Lettie curled up together next to their big keeping room fire and they look too serious for light conversation. "Rus, go and have a visit with the mayor. I wonder what the town will pay to have you fly the mail? I'm sure it wouldn't be much but the sky-tops need to do something to help us support them."

"You know, Lettie, Bert understands more ever day. I will try and have a serious visit with him. He could fly the mail, if he would. No one would even have to go with him."

"That won't work. The birds need to have a rider to deal with the people. No telling who would shoot at them. It's not right to ask him to go alone. I thought you liked to fly. Why don't you fly the mail?"

"Lettie, I'd love to, but I can't be gone and leave you here with the boys alone."

"You did this past summer and we made it just fine."

"Yes, and it was summer. Taking care of things in this cold is not fair to ask of you."

"You didn't ask. I'm volunteering to take care of everything here so you can do this. Somehow, I think it's just what this family needs." She smiles a provocative smile and pokes Ruston in the ribs.

"What are you talking about? What is it this family needs?" Ruston is a little miffed and confused with his wife's attitude.

"Ruston Lynn, you've been in a huff over these sky-tops for months now. You wanted one for yourself and now you have one. One so big and so beautiful that even I feel safe when you are with him. You complain about the cost of the feed that you didn't get to sell this year and you wonder how to support the birds. You've been offered a solution and I suggest you look into it. That's all."

"You mean you'd feel safe here with me gone."

"Ruston, haven't you noticed. Everyone is scared half silly of the sky-tops. Do you think anyone is going to bother us?" Giving her head a shake she continues, "No, not one little chance, and besides, Samuel is here almost as if he was living under our roof. He's a talented young man, and Jason and Hunter love him. They are working well together. The boys like his help and he is glad to be here." She pats Ruston on his chest and snuggles in closer to him and almost purrs, "No, Ruston I'd be fine, the boys would be fine. I think we should give it a try. Samuel wanted to pay for his flight home and there will be others. Why not let people pay to be flown somewhere?" She finishes giving Ruston much to think about.

A few days later Mayor Daily and young Samuel arrive with a proposal and Ruston is ready to listen. The passes are closed and there can be no mail until the spring thaw, and even then it will be quite some time before the road will be passable. Samuel wants to fly the mail on one of the sky-tops and the mayor feels this will solve the problem of the Lynn boys being too young for such responsibility. Ruston is handed a hefty sack of gold coins, and pressed for commitment. The pay offered is enough to make both Ruston and Lettie gasp with startled realization. The proposal offers a very nice solution and a new door opens.

Chapter 8

RUSTON'S WISH

The moon shines an extra bright glow through the windows of the massive barn, but Hunter doesn't notice. He doesn't even care. He is in his pajamas with a rather tattered quilt wrapped around his small shoulders, seated cross-legged in the straw with Topper and Queenie. Topper and Queenie are his friends and he likes to talk things over with them, especially when he is upset and no one will listen. Everyone else at Lynn Farm is fast asleep, even Dexter. Usually Dexter loves to be rubbed and played with, but tonight he just rolls over, waving his big paws in the air and doesn't want to listen to the things Hunter keeps trying to tell him. Now he is asleep and certainly isn't paying any attention. Hunter is more than a little cross because tomorrow morning his father will fly west over the mountains to Mooreland, and will be gone a whole week, and he and Jason do not get to go with him. No, they have to stay home and take care of their mother and all the chores while their dad is away. He always has to stay home. Everyone keeps telling him he is too young, or too little, and he finds it very hard to bear.

With careful deliberation, Hunter goes over in his mind all the arguments he might use to convince his father he is old enough to make the long flight with him, but he can't find one he hasn't already used. Jason had put up a pretty good argument too, and he hadn't had any better luck, and he's been fourteen for months and months now. *How old will I have to be before Dad will let me go? Man-oh-man, Jason is fourteen and can't go—it'll be years, and years before I get to do the fun things I want to do?* Sometimes Hunter feels his dad is much too strict and he doesn't like it. No, not one little bit.

It is boring to stay home all the time, while messages, mail, and even passengers are flown all over the place on his sky-tops. Hunter doesn't like watching other people fly on his sky-tops, especially when he has to stay home. Now Samuel Rickard is okay. Samuel is a big help and since he's been around the chores are easier. Besides, Samuel laughs and is fun. *Yes, Samuel may ride my sky-tops, he's pretty cool.* But sometimes Samuel gets to go with Hunter's father while he has to stay home, and that isn't okay. Being too little or too young isn't much fun and his mom and dad just don't understand how important it is to do something really exciting every once and a while.

Hunter pats Queenie's neck, and looks into her soulful eyes; of the two sky-tops, she is the more sympathetic and talking to her always seems to help him think. Right at the moment, Topper seems more interested in sleeping than he is in listening to Hunter's complaints.

"Queenie, if we have to stay here and take care of Mom, like Dad says, we are going to have to think of something really cool to do while Dad is gone." Queenie seems to agree because she nods her long slender head. "Topper, help us think, we want to do something really cool, something different. It would be even better if we could surprise Dad with something extra special." Hunter reaches over and shakes Topper's beak. Topper is sound asleep and Hunter gives him a good thump. "Top, how can you sleep at a time like this? Summer's coming! There will be so much work to do; we won't have any time at all to play. We've just got to do something really different and exciting, and I have to figure out just what it is that we are going to do. If we can't go to Mooreland with Dad we'll do something else that's as good or even better. Wake up, silly bird."

Topper doesn't move, and Hunter crawls over the straw to where Topper's head rests. He hesitates a moment before he bends over Topper's huge head and with his little fingers pries one huge eye open. "Are you in there Topper? I like it better when you help me with my thinking." He lifts his fingers and the big eye snaps shut. "Does he always sleep like this?" Queenie nods and opens her big beak and laughs a quiet laugh. "It is not cool to sleep like that. Look at him! He's really zonked!"

Some time later Ruston, finds his youngest son rolled up in his blanket, half buried in the clean straw between the two sleeping sky-tops. Gently he lifts him in his arms and carries him back to his comfortable bed. "Dad," Hunter mutters as he is lowered into his soft feather bed, "Do I really have to stay home tomorrow?"

"Yes, son, we've been over that too many times already."

"But when will I be old enough to go?"

"That depends a great deal upon you and your mother. You know she is still frightened even by the thought of flying. You need to remember and be grateful that she lets you and Topper fly together here close to home. There will be other trips and one of these days you will be old enough to go with me. Until then you must practice becoming the right kind of young man. If your mother knows she can trust you, it will be easier to persuade her to let you go."

"I have trouble remembering to be good sometimes, don't I?"

"Yes, sometimes you do. It's a part of growing up, and I want you to know, Mom and I love you just the way you are, but because you don't always remember to do what is right, we cannot let you do some of the things you want to do right now. When we know you will not make 'Hunter Mistakes' then your mom will be much more apt to let you fly with me."

"Will Jason get to fly with you before me?"

"Very probably, Jason is doing very well at remembering to do what is right. And, I know, as you get a little older you will too. Every day you get better at remembering"

Ruston turns to leave and Hunter whispers, "I wish Mom liked to fly, then she would let us all fly somewhere together. If Mom liked to fly she could fly right next to me and make sure I don't make any 'Hunter Mistakes'. She wouldn't have to worry then. Wouldn't that be cool, Dad?"

"Yes, Hunter that would be cool, really cool," Ruston sighs and shakes his head a little as he leaves the room.

The next morning Ruston tromps in from the barn where he has just finished feeding and getting Bert, ready for their flight to Mooreland. Glancing at his muddy boots he stops and scraps them on the stone sill just outside their front door. The mud won't come off and he's making quite a mess on Lettie's clean front step. She says he's as bad as the boys at tromping mud all over everything. He stares at the mess he has made and giving up, takes his boots off and sets them beside the door. Lettie, is a very clean house keeper and she and mud don't get along and it's such a muddy time of the year. The muddy time of year comes as the winter snows melt and turn into muddy mush. It is usually so bad some feel there should be five seasons rather than the traditional four. Summer, fall, winter, mud, and spring are a much better description of the seasons.

This morning is one of those best or worst days in the middle of the "mud season." Ruston steps in his stocking feet into the family keeping room with his saddlebags draped over his powerful shoulders looking for Lettie. How he wishes she would fly with him. He pauses, thinking of his lovely wife. For a moment he pictures her slender figure, her large expressive blue eye, and her glistening auburn hair. He loves her and wants her to enjoy the things he enjoys and asks himself, *What can I say that I haven't already said? I will ask her one more time. Perhaps, I can tempt her with seeing places she's never seen before, she's never been over the mountains or near the coast. Surely she'd like to go?*

A few minutes later Ruston has his answer. Lettie takes a deep breath and says, "Ruston Lynn, how many times do I have to tell you I'm not getting on that sky-top and going with you? I don't care how beautiful it is up there, or how safe or what fun it is to fly about all over the country. I'm not going—I never will go—do you understand?" Lettie raises her voice until it's almost a shout. In one hand she holds a sturdy broom and in the other a scrub brush which she waves around with real intent, and Ruston retreats a short distance and smiles at his wife. Lettie is a very spirited woman, and Ruston knows her stubbornness is only a part of her being uncommonly smart and assertive in her ways. She is right, you have to be a little crazy to think flying around on a dinosaur is safe, even though he is a tame and gentle dinosaur. Staying on the ground is safe and that is where they all ought to be, according to Lettie. She is right, but she is wrong too, all at the same time. How can he help her understand? While he likes Lettie just the way she is, he still wishes she would fly with him. If there could be a way to make a magical wish and have Lettie like to fly, Ruston would make that wish.

Within the hour Ruston and Burt vanish in the distance and Lettie shields her eyes as she watches them go. For a moment her heart flutters with sadness, she knows how much Ruston wanted her to go with him. Part of her wanted to go, but another part kept telling her to stay on the ground. With these thoughts she sighs and attacks the clunks of mud Ruston had left on her front door step. She hums as she sweeps and scrapes, then for a moment stops to listen with a frown at the noises erupting out of the hen house. Jason and Hunter are supposed to be cleaning the hen house and making sure all is dry and clean; but it sounds more like a war than a serious cleaning project.

After many minutes of shouting and great banging and thumping Lettie decides to see what the boys are up to. Curiosity and mischief make her tiptoe in to have a peek. There she finds both boys covered in mud, manure, and feathers with Hunter backed into a corner protecting himself from Jason's pretend attacks. Hunter howls like a wild banshee and whips away with a blunted wooden sword. Lettie makes the tiniest sound and Jason glances her way and lowers his wooden sword. Hunter makes the most of Jason's distraction and ducks out of the corner giving his brother a quick swat with his sword as he dashes by.

"Is the hen house all clean?" both boys hear their mother ask.

"Almost."

"Your father left a list that wasn't too long for you boys to do today. If you really work hard you can be finished and have the rest of the day to play. If you feel you have time now to play I will add to your list. I still have to shake out the rugs, hang out the wash ....," her words trail off as Jason and Hunter grab their pitchforks and attack the soiled bedding on the large hen house floor. Lettie watches for a few seconds and nods her head with a little smile before returning to her cleaning.

***

Time seems to time pass slowly while Ruston and Bert are away and Lettie is very glad the boys are taking such good care of her and all the many chores that have to be done. Lettie doesn't need any excitement and is happy because nothing the least out of the ordinary has happened. In fact, things are going so well she should have known something was going on, of which she is not the least aware.

A couple of days before Ruston is due home, Lettie is busy folding a pile of clean laundry when she hears a very startling noise which takes her at a run out into the front courtyard. But, by the time she reaches the yard, all is quiet. She stands listening, wondering what could have possibly made such as strange sound. As she turns to go, a wild whooping screech makes her jump and stumble. Mere seconds later Queenie bounds over the stone fence between the hen house and the lambing barn, with Hunter clinging to her back. His shrill voice screeches as if he might be in serious pain. Only it isn't pain, it's shrieks of laugher.

"Told you so, Jase, I told you so. Queenie can jump just as high as Dad's biggest horses. She can run just as fast too," he shouts over his shoulder as he and Queenie race out of the central courtyard.

"There is no way Queenie can outrun any one of dad's horses," Jason shouts after him.

Lettie watches Hunter and Queenie with suppressed laughter. It's too silly, a sky-top racing across country, hopping over fences! As she watches, Hunter aims for one of the big stone fences walling the lower paddocks and Queenie spreads her wings and bounds over with Hunter whooping and hollering at the top of his voice. "Has he ever ridden Queenie before?" Lettie asks Jason, who now stands just behind her, and is as amused by Hunter's riding experiment as his mother. Both of them pause for a good laugh. Hunter and Queenie's great running leaps over the farm walls is without doubt out of the ordinary, but add to this, Hunter's wild shrieking shouts of glee, his bouncing little body, and the whole situation is enough to crack a smile on even the most sober face.

Jason manages to get his laughter under control enough to answer, "Hunter decided since he couldn't go with Dad to Mooreland he would surprise him with something special on his return." Jason pauses and does his best not to start laughing all over again. "He's had a little difficulty deciding what the great something was going to be until he hit on the idea of flying with Queenie. The riding part has gone without a problem, it's the take off that they can't figure out. Queenie's not strong enough to take off with him yet. She needs to grow a little more."

Jason's smiles turn again into laughter as his mother asks, "Does your father have any idea about what Hunter is up to?"

"No, Hunter waited until Dad was gone before he started. He's been working with her just the way Dad starts his young colts. Queenie loves it and I couldn't see how it could possibly be wrong. Hunter is sure she will be just as perfectly trained as Topper before Dad gets back."

"But Jason, they are running through the fields jumping the stone fences. What could have possessed Hunter to start that?" Lettie is serious, but laughing too. The image of Queenie's spread wings, Hunter's shrill voice and their blurred bodies hurling over the fence still vivid in her mind. "It can't be safe. Who would have ever thought of such a ridiculous thing?"

And both answer together, "Hunter!"

It's difficult for them to be very serious. Jason wrinkles up his face and explodes into laughter all over again. "They've been racing up and down in the cliff pasture getting in shape and trying to take off for three days now. Queenie flaps her wings and tries to get off the ground, but just can't quite make it. Sometimes they will fly about two feet off the ground a little ways." Jason stops to wipe a tear from the corner of his eye.

"I'm not sure what I think of them jumping the fences." Lettie shields her eyes for a second and tries to see across the far field where she can hear Hunter's voice.

"They jumped the lane gate by mistake I don't think Hunter remembered it was closed, and he's been jumping everything he can find since then."

"Well, next time he comes through, please, tell him I want to visit with him. Queenie is so young we don't want to hurt her."

A little while later, Lettie has a feather mattress bundled in her arms and is headed out the back door when she hears Hunter's shrill call. This time he's in the sheep pasture behind the house. Hoisting the mattress on to the hedge next to the other mattresses she spreads it out thinking how nice they will smell when she brings them in that night. A sudden screech and the stampede of running hooves accompanied with panic stricken "baaaaing" sounds, causes her to spin around just in time to see the sheep running right toward the house. She can see over the top of the big old wooden gate set in the stone wall that edges her precious garden. This big gate opens into what they call their "lambing pasture" and at this time of the year it holds all the ewes and their newborn lambs. Before Lettie has a chance to think, a big old ewe bolts over the gate and is followed by a tremendous crash as one of their biggest rams hits the gate head-on and keeps right on running—he now wears part of the gate around his neck. He passes Lettie at a dead run, along with about twenty, give or take a few, ewes and lambs. The gate isn't slowing the ram in the slightest. The running sheep stampede through the deep mud of what is supposed to be Lettie's herb garden and duck around the far side of the house.

Now Hunter is no dummy. Seeing the sheep bolt and run he thinks fast, and whirls Queenie around. They are now going in the opposite direction. This is a good thing, because his mother is very angry. Hunter knows he should help put the sheep back where they belong, but he also wants to be far away. This troubles his young mind because it is difficult to be two places at once. As it is, it turns out to be good Lettie has a few minutes to recover before Hunter meekly shows up to help. By the time he does appear with Dexter, more as moral support than to help with the sheep, Lettie is no longer dangerous to a small boy's person.

Together, Lettie and the boys move the sheep into a different pasture and then Hunter and Queenie are exiled to the cliff pasture. With these restrictions in place, along with firm commitments from both boys to stay out of trouble, Lettie returns to her laundry thinking, *What possibly can go wrong now?*

Jason gathers his fishing pole and calls Dexter, then heads for the cliff pasture. Hunter watches them go with little clenched fists. "Every time I do anything really cool something has to happen to spoil it!" he mutters under his breath and Queenie nods her rubbery head in agreement. With a sniff and a sigh, Hunter turns Queenie toward the cliff pasture, and together they plod up the well beaten track. Hunter sits slouched in the saddle muttering about things not being fair and Jason never getting into trouble.

Topper and Race circle overhead and watch Queenie's dejected walk. Even from way up in the air they can tell something sad has happened. The big sky-tops swoop down and land on either side of Queenie and Hunter.

If you could see Hunter and Queenie as they clump along with Topper and Race, you would have to agree Hunter has to be a very strange little boy. How many little boys do you know with three pet sky-tops? Not very many, I'm sure. Well, it is even stranger to see a bored and sad little boy with three pet sky-tops. How can a little boy with three sky-tops ever be bored? I don't know either, but Hunter is sad and bored.

Sometimes little boys and even grownups, decide they want something right now and sometimes they cannot have whatever it is they want exactly when they want it. Not all things go just as we want them to. It's one of those simple facts of life and Hunter wants to fly Queenie right this minute. Only Queenie is not strong enough to lift them both off the ground. It is a problem and will always be a problem when something too small tries to do something too big.

Queenie hangs her head and looks just as sad as Hunter. Both are proving to be a bit difficult to cheer up. Topper and Race cock their great long heads and study the sad pair wishing they could make them smile. Their sad faces are enough to spoil a beautiful day.

When they reach the cliff pasture, Hunter slides from his saddle and with mutters and grumbles he lifts it from Queenie's back. As he turns to put it on Topper, Queenie whimpers a soft cry. In an impulse Hunter puts his small arms around her neck and gives her a tender hug,

"Queenie, we'll get this figured out and we will fly. You'll see! I'll figure something out."

When Hunter and Topper take off, Queenie and Race follow, and the four circle their valley with big lazy circles around and around on the rising air currents. What makes Hunter decide to land on the edge of the great cliff over their home we will never know, but he does land, and that changes everything.

Hunter and Topper sit on the edge of the cliff looking down at Lynn Farm stretched below them. Together they watch Race circle and land at the big barn. They can see Jason and Dexter on the edge of the stream, and Hunter laughs as he watches Dexter dive at something in the water right next to Jason. It's funny to see Jason get all wet, he can hear him yelling. It is never a good idea to take Dexter fishing.

While Hunter and Topper watch Jason, Queenie slips out of the air and lands next to them. Right then an idea clicks into Hunter's mind and soon he is off Topper and moving his saddle back to Queenie. A very few minutes later Queenie dives from the cliff with Hunter and carries him over the valley below. Hunter's idea works! Queenie didn't have the strength to get Hunter and herself off the ground, but she has plenty of strength to fly with Hunter from the top of the cliff. It was so very simple. Hunter soon learns Queenie doesn't feel as safe as Topper. She isn't as easy to sit on because her back is much smaller. But its okay, they are in the air flying.

Have you ever noticed when things are going well and are fun you forget what time it is? Well, this is exactly what happens to Hunter. It is such fun to fly Queenie that he forgets all about the time, he forgets about eating, and his promise not to get into trouble. This is another "Hunter Mistake."

***

Later that afternoon Jason carries a nice string of trout into his mother's large farm kitchen and lays them on her big work table. They will have trout tonight for dinner. Jason starts getting the things he needs to clean the fish and seeing his mother outside the big kitchen window, he shouts. "Mom, I have five big trout for dinner tonight."

Lettie steps into the kitchen and seems rather preoccupied, "I haven't seen Hunter in hours, have you seen him?"

"Nope, the last time I saw him he was all in a huff. He and Queen were headed toward the cliff pasture."

"Well, we'd better find him." She sighs as she looks over Jason's shoulder and sees his fish. Then reaching to take the cleaning knife from Jason's hands she smiles and adds, "These are big nice trout. Here, I'll clean the fish and you find your brother. I wish your father could see these fish—he would be very proud of you." Lettie gives Jason's shoulder a little squeeze and he feels good all over.

Jason starts his search in the barns and continues through the pastures then on to the stream by the cliff. He remembers seeing Hunter flying with Topper and Queenie, but they are no where in sight now. They could be anywhere. He calls and calls, his voice rebounding from the mighty cliff walls. The sound of his returning voice feels empty. Jason turns and runs back down the long hill by the pasture gates and walled corrals until he reaches the big barn. *Race will know where to look,* Jason decides as he grabs Race's saddle and straps it in place. Almost as an after thought he grabs his bow and quiver full of arrows as he and Race hurry out the tall barn doors. Jason has a tight uneasy feeling inside. Something is wrong—he feels he must hurry.

A few minutes later Jason and Race find Hunter up on the edge of the cliff. Hunter has broken a strict rule and gone beyond where he can see their home. Jason and Hunter do not have to ask for permission to go anywhere within sight of the home buildings. To go farther they need permission. When parents make rules like this they are not trying to be difficult or mean. They want their children safe, so they set certain boundaries and rules to help them stay safe and to keep mothers from worrying. It's important to keep mothers from worrying, things go better when moms are not worried.

Jason and Race can see Topper and Queenie on the top of the cliff and they know Hunter cannot be far away. As Race slides out of the sky, Hunter runs to them. He is streaked with dried mud, blood, and tears.

"I think he's dead, Jase, I think he's dead." Hunter sobs as he looks up to where Jason sits on Race's tall back.

"What are you talking about?"

"Topper found him, come and see. Come!"

Before Jason can stop him, Hunter turns and runs back into the tumbled rocks and scrubby bushes away from the edge of the cliff. "Stop, Hunter, we aren't to be up here." Jason shouts after his brother as he disappears into a maze of boulders. Jason hesitates only a second before following. When he finds Hunter, he is kneeling in a pool of blood beside the outstretched head and neck of a wounded sky-top.

"I gave him all my water, he's worse than Topper was when I found him, he hasn't moved in a long time. Look at the cuts all over him. He must have had a terrible fight. What could do that to a sky-top?"

Topper stands over them growling a steady flow of strange guttural sounds. Topper knows exactly what happened to the sky-top lying before them. He knows only a sawtooth could do this to a sky-top.

Jason slips down Race's side to the ground and stares in paralyzed fascination at the monstrous torn wings, body, and head. Blood is splashed everywhere over the rocks and the crumpled body. Race steps toward them and strokes the creature tenderly with his big beak. Gentle clucking sounds come from his throat as he straightens the wings and moves the rocks to make his friend more comfortable. As he works the clucking never stops. Then very faintly a tiny clucking sound comes from the wounded sky-top.

"He's alive, he's alive," Hunter shouts.

Jason knows the sky-top could die if he and Hunter don't do something, and struggles within himself trying to decide what they should do. His mother had told him to bring Hunter home and that is what he needs to do first. Gently he puts his hand on Hunter's shoulder, "Hunter, we have to go home and tell Mom what has happened." As he speaks he wonders what had happened on the cliff over their home. It was frightening to imagine what could have made those terrible wounds. "Let's go and get help, there isn't anything you or I can do. Someone will have to come and help us."

Race stands over the sky-top and makes a very strange sound as Hunter lets Jason pull him away. Topper makes a terrible growling sound and Jason gives the birds a careful glance—the sounds are frightening in a soft eerie way. This is not the pleasant clicking sound sky-tops use when everything is right. Race's sound is more like a warning as he stands his full height searching the sky. His whole demeanor is fierce and threatening. Never before had any of the sky-tops acted like this.

Jason gives Hunter a forceful shove toward Topper and Hunter mumbles through his silent tears, "Isn't there anything we can do? We can't just leave him there like that!"

Jason never has the chance to answer, Race screams a scream that isn't like anything Jason has ever heard before and turns back in time to see a monstrous sawtooth coming out of the sky, right at them. His mouth open and snapping with his feet extended forward with giant knife-like claws. A person would be like a rag doll in his grasp. The wings look as big as a house. The sawtooth screams his challenge and Race rears up stretching to his full height screaming back.

It is not a time for slow thinking and Jason is not the sort to be wishy-washy about anything, especially with a sawtooth about to drop out of the sky and slaughter them. He takes no time to think, in his dreams and his games of pretend he has faced dragons and demons of every sort and he knows what to do. He is a trained archer. He is a master marksman, even though he is only fourteen years old. Age has little to do with slaying dragons or flying dinosaurs, for that matter. Courage and skill are what count at this moment—far more than age. Jason is going to kill the sawtooth and there is no back up in him.

Grabbing the bow from his back he shouts, "Hunter, run, get down under that ledge. Hurry! Go as deep as you can and stay there."

Topper takes Hunter by the back of his pants and lifts him over the rough ground and pokes him under the ledge before turning to defend him. Race is frantic in his cries and wants to jump into the air, but is reluctant to leave Jason alone on the cliff. He takes great bouncing leaps, his screams enough to terrify even the bravest of souls.

"Race, stop! You have to wait—let me get some arrows in him first. Then you can have him." Setting an arrow he draws the bow, "I have to stop him. Don't get in my way," Jason shouts as he stands tense, ready and waiting. The attacking creature screams and Race rears up giving a raging scream in return. "Stay back, steady Race. Steady," Jason's shouts. The sawtooth is almost within range. Jason waits, it seems like a long time for the sawtooth to be close enough for his arrow to have any effect. When he is still too far away, Jason lets his first arrow fly. It is a near miss and only rips a hole in one of the huge wings. Jason's heart pounds as he opens his fingers and sets his second arrow free. Zap, it sinks deep into the huge creature's lower neck and chest making it jerk up with a violent screech. Then with a new burst of speed he dives back down with an ear splitting scream, and Jason shoots a third arrow, right through the open mouth into the back of its horrible throat. Then it is too late—the sawtooth falls, thrashing with convulsions, and as Jason turns to run he trips and falls underneath Race, who in the same instant leaps into the air and throws himself into the falling monster, and manages to knock it away from Jason and the wounded sky-top. In the commotion one of Race's wings whips Jason a savage blow slamming him into the jagged rocks. Jason cannot see his arrows buried deep in the sawtooth's throat and neck. He doesn't hear its chocking screams of pain and rage or his little brother's voice, because he is unconscious. Jason lies still on the rocks.

Chapter 9

A WISH GRANTED

"Jason, Jason, get up," Hunter screams as he scrambles out from under the ledge and runs to his brother. While Race and Topper make sure the evil sawtooth will never bother anyone or anything again, Hunter fears they may step on Jason and he yanks and pulls on his brother trying to move him, but he's too heavy. "Jase, you've got to wake up. Race may not be big enough to finish that thing off. That awful sky-top may have friends and they'll be really mad. Oh, wake up," Hunter shouts, but it doesn't do any good.

Jason lies in a heap with his body sprawled on the rocks. His head hangs to one side, almost on his shoulder. There is a big rock in the middle of his back that makes his chest stick up funny, and one of Jason's legs is tangled under him. Hunter cries as he gently touches Jason, but Jason doesn't move. Ever so carefully Hunter unwinds Jason's leg from under him and eases him from the big rock. Now he looks just fine, but he doesn't wake up.

"Jason, Jason!" Hunter sobs and screams. "Can't you hear me? Open your eyes—we have to get out of here." Hunter rocks back and forth as he sits rather scrunched in the rocks next to his brother, all while trying to make his young mind know what to do. He can't lift Jason into Race's saddle. He knows Jason wouldn't stay on, even if he could lift him. *Could Race hold Jason in his mouth and fly home'* he wonders.

"Race, leave that thing alone. It's dead, shaking it now isn't doing any good," Hunter tries to reason with Jason's sky-top. "Race, you have to go and get Mom. She will come, I know she will and she will know what to do." Race turns and gives Hunter a rather strange and challenging look. Race doesn't want to leave Hunter and Jason, he knows they need him. "I can't leave Jason, Race. It would be wrong to leave him here like this. I have to stay with him. He's my brother!"

These last words are said in just such a manner that should explain everything to anyone anywhere who knows about brothers.

Hunter continues to rock back and forth with his large eyes streaming tears and his arms tenderly cradling Jason's head to his chest. "I can't go, Race, you go, you have to get Mom. She has to come—she has to," Hunter gulps the words around his tears. "Race, go! Go fast, really fast."

Race makes a rather odd looking circle or two, as if he can't quite decide whether he will go or not. The deadly sky-top still twitches and jerks, and Race shakes his head and points his beak toward Topper. Topper nods and bounds to the edge of the cliff and dives over the side headed for Lynn Farm.

Now Moms are strange creatures—they have understandings that cannot be easily explained. Sometimes moms know about things and we wonder just how they know them. This is a special gift all mothers are given, yet few understand.

Lettie hums a happy tune as she finishes rolling Jason's fish in a bowl of corn meal and smiles to herself, *Jason is getting to be such a fine young man. He takes such good care of Hunter and me.* She sighs as she wipes her hands clean and decides it's time to bring the feather beds in from outside. It always amazes her the way the feathers expand and the feather beds grow larger as they soak up the sun. They will smell like sunshine when she carries them back inside. As she is about to gather one of the large feather mattresses into her arms, her eyes pass over her damaged herb garden. Some of the hoof prints are very deep and many of her precious plants are ripped and torn. For a moment she considers, *Hunter needs a meaningful consequence—he must learn to be more careful.* A smile crosses her thoughtful face as she thinks of her youngest son, he is so smart and happy, but sometimes he does things without thinking. *Yet, how was he to know the sheep would stampede right over the gate? Maybe it was part my fault, I could have stopped him when I first realized what he was doing, but I didn't.*

"Oh," she sighs with motherly thoughts sweeping through her mind, *raising children is so hard. How can Ruston and I help the boys understand and learn to think, at least a little, before they do such surprising things?* As Lettie's heart and mind considers her boys a sudden tight feeling causes her to turn and look toward the cliff. Little does she know at this very moment Jason is on the cliff staring at the injured sky-top.

Lettie shakes her head in a little jerk trying to free herself of the strange feeling—only the feeling won't go away. On the contrary it grows and she can't seem to control her growing concern. Lettie walks back into the house and tries to do something to calm herself. Fear can creep in and spoil everything, it can make everything unhappy, even frightening. Lettie tries to get rid of the feeling and then makes the sudden decision, she must find the boys. With maternal understanding she knows something is terribly wrong and runs out the front door calling. Nothing happens, not a sound, there is no answer. Dexter runs to her and Lettie calls again and again. Her heart begins to pound and the strange frightened feeling grows inside her until she trembles and tears almost choke her. Running into the huge main barn she calls at the top of her voice. Dexter understands and barks and jumps and howls. He is upset and Lettie looks at Dexter remembering, he had been with Jason when he had gone to find Hunter. Glancing around she realizes the sky-tops are gone. The vast barn is empty.

From somewhere outside she hears a frightening screech, and rushes back out into the courtyard in time to see Topper hurling out of the sky and calling again and again with a loud horrible sound confirming her worst fears—something is terribly wrong. She feels a dizzy sick feeling inside. Topper's saddle is empty—so he'd taken Hunter somewhere. *Has Hunter fallen off? Is he hurt and lying somewhere broken and dying?* Lettie's mind wonders all kinds of horrible things as Topper lands and flings himself to the ground in front of her.

Topper knows Lettie doesn't want to fly, he knows she has said nothing could ever persuade her to go up on a sky-top. Topper doesn't know how he will persuade her to come with him. Making himself as low as possible, so the climb on will be easier, he clucks and clicks and begs in his own sky-top language. Will she understand?

"Topper, what has happened? Where are the boys?" Her words fade as her eyes rest upon Topper's huge blood smeared feet. The blood is fresh enough to make smears on the paving stones. "Has there been an accident?" Relief fills Topper as he nods his head and motions with his head and neck for her to get into his saddle. He scarcely has time to finish nodding before Lettie scrambles up his leathery wing and fastens the harness into place.

"Go, Topper, let's go. Please hurry."

Sometimes people do very remarkable things just because they love someone. Fear does different things at different times. Sometimes it makes us want to run away and hide, it can make us mean and forceful, and it can make us stronger and braver. Yes, Lettie is afraid to fly, but she is more afraid for her children. When you love someone you don't think about yourself and what you want or don't want, so it is with Lettie. Having Jason and Hunter safe is many-many times more important to her than her fear of flying. She didn't have to think about whether she would fly or not. If it means saving Jason and Hunter from some danger—of course she will fly.

After Topper's wild run for take off and his leap into the air, Lettie has a minute or two to consider what she has done while they circle for enough height to get over the edge of the cliff. She comments to herself, *Lettie, you are flying on a sky-top and glad you have Topper to take you to wherever the boys are.* She pauses to consider, *and this is so comfortable. I don't have the least feeling that I might fall.* She is surprised to discover she is not afraid; her only fear is for what she will find when she finds the boys. All she wants right this minute is for Topper to fly faster. Topper feels her pressure and her words asking him for more speed. With all his strength he sweeps the sky with his great wings, he too is worried. The wind whips Lettie's face and hair, and tears at her long skirts as they billow around her, but she is not afraid.

Hunter holds Jason's head in his lap and leans over him as he cries and prays all at the same time. Race stands with his huge clawed feet on either side of the two little boys as he watches the sky. He understands Hunter's fear. He knows the now dead sawtooth has friends somewhere. Queenie cries and whines softly from a few feet away and Jason still hasn't moved.

Hunter doesn't see Topper as he lands with his mother and misses her tumble to the ground. Hunter just knows his mother is suddenly there and he immediately starts to tell her about the horrible fanged sky-top and its attack. If Lettie would look she would see Race, Topper, and Queenie all nodding their heads while Hunter tells his strange story. As it is, Lettie scarcely pays any attention. Jason lies before her and he is deathly pale, with his breath coming in very shallow little jerks, and there is blood everywhere. Lettie knows she must get them all away from the cliff as quickly as possible, but what if Jason's neck is broken? Is his back all right to move? Will it hurt to move him? All these questions come into her mind, as she wants to lift him in her arms.

Deep heavy growling sounds come from Race and Topper's throats and Hunter shakes Lettie's shoulder, "Mom, they made that noise just before the other sky-top came. We've got to get out of here."

Without further thought, Lettie gathers Jason into her strong arms and struggles to raise him from the ground. Race moves toward her and sits very low inviting her to step into his saddle, but she can't reach the stirrup, much less pull herself into the saddle, and hold Jason all at the same time. She stands confused for only a second before Hunter pushes her back toward Race and holds the stirrup out for her. At the same moment, Topper puts his big head and beak behind and under her and lifts. Slow and steady, up she goes, carefully she pulls and eases herself into the saddle. Hunter pushes with Topper as best he can and helps her not fall backwards. Lettie is very clumsy, and if it wasn't so serious it would be quite funny. But no one else watches, and Lettie and Hunter certainly don't feel like laughing.

Race is ready to plunge over the edge of the cliff, but Lettie isn't ready at all. The courage and fear that had carried her up to the cliff has changed to anxiety for their safety, and now Jason hangs limp and unconscious in her arms. She cannot hang on to Race and hold Jason too. She is afraid she will lose her grip. There is no room for error here. So it takes a few minutes for her to readjust the safety harness to encircle both herself and Jason's still form. As she fastens the last buckle she whispers, "Let's go Race, take us to Doc Hanlin."

She is not prepared for the dive from the cliff. It is Race's usual habit to slip gently from the cliff and make the start into the air easy for his passengers, but today he is in a hurry and leaps from the edge. It's a good thing they are well strapped on because Lettie just might have turned loose and dropped Jason. She also might have hung on too tight and strangled him. We will never know, because they are buckled tight and quite safe.

Race's dive from the cliff does two things. It makes Lettie close her eyes and it causes Jason to jerk and squirm in Lettie's arms. Lettie gives a little cry and she opens her eyes, holding him tighter. Jason's eyes flutter open and can't quite focus. Everything is all blurred, so he squints and asks, "Mom, what are you doing here?"

Lettie is too choked with tears to answer and Jason takes a deep breath and closes his eyes, then opens only one eye and looks up at his mother, "We're flying!"

Moms sometimes cry at funny times and this happens to be one of them. Lettie's tears make it difficult for her to answer. Bending down she gives Jason a gentle kiss on his pale forehead. "Oh Jason, you gave

101

us such a scare." Her voice breaks and she chokes on her tears with a little strangled cry.

"You are on a sky-top—Mom, you are flying?" a slow smile begins to spread over Jason's ghostly face. Rather feebly he tries to turn his head to see where they are. Then he gives a sudden jerky twitch and cries, "I hurt, oh, man do I hurt. Oh …. Oh!"

"Just lie still, we will be at Doc Hanlin's in a few minutes. Don't move, please try to relax."

Jason closes his eyes and draws his brows together in a little frown, "Is Hunter okay? I can't remember what happened. I fell on the rocks underneath Race and I could hear him screaming. That's all I can remember."

"Yes, Hunter is fine. He took good care of you."

Lettie looks over at Hunter sitting so tall and brave with his little chin up making a rather determined profile. Looking her way he shouts, "Has Jason opened his eyes yet?"

"Yes, he's awake. He seems fine, but really hurts."

Hunter's shout of pure joy is enough to make them jump. His shouts continue like a funny singing shriek. Waving his hands over his head he lets the world know his relieved feelings, in what Lynn's call a "Hunter Yell." Lettie has to laugh in spite of herself. That's just the way Hunter is. Sometimes Hunter can't find the right words so he makes a joyous sound. Right now his high pitched voice is a beautiful sound because they all share his feelings. They all want to sing out, but they are much too grown up.

Jason takes a deep breath and he feels his mother give him a tender squeeze, "It sounds as though Hunter is just fine." He tries to laugh and it hurts too much, so after a little pause, "I can't believe you're flying, Mom. Boy, won't Dad be surprised." Jason speaks with his eyes closed. He can feel the rhythm of Race's powerful wings and the cool air rushing over him. He can feel his mother's arms and is glad she had come to get him and that she had decided to fly. "Thank you, Mom, for coming to help us. It was pretty bad up there."

"Don't think about it."

"No, I want to think about it." Jason pauses and adds, "There is something strange about the sky-top that attacked us. It has teeth and fangs. It's not a sky-top, Mom, it's something else. I've always wondered how Topper got himself all tangled up in the trees at the base

102

of the cliff. I've always thought it looked as though he'd been in a fight. But it seemed impossible. Well, now we know. I don't know what that creature is, but it's not a sky-top. It's more like a fanged lizard than a bird."

Race swerves and dips to miss a swarm of swallows circling in a large mass. Lettie holds her breath and tightens her grip. "What was that?" Jason asks as he opens his eyes again and can see the worried look on his mother's face. "Does this really scare you?"

"No, Jason, it doesn't and it surprises me. This is not frightening at all. It's not what I expected. You can see everything from up here. My feather beds looked so funny all strung out on the hedges at home. The farm roads look like little brown ribbons winding around the green hills. And now I can see Glendale up ahead and it looks like a bunch of little dollhouses. I can see why none of you want to take the cart, or buggy or even a good horse any more. This is so comfortable and so fast, and Race, he is ..." she pauses with a lack of words. "He is ... well, let's put it this way; he doesn't feel as though he would ever fall out of the sky." She laughs at the thought. "He is so solid."

Race can hear her words and gives a funny trumpeting sound almost like Hunter's shouts of joy and they all feel much better.

"Dad is going to be so happy to see you fly," Jason tries to move then relaxes back with a slight grimace.

"Right now let's make sure you are all right and let's not think about me flying any more. I'm up here right now because I love you. As for more flying, let's not say a thing to your father."

Once on the ground at Doc Hanlin's, Lettie's head swims with unanswered questions and the decisions she must make. Jason is rather battered with bruises and he's rather dizzy when he tries to stand, but Doc feels a few days quiet and he will be back to himself. While relief fills her soul. Hunter is not giving her a moment's peace. He keeps reminding them there is a sky-top alone and hurt up on the cliff, and must have help immediately—if not sooner. He also says there is a bad sky-top with two of Jason's arrows in it lying not too far from the good sky-top, and he wants to go up on the cliff and cut its head off, just to make sure he won't bother anybody ever again. Lettie understands how he feels, but doesn't want any part of his plan.

Doc listens to Hunter's pleas and suggests Jason remain with him for a day or two. He thinks Lettie has a bit too much on her mind at the moment and he's afraid there will be far too much excitement at Lynn

Farm for an invalid, especially one who could prove difficult to keep down and quiet. He suggests Lettie go home and send Race back for him, then he and Hunter will go up on the cliff together and see what should be done.

"We'll take young Master Rickard along, and if the sky-top up there can be saved we will do our best." Sensing Lettie's coming refusal, he argues, "Lettie, Hunter and Jason are right, we need to know what's going on up there. I want to see for myself. If these creatures are hostile in anyway we need to know and be prepared. If there really are good sky-tops and bad sky-tops with teeth—then we need to save the good one and learn all we can about the one that attacked them. We have a confusing circumstance here—we must understand, Lettie."

***

It is very late that night before Doc Hanlin and Hunter arrive back at Lynn Farm. "He's a good boy, that one is." The doctor watches Lettie embrace Hunter and send him off to bed. Shaking his white head, he grins, "He stayed right with me spooning water and medicine into the creature's mouth and clicking and cooing like you wouldn't believe. And Race seems to understand our words. He acts as though he knows exactly what's going on. At times I think Hunter can understand them, they click and clack back and forth. I am fascinated with the boy's relationship with these birds. It's really quite touching."

Stopping, he stares at his feet a moment before continuing. "Lettie, I don't want to frighten you, but something strange is going on up there. The sky-tops are frightened of something. They watch the sky with a sense of fear. It is almost as if something beyond our comprehension has happened." He pauses and shakes his tired head, "Lettie, the feel up there is almost evil—I can't explain. That dead sky-top, the one Jason killed, is different. His head is a different shape—he doesn't have a beak, instead he has teeth with savage fangs. His head is more like a toothed lizard or a snake than a sky-top. The sky-tops have beaks, they don't have teeth or fangs. I want to go back up and have a better look in the daylight."

Lettie stands looking up at this gentle kind friend, her mind a coil of relief and confusion, "Is the sky-top still alive?" She is almost afraid to hear the answer.

"It is, only just barely. Samuel stayed up there to take care of him. He insists he will be safe enough. He figures if he can save it, maybe it will be his. I think Race will go up and stay with him, but I don't think it's safe up there. Samuel promised he would get into a deep crevice between the rocks at the first sign of danger." Turning toward the door he mutters something about not liking the situation, then almost in an afterthought, "Will you need Race tonight?"

No, Lettie doesn't need Race, she just wants him there at Lynn Farm with them. She shudders at the thought of Samuel spending the night up on the cliff with a dying sky-top, yet she understands why he wants to stay. *Samuel, delightful helpful, Samuel,* his image swims before her eyes. His mother, the sweet Rosie Rickard, a widow, depends upon Samuel for everything. *Yes, Samuel needs a sky-top of his own. With a sky-top he could expand his current mail route and take much better care of his mother. They could pay the mortgage on their farm and be quite comfortable.* With a sigh, Lettie whispers in her heart, *Ruston, hurry home. Please.*

***

Ruston Lynn sits up with a jerk, "Lettie, are you all right? ... Lettie?" he whispers. Lettie's words linger in his sleepy mind. Staring into the darkness around him, he can feel her plea for his return. Can this be a trick of his imagination? He eases back down in his bed and closes his eyes and can see Lettie in his mind—she is still up and dressed, even at this late hour. Then the puzzle becomes more troubled as Ruston feels he can see Doc Hanlin with her. Sleep is no longer a question.

Whether Ruston was asleep or awake we will never know, and so it is with an inner pressing force, Ruston is up and moving. He doesn't question, instead he acts. Some Dads are blessed with insight they themselves don't understand; they are very like moms in that they sometimes know things there is no way for them to know. Some say it is a special gift moms and dads are given to help raise and protect their family. Sometimes moms and dads don't understand this special gift and choose not to pay attention to it. When this happens, things usually don't turn out very well. In this case, Lettie whispered the words for Ruston to hurry home, and Ruston heard her.

Throwing back his covers, Ruston gets out of bed and walks to his open window. The night air is cold and fresh on his sleepy face. Taking a deep breath he whispers Lettie's name. Leaning on the cold stone sill he looks out into the night, thinking of his family. As his mind clears he knows they need him and he is a long ways from home. Within the hour he and Bert soar over the star covered mountains that separate Ruston

105

from his home and family. Bert seems to sense the urgency and slashes the sky with powerful strokes, pushing the miles behind them.

As the night sky whips past Ruston's face with cold fresh awareness, Ruston hopes his letter of apology and explanation will be well received. Cutting his visit short by a day shouldn't cause a problem. He grins to himself as he considers the reverence with which he and Bert had been received and treated during their visit.

Ruston had been asked to arrive at The Governor's Palace in Moreland just before noon almost a week ago. The governor had prepared a special ceremony for the arrival of the great sky-top rider and his fearsome sky-top, Black Bert. The population had come in literal droves to wait for his arrival, some of them arriving the day before. Despite their previous knowledge and all the preparation, no one, and least of all the governor, had been prepared for the reality of the situation. Bert had screamed a great blasting scream as he dropped out of the sky into the crowded palace courtyard and the crowd had fled only to creep back and stare in open wonder at the splendor of Bert and his rider. Bert had thoroughly enjoyed creating a sensation. Bert is usually a very quiet sky-top. When you are as big as Bert, you don't need to do any thing loud to be important. On this occasion Bert had used his huge voice to excite his public. If the truth is to be told, Ruston enjoys Bert's theatrical moments as much as Bert does. Creating a sensation is fun. The people came to see something exciting, so what's so wrong with giving them something exciting?

The government officials accepted him as being something very near deity and all but worshiped him and the power he and his sky-top offered as future possibilities. The fact one sky-top had been trained meant it could be done again. Moreland's governor envisions flying guardians protecting their costal city.

Ruston's note states he had received an emergency message for his immediate return. *Let them wonder how the message arrived.*

***

The next morning Hunter gobbles his breakfast and asks, "Mom, Jason is still at Doc Hanlin's and Samuel is up on the cliff so that means we're the only ones here this morning, right?" He takes a gulp of milk and pauses to consider, "Things are way to quiet without them." Another gulp of milk and he asks, "Who's going to do all the chores?"

"Well Hunter, it's up to you and me. In case you're worrying, I milked and fed the calves before I woke you up. I thought you needed a little extra sleep. But all the rest of the chores are yet to be done."

"Thank you, Thank you. You knew I didn't want to milk. That old Bossie Cow hates me. She 'bout killed me the other day." Hunter rubs his head remembering how hard she's kicked him the last time it had been his turn to milk. "Tell you what," he tips his head a bit, then with a little wrinkle to his brow he decides, "I'll take care of the pigs and everything in the big barn and south pasture if you'll take care of the chickens and the lambs." Taking the last bite of his breakfast he finishes his milk and asks. "That's everything, isn't it?"

Seconds later, Hunter races out the door and Lettie watches him go with a puzzled smile. *He's growing up. Responsibility becomes him.* A little later, she is pleased to find him with the pig slop buckets all rinsed clean, the pig troughs filled and the pigs enjoying their breakfast. "Do you need any help with the chickens or the sheep?" Hunter calls out to her.

Appreciating Hunter's mature acceptance of their situation, Lettie assures him she can manage, and smiles as she watches him head for the main barn with a little prance to his step. What Lettie doesn't know is Hunter has a plan and he's hoping nothing will happen to spoil it.

A little later a shrill trumpeting sound comes from the front courtyard and Race lands and trots up to the front door. As Lettie answers his call and opens the front door, Race reaches toward her with a note written in Samuel's bold scrawl.

"So it's breakfast, he wants?" Lettie looks at Race who answers with an enthusiastic bobbing head. "Now I'm a short order cook." She comments to no one in particular as she turns back inside and calls over her shoulder. "Give me a few minutes and I'll send up something for him."

When a little later, Lettie carries out a nice hamper filled with the basic necessities for a day on the cliff, she can't figure out how best for Race to carry it. The saddle bags aren't the right shape for her picnic hamper and she doesn't want to pack the food all over again. Standing there wondering how to manage she puts a foot in the stirrup and swings into Race's saddle. "I'll just go up and see what's going on"

As Race bounds into the air, Lettie feels a little thrill and wants to shout, a Hunter sort of shout. No wonder her boys, or her men, enjoy this so much. As Race touches down after their very brief flight what does she find?

"Hunter! What are you doing up here?"

Hunter kneels beside the injured sky-top patiently squirting water into its open mouth. "I finished the chores, Mom, and I knew Samuel would need me, so Top and I just bounced on up to see if we could lend him a hand."

"Thanks, Lettie," Samuel interrupts before she has a chance to say the sharp words resting on the tip of her tongue. Taking the hamper and giving her a hand to help her from Race's saddle, Samuel leads her over to Hunter's side.

"I don't have Hunter's touch. I couldn't get him to drink for me. The poor creature looked so frightened until Hunter got here. See, he's peaceful now." Finding a comfortable rock—if there is such a thing— Samuel sits down and opens the hamper. "That boy of yours is a wonder. I think, at times, he's speaking their language."

"I am, see I'll show you. Listen." Hunter then clacks two sounds, "That's my name, Samuel yours is," and a clickity clack follows. "Did I get it right, Topper?"

All the harsh words Lettie wants to speak melt away as she watches her youngest son. Confusion makes her feel suddenly out of place and wrong about so many things. Lettie glances off, seeking help in her confusion. Studying the body of the dead sky-top, she moves closer and sees Jason's well placed arrows. A shudder shakes her, and a tear wells up and spills over her cheek. One arrow rests at the base of the throat. The other must have entered the bird's brain as it passed through the open mouth directly into the back of the creature's skull. And there, clear for her to see are the teeth, a row of jagged razors rimming the entire mouth with two deadly fangs in the front. Jason was right, this is not a sky-top. Tears stream freely down her unashamed face. Taking the end of her apron she tries to wipe them away.

Race steps up beside her, his long beak and head very near her side. Lettie strokes his shining beak, "Thank you for saving Jason." She chokes, "Jason might have been under him, mightn't he?" Race nods. "Can you really understand Hunter's clacks?" Race wags his head and makes a funny nod. "Is that a sort of?" Then he nods the affirmative and Lettie laughs through her tears. Race's big head is low and in a moment of tenderness, Lettie encircles his long beak and gives him an affectionate hug. "Thank you again."

The morning light baths them in warmth and fills the area with dazzling brilliance. Lettie takes a deep breath of cool sweet air and fights back her tears, then looks again at Hunter who has scarcely moved. For several minutes she watches her little boy and recognizes he seems to have a special gift. Is it a gift of healing or for working with the sky-tops—whichever, it doesn't really matter.

Minutes pass and Lettie knows she must go back down and asks herself if she should insist Hunter come with her? *And break his heart,* her thoughts fill her again with confused sadness. Walking toward the edge of the cliff she looks down upon their home. It's beautiful. Ruston has provided well for them. The two feed cribs stand tall and proud. She smiles as she thinks of the jokes they have shared about filling the cribs and keeping enough feed for their hungry pets. So much has changed.

Thinking of Jason, she realizes how much he has changed in the past year. It was only a little while ago he was content to build tree houses, swim in the creek, and sail homemade boats with his little brother.

Hunter distracts her thoughts for a moment as he mixes pig feed with water and a little of Samuel's milk and starts spooning it into the sky-top's mouth. His cheery voice announces, "I think we need ta call him Blinky, 'cause it's all he can do. Look, blink, blink, blink. He must have a powerful headache." He dribbles another ladle of pig food into the waiting mouth, "Am I right? Course I'm right."

Sometimes understanding is slow in coming. Many times we fail to recognize the good that comes from times of trial, and we must remember the sky-tops have been a real trial for Lettie. Since Topper's arrival, her once secure life has turned end over end, and at times she has felt as though she had no control over her boys and their safety. So much has changed. While she hardly recognizes Jason, Hunter seems to be the same Hunter. *Or is he,* she wonders?

In a moment of reflection she realizes the changes in her boys are because of the fearsome sky-tops. It is because of them, Jason is now a true marksman with the courage and the confidence to stand and defend himself in a manner most men could not have managed. It is because of the sky-tops and the experiences they have brought with them that her boys are learning to work and take real pride in a job well done. Realization sweeps over her as she acknowledges her little boy, Jason, isn't like the Glendale boys anymore. No, he's different. Hunter isn't like his old friends anymore either. Why are they different? Ruston has told her over and over again that boys don't become men by making things easy for them. He has insisted, much to her dismay, they work beside him and accept responsibility at as early an age as possible—and if they fail they must have appropriate consequences. She has felt him to be too hard in some of his consequences. Then with strange realization she accepts the fact that on each of these occasions the mistake has never been repeated. At least Jason has never made the same mistake twice. Hunter has had a little more difficulty with his self-discipline.

Now she watches Hunter and can hear his gentle clicking and is deeply touched as Race bends over him as if supervising.

We are creating incredible young men, Lettie remembers Ruston's words.

With clearer understanding, she moves to Hunter and kneels beside him. "Hunter, what are you going to do with Blinky?"

"Well, I gotta get him well first. But I think maybe he and Samuel will be right for each other. We'll see, 'cause they both have to like each other. We'll let Blinky decide."

"Doesn't it frighten you to be up here?"

Hunter looks up and around him, "Race is right there and so is Samuel. Race'll let us know when it's time to run."

"Where would you go?"

Hunter turns half around and points to a mountain of rocks that stand piled high above them. "Samuel has found a nice hole for us to get into. He says he'll stay out and help Race, 'cause Mom, Race can't fight teeth like that. That dead thing over there is not a sky-top. It may look like one from a distance, but they are not at all the same. I think the sky-tops call them sawtooths. At least I think that's what Topper has tried to tell me." Pig feed drips down Hunter's arm and he notices and pours it into Blinky's waiting mouth.

"Hunter, I'm really proud of you and how well you take care of the sky-tops."

Hunter stops and looks at his mother, "Gee, thanks Mom, I was afraid you might be mad. Thanks a bunch." And another scoop of watery pig feed goes into Blinky's mouth and Hunter purrs with soft clicking sounds.

Topper carries Lettie first to Doc Hanlin's to see Jason, who wants to come home right now, and then back to Lynn Farm where she lands only minutes ahead of Ruston and Bert.

The next few hours are hours Ruston will never forget. Standing on the cliff staring down at Jason's arrows embedded deep in the body of a toothed sky-top—which Hunter tells him is really a sawtooth—is not an easy experience for him. *Too close, way too close,* he doesn't even want to consider what might have happened, *And what shooting!* A sudden weakness shakes his soul as he remembers how close he had come to relenting on his requirement to have not only accuracy, but speed in Jason's shooting as well. Accuracy and speed had saved him; that and a good mind, to say nothing of courage. For a brief second he smiles as he remembers Jason's disappointment at being kept at Doc's. A little black and blue, but other than that, he was ready to come home and go back to work.

It doesn't take Ruston very long to realize they cannot safely care for Blinky and remain up on the cliff. The sky-tops are all on edge as they keep searching the skies. Yet, moving a bird the size of a small building is not an easy thing to do. Ruston's mind buzzes with the possibilities of how it might be done. What will he need, ropes? Yes. What about the huge nets and tarps covering the large haystacks? Could he rig some kind of a hammock to carry Blinky? And can the sky-tops carry the invalid? Are they strong enough? Maybe, if he could figure out how to get the bird into the net and create a way to pick him up.

Lost in deep thought, Ruston stares down at Blinky's limp body. His eyes wander over the lacerations and swollen blue flesh, noticing Doc Hanlin's masterful job of stitching and patching together the sky-top's many wounds.

Blinky stares up at him out of the corner of one eye and Ruston is filled with the sense of the sky-top's appreciation. It's strange how these feelings can be so powerful.

"You almost lost it, big fellow," Ruston comments and is startled to hear a feeble answer. Ruston places a hand on Blinky's massive cheek, "We are going to do all within our power to pull you through this." He pauses considering the enormity of the situation, "Somehow, we have to get you down to the barn where you can have the care you need." Burt nudges Ruston's arm and nods his giant head in agreement. Topper and Race nod and clack, it seems the great birds all agree— Blinky must be moved down from the cliff. Even Blinky tries to nod his head and flinches with a jerk that ends in a giant shudder.

Getting the nets around and under Blinky will be very difficult and Ruston fears moving him might cause serious complications. "Bert, moving him could kill him. He's cut and torn in so many places. I hate to do this to him." Bert answers with a distinctive shove that leaves no doubt as to how he feels about the risk. Move him from the cliff—they must.

How will they ever manage to get the net and tarps under Blinky? There seems to be no way possible. A little later Ruston arranges the netting up against Blinky's body. Bert suddenly understands and almost barks out a couple of orders. He and Race stand on either side of Blinky and placing their huge beaks underneath the injured bird they lift. Blinky gives a little cry and Ruston and Samuel dive beneath them and move the netting as far as possible. It takes three lifts before the netting is secure under Blinky's body. After a great deal of pushing and shoving and adjusting and readjusting the straps and the net, Blinky is ready to move.

Ruston and Samuel begin stretching the ropes out when a scream from Hunter makes them jump and feel a moment of panic. There in the northern sky are several full sized sky-tops headed right for them. In an instant Hunter dashes for his hole while Ruston and Samuel make a dive for their bows. Bert grabs the back of Ruston's shirt and makes a terrible threatening sound and Hunter shouts, "No, Dad, they are good sky-tops. Listen to Bert." Topper bounces up and down clacking happily, he seems to think this is amusing.

Seconds later, Queenie lands with three sky-tops right behind her. The birds are magnificent, each so different from the next. One is the brightest red sorrel color with pale wing tips. Another is pale gray with black edging, and the third a deep smoky gray. Ruston and Samuel stand well to one side and watch as the birds gather around Bert who clacks his greeting and seems to be giving instructions. After much clacking and bobbing of heads, Race and the three new sky-tops fall into place around Blinky, then Bert looks back at Ruston and clacks.

"Dad, he wants you to help them with the ropes," Hunter shouts as he hurries toward his father.

After considerable adjusting and readjusting the ropes, it is time to lift Blinky and carry him down to Lynn Farm. To Ruston the likelihood of being able to fly a sky-top in a net is next to zero, but Bert is positive. Hunter moves with his father and Samuel out of the way and watch in wonder as the sky-tops, each carrying a rope in his beak, lift well over a thousand-pound bird and prepare to fly with him. If the sky-tops drop the net the helpless bird will fall into the trees beneath the cliff, just as

Topper had done well over a year ago. In fascination they watch as the huge birds lift and hold Blinky off the ground while they adjust their distances. They then do an interesting thing. Slowly they spread their great wings, all while standing still. They cluck and clack. The wings over lap and the birds move until they are wing-tip to wing-tip.

The effort involved is beyond belief. All four sky-tops hold the ropes clamped tight, their frames rigid against the immense weight. The grand red sky-top is at one corner with Race behind him on the same side. The two grays take the opposite side. Bert seems to make suggestions and they gently set Blinky back on the ground. Bert reaches for a long section of unused rope and brings it to Ruston and clacks some kind of request.

"Dad, he wants you to tie the rope someplace," Hunter takes an end of the rope and carries it to Blinky then, much to Ruston's surprise, Bert taps where he wants the rope tied.

When Bert is satisfied, the birds take their corners and slowly, together they lift Blinky from the ground. Their muscles bunch and knot as they half squat and then rise to their full heights. It is wonderful to see. Hunter can't imagine how their necks can hold the weight, but they do hold it, and that's what counts. Slowly they carry Blinky to the edge of the cliff. Then their wings spread and they seem to be measuring and making final adjustments. They click and clack in soft tones. Bert stands to one side holding his long length of rope. With great sweeping wings, the giant birds work in unison then together they scrunch down and spring into the air. Bert leaps into the air over them flying up straining against his rope. His great wings throbbing upward as he strains to relieve as much of the weight as is possible. There is no question of circling. All five sky-tops strain against the impossible weight as they slide through the air straight down to the courtyard. With their wings stretched to their fullest they sail gently down into the Lynn Courtyard.

Jason missed all the excitement. It isn't until after Blinky's amazing flight down to Lynn Farm that Ruston and Bert carry Jason home where Lettie has his bed all ready for him. Only Jason doesn't want his bed he wants a meal, a real meal. No broth, no sweet sticky medicine, he wants real food! It is obvious, Jason will be quite himself very soon.

It's now very late. Blinky is asleep and resting comfortably. Ruston, tired from the long fast flight home and the day's incredible events, stands for a moment looking up at the cliff. As he watches, Bert steps out of the main barn and Ruston hears the big doors clang shut behind him. A second later, Bert takes two running leaps and jumps into the air. *Where does he go and why?* Ruston wonders, he has so many questions and has so few answers.

***

Several nights later, after all the excitement has died down, Ruston takes Lettie in his arms and holds her close, "What did you do when Hunter brought Jason home like that? You've never told me and we've been so busy I keep forgetting to ask."

Keeping a very straight face Lettie answers, "Hunter didn't bring Jason home, I went up and got him."

"No, I mean …." Ruston pauses, a little confused.

"Topper came home screeching something terrible and his saddle was empty. I knew something was wrong and so Topper took me to where the boys were on the cliff." She smiles with a devilish twinkle in her eyes.

"You mean you flew Topper?"

"Yes, I did; and if you'd given it any thought you would have known that was what happened. Race and I have been coming and going ever since you got back. That's how I've been able to get back and forth so easily. I think Race enjoys it as much as I do. I kept thinking you would see us." She pauses with a fiery sparkle in her eyes. "You didn't seem to notice that I hadn't taken a horse and buggy to Doc Hanlin's and you knew I'd been there just before you went after Jase. Where was I? I was here when you and Jason got here, wasn't I? How did I get home so fast? Race took me there and brought me home. And you never noticed." Lettie enjoys teasing her husband.

Ruston is too surprised to even make a sound.

"I wanted to surprise you. The boys know and we've been keeping it a secret."

Ruston gives her a squeeze, "Am I hearing this right? You've been flying several times and I haven't known it? How could you?"

"I'm sorry Ruston. I wanted to be really good before you saw me. I wanted to practice first, but I'm glad you know."

"I am surprised! You always said you would never, ever go up. I've been afraid to mention it again."

114

"Oh, Ruston. I've wanted to go up, but I was afraid. It's crazy to fly around on huge sky-tops that everyone else is afraid of. When I think about it now, I feel I'm crazy to want to fly again. But I do. I will go with you now, whenever you want to take me."

"Now! I want to take you now! The boys are asleep, everything is peaceful the weather is perfect. Come now!" He laughs as he pulls her toward the door.

"I'm in my nightgown, Ruston. You've got to be kidding. We cannot just go flying about just because."

"Why not, give me one good reason," he laughs and pulls her out the door. She laughs and tries to get away, but he's holding her too tight. Hunter hears them and wonders what is so funny as he rolls over and puts his pillow over his head.

"Ruston, I want to put some clothes on."

"No, I like you better this way. This is our secret. We are going to fly over Glendale with you in your nightgown. We will laugh over this for years to come. Come now," he teases.

Lettie laughs with him as she pulls herself free and races Ruston to the barn where they wake up a surprised Race. Soon they are flying in graceful circles in the cool night air over their beautiful valley. Ruston's wish has come true. Lettie loves to fly.

It's sort of funny how sad and scary things can help make wonderful things happen.

Chapter 10

THE BET

"Why you runny nosed little brat!" Chat Dixon stares down at Hunter. His deep dark eyes taunt with mocking laughter. "My race mare, Trixie can run rings around any one of your stupid sky-tops!"

Hunter steps closer to his life long enemy, his small fists clenched, "Don't you call my sky-tops stupid, you'd be surprised at how smart they are." And he would too. "If there's anything stupid around here it's you and your fat friends."

Chat cracks his knuckles and smashes his fists together, "I'll teach you a thing or ..." only he doesn't finish because Topper is there standing over them, his low guttural growl gives a subtle warning. There is a strange glint in his eyes and frankly he'd like it very much for Chat to take a swing at his Hunter Boy. It would give him a good reason to pick him up and shake him around. Cocking his great head to one side he leans over the two boys listening while inserting a word, or rather a few clicks and clacks here and there.

Chat is four years older and two heads taller than Hunter. His father is the size of a small ox, he even looks like a big ox, and Chat shows every sign of being every bit as large. One wonders why he would bother picking on Hunter, but he makes himself feel big as he makes others feel small, and it's been very easy to make Hunter feel small.

"I don't even have to run Topper against Trixie to beat her with a sky-top. Little Queenie will run rings around her—I'll leave you in the dust!"

"You mean that scrawny little blue thing that follows you everywhere?"

"She's not scrawny, she's just a baby and still growing. She'll be bigger than Topper, you just wait and see." Hunter takes a gulp of air and challenges, "She'll out run your Trixie if you're not afraid to run."

"Me, afraid? Never!" Chat gives Hunter an evil look and suggests, "This coming Saturday at noon—now what ya gonna bet?"

Hunter isn't ready for this and steps back, rumpling his already rumpled hair—he thinks fast. "I don't bet, my Dad doesn't bet, and you know it. Queenie and I will race to make you keep your big mouth shut about me, my family, and my sky-tops. Any one of them can outrun your fastest horse, and Queenie and I are gonna prove it!" Hunter almost shouts up into the bigger boy's face.

***

It's about an hour later when Ruston pauses in his work at the forge in his shop and listens. There is an unusual amount of noise coming from the main barn telling him the boys are home from school. With careful precision he cuts a red hot band of steel into a beautifully shaped hinge then places it back in the hot bank of coals and pumps the bellows. *The boys are certainly noisy, I wonder what's so funny? Whatever it is certainly has them in high spirits.* Only moments later, Jason bursts into the shop laughing at his little brother and what he has done. As Ruston listens to Jason's explanation, he pulls a glowing hinge from the embers and dips it in a barrel of water before setting it to one side. A look of, first disbelief, and then confused anger flickers across his usually kind and pleasant face.

"Hunter did what?" he demands. "I'm not sure I understand."

Taking a deep breath, Jason is surprised at his father's reaction. His news should be funny and make his father laugh. Only it doesn't. Carefully he tries again, "He bet Chat Dixon, Queenie can outrun his race mare, Trixie. They are going to run on Saturday from the Village Square to Neeiler's corner and back." Jason watches his father in growing apprehension, all his laughter forgotten in his father's unexplainable reaction.

"What could have possibly prompted this?"

"Dad, Chat is a nasty cheat with a big mouth and he makes our days miserable. He's hounded Hunter and me to let him ride Topper or Race ever since he's known about them. He's even threatened all kinds of things. Hunter don't like him."

"Doesn't, Jason, doesn't," Ruston corrects.

"Hunter doesn't like him and neither do I. He and his gang follow us around teasing and being worse than just rude to anyone that happens to get in their way. It's a game with them. You know they beat up

Hector Manning last week because he wouldn't give Chat part of his lunch." Jason takes a passionate breath and continues, "Chat called him some terrible things and everyone laughed so Hector hit him. Hunter and I haven't eaten our lunches out on the school grounds since then. We sit on the school steps and eat our lunch there where Chat can't corner us."

"I know, I heard about it." Ruston closes down the damper and arranges his tools in a neat row before picking up several new hinges. Turning, he studies Jason a moment, "School will soon be out for the summer and then we won't have to worry about Chat's gang for a while. In the meantime I wish you two would stay clear of Chat and his friends."

"Dad, that's impossible. For the past two weeks they, or at least one or two of them, have followed us everywhere. We are careful never to be caught alone, and we make sure Topper or Race is there to pick us up just before school lets out, so we've been all right."

Dexter interrupts as he bounds in through the open doors, his pink tongue hanging to one-side, and a great smile on his face. He wants to play and things look much too serious in here. Glancing around he bounces his big body into Jason who responds with a rather distracted pat on his head. When Dexter doesn't get the attention and activity he wants, he bounces right back out again hoping Hunter will be more rewarding.

Jason watches his father and is very puzzled over his strange attitude. It's disturbing to see the frown on Ruston's face grow as he considers the situation.

"Frankly, I don't like this one bit."

"Why, I thought you'd laugh," Jason almost pleads.

"Jason, this won't solve the problem. If Hunter loses, the teasing will go on and we must remember your little brother has a temper. It's buried rather deep, but when he's mad he doesn't think very well." Ruston pauses, "None of us think very well when we are angry. Anger is a dangerous thing." For a moment Ruston stares out the window, the afternoon sun on his face. "I've known Chat has been pushing you both, but I didn't realize it had gotten this bad. They are a rough bunch and are going to find themselves in serious trouble one of these days and I'd rather we not be the ones to trigger the situation. It's already dangerous, let's not make it worse." Glancing down at Jason he continues with, "You know Chat's father can be more dangerous than his boys."

"But Dad, I don't think Hunter will lose," Jason hopes this will ease his father's concern.

"Winning may be worse than losing. You see, Chat makes himself feel big by making others small. He doesn't realize to be big, really big and important, you must lift the little fellow and carry him. You must prove your strength not by destroying, but by building and lifting others around you." Ruston looks down at the hinges in his hands and shakes his head, feeling the need for a simple solution. "No, if Hunter loses, Chat has become the bigger, and the better in his own eyes and in the eyes of his friends. You see some people seem to feel they have to be bigger, better, faster. Some of these people need to feel big almost as much as they need to eat. It is a kind of appetite."

How can I possibly help Jason understand? Ruston's mind pleads.

Shifting the hinges to one hand, he carries them to a shelf in a far corner. "On the other hand, if Hunter wins and proves Queenie is the faster, he will have made Chat the smaller or the slower, or whatever. The thing we are faced with here is Chat's ego, and unfortunately Chat feels he has to be best at everything. It is not a simple race. No matter how hard you try, you will never solve the Chat problem by beating him." Taking a deep breath he continues, "Jason, if Hunter wins the only retaliation Chat understands is to crush Hunter, and that is what I intend to prevent."

A little later they find Hunter under a tree in the apple orchard reading a book. Soon Hunter understands the nature of their visit and is most upset, "You want me to loose the race! Dad, I can't do that! That makes me sick all over." Hunter looks up into his father's eyes hoping to see a teasing smile, when he doesn't, he slams his book shut and with a clenched fist exclaims, "Chat, has called me every name in the book; he pushes and shoves me around, remember when he pushed me into the mud puddle and stood on me? Yesterday he squirted perfume on me and everyone laughed." Hunter quivers with emotion as he continues, "He's been following me and Jase, and pushing us and our friends around 'til none of them dare do anything with us. It's bad, Dad, really bad. I'm sick of it!"

"I know, and I want to work it out, but a race to put Chat in his place won't serve the purpose. Win or lose you will still be a target for Chat's anger and jealousy."

"Awh, Chat isn't jealous, he's just plain mean."

"But he is jealous, Hunter. It's why he does the things he does. Until you became important and rode around on sky-tops he hadn't paid much attention to you or Jason. Then you became the village heroes and he became jealous. I promise jealousy is at the base of this and he feels he must take you down and damage you in some way to make himself feel better. Some people feed on this sort of thing."

Later that evening Hunter is in the barn curled up in the straw with his nose buried again in a book. Blink is sound asleep next to him and Queenie seems interested in the book. As Samuel forks hay into the various stalls he pauses in his work for a moment and glances over at Hunter. *He surely does like to read. It almost looks as though Queenie can read the way she studies the book over his shoulder... Guess I ought to read more. Ruston says it will make a difference in my future.* For a moment Samuel leans on the pitchfork and considers the thought.

"What are you reading?" he calls to Hunter who looks up, and it's obvious he's been lost in another world.

"It's one I borrowed and it has a cool race in it. It gave me the idea of challenging Chat to a race. I wanted to let him know he wasn't so great," Hunter pauses then looks up into Samuel's face and finishes, "But Dad wants me to stop the race."

Samuel squats down next to Hunter and asks, "Why would your father want to stop the race. It will be a great race, one everyone would like to see."

When Hunter shrugs with a sad look and opens his book, Samuel presses and wants to know why. As Hunter shares his father's feelings he is a bit glum and finishes, "But, I guess it's all right, I talked Dad into letting us run, and I will let Queenie stay right with him and worry him a lot and then let him beat us by only a smidgen." Then with a little grin he smiles a fiendish smile, "I'm gonna worry him bad, he'll know Queenie is fast. It'll be fun to make him sweat." Giving Samuel a serious glance he notices Samuel suddenly looks quite ill, and asks, "Why, did I say something wrong?"

"No, not at all," Samuel almost chokes, "I just remembered I need to tell your father something."

Ruston is out with his mother cows checking the new born calves. He looks quite content as he watches the playful babies.

"Good evening Samuel," then pausing he senses something is wrong. Samuel is pale and obviously upset. "What is it?"

Samuel starts with a confused sputter, "Master Lynn, I'm afraid I've made a mistake. I'm afraid you will be terribly disappointed in me. I've come to beg your forgiveness."

"Samuel, I've known you too long to be terribly worried about anything you might do. I don't see how you could disappoint me."

"You don't understand, and I didn't understand when I did it!"

"It's okay Samuel, people make mistakes and we manage to get over them. Now what is it you've done that is so terrible?"

"I bet Arnald Dixon, Queenie would win!" He blurts, and then fumbles to explain. "You see, late this afternoon, I went to Simson's Store and Chat's father, you know Arnald Dixon, was there with a crowd of men all gathered round talking about the race. Dixon is so crude and loud, he makes me want to hit him. I listened to him and he made me mad." Samuel stands twisting his hat in his hands while keeping his cool gray eyes steady on Ruston. "I listened to the things he said about how stupid Hunter was to make such a bet and how impossible it would be for a clumsy sky-top to beat Chat's mare and I knew he was wrong. Why, Master Lynn, I've watched Hunter and Queenie run and they don't even have to try to outrun a horse. Queen's legs are more than twice as long as a horse's, all she has to do is trot to keep up." Samuel swells with indignation as he remembers the insults. Taking a quick breath he announces, "I know what Queen can do and I told him so. Then he told me to put my money where my mouth was and he prodded. He turned on me like a spider plays with a fly caught in its web." For a moment Samuel is still and sighs, "You know I don't have any money to bet with, but I do have two strong hands and I'm a good worker, so I bet him my labor in rebuilding and repairing the fencing around his place, plus repairing their big barn against the mortgage he holds on our farm."

With the truth shared, Samuel takes a deep breath and looks for encouragement and understanding from Ruston, his mentor and friend.

"I see …." Ruston almost whispers. "You know I've asked Hunter to give the race to Chat or to let Chat and Trixie win."

"I do, and I understand, but I wanted you to know what I've done. I wouldn't have done it if I'd of known how you felt. Dixon was so rude and making fun of Hunter and I just couldn't stand it. I wanted to put the big man in his place."

"A bet never puts anyone in their place, and someone always loses. You need to remember that," Ruston almost whispers.

Picking up the pitchfork Ruston sets it over his shoulder and turns placing his other hand on Samuel's shoulder and nods saying, "This definitely changes the whole situation. I think we need to go have a little visit with Hunter and Queenie."

***

On Saturday morning the weather is glorious and everyone's spirits are high despite the complications with the race and Chat's gang. Samuel and the Lynns circle on the sky-top's silent wings over Glendale and look down at the town. Ruston is dismayed to see Glendale's population has turned out for the race. Hunter's little problem seems to have grown into a town spectacle. With growing disquiet, Ruston fears for the outcome of the day's events. It doesn't take long before he realizes the depth of his worst fears.

"Rus," a booming, yet somehow unpleasant voice shouts above the noise of the crowd and causes Ruston to turn. "Glad to see you here. Foolish thing that boy of yours did to bet my Chat his littlest sky-top could outrun his race mare, Trixie. Absurd, absolutely absurd." The huge, smooth talking Arnald Dixon, smiles down at Ruston with a slight curl to his lips. This man makes their village smithy look small. His head is big and round and covered with slick black hair, his eyebrows are all black and bushy over little black eyes that always sort of squint. His neck is huge, and makes his head even look small. It's a wonder how he manages to button his top shirt button.

Looking square into the big man's eyes, Ruston covers his anger with a cheerful greeting, then finishes, "Yes, it's a little foolish to run a sky-top against a horse, but it will be something both boys will remember. It's good to let them have their fun." He steps back turning to go with the words, "May the better pair win."

Dixon steps forward reaching to grab Ruston's arm, but somehow, Ruston manages to slip out of his reach. Irritated by Ruston's ability to control the situation he pursues his attempt to retain him, "What'll you wager, your sky-top for my horse?"

"This is a kid's game—you said yourself it was absurd. Let's keep it that way." Ruston smiles a pleasant smile and wishes he could punch the big man in the face. It might make him feel better, but it wouldn't solve the problem. With a sigh he wonders how he might reach through the pride of this mammoth man.

"What, you afraid to bet?" Dixon taunts with contempt seething through his smug smile.

"I'm not a betting man, Dixon and you know it. We've had this little talk before and it won't serve." Ruston again turns to walk away.

"Everybody else is betting."

Ruston pauses as Dixon continues, "That fool Harold Simson bet me a whole lot more than he can afford. I'll ruin him!" Dixon's smile widens showing the flash of a gold tooth, won, he claims in a bare knuckle fight.

The next hour is a nightmare for Ruston as he learns how many of his friends have bet on Hunter and Queenie. With a sick feeling he finds Hunter and they retire to the edge of the village to wait for the race away from the crowd.

"Hunter, Samuel isn't the only one who has bet on this race." Ruston's heart aches as he continues. "Son, it's not just yours and Chat's race any longer. It's become a public race because the town is betting and the race must be fair. As your father and representing a small community that believes in you, I must ask you to run a fair race, don't hold Queenie back, and if possible you need to win. Some of our oldest and dearest friends have bet on you to win."

Hunter looks up at his father with wide eyes, "Dad, I know what Queenie can do and we will win. I'll win for them," he pauses and with a smile he realizes, *and I'll win for me and Queenie too!*

Standing next to Hunter, Ruston places a gentle hand on his son's small shoulder and tries to explain, "Son, they don't understand. They don't realize with every bet there is a winner and a loser. No one ever considers the fact they could lose. Some of these good people have foolishly gotten themselves involved in something that could cause them great suffering. Dixon has mortgages on a number of homes and shops here in town—he could ruin these people." The consequences of this day's foolishness are frightening to consider and Ruston is sick inside as he contemplates the possible outcome.

"I will win, Dad?"

"Well, Son, all I can ask is that you and Queen do your best."

At the starting line the crowd presses close on either side of the road. The Glendale Band plays a loud bouncing tune that sounds a little off key amid the excitement. Queenie loves to be the center of attention and stands tall and grand, or at least as tall and grand as is possible for a very large featherless bird. She is quite calm as she looks down on all the people. The bright red fringe and tassels on her bridle and saddle, dance as she moves and she gives her head a little shake, liking the sound of the fringe in the refreshing breeze. Cocking her slender head to one side, she watches the nervous and very nearly frantic race horse bouncing and pawing next to her.

The crowd parts as Mayor Daily steps to the starting block with a big bright red flag.

As he clears his throat he unrolls a piece of paper and begins to speak. Hunter doesn't know whether to laugh or cry. The mayor is about to give a speech. Queenie stretches her long blue head and neck over the mayor and looks at his paper and everyone laughs. Snatching the paper to one side, the mayor blusters a bit then bellows louder. Without his knowing it, his impromptu speech grants Queenie an unneeded advantage. While she is relaxed and content to stand amid the confusion, Chat is rapidly losing control of Trixie. Queenie clicks and clacks down at the frightened horse trying to comfort her, but this doesn't help. Rather it creates the opposite effect—Trixie isn't the least comforted and shies away. In a moment of frantic plunging, Chat's father grabs her bridle and does his best to keep her still. No one seems to be listening to the mayor. By the time his speech ends, Trixie's sweat glistens and runs down her lean legs. When the flag finally drops, Trixie leaps forward and Queenie begins with a delighted trumpeting squeal and a huge bound.

"Stay on the ground, Queen, if you fly one step we are out and all those people will lose their money to rotten old Dixon." Hunter stands in his stirrups hanging onto the secure straps in front of his saddle. "Stay on the ground, girl," he pleads with serious anxiety, fearing she might forget. But Queenie understands and lengthens her stride settling down to a comfortable run. At least as comfortable as a two legged sky-top can be.

Trixie is ahead by about one horse's length, but Queenie doesn't mind. She enjoys running and for the moment, watching the horse in front of her is fun. Hunter feels her efforts and knows she hasn't yet started her race. Leaning over her long neck he shouts, "As we pass that hay meadow up ahead let's pull up along side and see what happens." Queenie nods and as they race along the edge of the field she eases up beside Trixie, and Chat looks up at them, his face murderous.

With an impish little smile, Hunter waves and urges Queenie on. Down the farm road they run. "Yeeee owwww," Hunter shrieks with sheer joy waving at the crowd gathered in front of Neeiler's and along the road, as he and Queenie race with huge strides round the curve and turn back toward Glendale. Standing in his stirrups, he leans into the wind and Queenie gives a little snort. "Wait a little, Queenie, we don't want to beat him too bad. Dad, says this is not a time for pride."

As Queenie relaxes her pace, Hunter hears pounding hooves moving up from behind and looks back. "Slow up Queenie, a little more, let's let them catch up for a moment then we'll sprint into town." Queenie relaxes her strides and glances over with a friendly click and clack as Trixie pulls up along side.

Chat looks up, hurling verbal abuse toward Hunter, who is repelled by his words and his look of uncontrolled hatred. Easing Queenie back even with Trixie, Hunter wonders what Chat must have going on in his head to look like that. Leaning down low on Queenie's neck, he tries to have a better look at Chat's face. Never has he seen such crazy anger.

"Getting tired?" Chat shouts, "You goose faced idiot, no one out runs me and Trix." Then slashing his whip into Queenie's face he gives her a stinging blow while shouting disgusting insults. For a brief second, Queenie shies back and Trixie lunges into the lead.

The crowds gathered at the square in Glendale can see them now as Queen and Trixie run toward the finish line. Trixie is in the lead and this is not as planned. The gatepost at the edge of the village square is the finish line and Hunter knows it is time to win and shouts, "Queenie, now run! Go, girl, pass them and beat him good." Gone is Hunter's resolve to make the finish close. Queenie stretches out her long neck and lengthens her stride and runs. The wind is terrific and the speed thrilling—never has she run so fast. Standing tall in his stirrups, Hunter gives a "Hunter Yell" before flattening low on Queenie's neck. For a brief moment they are beside Chat, who lashes Trixie with his whip. Anger fills Hunter's soul at the abuse, and Queenie growls a deep throated growl causing Trixie to swerve to one side before she explodes past. The last quarter of a mile proves beyond all doubt which of the two contestants is the faster. As Queenie settles down to run, the distance between the two racing figures widens and continues to widen as she hurls past the finish line.

Trixie and Chat cross the finish line many lengths behind, but few are there to notice. They have followed in Queenie's wake and have gone mad with roars of approval. To most of Glendale's way of thinking it was a marvelous race. Those who had made bets on Queenie are especially exuberant, and shout and pound, one another on the back. Some faces glisten with tears of joy. Bert, Race, and Topper stand in the road blasting the air with their huge voices. They seem to have enjoyed the race as much as Queenie and Hunter. Their enthusiastic bounces make them dangerous to be near at the moment and the area around them is quite empty, but no one seems to mind.

As Hunter swings Queenie back, he catches a glimpse of Chat who has lost all control. In his anger he yanks Trixie's bit and beats her with vicious blows, his face distorted with rage. Urging Queenie back, Hunter rushes toward them and in their haste almost knock the trembling mare down. "Get the whip, Queen." Hunter shouts, and Queenie willingly snaps the whip from Chat's hands. A sudden hush comes over the excited people around them and they hear Hunter's voice as he shouts, "You can't do that, Chat. She ran her best. She's a fine animal, you should be proud of her."

"Why you skinny little brat," Chat turns on Hunter. "You are going to regret this."

As Queenie lunges toward Chat, Hunter pulls hard to stop her, "No, Queen. Wait. He didn't mean any harm, he's just mad."

Chat ducks away from Queenie shouting, "You better believe I meant it. You just wait. You won't have a precious sky-top to protect you one of these days and I'll give you a taste of my fists."

"It was just a race," Hunter is quite serious as he tries to smooth the situation. "It really doesn't matter. I made the bet so you'd quit calling me names and shoving me around. Remember?"

As it is, some go home happy while others are devastated. Harold Simpson will now be able to pay off his mortgage; he will be free of Dixon and hopefully a wiser man. There are others too that have fared quite well with the morning's work and these are joyous and thump Ruston on the back, delighted with their good fortunes. But Ruston has no desire to celebrate with them and wants to leave. As he gathers his family together and ushers them toward where the sky-tops watch from a little distance, he catches a glimpse of Arnald Dixon. Their eyes meet and Ruston is startled by the hostility he recognizes, even at a distance. With a heavy feeling he knows they have made an enemy with this day's work and fears his boys will not be safe from Chat's brutal fists.

Much later in the day, while Hunter and Jason clear the table from their evening meal Hunter asks, "Dad, why was it so bad? I mean, the race was fair, everybody saw it. I didn't cheat and hit Chat with a whip."

Ruston leans back in his chair, his face serious. "Who do you think has to pay off all those bets? The money has to come from somewhere." Hunter stops with a pile of plates in his hands. "Hunt, it was Master Dixon who made the bets with all those people and if he is to remain in Glendale with any degree of honor he must pay every single person he made a bet with." Pushing himself back from the table, Ruston stands, "I don't know the full amount of what Dixon bet, but I know of three that were very large amounts. The race could be the end of Master Dixon's affluence. You see all wealth has its limits. I am afraid he may have over extended himself."

"You mean Dixons might be poor because of this?" Hunter is incredulous.

"It is possible. More than likely they will have to do without some of their fancy things. Let's hope it's not more serious than that."

"He shouldn't have made those bets."

"You are right. He shouldn't have, but he did and now he must pay them. A town like Glendale will not forgive someone who bets and then isn't good for his bet. Dixon will have to pay if he is to remain in Glendale and live happily here." Starting toward the door he picks up his hat, and Hunter follows.

"Why did he do it then? I mean make all the bets like that?"

Ruston turns back toward his son, "The same reason Chat beats up the kids at school—it makes him feel big and important. Arnald Dixon thought he could make himself bigger, richer, stronger, and all those things by betting and winning, and taking more from the people of Glendale." Placing his hat on his head he looks down at Hunter and Jason who stand listening, "It's not a very pretty picture. Arnald is smaller and poorer today than he was yesterday, and he won't forget who did this to him."

"But Dad, he did it to himself," Hunter explodes with defense.

"Yes, he did, but he won't see it like that. All he will remember is that you and Queenie beat him, and made him look small. Then there's also the fact you have cost him a great deal of money."

"No, no, no! He cost himself all that money. It was just a silly race and a silly bet. He's the one who made it cost a lot of money," Hunter argues, his face red with anger and eyes glistening with the hint of tears.

"You're right, absolutely right. But it won't change things. All Chat and his father will remember is that you beat them and because of you, they have lost a great deal of money."

Hunter takes a deep breath, and Ruston raises a gentle hand to silence him, then with a smile, he quotes a favorite family saying, "Convince a man against his will and he'll be of the same opinion still."

"But ...."

"No, buts. That's just the way it is regardless of how wrong or silly it is. Grownups can be just as childish as kids, only when they are childish it seems to mess things up a whole lot more." Pausing he takes a deep breath then continues, "We all need to understand that, unless I'm mistaken, Chat Dixon will now be meaner, and more violent—and somehow I must protect each of you. I'm afraid we don't understand the Dixon way of thinking and just to play it safe we had best prepare to defend ourselves."

With these words Ruston steps out the door leaving Jason and Hunter watching after him.

"I'm glad you can shoot Jase," Hunter whispers.

"Ya, but I can't shoot somebody. I can't carry my bow everywhere. The bow isn't the answer," Jason answers as he piles the dishes in their big wash tub and carries the steaming kettle of hot water from the stove. "You just don't go around shooting people because you don't like them."

***

The following day Jason saddles Race for Samuel who is about to leave with the mail and Hunter runs out with a small bundle for him. "Samuel, please take this to Grandpa, I've put the direction on it." Hunter stops considering his package, "Did I do it right, I've never mailed anything before."

Samuel smiles and looks at Hunter's parcel, "Well, let's get it addressed right and I'll take it for you. The address has to be right because I only take it to the town mail office and someone will take it on to your grandparents from there." Curiosity causes Samuel to ask, "What's in this lumpy package anyway?"

"A letter and one of the sawtoothed sky-top's teeth. I thought Papa'd like it. I also put some of Mom's cookies with it."

"Only Hunter," Samuel whispers to himself with a little chuckle as he slips the package into his large saddle bags and then climbs into Race's saddle. *A huge tooth and cookies!* He laughs and waves to Hunter as they turn to take off—*Only Hunter!*

At this same time Ruston is busy with a new project. He is about to hang something rather big and long, round, and brown. It looks like a giant sausage and is almost as big as Hunter. Ruston plans to hang it from one of the beams inside the main barn not too far from his shop door.

It's time for lunch and when Ruston doesn't come, Lettie sends Hunter out to the barn to find his father. As Hunter and Dexter hurry toward where Ruston stands staring at his handy work, Hunter stops and studies the huge sausage. "What's that crazy looking thing for?"

"It's a punching bag."

"What's it for—punching?" Hunter giggles with little snorts. *What a kick, a bag for punching.* This is really funny.

Ruston laughs at Hunter's ridiculous laugh and punches the heavy leather bag with his powerful fist and the huge bag swings from its long ropes. "That's exactly what it's for. It's time for you and Jason to learn how to defend yourselves." Pausing, *I wish we'd started months ago.* Then aloud, "Now let's see how hard you can hit it. Come on; give it all you've got."

"Wham," Hunter's right hand smashes into the leather and Dexter barks with excitement. "Oooooh, ooooouch." Hunter cries and looks at his throbbing hand.

"Here Son, you have to hold your hand like this. Make a tight fist." Ruston speaks as he shows Hunter his fist, then gently curls Hunter's fingers into a tight ball. "Now try again." Looking up into his father's face, Hunter looks down at his clenched fists. "Use your left fist if your right one still hurts."

Hunter gets set with grim determination and attacks the heavy leather bag, and it actually moves. With a shriek, Hunter pounds with both fists again and gives it a sound kick, just for good measure. The big bag bounces a little and Hunter laughs as Dexter starts to jump and bounce with both front feet trying to push the moving bag.

So this is a beginning.

Chapter 11

THE TEST

Glorious morning sunshine spills across Hunter's bed and warms his sleeping face. Opening his eyes, he is blinded with the unwavering light. "Ug," he groans and rolls over pulling a blanket up over his head.

School is out for the summer and he'd asked to please be permitted to sleep late, just this once. Closing his eyes he takes a deep breath and snuggles down deep in his feather mattress and tries to go back to sleep, but his mind is too busy. There is no school today, or tomorrow, or the next day!

Nope, sleep is gone. He stretches and lies there thinking. Everything is too quiet.

"Why is everything so quiet?" He wonders out loud and tries to see out his half open door into the hall. "Houses aren't supposed to be this quiet. People make noise and I should hear something." Sitting up he listens—silence. *It's way too quiet*, he decides, and swings his feet out of bed. The windows are open and the day is warm as he plods his way through the quiet house. "Where is everybody?"

"Mom," he calls at first in a polite voice then much louder. A minute or two later he finds his mother at the back of the house sewing.

"There you are—I've been lookin' all over, where is everybody?"

Lettie looks up, her needle hovering in mid-air, "Your father and Samuel are over at Crawford's working on plans for their new barn, and Jason took a crate of eggs to the Red Lion."

"Awh, that means he won't be back for hours and hours." Hunter mutters in disgust as he plops down on a big over stuffed chair.

"Why would you think that?" Lettie looks up again to see a rather terrible frown covering Hunter's usually happy face.

"Cause, Emily Foster lives there, and Jason thinks she's pretty. He's always watching her. Makes me sick!" He finishes with a gagging gesture.

Lettie has a little difficulty hiding her desire to laugh. "Why is that so bad? Jason is right, Emily is a beautiful girl?"

"But he likes her, Mom, and that's terrible! Terrible!"

"How old are you now, Hunter?"

"I'll be eleven soon," he answers and is puzzled as to what this has to do with Emily Foster.

"Yes, and Jason is fourteen and because he's fourteen, girls are getting prettier and prettier to him." Lettie can't look at Hunter's face she's afraid she might laugh. He looks sick. "When you are fourteen they will be pretty to you too."

"Mom, that's disgusting!"

"Maybe so, but that's the way it is. Then one day you will find a girl so perfect, so beautiful, and so wonderful, you will want to be with her for ever and ever. But you needn't worry—liking girls starts sort of slow and easy." Glancing up at Hunter she finds him, for once, speechless. A laugh betrays her and the laugh won't stop.

"You're teasing me, Mom!"

"No, I'm not. You ask your dad how it is. He used to think girls were yuck too, until he met me." She gives a smug little smile, and turns back to her sewing.

Hunter watches her for a minute—not at all sure what he should say. Sunshine spills over his mother's bent head and her auburn hair glistens with a halo of red.

So Dad thought girls were yuck before he met Mom, Hunter leans forward wanting to see his mother's face. Satisfied he leans back thinking, *Mom really is pretty and she's cool to. There aren't very many moms who will fly around on sky-tops, and run races, and can make awesome pies and sweet rolls.* Then his brow wrinkles and a little frown appears on his thoughtful face, "But Mom, there's only one of you." Hunter wants to shout. "And Dad took you for himself."

Crawling out of the big chair, he heads out the door, and Lettie calls after him, "There are sweet rolls on the kitchen counter and fresh milk in the well house."

A little later Hunter tromps out across the paving stones toward the main barn. Dexter prances next to him hoping for a taste of the sweet roll, but Hunter doesn't seem to notice. Taking a huge bite, he stops a moment to chew. Dexter whines and gives him a nudge, hoping he will share. No such luck.

Shoving the last of the sweet roll into his mouth, Hunter has difficulty chewing and his cheeks make him look like a greedy chipmunk. Then wiping his hands on his pants he sputters through his mouth-full, "Come on Dext, let's see how Blinky is this morning." Breaking into a run, Hunter wonders, "Maybe it will be Blinky's day to fly. Dad says he'll be ready to fly again just as soon as he's strong enough to get off the ground. That will be so cool. "

The beauty of the morning accompanied with the thoughts of time all his own have vanished Hunters doldrums, and it is with wonderful enthusiasm and energy that he and Dexter explode in to join Blinky.

The giant bird is sound asleep in his comfortable bed of straw. Opening one eye he studies his noisy visitors. "Come on Blink, this is no time to sleep. You need to be outside exercising and getting ready to fly." At which, Blinky moves his great head and opens his other eye. Blink, blink goes his eyes then with a mammoth sigh he makes a soft "click, click."

"Yep, I know," Hunter laughs and gives the big bird a fond pat before sitting down in the straw, pulling Dexter down with him. "This is going to be an awesome day, I've decided I will first go up to the cliff pasture and rebuild my city." Pausing, he tilts his head to one side and looks first at Dexter and then at Blink, "I'm going to tell you a great secret."

Blink moves his head nearer and opens his eyes a little wider, "Click, eeeerk, clak."

"It's a wonderful secret." Hunter pulls and ruffles Dexter's fur as he talks and Dexter rolls to his back hoping for a tummy rub. "Dad had some cement in some old tubs and sacks, some of it got wet so he was going to haul it off. I dug through it before he left and found enough to fill one of my buckets. I've been wanting to cement my city all together so the rain can't mess it up." This thought makes Hunter smile a very happy smile, "That'll be really cool." Turning to Blinky, he leans and drapes himself over the sky-top's head and neck giving the bird an affectionate huge, "Then I think it's time for you to take me for a ride. Dad has your saddle all ready—he told me yesterday he needed to fit it to you." Dexter moves closer and pushes, wanting Hunter's full attention and is rewarded with a firm embrace. "I can fit the saddle for Dad and you can have your first lesson in how to carry me. It's really easy."

Blinky snorts a little snort and smiles a huge sky-top smile with a string of clicks, clacks and rurrrrrs all mixed together.

"That'll be the greatest. Now you get up and get all limbered up, you might even spread out your wings and exercise them. I want to fly with you really soon. Okay?" Giving Blink a firm pat, he pushes himself up to his feet. Blinky watches him a moment then draws his great legs in under himself and sits up stretching his long neck up toward the ceiling and opening his immense beak in what must be the biggest yawn ever made. "Great! You're gonna love your saddle. The sheepskin is the softest yet." Hunter stops to give Dexter's itch a good scratch and looks back up at the huge bird, "Then, Blink we might even go into town, we can go all over today, only you've got to get up and have your breakfast first." Motioning Dexter to come with him he skips out the door into the morning sunshine.

Watching them go, Blinky yawns again and looks out one of the big windows where he can see Hunter and Dexter cross the front of the barn and head up the cart track toward the upper pasture. The bucket of cement must be heavy, Hunter looks rather stooped as he half carries and half drags it along.

Once at his sand city, Hunter drops to his knees and goes to work. Soon the miniature buildings begin to take shape, along with the roads and canals. Rather than rebuilding the castle, Hunter takes it apart, setting the rocks in neat rows. He then digs a hole and fills it with cement and mixes it with water and a little sand. He stirs and hums a little tune. He's watched his father build barns and fences and he'd even helped build the new back porch on their large home, and he knows just how to mix cement and how to set the stones. One rock at a time he smears the cement and puts the rocks in place. The castle gate is a bit tricky; the rocks must be carefully balanced.

A little rabbit watches from under the edge of a nice bush. He sniffs and decides he wants to nibble some of the grass at the edge of the sandy beach. Little tip toe steps he takes. The big yellow dog is sound asleep and all is safe, or so the rabbit thinks as closer and closer to the green grass he creeps.

Hunter doesn't see the rabbit, he's busy. He mixes more cement and starts on the castle's inner court. The cement works beautifully. This will be a perfect city. The minutes tick by, Dexter sleeps, and the rabbit enjoys a feast, nothing could be better, except for a pesky fly. First the fly sits on Hunter's ear, "whop" Hunter shoos it away. Then it buzzes his forehead, round and round it goes and Hunter swings at it flipping cement in every direction. When the fly lands on Hunter's nose, Hunter yells out with a loud bellowing sound and Dexter sits up and the rabbit jumps, Dexter sees the rabbit, and the rabbit runs. With a wild scramble Dexter is up and running. Down the pasture they go with Dexter barking a funny yip at every stride. Hunter raises up on his knees and watches. "You'll never catch him Dext, it's a waste of energy," Hunter raises taller on his knees as he laughs and shouts. Dexter and the rabbit are tiny little shapes now headed down the cart track and Hunter is alone.

Less than a minute later Hunter is startled by a sound that isn't right. The crunch, crunch of big feet on gravelly sand is just behind him and he turns and looks over his shoulder. There not twenty feet away is Chat and his buddy, Dorf, a nick-name for dwarf because he is so huge. They smile evil smiles, and Hunter knows he's in trouble. Chat opens and closes his fists, the way Ruston does before he hits their punching bag.

Hunter watches as they slowly step closer, seeming to enjoy their triumph in finding him alone. *Dad says if I get into trouble I have to keep a cool head and think—use every advantage. A fight is not a time to panic or run scared—I have to plan my best defense, and keep thinking.* Hunter remembers his father's words of counsel given during one of their punching bag lessons. *What do I have?* he ponders as his hands clench into the sand beneath him. *I have sand and they have eyes.* Digging deep with his fingers he grips two fists full of sand and crouches ready to throw and run. *Run where?* Remembering the thorns and the low tunnels surrounding where Topper had once been caged beneath the cliff, he gets set, his mind racing.

"We've got you now—no dirty little punk gets away from me," Chat gloats, "Nobody here to protect you. No dog—no scrawny brother—and not one of your big sky-tops—all alone, little boy." He crunches his knuckles and grins an ugly grin, "We're gonna rub your nose in the mud and make you eat dirt. That's before we break every bone in your puny body."

One step closer, then another step, both are now side by side and Hunter comes off the ground with an ear splitting scream and slams sand into Chat's and Dorf's faces. He throws with all his strength, just as his father had taught him. Knowing whatever he does the first few seconds makes all the difference and it has to be with all the strength and speed possible. Hunter throws aiming for their eyes and without waiting to see the results he whirls and runs. The stream is a bit high at this time of year and some of the rocks Hunter uses as stepping stones are underwater, but that doesn't matter he knows where they are and bolts onto the boulders hopping and half falling as he scrambles from rock to rock. He can hear Chat and Dorf bellowing and knows he's slowed them a little. The tangle of stickery bushes are still there edging the stream and the opening his father had cut for Topper is well grown over, and for once their thorny branches are welcome in Hunter's way of thinking. As he reaches them he dives into the undergrowth, glad of his heavy pants and shirt. He wiggles and squirms and reaches the trail leading into Topper's old clearing and lurches to his feet racing forward wondering just where he should go. Remembering their favorite climbing tree he makes a dash and begins the climb. He can hear Chat and Dorf cursing and yelling and he wants to grin and shout, *hey, up here you sorry oafs.* But he doesn't and keeps climbing higher.

Only a few moments later his pursuers burst into the clearing and stop to look around. Their obscenities make Hunter's ears and face burn with embarrassment. He's not quite sure what all the words mean, but he is positive they aren't nice and that his parents would wash his mouth out with soap if ever he uttered even one of them. Fascinated he watches while they prod and poke into the bushes, looking into every possible hiding place. The situation is quite funny and Hunter grins to himself and is quite pleased with his situation. Then an unfortunate thing happens. A small branch breaks loose under where he sits and clumps down to the ground and Chat looks up.

"There he is!" he shouts and points. "Hey, Dorf, up there, look up there!" Chat stares up at Hunter with a cruel gleam in his eyes and Dorf lunges for the tree while Hunter eases up the next branch higher, watching and praying for another miraculous solution.

Dorf is both clumsy and heavy. Some of the branches break beneath his weight making his progress slow. Chat curses Dorf's slowness while Hunter watches and tries to decide what to do next. Ruston has told Hunter to run if he can, and if he can't, to use whatever is at hand and right now all that's available is height, hands, feet, teeth, claws and an unsinkable will. Since he can't run, Hunter decides he must attack, only how? He's a good twenty feet off the ground and keeping from falling is a problem, because hanging on is a necessity. Dorf provides the answer when he reaches up and tries to grab Hunter's foot. Snatching it away Hunter almost falls. As he struggles to right himself his foot lands within Dorf's reach and he feels himself being dragged down. Then seeing a perfect target in Dorf's huge face, he kicks and there is a terrible crunch as Hunter's heavy work boot hits square into the middle of Dorf's nose. One, two, three kicks fly forward toward the brutal face with all the strength and speed Hunter can muster. Blood runs down Dorf's face and his screams are beautiful to Hunter's ears, only Dorf doesn't turn loose. For a brief moment they hang suspended, almost motionless in the air as the branches strain and start to break. Thrashing, twisting, and squirming, Hunter tries to pull free of Dorf's fingers. A loud cracking sound tells Hunter the branch he's sitting on is about to drop him. He kicks again, this time right at Dorf's front teeth. His boot makes a sickening crack as it hits. Dorf turns loose, trying to protect his face from another blow, and Hunter kicks savagely. Losing his hold, Dorf falls, snatching at any and everything as he goes down. The limb under Hunter gives way with a sudden snap and down he goes. A big leafy tree limb slaps Hunter in the face and he grabs for it. His small hands rip through the leaves and down the branch into the rough bark. It must hurt, but he doesn't seem to notice. Hunter's hold jerks him into a better position and his feet touch down on a lower branch that sags dangerously under his weight.

Looking down, Dorf is flat on his back looking up—he's not moving. Blood streams from his nose and Chat steps toward him, "You okay?" When Dorf doesn't answer he bends over him, giving him a little shake. In this instant, Hunter jumps, aiming right at Chat's back. Chat shifts a little to the left, exactly in line with Hunter's fall and "whop" he lands grabbing at Chat's ears with his full weight across his back.

"Yeeeeeaaaaaaooowwww," the howl is horrible as Chat is knocked forward onto his knees. Heaving himself back onto his feet, he staggers and thrashes around trying to rid himself of the demon on his back. Locking on with both legs wrapped around Chat's neck and body and his hands pulling hard on his ears, Hunter gets set for a wild ride. Chat claws at Hunter's hands and legs trying to rip him free. Slipping on the rough ground he goes down and Hunter manages to stay on clamping his legs even tighter.

The blow from Hunter's fall, combined with the surprise has disoriented Chat for the moment and he wallows around on the ground making all kinds of obscene noises, and Hunter doesn't turn lose. Once on his feet again, he whirls around while yanking on Hunter's legs. Grabbing his hands he tries to pull him off and Hunter kicks with wild furry, landing a couple of sound blows into Chat's mid section. Then tripping over a limb, Chat loses his grip and they both fall in a heap. Before Chat has time to right himself Hunter jumps up and kicks, giving Chat a terrible blow in the back of the head before darting into the underbrush. Chat's rage is horrible, bellowing like a mad bull, he lunges to his feet and plows into the brush. Hunter knows he has little time and hurls himself along on his hands and knees through the thorns and jagged limbs. Ducking behind a log he burrows deep in the thorny shadows and holds very still, his heart pounding as if it might explode through his ribs.

Listening, he can hear Chat cursing as he fights his way through the painful undergrowth. Hunter feels certain Chat must be able to hear his heart and his frantic breathing. Doubling over, he makes himself as small as possible and tries to plan his next move. Closer and closer Chat comes, beating and stabbing through the bushes with a large heavy stick. *Should I move farther back and risk being heard or seen? He's almost in front of me now!* Hunter worries and begins to ease his way deeper and deeper into the massive thorn bushes. Inch at a time he scoots until a down tree blocks his retreat. *I'm trapped.*

Several minutes pass while Chat smashes and thrusts his way through the bushes until Hunter can see his feet and realizes he is within the reach of Chat's battering stick. It's too close and Hunter bolts up, out, and over the log, only he's too slow. Cruel hands catch him and yank him backwards. Wiggling, kicking, and screaming at the top of his voice Chat drags him by one leg back through the sharp brambles toward the clearing.

Hunter's screams shatter the air and echo from the cliff in eerie waves and Dexter raises up out of the hole he's been digging. The rabbit can wait. He sniffs and listens, yes something of some importance needs his attention up there where he'd left Hunter, and he starts to run. His long strides both quicken and lengthen as he recognizes his young master's shrill yell. Faster and faster his legs carry him until he is a literal streak of yellow hurling up the cart track.

"Dorf, you idiot, get up off your back side and help me. I need you to hold him," Chat is vicious as he yanks and pulls Hunter over the brutal ground. "I'm going to beat the kid to a bloody pulp. Get up, Dorf," he snarls, "Somehow I don't think he'll stay still for me while I poke his eyes out."

Dorf has his own problems right at the moment. The fall he'd taken has battered and bruised his whole body and his eyes don't want to focus as he staggers to his feet. Picking up a handy stick he stands, wishing his head would quit spinning. There seems to be two of everything, and everything is tipped and wobbling. The pain in his head is incredible and he thinks he might be sick.

"You're a lot of help!" Chat screams at Dorf, as he yanks Hunter toward the clearing. "Why I ever decided to let you come along I'll never know. You can't climb a simple tree, and when you fall you just lie there moaning like a baby. I outta punch you." Dorf doesn't seem to hear, he stands rubbing his shaggy head where a giant goose egg is making its presence felt. His face is swollen and turning a sick color. He definitely doesn't look as though he feels very well.

"Ahhhhhhggggg," Chat jerks Hunter over a wild rose bush. "Hurts don't it?" he gloats as he drags him the last few feet into the clearing. Then grabbing Hunter up by his shirt and pants, he yanks him to his feet and heaves him in the air and whirls him around over his head with the intention of slamming him into the ground.

"I'm going to jump on your face!"

Making a wild squirm around inside his loose fitting shirt Hunter manages to turn and sink his teeth into Chat's hand. He bites down for all he's worth grinding his teeth into Chat's flesh. The reaction is instant. Chat screams and drops Hunter, letting him fall, only Hunter doesn't fall to the ground where Chat can stomp on him. Instead Hunter has hung on and is now over Chat's shoulder, where Hunter sinks his teeth into Chat's ear. For a brief second Hunter's legs flail and kick and batter Chat's back side while Chat staggers and lunges around trying to rid himself once again of the small demon that is now attached to his ear. Hanging on for dear life, Hunter finally manages to get his legs wrapped around Chat's body.

"Hit 'im, Dorf. Beat 'im in the head," Chat orders while Dorf waves the big stick and wishes his eyes would focus enough to find the kid's head. *Mustn't hit Chat, you know. That'd make Chat mad.*

138

"Don't just stand there, hit 'im," Chat bellows again and Dorf swings.

Somehow, Hunter sees the blow coming and manages to push himself away just in time. The stick glances off Hunter's shoulder and strikes Chat a wicked smack in the head and he goes down. Hunter is off at a dead run only to feel Dorf's powerful hands lift him from the ground.

"Got 'im for ya," Dorf gloats over his catch.

Hunter makes a rapid twist and lashes out with a wicked kick right where it will hurt Dorf the most, and he's free, but before he can run, Chat has him. He is wild with rage. Blood streams from his nose, there is a terrible mark on the side of his face. He staggers barely able to stand and swings a fist into Hunter's face. As Hunter falls he grabs Chat's legs. The surprising tackle catches Chat off guard and he rolls to the ground again and Hunter does his best to get away.

It's a mad mixed up moment of frantic thrashing around in the dirt and brambles. Hunter grabs a fistful of dirt and leaves and throws them into Chat's face. One moment he is about to get away and the next he's on the bottom and doing his best to not let Chat get a good grip on him. Chat strikes and curses while trying to get a firm hold. But Hunter doesn't give up; he squirms, bites, kicks, and screams. Dorf stumbles over to them and a horrible sound stops him. From out of nowhere a yellow streak lunges into Chat with savage teeth and snarls.

Chat screams and screams again as he and Dexter roll over and over on the clearing floor. Hunter is loose and rolls out of the way. When Dorf steps in with his stick, Dexter whirls to meet him. Dexter, Hunter's wonderful dog, is a wild ball of yellow fury. Forgetting the danger of his situation, Hunter cheers Dexter on. He isn't paying attention to Chat who makes a lunge and grabs him. Not waiting to see what happens next, Hunter kicks with nasty thrusts and his opponent doubles over, but not before belting Hunter in the face with his fist.

Hunter rolls backwards into the tall grass and brambles thinking his head must be broken. Grabbing up a handy club, Chat starts for him. This is no time to cry over a smashed face and Hunter lunges to his feet breaks into a run for someplace far away. A howl and a heavy crash causes Hunter to glance back in time to see Jason lunge into Chat. Fists fly in every direction. Hunter dashes back into the brawl only to be thrown backwards into the bushes. Again he races to his brother's rescue. A kick in the rear—a fist in Chat's back side and "OOoooow…"

a slam back in his own face—that one hurt. Hunter staggers and realizes Jason is barely staying out of Chat's reach. He must do something.

"Dext, stop Chat, I'll take care of Dorf," Hunter yells, and Dexter hurls himself into Chat's back side and both go down in a snarling screaming whirl of dirt, and leaves. "You move one inch and I'll call him back on you Dorf. You just sit still." Hunter picks up a big stick and stands over Dorf as if he actually thinks he can make him sit still. However, Dorf seems perfectly willing to stay where he is.

"Dexter!" a booming voice rings over the racket. "Back off, boy!" Ruston commands and Dexter backs away from Chat and turns and trots to Ruston's side smiling his happy smile. "Good boy," Ruston gives him a tender rub before turning back to the situation.

Chat holds his club and whips it back and forth in a taunting challenge, anger having taken control of his better judgment. "Chat, you'd better give that to me. It's not going to do you any good," Ruston speaks as he moves toward Chat and reaches out to take his weapon. Chat jerks away and hurls the club at the side of Ruston's head and somehow misses. Ruston is quick as he ducks under the swing and grabs Chat's arm, jerks him around, and pins his arm to his back. "That will get you into serious trouble, young man." Ruston speaks with a gentle voice while prying the stick from Chat's fingers. Chat winces in Ruston's crushing grip, and struggles to free himself as he is pushed toward the center of the clearing where Jason and Hunter stand with Dexter. Dorf sits cross-legged not too far from where he had fallen and looks as though he's had enough. There's no fight left in him.

When the excitement in the clearing is under control they are able to hear the sky-tops beyond the thorny thicket near the creek. Their voices trumpet their frustration and anger at their separation. Ruston knows exactly how they feel and can't help himself when he smiles and wants to shout with praise at the courage he'd witnessed in his two sons.

Yet, praise must wait. Now he wonders what he is to do with the rebellious Chat, and poor Dorf? As he gives this some thought, he glances toward Jason and sees he's all right, despite the cut running across his forehead and the blood running in a slow oozing trickle down his face. He's certainly messed up with scrapes and scratches, but there is a huge smile across his face. *No serious injury there.* Shifting his gaze, he studies Hunter, who stands over Dorf and seems to be total master of the situation. However, this son doesn't look so good. His shirt is ripped in several places; he is covered with dirt, leaves, and little sticks and thorns. His hair and clothing is a matted mass of vegetation. His face is covered with blood, and he can see blood seeping through a couple of spots on his shirt. There is also blood on Hunter's hands and it looks as though the side of his face is swollen. But even this son is triumphant and grins back at him. *He obviously took a pretty bad beating, but it seems there's no serious injury there either*, Ruston sighs with gratitude. *Lucky I left Crawford's when I did. A few minutes longer and things might have been much worse.*

"Let's go. Come on, up with you Dorf. Jason, it looks as though he may need some help. You two lead the way and Chat and I will be right behind you." As they start down the overgrown path leading back to the creek, Ruston is alarmed at what he sees in Dorf, and decides to take him immediately to Doc Hanlin.

"How'd you know where we were?" Hunter asks as he follows Dorf and Jason.

"I didn't find you, Bert did. We were about ready to land at the house when he suddenly swung up here. We could see Race and Topper on the ground up here near the creek and could tell something was wrong. It's a wonder you didn't hear them. However you were making enough noise it's no wonder you couldn't. You know this wasn't a very silent fight. Even without Bert, I'd have heard you." He gives his head a little shake remembering the racket.

"That's how I found you," Jason calls back. "I saw their horses out by the road and wondered, so I made a circle up here and heard you; I came as fast as I could. Topper was with me and Race, and he was ready to come in after you. Only he wouldn't fit—he's grown too much."

"Yea, I'da been toast if you hadn't gotten here when you did. He was gonna poke my eyes out."

"Ahhhhhhh….," Dorf's pitiful scream interrupts as he does his best to run back into the thicket only to be met with Dexter's persuasive snaps and snarls. In an effort to rescue Hunter, Topper has wedged himself through the trees down the narrow trail. He fills the entire path. He is stuck and he is mad.

Poor Dorf sinks to the ground covering his head with his hands. It's very good Topper is too big to scoot any farther down the trail or he'd be able to reach Dorf, and as mad as he is he might be difficult to restrain.

"It's okay, Topper," Ruston tries to reassure the excited bird. "I know these boys deserve to be given a good sound beating, but we are not going to be the ones to do it. We'll let Chat's father take care of the situation."

"No, no," Chat almost screams, "I won't go to my father." As he turns toward Ruston, Topper makes a huge lunge breaking limbs and branches as he gains a few feet more along the small trail.

"No, you don't, you big lummox," Ruston shouts thrusting himself between Dorf and Topper.

But, Topper has no intension of backing off and Hunter wraps his hands and arms around the bird's neck. "No, Top," he persuades, "you have to back up and let us out of here. Now, back up." Hunter pushes with all his might against Topper's chest. "Back up, you got in here, now you gotta scoot back out." As it is, it takes more than a few minutes to get Topper out of the way and even longer to cool his temper.

***

Sometime later we find Lettie and the boys around the big family table in their keeping room. Hunter sits on the edge of the table inspecting his bandaged hands. "Man, Mom, I won't be able to do anything with all this on my hands." Holding them up for his mother to see he says, "Look they won't even bend."

"I'm amazed you even want to move them. They are torn to shreds," Lettie answers.

"But that stuff you put on them didn't even hurt and they sting a little now but not too bad." Hunter turns his bandaged hands over and checks out the other side. Then moving his swollen jaw back and forth he explains, "The side of my face hurts worse than my hands do."

Jason reaches out and tries to touch Hunter's eyebrow and Hunter swats his hand away. "Sorry, it looks like there's another splinter there." Jason reaches again and this time Hunter is still. "Mom, he's got another one. Look, right here."

Lettie sets the basket of bandages back down on the table and looks at Hunter's eyebrow and sure enough, there's another sticker. "I honestly don't see how it is possible for you to have so many thorns all over you and your clothes?"

"I told you, Mom! I tried to hide in the thorn bushes so he wouldn't come after me and when he caught me, he dragged me through

142

the rose bushes and I fought like a wildcat." Hunter explains while his mother works with a pair of tweezers on the reluctant sticker.

"Ouch, those stupid tweezers pinch." Hunter rubs his swollen eye a second then lets his mother try again.

"Your eyes are turning black you know," Lettie comments as she works.

"Figgers, when he hit me, for a second or two I couldn't see very well." He takes a deep breath then yawns. "What did you put in that nasty drink? I think you put somethin' in it ..." he yawns again.

"I put some of Doc Hanlin's herbs in the drink to make you sort of numb. It's amazing the way it works. Doc says it's a powerful pain killer and I thought you'd rather not feel all the cleaning and scrubbing I've done. You were quite a mess. I'm afraid you will feel your hands much more tomorrow."

"An'... my face, an' my back side ..." Hunter doesn't get to finish because Dexter leaps up out from under the table in a wild rush to greet Ruston as he opens the door and joins them.

"What'd you do with them, Dad?" Jason can't wait to hear.

Giving Dexter an affectionate rub, Ruston answers, "I took Dorf to Doc Hanlin's—I think he may have a mild concussion. Then I went to Dorf's parents and explained to them."

Jason can't be patient and asks, "What did you tell them?"

"I really didn't tell them anything other than he'd taken a fall out of a tree and that I'd taken him to Doc's."

"Why didn't you tell them he was going to help Chat poke my eyes out?" Hunter raises his voice and wants to know.

"I thought about it and decided I'd let Dorf tell his parents. I don't think Dorf is very happy with the outcome of today's adventure. Doc and I agreed that the fewer people who know about today the better."

"Why!" Hunter almost explodes.

"Gossip is a terrible thing, Son. The town is already divided against Dixons and what we want is not revenge, but to get along with them."

"That's impossible." Hunter waves his bandaged hands around and glares at his father. "That Chat is about as mean as a bad bear. I think I'd rather run into a bear in the woods as I would Chat again."

"But bears are just being bears, and Chat is just being the way he's been taught." Ruston looks at his youngest son and his heart aches as he sees the welts and bruises and the two bandaged hands.

"What's that supposed to mean?"

"Most bears won't bother you if you don't bother them. If you take their food, or bother their babies, then you're in trouble. That's just the way bears are, so getting along with them isn't that difficult."

"Well, Chat better look out then, 'cause he messed with my mom's babies." Hunter is defiant and Lettie almost chokes with laughter despite the seriousness of the situation.

"Chat's not a bear, though, and as far as that goes, neither is your mother," Ruston knows better than to look at Lettie, although he wants to join her mirth. He's also very glad she is able to laugh. He'd been more than a little worried about how she would take the whole situation. *Yes, a little laughter here is a good thing. We all can use a nice refreshing laugh.*

Giving in, Ruston chuckles, "Your comparison is excellent, Hunter—so let's take it a little farther. You understand there are ways to avoid trouble with a bear and to even get along with them, and Chat is not that different. There is a way to get along with him too."

"Maybe I don't want to," Hunter challenges.

"I don't blame you. As a matter of fact, one of the most difficult things I've done in a long time is to not level Chat with my fists when I got there and had the chance."

"I wish you had. That'd be great."

"No, it wouldn't have been great, because then his dad would have to come and he'd have a right to be really angry with me and might want to fight. What would a fight between us solve?" Ruston watches his boys' reaction and knows they understand this consequence.

"That man is the size of a mean bull," Jason almost whispers.

"Exactly, and I think I might look worse than Hunter here after he got through with me," Ruston speaks as he helps Hunter off the table. He then pauses a moment and watches while Lettie begins putting the ointments and bandages back in her basket.

"What'd you tell Chat's dad?" Jason asks.

"I didn't tell him anything. I'm not at all sure what Chat will tell him, because he certainly will be asked. Hunter, I think his black eyes and face are going to look worse than yours. And his ear is a mess."

"Yes, yes, yes!" Hunter is triumphant as he waves his bandaged hands in the air.

"What did you do to Chat's ear?"

"I tried to bite it off," Hunter looks as though he'd do it again if given the opportunity.

"What'd Chat's dad do?" Jason interrupts.

"He didn't do anything, he wasn't home when we got there." Ruston pauses a moment then finishes, "So, I didn't tell him anything. I left that for Chat to do.

"Did either of you happen to hear Chat when he told me he didn't want to go to his father?" Both boys nod and Ruston continues, "I asked a few questions and I am absolutely certain Chat is afraid of his father. I'm also rather certain Chat is not the real problem." Pausing he gives his head a tired shake as if to rid himself of a nasty memory, "I learned that Chat told his dad he wanted to ride on one of the sky-tops and he was told to make you take him." Jason's, Hunter's and Lettie's eyes are wide with disbelief. "Yes, you heard me right." Ruston continues, "Chat's father told him to make you, Hunter, or you, Jason, take him for a ride. So Chat tried everything he could think of. Then when Hunter and Queenie beat the socks off Trixie and Chat, his father told him if he was a man, he'd go and pound the stuffing out of a certain Hunter Lynn.

"I honestly don't believe Chat wanted to do any of this. His father told him he had to make you boys respect him, and to make you do the things he wanted you to do."

"Make them respect him!" Lettie steps toward Ruston and asks, "How can any father be so ....."

"I know, I'm just repeating what Chat told me." Noticing their questioning looks he continues, "I asked him why he hadn't come to me and asked if he could go up for a ride on one of the sky-tops, and all of this just came tumbling out."

"Were you at Doc Hanlin's so he heard all this?" Lettie wants to know.

"No, we were on the way to Dixon's," Ruston sighs and turns to his wife for a moment forgetting his children. "Lettie, when Dixon wasn't at home I went in with Chat and helped him get cleaned up. I wanted to be sure he wasn't seriously hurt, and once Chat started to talk and to share some of these things it seemed he couldn't stop. It was as if he wanted to unload a million miseries. He told me things I still can't believe. Did you know his father has taught him that to be a man, a real man, he had to make people respect him. Chat's understanding is that respect is gained only by brute force. He has to make people afraid of him to be respected. This is his honest concept."

"And Arnald, his father, has taught him that?" Lettie is incredulous.

"He has, and equally as bad—he takes him to the gaming dens and gambling parlors when they go to Lakeland. He learned to gamble at cock fights when he was Hunter's age! Chat told me these places are part of his education in being a real man."

Hunter moves toward where his mother and father stand and gives Ruston's elbow a little shake. "What does it take to be a real man? I'd like to know—'cause I'm wondering."

"Oh, what a question!" Ruston can't help but smile. "Think of every opposite of Chat. Come on, think of opposites."

"Someone that doesn't get mad if they get beat in a race."

"Yes."

Hunter frowns and thinks while rubbing the top of his head, "Someone that doesn't bet and use money in silly ways."

"Yes."

"Someone that doesn't use their fists to get what they want."

"Yes, Jason you think of one."

"How about someone who shares their money rather than taking it away from others?"

"And he can't cheat," Hunter adds.

"You're getting the idea."

"What about being nice, and happy, and cheerful?" Jason is beginning to understand.

"I know, I know," Hunter is elated with his idea, "To be a man, I have to be just like you. You are all of those things, Dad, you are, you are!"

Ruston is deeply touched and puts a strong arm around Hunter's shoulders. "Boys, I want you to remember this—it is so very important.

To be a man, a real man, the kind others respect you have to lift others rather than tear them down. You have to help them, serve them, and be honest with them at all times. It's not a sometimes situation. You can't be part way honest, or to have wavering integrity."

"Dad, how do you lift somebody? I'm not big enough," Hunter is quite serious.

"Doesn't a smile lift a person's spirits—how about your mom's pies, don't they lift your heart and make you want to sing, doesn't a sincere thank you give you a lift? When my family is happy it gives me a lift, just to be with you is a wonderful lift. You lift me, Hunter, every time you do something right. And today you managed to protect yourself and I'm so proud of you I could pop. Being proud of you gives me a lift." Then turning to Jason, "And I am so proud of you, and your willingness to defend your little brother. Both of you proved to me you are rapidly becoming real men. The kind of man Chat wants to be, and doesn't know how."

"Well," Hunter gropes for words. "Chat will never be all those things. ... I just don't see how we can make all this right, and if you didn't tell Master Dixon, we don't know what's going to happen," Hunter gives an expressive gesture with his bandaged hands. "So…what do we do now?" A little worried frown makes a wrinkle between his eyes as he looks at his father and waits.

"I have told Chat he must come here and apologize to you, Hunter, or I will have to go to his father."

"Oh my," Jason and Hunter can hardly believe what they've heard.

"What did Chat say?" Lettie asks.

"He didn't like it. He told me his father says, 'Dixons don't apologize to anyone, ever.'"

"You're kidding."

"No, but if Chat manages to come and apologize we must receive him with kindness. It will take courage to apologize especially after today's blow up.' Ruston sighs, "How about you Hunter, and you, Jason, can you be polite to Chat when and if he comes?"

"I think I'll kick him once more just for good measure, then I'll be nice," Hunter looks as though he might do it too.

"Jason?" Ruston questions.

"I can do it, but I won't like it."

"Well that's a start, but there's much more to it than that. You asked about what it takes to be a man, well I'm afraid the next few weeks will be a test of what kind of men you will be. You see, being nice to Chat isn't enough—you must forgive him as well. It is much easier to hate and to be angry and mean, than it is to be kind and good to someone who has hurt you. It is easier to want vengeance, and to get even, than it is to forgive. The real men in this world are able to forgive and to be nice, even when they don't want to be. This will be a proving ground for both of you—it will be a test that can be a turning point in both of your lives. Remember some people never pass this test and they go through life sad, cross, and many times, mean. And they are never happy."

"I'd be happy if I can smack Chat 'till he can't get up." Then holding up his hands, his face burning with anger, Hunter raises his voice and blurts, "He did this to me and you expect me to forgive him? I can't do it!"

"I know exactly how you feel, but if we want to stop the Dixons from haunting and hounding our family we must be ready to be kind to Chat when he comes. This is the only way to solve this problem. If we are mean and retaliate, things will be worse, and when it happens again I may not come in time, and Jason and Dexter may not be near.

"Hunter, will you help us stop this silly mess, will you be nice and kind when Chat comes and apologizes?"

"You mean if he comes," Hunter challenges.

"Then, if he comes, will you be kind and accept his apology?" Ruston is firm in his question.

Hunter gives a little shrug and nods his head, "I'll be nice, but you can't make me forgive him, 'cause I know he won't come. I know he won't. He's too mean."

Ruston is sad as he looks at Hunter's angry face, "I'll accept your word on this, Hunter, but I want you to think about the test. Some tests are easier than others. You passed a great test today when you managed so well against Chat, but today's test was the easy one. Forgiving is many, many times harder than what you did so well today. I want you to think about this and know that every man, if he's to be a real man, one who other's respect, must learn to forgive—not just be nice and kind, but to forgive and forget, and not remember anymore the bad things you are thinking right now.

"Will you give this some thought?"

Later that night, Hunter invites Dexter up into bed with him and covers them both with a layer of soft quilts. Hearing his mother coming down the hall he whispers, "Shhhhh ... hold very still and Mom won't know you're there and make me kick you out." Dexter understands perfectly and doesn't move. He doesn't like sleeping on the floor so both pretend they are asleep.

Lettie tip toes in and peeks down at Hunter who is sound asleep, or so she thinks. Leaning over, she gives him a tender kiss on his forehead, before turning to where Jason is supposed to be. But he's not in his bed. So she tip toes back out the door and Hunter giggles. Lying there he rumples Dexter's rich fur with his bandaged hands and whispers, "Dex, you've got to help me. I will never ever forgive Chat—I can't—I just can't, but I want to be a man, a real man, just like Dad. What am I to do?"

Dexter doesn't hear. He doesn't even make a sound. He's already fast asleep.

Chapter 12

Grandpa's Gifts

Weeks later, "Shhhh," Lettie leans over Jason's bed motioning for him to be very quiet and not wake his brother. Jason opens his sleepy eyes and grins remembering what day it is. When Jason is dressed he hurries to find Dexter; he is to bring him upstairs and hang onto him so he won't jump in the middle of Hunter's bed before everyone is ready. In a very few minutes all four are standing in a circle around Hunter's bed.

"Happy Birthday, to you!" their voices ring in the familiar melody as Dexter pounces right in the middle of his little master. He covers Hunter's face with wet sloppy licks and Hunter sputters and laughs as the "Happy Birthday" song finishes. At the end of the song Ruston places a big package on the bed between Hunter and Dexter.

Pushing Dexter off to one side, Hunter attacks his package with fiendish glee and finds a big nice bucket and inside leather tools!

"Yeow-eeeeeeee," Hunter shouts as he rummages through the tools crowing with delight.

"There's another surprise waiting for you downstairs," Ruston interrupts Hunter's happy sounds.

Throwing back his covers he grabs his bucket and jumps to the floor, "Let's go!" and he heads for the door which Lettie blocks while holding out Hunter's clothes for him. With a jerk and a scramble he is dressed, well, sort of dressed. He's omitted the socks and his pants go on over his pajamas and his shirt is buttoned crooked, but it doesn't matter.

Out into the hall and down the stairs he goes with Dexter and Jason right behind him. They explode into the keeping room and run right into Grandpa Lynn, or Papa as the boys call him, who is a very nice older version of Ruston. His hair is not as blond as Ruston's and it has some gray running through it. He's a little taller but not quite as wide in the shoulders. He has the same gray eyes, the same funny twinkle, the same laugh, they even talk alike. But, Papa has lines on his face, he says they are his war lines and that he's earned every one of them.

Hunter and Jason are so glad to see their grandfather that they haven't seen their grandmother, who is not at all like Ruston. She is not broad and powerful, she is not blonde—no, her hair is kind of a gold brown with some gray streaks, and she has some war lines too, but we're not supposed to notice, because ladies don't have war lines. She's standing with Lettie watching the excitement. When Jason sees her, the hugs start all over again. The laughter and the hugs are great, but there are way too many kisses for Hunter's way of thinking. Hunter should be grateful his grandmother is a petite lady, if she was a big husky lady he might never have gotten away.

Then Hunter notices a number of neat and rather large leather bags spread out around their keeping room floor and asks, "What're all these?"

"Shall we open them and see?" Grandpa's eyes dance with delighted sparkles. Without waiting for an answer, he hands one to Hunter and one to Jason and there's one for Ruston too. Hunter's bag is almost as long as he is tall and is very heavy. This is a wonderful birthday.

Inside the bags are swords for each as well as foils. Hunter is a little dismayed when he discovers they're not sharp. "Can you sharpen these?" he asks.

"Oh course," Grandpa answers. "But these are practice swords and before I sharpen them, you must be very, very good with these and that will take some time."

The thought of getting to practice with a sword, even a blunt sword, is the most exciting thing ever, and Hunter can hardly wait to begin his first lesson. But there are three more leather bags waiting to be opened. Hunter doesn't know how to wait and be patient very well; he can't stand the suspense and opens the largest bag. It is heavy and he rolls it out on the floor and unties the leather thongs holding it together.

Inside is a very interesting variety of weapons. "What are these?" Jason and Hunter ask at the same time.

"These are for the sky-tops," Grandpa answers. Reaching down he picks up a wicked looking blade. It's almost as long as Hunter is tall and curves down with razor edges and ends in a dagger point. The hilt of the blade is a funny concave shape with heavily padded leather straps attached to either side.

"These are not for practice!" Hunter notices their gleaming edges.

"You are right—these are for the sky-tops. They are spurs and will fit right over Bert's short stubby spur claws and give him a serious weapon. That is, if I've made them just right. If not, I will make some adjustments and he will have fighting spurs." Holding the spur out to Ruston he is pleased with his son's reaction.

"Dad, I'd had the same idea, only I haven't had the time ..."

"I know," Grandpa doesn't give him time to finish. "Your mother and I know how busy you are and we wanted to help.

"Hunter sent us a tooth from the creature Jason killed, and your mother and I kept thinking about your sky-tops and the fact they have no teeth or real claws. That tooth is razor sharp and huge." Papa shakes his head in distressed disbelief. "Hopefully these spurs will even up the odds a little and give your birds some serious weapons, and a fighting chance."

Hunter is on his knees sorting out the various blades and notices the different sizes. "There are five pairs," he almost squeals with delight. "Let's go out now and see if they fit. Topper will be so excited. He loves presents."

There is only one thing wrong with Hunter's idea, no one has noticed Dexter's crying or his tiny scratching at the front door. They've been too busy and too loud. They don't know all the sky-tops are gone.

When Hunter hears Dexter's little cries, he feels bad and opens the front door and invites his pet in. But no, Dexter doesn't want to come in, he wants Hunter to come out, so it is with tender pats and lots of love Hunter tries pull his pet inside. When Dexter refuses to budge or be comforted, Hunter follows him into the barn and finds it empty. For a second or two he stands with one hand resting on Dexter's shoulder and wonders what it is he feels down deep inside. It's not a nice feeling. It makes all the happy feelings of his birthday and having his grandparents there sort of vanish with a strange tight feeling. He calls for Topper and Queenie and his voice is dull in the empty barn. It is with a strange, upset sense of urgency he hurries back to the house.

"Dad, the sky-tops are gone," Hunter stands at his father's elbow and wants him to stop talking and listen.

"Dad, the barn is empty and Dexter is all upset."

No one pays much attention at first, then when they do listen no one seems to care.

"So the barn is empty. Samuel left with the mail very early this morning on Race. They were all here when he left, so now they're gone. You know the sky-tops don't stay inside all the time," Ruston reasons.

"But Dad, Blinky is gone. Blinky—he's never been gone before," Hunter protests and no one understands. While not liking this, Hunter knows finding the sky-tops, when they could be anywhere within a hundred miles is impossible so he does his best not to let their absence spoil his birthday. After all, you are only eleven once.

"May Jason and I have a fencing lesson or will you show us how to fight with a sword?" Hunter asks, then adds, "I wish they were real swords and sharp." As he speaks he makes funny little wrinkles between his eyebrows and look's positively devilish. Then picking up his sword he gives it a little heft feeling the weight and gives a fiendish grin. "Still, a whack with this would hurt something terrible."

"Exactly." Lettie interrupts, "And that's why Grandma and I have made padded vests and arm guards for you to wear." As she speaks, she holds up a Hunter sized vest.

"Wow, it's just like the ones Dad wore when he was in the Royal Guard," Hunter is elated, and then noticing his grandfather, asks. "Grandpa, what's that?"

"This is a fencing mask. It's to keep your eyes and face safe."

"Looks sorta like a bird cage," Hunter isn't sure he wants to wear it on his head.

There are even protective gloves to cover their hands, and as Lettie holds a pair out to Hunter she asks, "How are your hands—let me have a look at them." Obediently, Hunter holds out his palms to her, he's gotten rather used to this. "They look as though they are still a little red and tender in places," Lettie looks concerned. "Do they still hurt very much?"

Hunter shrugs and answers, "Not really. I'm careful, and it's only when something scrapes or pokes that they bother me now." Then looking up into his mother's face he asks, "Chat isn't going to come, is he?"

"I guess not. Your father is very disappointed in him."

"Yeah, it would 'a been nice. I'm still mad at him, I really wanted him to apologize. I think I'd feel better about everything. I want to think it will never happen again."

"I know, we all would feel better about a lot of things if he'd come."

"Mom, are the swords because of Chat and his father?"

"No, your father and Papa have planned this for a long time. They've been waiting for you to be old enough and big enough not to make 'Hunter Mistakes' and hurt either yourself or someone else with foolish play." Lettie pauses a moment then adds, "No, the swords have nothing to do with Chat or his father. They are only a part of growing up and knowing how to defend yourself and the family you will have someday."

"I'd fight for you Mom, I would. I'd rescue you! I really would."

Lettie gives Hunter a little squeeze and tells him, "I know you would." Then as she helps Hunter into his padded vest and gloves, "You know Papa taught your dad to shoot, and to fence, and use the saber. He taught him to fight with his fists and to wrestle and helped him become good enough to be chosen as a member of the king's personal guard. Papa has been planning to come and work with both you and Jason ever since you were very little. He'd have come a long time ago, except your father and I didn't think you were ready."

"Did Papa teach Dad how to do what he did when he just zip, took Chat's club away from him. He made it look so easy. I wanna learn to do that."

"That is exactly why Papa is here. He wants to teach you the same skills he taught your father."

"Dad is going to help, isn't he?"

"He wouldn't miss it. We hope Blinky will want to go home with Grandma and Papa. That way they will have a sky-top and be able to fly back and forth and be here with us more often."

"I could even go sometimes and stay with them," Hunter is elated at the thought.

"Indeed you may," Lettie appreciates Hunter's thinking into the future and adds, "Let's hope Blinky will choose to go and live with them—it would be a help to us. He eats as much as Bert and if he goes your grandparents can go back and forth, and we can pick up another group of mail routes farther south."

"So we can buy more pig feed ....." Hunter understands his father's constant concern over the cost of feeding five sky-tops.

A clatter of steel against steel interrupts. Jason and Ruston have moved out into the front courtyard and have already started Jason's lesson. A few minutes later, Hunter and Papa cross swords and Hunter's first lesson begins

"Papa, this is for you," Hunter yells as he makes a wicked thrust and misses. "If you'd stand still I'd get you."

"But that's the whole point. You never stand still so someone can strike you. You keep moving and you make yourself into as small a target as possible." Grandpa reaches out and turns Hunter sideways so only his shoulder and sword arm is toward him. "When you attack me head on or facing me like that, I can slash right across your stomach. That's an ugly way to die," Grandpa looks serious. "This is no joke—now stay with only your weapon arm facing me."

When Hunter makes the necessary adjustments, Grandpa tells him, "There, that's better, now; 'On Guard.'" Hunter lunges at his grandfather attacking with wild whips and slashes of his sword and Papa easily parries each of the blows until Hunter stands huffing and puffing.

"It's not fair, I didn't touch you once."

"That's why I'm the teacher and you are the student." Grandpa studies his red faced and puffing grandson a moment, then suggests. "Look at Jason and your father. Notice, Jason isn't just swinging and whipping his sword all about."

At the other side of the court yard, Jason and Ruston are blade to blade going through some simple exercises, the parry and the thrust, the retreat and the feign. Back and forth they move, almost in slow motion.

"They aren't fighting, they look more like they are doing a funny dance," Hunter complains.

"That funny dance is how you must begin. Jason is learning where to put his feet and how to protect himself from his father's blade. You must learn to parry the blade or to block your opponent's sword first. The sword must protect as well as attack. You first learn to defend and to control your opponent—the attack comes when you are sure you can block your enemy's blade. Many a soldier has died because he made his thrust without making sure his opponent's sword was safely out of the way. When you are striking or thrusting you have no protection. First you study your opponent's way of moving and you learn how to lead him with you body. You can actually lead a person to attack just how you want them to, which will leave you the opening you need for your blade. Learn the dance first. One good strike with your blade and the battle is over. There is much more to this than just slashing away at each other."

Hunter watches his brother a few seconds, then with a big sigh looks up into his grandfather's loving face and smiles. "I guess I'd better learn to dance."

It is mid-afternoon and Ruston is worried. Samuel and Race should have been back well over an hour ago. They've never been this late before.

Hunter is most aware of the situation and doesn't hesitate to voice his opinion. "You're worried about Samuel—I'm worried about Samuel and all the sky-tops. Dexter tried to tell us something was wrong. I think Bert came and got Topper and Queenie, and that Blinky decided to go with them. I think something happened and Bert needed all of them. That's what Dexter was trying to tell me, only he can't talk and so he cries and worries and wants us to do something. Just look at him," Hunter points out into the front pasture where they can see Dexter sitting watching the northern sky. "He's been like that all afternoon. He knows they need us." Hunter finishes, his fists clenched and his face a little pale. "They need us."

"Have you remembered to pray for them?" his father asks.

"I don't forget, ever."

"Then all we can do now is wait, and remember there is no faith so long as there is worry."

Not worrying is not easy. Waiting is many times more difficult than hard work. The next hour is not a happy hour, and when Ruston finds Hunter with his bow and arrows shooting at his target he is at first pleased that Hunter has found something to do. Then he discovers there is a face painted on the target and asks about it.

"That is Chat Dixon and I'm putting holes in his big fat head," Hunter is passionate as he draws back his bow and lets the arrow fly. "Smack," right into the face it flies. Hunter's shooting has improved only Ruston isn't pleased.

Taking the bow from Hunter's hands he turns his son toward him, "I see you haven't forgiven. So long as you want to shoot at Chat I know you are not passing the test."

"The test," Hunter almost shouts, "How can I forgive Chat when I can still hear him telling me he's going to poke out my eyes. I can still see him with that club and feel his hands dig into my back." Taking a gulp of air, his body shaking, he continues, "Dad, I wake up at night scared almost silly. I see him every night and sometimes I don't even want to go to sleep, because I know he will be there." Tears fill Hunter's eyes and roll down his cheeks as his father pulls him into his strong arms.

Dexter's wild barking rips through the afternoon. He leaps in the air and races to find Hunter, he wants to tell him the sky-tops are coming. Finding him, he licks away his tears until Hunter is very glad when he decides to attack someone else with his exuberant attention.

As the five sky-tops land, Hunter's eyes can only see Samuel, who hangs limp in Race's saddle. Blood streams down Race's side and legs, and Samuel doesn't move.

"Samuel, Samuel," he hears himself scream as he runs to Race and tries to scramble up the sky-top's side, but his father is already there and has Samuel in his arms. Ever so gently he eases him out of the saddle down to his grandfather.

"He's alive," Ruston shouts with relief.

"I don't think all this blood is his…" Papa doesn't get to finish.

"It's Race, it's Race's," Hunter shouts as he points to a deep gash on Race's shoulder.

Hunter is furious when his mother refuses to let him in the room with Samuel. He wants to help, but he is told to wait outside. Sometimes mothers really get in the way. Sometimes he would like to be the boss, even if for just a little while. Maybe his mom could take his place and see just how he feels.

Wait outside with the sky-tops and Dexter. I'm not an animal, Samuel is my friend and he needs me. Hunter's mind will not leave him alone. Things are a little better when Doc Hanlin arrives and maybe it's not too bad, Jason has to wait outside too and is every bit as cross as he is.

Together they wander out into the courtyard and find Race still standing there in a pool of dried blood.

"I was supposed to take care of him," Jason whispers to himself as he rushes to the tired sky-top. "Come on boy, let's go in the barn and take that saddle off. I'll get you cleaned up. Man-oh-man, you are a bloody mess." Race sighs and follows Jason toward the barn and Jason shouts at Hunter, "Get us a big bucket of hot water and some of Mom's towels so we can clean up Race's shoulder."

A few minutes later we find Race resting comfortably in his straw bed with Jason and Hunter scrubbing him with nice warm water. The only thing bad about this is Hunter's selection of towels. Jason told him to get some of his mother's towels and you don't wash a wound with old dirty towels, you use good clean ones. At least this was Hunter's way of reasoning. So it is that Race is scrubbed and rubbed with very nice towels, and Topper and Queenie want to help and manage to get in the way. Queenie insists on a towel for herself. She makes very funny whistling sounds and keeps putting her big head right next to Jason as he tries to clean away the blood. Finally in desperation he gives her his towel and gets another for himself. Queenie is fascinated with the big tub of hot water and dips and re-dips her towel. When she won't move Jason swats her with a wet and bloody towel and sends a spray of hot water in every direction. Queenie steps back for a moment and waves her towel around watching Jason. Then when his back is turned, "whap," right up the side of the head she swats him with her wet towel.

Needless to say none of them manages to stay dry. The hot water soon disappears and more water is dipped from the well and the wet towel battle goes on. Race watches and gives funny sky-top laughs until a wet towel smacks him right in the face. Whoever threw the towel made a mistake, because Race didn't like it. For a second the towel hangs over his long beak and drips water in very wet splashes that stream down his chest and into his clean bed. Then the towel slowly starts to slip. In slow motion it slides off his nose and as it drops, Race growls. There is no need for a translator, and repentance is quick. It is a good thing sky-tops are nice, at least usually, because if they were not nice creatures, two boys and a dog might now be bird food. As it is, Jason and Hunter, as well as Queenie are wise in their immediate apologies. Once said, they stand looking toward Race, who studies them through narrow squinted eyes as though deciding what to do with them. In the end he sighs and gives a few clacks and is content to let Jason and Hunter finish cleaning up his shoulder.

"He needs stitches," Hunter comments.

"I know," Jason answers.

"Mom, has that powder that makes things quit hurting. You know the stuff she put on my hands after the fight with Chat."

"Do you know where it is?"

"Yup, I'll get it and I know where her sewing stuff is too."

Believe it or not, they intend to sew Race up themselves. The wound is clean and they have filled it with their father's slave, the kind he uses on his horses when they have big cuts, and now the next thing is to sew it up. Thankfully, Doc Hanlin comes out to see Race's wound about the same time Jason discovers the difficulties in threading a needle. Having never done this before, it has proved to be beyond his ability. From now on he and Hunter will not look at their mother's sewing as easy girl work. The thread simply will not go through the tiny hole in the needle—which is just as well.

Doc is pleased with how clean the wound is and is most complimentary. He is in the middle of his compliments when Lettie comes out to find the boys and sees what is left of her best towels. Not one person, or sky-top present realizes Lettie's feelings at this moment. The stress of the day, especially seeing Samuel unconscious combined with now seeing what's left of her towels is enough to make any nice woman lose her temper, but somehow Lettie manages to control her feelings and listen to Doc's compliments. She studies her boy's intent faces as they watch each and every stitch. For a moment she stares off into space then sighs—it's not every day a boy has a lesson in sewing up a sky-top, and who is she to spoil it? Still her towels will never ever be the same again. Sometimes being a mother is not very easy. *We will discuss the first and best use for my towels a little later,* She decides. Then in a moment of compassion she lays a hand on Race's neck and gives him a tender caress.

"Thank you for bringing Samuel home," she whispers. With a last look back at the boys she gathers up her towels and leaves them alone with Doc Hanlin and Race.

***

That night when Samuel is awake, Hunter and Jason are invited to go in and see him. They know Samuel has lost a lot of blood and is very weak, but still they aren't prepared for how pale or how weak he looks. It's a bit of a shock. He's as white as Lettie's sheets and his eyes have big dark rings around them. His left leg is all bandaged and propped up on pillows.

"Samuel, can you hear me? Are you going to be all right?" Hunter asks as he tip toes near.

Samuel's eyes flutter open and he gives them a weak smile. "I thought I was going to lose it, boys," he answers and reaches out a hand toward where Jason stands. "That sky-top of yours saved me a dozen times."

"What happened?" they both want to know.

"We were on our way home, when a sawtooth came at us out of nowhere. I thought maybe Race could out run it and I pulled my bow and tried to get some arrows into him. We flew for miles with the sawtooth literally on our tail. He'd snapped and somehow Race would manage to swerve and get out of the way. I thought we were goners for sure." Samuel manages a weak smile and motions for the boys to sit down on the bed with him.

"How did you get away," Hunter can't stand not knowing.

"When the sawtooth was right up with us, Race would roll and dive and in the middle of a dive, Bert was there. I didn't see him coming, he was just there and he hit that sawtooth with all the strength he had and the two of them fell. Well, Race dove right after them. Bert and the sawtooth were rolling and tumbling down below us and I thought at first, they were locked together. But then they broke loose and Blinky and Topper charged and gave the sawtooth fits. Those birds are game—they know how to attack and stay out of the way of the teeth and claws. It was something to see."

"Did they kill it?" Jason asks.

"Well, while Race, Topper, and Blink kept the sawtooth busy, Bert came right up under him and grabbed him by a leg and literally yanked and thrashed him with those snapping teeth just missing him time and again. Its amazing Bert's not ripped to shreds. When Bert let go, it turned on him and Race dove into it and it turned on us and that's when he got us. Race was too close and its teeth got his shoulder and my leg all at the same time. Race rolled and tumbled and we fell and I was sure the harness would break. I couldn't believe it was possible to roll and fall like that and live to tell about it."

"Is that how the blood got all over you, I mean when you rolled. You were covered and we thought you were dead," Hunter asks while patting Samuel's hand.

"I guess so, I didn't have time to think, but there was blood everywhere and we were upside down as much as we were right side up."

"Were you scared?" Jason whispers.

"Scared? I've never ever been so scared in all my life. But you know what?"

"What?"

"Our sky-tops licked that sawtooth. They pounded it to death. When Race broke free from our fall, Bert took the sawtooth to the ground. He rode him standing on his back. He shoved it into the ground then the three of them finished it with their beaks." With a feeble smile Samuel finishes, "So we won. Our birds are absolutely fearless. They would not give up."

"Is it only your leg Samuel? Is that all that is wrong?" Hunter asks.

"I feel as though I've been yanked into pieces, but yes it's only my leg and Doc says I've lost too much blood for his liking—but he says I'll live." Samuel finishes and smiles at his young visitors appreciating their genuine concern for his well being.

As the boys leave the room, Samuel calls after them, "Hunter, will you or Jason please tell Bert thank you for me. Had he not come when he did, Race and I would not have come home and you might never have found us. Bert and Blinky need to know how grateful I am."

Chapter 13

THE ATTACK

The next morning we find Grandpa and Hunter out in the courtyard "dancing" with their swords. "Step, step, parry, parry, slash, parry, stab," they count and move together in even steps, their blades making simple but very precise movements.

"When do we get to put Topper's spurs on him, Papa?" Hunter wants to know.

"Just as soon as your father gets back, Careful," Grandpa cautions, "Better keep your blade up, I could have taken you that time."

Back and forth they go working their blades deflecting imaginary blows.

"I told Topper we had presents for them and he doesn't like to wait."

"Waiting is good for him, it will teach him patience."

A little later Race, Topper, and Queenie are out in the courtyard watching Grandpa spread his sky-top spurs out on the paving stones. They understand these are gifts from Papa, B*ut what are these metal things for?* Hunter tries again and again to tell them how the spurs are to be used, and still they don't understand. In desperation Hunter picks up his own little sword and rushes with it toward his archery target leaned up against the side of the barn and thrusts his sword deep in the tight straw.

Topper knows what a target is and understands the importance of Jason's arrows. He's seen what an arrow can do and appreciates the fact Blinky is alive because of Jason's well placed arrows. However, Hunter has just attacked the target with a sword. The sky-top spurs lying at his feet are not little like Hunter's sword—no they are sky-top size and look to be as sharp or sharper than Jason's arrows. He snorts and clacks his big beak together and carefully picks one spur up in his long beak. Then giving it a little shake he readjusts it in his mouth and makes a rather loud rrrringsssh sound, and Race moves closer. He watches Topper with keen fascination as he holds the sharp spur and whips it around with his beak then trots to the target and stabs it into the target with a wicked growl. His thrust is so powerful it knocks the target down. He seems to have gotten the idea and is very pleased. Race decides he must have a spur for himself and in very little time the two birds shred the target.

In the midst of this, Ruston starts to stop the excited birds in their demolition demonstration, but his father stops him. "Wait, Son let's watch. We learn as we watch. These are intelligent birds and they have needed a weapon, and are now recognizing what their gifts are for. The target has served a very good purpose. Let them learn and let us enjoy and watch. I'll make the boys another target."

While Grandpa and the Lynns are content with having their target torn to pieces, Queenie is not. She is quite sure the target should not be destroyed and sets up a rather loud whistling howl, so loud when Bert and Blink touch down a few minutes later they hurry to see what the noise is all about. As Bert intervenes, Top and Race are very still and look a little silly with the spurs and their straps sticking out of their mouths. Bert looks at the mess and clicks and clacks and Top and Race answer with a chatter of sounds. Then Topper makes a dive at what is left of the target and sinks his spur deep in what once had been the firm target's center.

"Snort. RRRRRRrrrr," Bert almost purrs as he retrieves Top's spur for him. For a moment he sort of waves the spur around and slides it up and down in his long beak. Topper can hardly contain himself and clatters a number of sounds then growls, before stepping back to watch his father. Queenie is quiet and watches with Blinky from a respectful distance, each wondering what Bert will do. They don't have to wait long, because Bert gives his weapon a few little thrusts with quick jabs into the air, then stabs the target with so much force it's a wonder the blade doesn't break. Yanking the blade free he makes a blasting trumpet sound. Great sounds rumble and clack from his throat and if it is possible for a sky-top to smile, then Bert is smiling.

In the next few minutes the oversized spurs are carefully strapped and adjusted over each of the sky-top's rather knobby short spurs. Now armed with terrible knives, they practice walking about the courtyard. The blades clank on the stones and Grandpa knows adjustments must be made and finds it very difficult to persuade the reluctant birds to let him remove their weapons so he can raise them up off of the ground. Blades that grind into the ground won't be sharp very long. But how do you tell a sky-top this?

Their excitement makes explaining anything all but impossible. When finally Bert permits Grandpa to shorten his straps and raise his spurs he is very curious. Cocking his immense head to one side, he holds his weapon foot in the air and studies the blade from every possible angle. When the adjustments are complete he stands a moment admiring his spurs, then walks a little ways. The spurs don't drag. They don't touch the ground, he can walk without the scraping noise. Making a couple of hop steps he then trots over to what is left of the target and stabs it again and again. Crowing with delight, he prances around the target jabbing it in a one legged dance. The dance is so funny no one can help themselves as they literally double over in laughter. He looks like a long necked elephant with wings hoping around on one hind leg. To make it all even funnier, Bert's immense beak is open in a great smile. He's so happy.

The sky-tops crow and whistle, their very most pleased sounds, and Blinky hits a very pleasant note almost like a musical hum. It is a very happy sound.

Now Grandma is quite interested in this sound and walks to Blinky and offers him a nice apple. This ends his song for a moment while he slurps and swallows. Then Grandma does a funny thing. She tips her little head and hums a note and watches Blinky who puts his big head right down next to hers and makes a strange purring sound. Then cocking his head to one side he watches her as she hums another note. "Come on, try it big fellow," she coaxes until a rich rumbling sound vibrates from somewhere deep in Blink's throat. Hunter and Topper listen and Topper makes an effort to copy Grandma's sounds. "Do you know, Hunter, I think these creatures might learn to sing. Listen to their voices, they are so deep and rich." Grandma reaches up and pats Blinky, "This big guy sounds like an orchestra of cellos. I think he needs to cultivate his voice," she laughs and asks, "Do you think we could fly home on him? Grandpa and I hope he will choose to stay with us. Our feed bin is full just waiting for him and any friend he chooses to bring."

"May I go home with you too? I won't eat near as much as he will. Pleaseeeeeeeese, Grandma, just for a couple of days?"

So when Grandma and Grandpa load up for their flight home, Hunter hurries to be ready and Dexter knows exactly what is about to happen and sits in the center of the court yard howling long mournful howls. As they take off Lettie and Ruston are comforted to see Bert take to the air and follow with them.

"That's an impressive chaperone," Lettie comments.

"I asked him to stop by on the way back to let us know they are home safely," Ruston comments. Then with a little chuckle he adds, "I think Bert wants to try out his new spurs."

***

The next few days are rain and more rain. Water runs off the roofs and across the courtyard, the stream rages with high water, the roads are mired with mud and it's a very good time to work indoors.

"What are you making?" Jason watches his father who works at his forge shaping a red hot piece of metal.

"I keep thinking about some of the things Samuel said about his battle and I want to give our sky-tops a little protection. The spurs give them a weapon, a badly needed weapon, but their heads and necks could do with some protection, so I'm making a helmet and I thought I might add a spike or something to it. What do you think?" So as the rain pours, Ruston and Jason keep the forge fire blazing and create some very unique helmets for their sky-tops.

A few days later they present Bert with his helmet. It is black and has metal that goes down between his eyes and runs clear down over his beak and ends with a wicked looking curved up spike. On top of the helmet are three spikes, one very long with shorter ones in front and in back. There are big arches running up over each eye, then the helmet back fans out and down a little ways over the back of Bert's neck and ends with chain mail running all the way down to his body. The effect is marvelous. Bert looks like a dragon with his black helmet and all the sharp spikes. If it is possible for a sky-top to be prideful, I think we would all agree Bert is prideful at this moment. He struts around the courtyard purring wonderful pleased sounds and if we could understand him, we would know his sounds are "thank you" said in a dozen different ways. Only we can't understand his words and neither can they, but Hunter understands and laughs, "Bert says, 'Thank you, thank you, thank you.'"

This is good, because even sky-tops need to remember gratitude and to say thank you. Especially if you want to receive future favors. This is a simple fact of life.

Now, Sky-tops aren't very different from little boys, or grown men, or any of us really for that matter, and Bert's helmet has caused a sensation and is to everyone's liking. However there is one problem, Race insists he cannot fly the mail until his is finished. So more helmets must be created and it is decided the mail routes from this time on will require two sky-tops in full armor. This is just in case another sawtooth decides to attack.

It is a week before all the preparations for flying the mail once again are made, and Samuel assures everyone that sitting on a sky-top would be good for him. He's tired of sitting around and wants to be up and away. It's little wonder his mother as well as Lettie wring their hands and try to persuade him to wait a little longer. In the end both Ruston and Samuel fly the mail with Race and Bert because it's time for Hunter to come home, and Ruston knows Lettie will worry unless he and Bert make the trip.

Queenie insists on going with them, but she will not wear her spurs or her helmet and Ruston is rather cross. It is difficult to understand why the other sky-tops are so thrilled with their spurs and helmets and Queenie isn't. Once more, Bert does not seem to feel she needs spurs or a helmet. This is something Hunter will have to figure out. By the time they leave with the mail, Ruston feels her refusal to protect herself is her problem.

Once Hunter is home and is aware of the problem, he decides to end the conflict—Queenie will wear the helmet and the spurs, or else. However, or else, may work with children and maybe friends smaller than you are, but not with an eight foot tall sky-top. Even a small gentle sky-top can be most difficult. After several heated attempts to force Queenie into letting him put the spurs on her, Hunter gives up in a huff. He is quite angry and Queenie knows it. After giving the situation a lot of thought, Hunter decides he and Queenie need to have one of their long talks. So later that evening, when Queenie is snuggled down in her bed, Hunter goes out to join her, and Dexter is most put out. He's not the center of attention and pushes and shoves until Hunter grabs him and pulls him into the straw for a tummy rub. Now things are all right.

Seated between Topper and Queenie, Hunter feels he needs to understand a number of important things. The first is why Queenie doesn't want to wear her spurs or the helmet. She must have a reason. Because he only understands a little of what the sky-tops say he has to ask "yes" and "no" questions. So with a limited sky-top vocabulary and nods and shakes, Hunter begins to unravel the mystery. After many minutes of searching Hunter exclaims, "Wait a minute Queen, you can't mean that." He shakes his head and argues, "Your job in a sawtooth battle is to fly high and keep watch, and that's why you can't wear your spurs?" When Queenie nods, Hunter scratches the top of his head in his thinking sort of way. "I don't see what that has to do with spurs?"

Queenie and Topper both talk at once, trying to explain and Hunter frowns and quits rubbing Dexter. For a moment Dexter is content then he shoves his wet nose into Hunter's face hoping to start the rubbing again, but it doesn't work.

"Fly fast where? I'm not getting it. The 'churp, clack, purrrrr' is something about mother?" Queenie is delighted and bobs and shakes her head and bounces her whole body.

Topper clacks and lets Hunter know she is talking about mother, only something isn't quite like their mother. Topper clacks, "All mothers."

"All right, you're talking about mother, not my mother. Right? Right." He pauses watching both sky-tops. "You are talking about your mother, how can that be all mothers?" When both sky-tops look frustrated, Hunter can't stand it. "I don't see what your mother or any mother has to do with spurs."

What Hunter is not able to understand is female or "mother" sky-tops are not fighters. They are to flee or run away, and if possible warn the others. Hunter doesn't realize a female sky-top's protection is their speed—the females are faster than the males. They are weaker and lighter, but much faster. To be weighted down with spurs or to be expected to fight goes against their culture or the way young sky-tops are raised.

Hunter's lack of understanding makes him cross and he tells Queenie so, "Hearing about your mother makes me mad. I've asked you about your mother so many times. I've asked you where you lived before you came here to live with us. I've asked you where Bert goes and who eats all the pig feed he takes with him and you just tell me mother and home. I want you to take me there and it makes me mad at both of you, why won't you take us there?"

In a huff, Hunter pushes Dexter out of his way and gets up. He has a mean scowl on his face and he almost growls, "I don't know why I can't see your mother. You see mine all the time. What's wrong with you, do you think we would hurt her? We want her to come here to live so Bert won't have to fly back and forth, stupid birds!" He storms toward the door.

Queenie's soft apology calls him back. She hangs her head and asks forgiveness, and Hunter turns back and gives her a big hug and reminds her, "I want you to take me to your mother. I want to see where Bert goes every night."

***

On a bright summer morning several days later, Bert and Blinky land together in the Lynn courtyard and Bert has something he wants to tell Ruston, only Ruston doesn't understand. He stands listening to Bert's growls and clicks and hasn't the foggiest idea what it is all about. As Bert jabbers the spikes on the top of his head wave about and are dangerous when he puts his head down near the ground. He moves too fast sometimes and doesn't realize how close his spikes are to other things—namely people and pets, and other sky-tops. So Ruston stands a little ways back listening.

Jason is out trimming his mother's roses along the yard fence and notices the situation and shouts to Hunter, who has a hoe and is vigorously attacking the weeds that are determined to take over the green beans. As far as Hunter is concerned, the weeds may have the green beans, but he can't fly with Topper until the hoeing is finished. So he works in a rapid frenzy to get it over with. The need for an interpreter is a welcome diversion and the hoe is dropped on the spot—so much for putting tools away as he hurries to see what's up.

Listening to Bert's sounds a moment, Hunter's face brightens, a huge smile covers his face and he sputters, "You won't believe it! You won't believe it! He wants to take us to his home. He wants all of us to fly with him and he will show us where he lives."

The news is electric. In no time saddles are in place, along with two huge picnic baskets filled with all the wonderful things Lettie feels essential to the occasion, which is far more than they will need. Water jugs, blankets and extra comforts. Bert laughs politely as he watches their excitement. He looks just like a proud host watching his special guests.

When they take to the air they are five sky-tops strong with four armed for mortal combat and all are so excited about the day's venture not one of them notices Dexter who sits in the courtyard howling. He doesn't like being left home.

Today's flight plan is slightly different in that Bert insists Ruston and Lettie ride Race and that both Jason and Hunter ride on Topper. While situation this a little strange, Ruston does not feel the need to argue. Once in the air Topper hums a happy sound and clinks his spurs together. They make a nice clear ringing sound.

While Hunter was at his grandparents, he and his grandmother had spent some time working with the sky-tops and Hunter wants to surprise his family. With the whole family together, this is the moment he's been waiting for. Giving a little singing note to Topper, he begins a familiar melody. Blinky is a marvelous base, his deep throated notes vibrate through the clouds like many cellos, while Queenie and Topper are much more like violins when they hum. Their singing or humming voices are not at all like their clacking voices. When they whistle, Queenie is a nice flute and Topper is a rather loud trumpet. Blinky's blasting voice is like nothing you've ever heard before and is difficult to describe. Perhaps a slightly off key brass band might give you an idea. For now it's best he be a cello and hum until grandmother has a little more time to work with him. Today he hasn't improved and Hunter asks him to hum, please and this goes very well. Jason and his parents are amazed and want to laugh and sing at the same time which doesn't work very well. Soon all the sky-tops add their voices and the melodies get mixed up, but it doesn't matter, it is a joyful time

Queenie dips and swoops over and around them dodging light fluffy clouds, her jubilant voice singing in heavenly melodies. It is fun to watch her play, for she plays as only a happy sky-top is able to play. She dips through the edge of a fleecy cloud and for a brief moment is hidden when suddenly, a terrifying scream rips the morning air. The sky-tops swerve in time to see Queenie dart out of the, too near, clutches of a sawtooth almost twice her size.

"Noooooooooo, run Queenie," Hunter screams aiming Topper right at the attacking sawtooth. "Hurrrrrrry Top—faster!" he shrieks as Topper hurls himself through the air at the savage sawtooth.

"Swoop in under him," Jason yells at Hunter's backside, "I want to put an arrow in under his wing. Then get us out of the way quick."

"There's another sawtooth a little ways back! Watch him, Jase," Hunter screams a warning.

They can hear their father shouting at them to get back and Hunter answers in a tense whisper, meant only for himself, "Get back! I will not get back, that's Queenie they're after." Then he yells a blood curdling yell, "Go Top! Get your arrow ready we' re ...... duck Jason!" he screams as Bert slams his body into the sawtooth right over the top of them, his glittering spurs aimed for savage results.

"Watch it, Jase!" Hunter shouts as Topper rolls away from the second sawtooth just in time. Blinky is there above them with his spurs slashing into the sawtooth's outspread wings. Swooping into position, Topper gives Jason an instant to whip an arrow into the unprotected sawtooth's heart girth and the creature screams and turns on them.

"Roll out of the way—NOW!" the boys can hear their father's yell as Race drops out of the sky onto the sawtooth's back sinking his spurs in deep. For a split second Ruston manages to shout and tell the boys again to stay back out of the way.

Topper makes a quick dive and falls back while Jason and Hunter twist in their saddle trying to see Race and their parents.

"Fill him with arrows, Dad," Hunter shouts as Jason places an arrow deep in the sawtooth's belly

"Man, that was crazy, Jase, you could'a hit Mom or Dad."

"But I didn't," Jason answers while notching another arrow. "Take me up under them again and let's help Race out."

"Looks to me as though Race has him whipped. Man-oh-man he's wicked with those spurs."

Race braces himself on the sawtooth's back with his spurs digging as deep as possible. For a brief moment or two the sawtooth jerks and tries to shake loose while snapping up across his back at Race, who dodges its vicious teeth. Then they fall.

"Nope, I don't think Race needs us, where's Bert?" Hunter wonders.

"Down there somewhere, he and that first sawtooth just dropped out of the sky." Jason searches the skies below them. I'm glad Mom and Dad didn't ride him today, those two birds went end over end, it would have been awful to ride."

"The one they're on right now isn't what I'd call a pleasure ride. Look at them. Man, my stomach would be right out the top of my head. They aren't flying Jase, they're just plain old falling," Hunter pauses then adds, "Go after 'em, Top, I can't stand it."

Topper dives after them and they watch as Race spreads his wings and breaks the fall and the birds roll in the air. Then off to one side coming in with deadly speed is another sawtooth headed straight at the unsuspecting Race.

"Goooooo, Topper!" Hunter howls, "Get him right on top of him just like Race did—use your spurs. Don't let him get Mom and Dad." Hunter's lungs feel as though they might split, his scream is so loud. Then leaning into Topper's dive, "Hang on, Jase," he shouts back at his brother a little too late to do much good because if Jason hadn't had a good tight seat he'd be straining at the top of his harness right now. As it is Topper folds his wings back and literally shoots with painful speed straight for where the sawtooth will be in a matter of seconds—and both boys are wishing him faster. Sometimes a second or two can seem like hours and as they watch the distance narrow between their parents and the attacking sawtooth, there is only one thought in their minds. Will Topper reach them in time? They hope and pray they will be fast enough. The air rips at their faces and clothes and they don't care, their parents are right in line with the sawtooth, and don't even know it. Then all of a sudden the sawtooth is there beneath them and Topper aims his deadly spurs and smashes with full force into it's back, knocking him out of line with Race and their parents. Hunter can't help himself and sheiks with his loudest "Hunter Yell," all his pent up emotions finding release. At the peak of his triumphant yell, the birds beneath them roll over and over in the sky. The wings are a tangled mass and things seem to move in slow motion while the boys hang on and try to know up from down. When it all levels out, they can feel Topper literally bouncing in giant shoves forcing the sawtooth toward the ground. Topper has his beak blade hooked into the back of the sawtooth's neck and head holding it still. This is much better than having to dodge those teeth.

"Keep watch, Jase, we don't want a sawtooth to come at us the way this one did at Mom and Dad."

"We've still got company up here. There's another sawtooth up above us, but Blink and Bert are giving him fits. Oh look, here comes Mom and Dad."

"I think this one is about done for—you okay Top?" Hunter pats his sky-top as he asks, and Topper gives him a funny whine. "What's the matter—you can't nod your head?" Hunter thinks this is funny and starts to laugh, and he sputters, "Can't talk very well can you? Busy beak, that's what you are." As Hunter teases they can feel the huge sawtooth falter beneath them and his wings almost stop their struggle.

"Top, I think you can let him go, he's done for. Go ahead turn loose, let him go. He's not flying, he's just going down."

Topper has no intention of turning lose, he's winning and intends to finish what he started. Race and Blinky swoop over next to them and chatter and clack as Topper rides his kill to the ground. As they fall the last few feet Bert is there too.

"We did it, we did it," Hunter crows over their victory. "We whipped them, we whipped them all!" He waves his arms over his head and shouts another "Hunter Yell" just for good measure. It's difficult to be too upset when you have Hunter along to cheer you up. So what if you've fallen hundreds of feet straight down in the sky, been rolled over, round and round, and end over end at a staggering number of RPMs, besides being slapped in the head a few times with a sawtooth wing. That's just the way life is sometimes and there isn't any point in getting too excited over it. At least that's Hunter's way of thinking, and his exuberant attitude lends a spirit of celebration to their adventure.

A few minutes later the sky-tops all fly in a great sweeping circle together, their jubilant trumpeting voices echoing into the distance. Hunter wants to bounce and shout, and Topper wants to bounce and shout with him, their racket is a joyful sound. And right now a little levity is needed. The boys haven't noticed their parents—neither are joining their victory cheers.

It was too close a situation for comfort and as they fly toward Bert's home, Ruston and Lettie can't help but wonder just exactly how many sawtooths there are left to contend with, and what might have been the consequences had Grandpa not given the spurs to their sky-tops. Without doubt, Papa's gift had made all the difference.

Chapter 14

THE PLAN

Topper and Queenie dip and swoop over and around Race, where Ruston and Lettie ride in rather sober silence. Watching his boys, Ruston wonders if they should turn around and go home. It's rather obvious the sky-tops haven't considered turning back and neither have Jason or Hunter. *How many sawtooths are there and where are they right this minute?* Ruston's mind is a sober maze of thoughts. He wishes he could be sure there are no more sawtooths in the area. Should he take his family home, he wonders and turns toward his wife and asks, "Lettie, do you want to go home?"

Leaning forward she wraps her arms tight around her husband and rests her head on his back. "Right now I'm close to falling apart. I don't' know whether to cry or to shout with the boys. I'm angry—I'm thrilled we've won—I'm grateful we are all safe, and another part of me is frightened—really frightened." Ruston can feel his wife's emotion in every word. She takes a deep breath and continues, "Ruston, we are faced with a choice, we either have to get rid of the sawtooths or we have to accept the situation and stay on the ground."

"And what would happen to the sky-tops? Do we send them away?" Ruston wants to understand.

"Do you want to be a part of another battle like that?" Lettie challenges.

"Of course not!"

"Then we have to get rid of the sawtooths—all of them, or we give up and stay on the ground. We can't just ignore them and pretend we are safe—we can't co-exist with creatures like that. I'm not ready for any of us to die in a sawtooth battle," Lettie sighs, and Ruston turning back can see tears gathering in her worried eyes.

Race's great wings pump steady sweeping motions through the morning air and after a few minutes he dips a little lower following a wide shallow river. Smaller streams of water can be seen joining the larger body of water and if the Lynns weren't so preoccupied with their thoughts they would be enjoying the flight, for they are over land few, if any, humans have ever seen. It is beautiful fertile land, the kind Ruston would love to farm, but he's not thinking about farm land or irrigation water at the moment, and it isn't until a wild "whoop" from behind causes them to jump, their nerves still being rather frazzled, that they are brought out of their preoccupied silence.

"Watch what we can do," Hunter shouts as Topper makes a dive in front of them and rolls a full three hundred and sixty degree roll-over. Hunter's shill voice screeches with laughter at the top of his lungs. Queenie is right behind them with a double roll all while whistling her delight. On the second pass in front of their parents, Jason's arms are held wide at shoulder height as Topper rolls gracefully, or as gracefully as a sky-top can manage, and Lettie almost strangles Ruston as she watches Jason suspended upside down in his harness.

"I wish they wouldn't do that," Lettie confesses.

"I'll talk to them about taking foolish chances. Yet, Lettie, in ways it pleases me. Our boys are not cowards. Twice now they've proven they can stand up against terrific odds and not panic. No, by golly, they are game little roosters, and like it or not, they saved us today."

"I've been thinking about that. Well, Chat was one thing, but this really can't even be compared."

"No, you're not seeing my point," Ruston pauses, then continues, "They didn't cry and want to go home. They certainly aren't crying right now, look at them," Ruston points after his boys. For a moment they watch as Topper and Queenie break away from the river and turn into a narrow gorge. "They don't seem to mind having just been attacked and jerked around in the face of death. They did what needed to be done and rather than cry they are strutting their stuff, they are as game as ever. I'm just as pleased as I can be.

"Lettie, a year or so ago this would not have been the case. They are growing up."

Race makes a sudden dip and drops down into the gorge and slips between sunlit walls of stone.

"I'm glad you are pleased, and well, I'm pleased too, but Ruston we can't just go on like we are. We'd all be dead right this minute had Papa not thought to make the spurs for the sky-tops. We have to do something."

"What would you have us do?" Ruston asks.

"I'm not sure. I was just thinking we can't know what is best until we understand what the situation really is. How can we hope to destroy all the sawtooths if we don't know how many there are, or where they are? They can keep right on surprising us—so we have to find them and surprise them. I've heard you talk for years of battle plans and the strategies you used in the wars. Is this so different?"

"No, not really," he pauses thinking. "You mean to say you would support me if I wanted to help Bert and the sky-tops destroy the sawtooths?"

Lettie considers a moment then adds, "You'd have to promise you won't take any chances. Our safety has to come first. Is that understood?"

"Absolutely, I'll go you one better, you can be a part of the planning, and we won't do anything you think is foolish."

The sheer canyon walls leading to Bert's home close in around them with soft hues of golden magnificence. Strange, bubble like, pock marks cover portions of the walls, giving evidence of having boiled with great heat in ages past. The holes grow larger as they glide between the walls of a narrow valley. Below a stream tumbles along a rocky bed and at times they can hear the water roar. They pass occasional waterfalls spilling into the stream and then there is a wide gap between the walls and the extra room is most welcome.

Ahead of them they can see Bert, Topper, and the boys, along with Queenie and two sky-tops they've never seen before, make a little swing to the left then with a swift turn back to the right, they fly straight toward the solid rock wall. Hunter's shrill voice is loud and clear and then they disappear.

"Ohhh," Lettie gives a worried gasp just as Race makes the same loop to the left rounding a strangely sloped slab of stone the size of a skyscraper that juts out into the narrow valley. On the far side, Race swoops a hard right and flies straight into the shadows of the leaning mass of rock. There before them seems to be an undercut with a sheltered shelf back in the depths of the dark shadows.

Race slows his flight as he slips under the protective cover of the immense rock overhang. Layer upon layer of massive and strangely shaped stone, tower over and beneath them, and every layer is different. Each layer seems to suggest the passage of time, and had left its story on the walls around them. Several layers of the wall show evidence of having boiled at one time with intense heat. Giant pock marks scar the surface while both above and below the walls are smooth. It is into one of these great pock marks that Race aims, his powerful wings whip a quick backward stroke as he prepares to land inside a dark opening.

Lettie holds her breath while gripping Ruston's shoulders then gasps, "Duck, we'll hit our heads!" as Race slides into the heavy shadows between the craggy outcroppings of the hole. Touching down on the dark shelf, he folds his wings and takes a few trot steps as the darkness swallows them.

Ruston and Lettie flatten against Race's back hoping the roof is tall enough for their height. When their eyes adjust to the dim light they are most pleased to find the roof is quite high. In surprised awe Ruston and Lettie search the perimeters of the hole, but Race doesn't give them a chance to look around and moves at a trot into the dark interior. They duck down a narrow passage and Ruston feels sure the ceiling must be right over their heads and reaches up to see if he can touch it in the total darkness.

Round a tight bend light spills upon them as they trot into a huge cavern. Actually the word huge isn't accurate. A small village would fit in the immense room. Light streams into the area from two holes in the ceiling and is most welcome to their hungry eyes. Looking up into the golden light, they see a tangle of roots and vines tumbling through the gaping holes. A surprising waterfall fills the cavern with its constant voice and gives the atmosphere a strange vibration. Beneath the falls is a large and what appears to be deep pool with a small stream overflowing across the uneven stone floor.

"This is unbelievable," Lettie grips Ruston's back and gives him a little shake. "Look at all the sky-tops. This place is ….."

She doesn't get to finish because they are surrounded with sky-tops all chattering and bouncing. One particularly nice sky-top reaches up and places its face right near Lettie and clacks some friendly sounds. A precious baby sky-top scampers up to Bert and he wraps his neck around the little creature. It's almost as blue as Queenie. As Lettie and Ruston step to the ground and Ruston begins unloading their picnic baskets the little sky-top wants to carry one. She takes it in her beak and tries to pull it from his hands. Queenie snorts and comes to the rescue. Taking the picnic basket away from the baby, she gives a sound reprimand and the small sky-top drops her little head and cries soft whimpers.

"It's okay, Queenie, let her carry it if she wants," Lettie intervenes and hands the basket back to the little blue sky-top. Lettie laughs as she watches, what she believes must be Queenie's little sister, prance around with their picnic basket in her beak.

Not many picnics anywhere on any planet have ever been quite like this one. What with the excitement over the battle, combined with the Lynn's excitement in seeing Bert's home, and add to it the sky-top community's excitement over the victory and their distinguished visitors, it is a real celebration. However, there is one very odd circumstance, they are so quiet. Even Hunter is quiet.

After the excitement has settled down enough to make questions possible, Lettie asks Hunter about the bird's muffled silence.

"Oh, it's not that quiet in here. That waterfall makes you want to shout over it, but Queenie told me to shut my loud mouth."

"Queenie said that to you?" Lettie has difficulty believing this possible.

"Not in those words but yeah, she said I had to be quiet so the sawtooths won't find the cave. They all whisper, except when they forget like when we first got here," Hunter pauses. "Could I have one of those?' he asks pointing to a rather squashed plate of brownies. Seeing his mother nod her head he dips his hands into the brownies and comes up with a chocolate mess that seems to please him very much.

"So they hide in here and hope the sawtooths won't find them?" Lettie asks.

"Right."

"But they must go out to find food. These birds need a lot of food."

"You ought'a see the back of this cave, they have it filled with food. There are bubble-like pockets in the rock walls everywhere and all the pockets are full of food. They could last a long, long time."

"But Hunter, they have to go out to get the food to bring it here."

"Oh, I guess you wouldn't know," Hunter takes another bite and chews thoughtfully for a second before continuing. "The sawtooths can't see in the dark and so they don't go anywhere after dark. The sky-tops do most of their flying at night. They work at night, fly at night, and are here in the day. They eat leaves and branches, the little branches, and sometimes during the day they work real quiet down in the forests making great piles of food to carry home at night. That's what they were doing the day Topper first took us to find the sky-tops. You know the day Topper called them out of the forest."

"And the sawtooths have never found them?" Lettie asks.

"I don't think they would still be here if they had," Hunter reasons.

Handing Hunter another brownie, Lettie gives the top of his head a nice rumple messing his hair up really nice and comments, "You are a wonder."

"Thanks!"

For a moment she watches as Hunter wanders off into the depths of the cave and isn't the least surprised when several very small sky-top babies crowd around him following almost too close.

Much later that afternoon as Ruston prepares to return home, no one can find Hunter. He and Queenie are missing. Topper is argumentative about their preparations to leave, and Race will not sit for his saddle to be placed on his tall back.

"This is a bloomin' nuisance! What's gotten into you, Race?" Ruston challenges and both Race and Topper answer with a jumble of sounds that none of them understand. "Where is your brother, Jason?"

"He was over by the waterfall giving a music lesson to that flock of babies the last time I saw him. Queenie was with them, but they're not there now."

With an exasperated sigh Ruston asks, "Do you know what's going on Jason, can you figure out what they are trying to tell us?"

"All I know is we can't go until Bert says it's safe," Jason answers. "Dad, have you seen the guards they have set up around this place?"

Turning toward Jason, Ruston comments, "I somehow have the feeling I should have taken my tour of the place with you and Hunter, rather than scouting on my own. It seems I missed some things."

Lettie gives a little chuckle, "I told you so."

Turning toward his wife, Ruston is a bit miffed, "Right now I really don't need reminding." He pauses and gives Lettie an angry frown, "At times I feel as though I haven't the foggiest idea what is going on around me. I live in two worlds, my own and a sky-top world. I can't work or do much of anything these days without first consulting my youngest son."

"If we could speak their language we wouldn't have this problem," Lettie reminds him.

"Don't start that again—I refuse to learn to squawk and click it's, ... it's..."

"It's what ......?" Lettie bites her lip and tries not to laugh. This has been an ongoing topic for weeks now and sometimes Ruston can be very stubborn.

"That's not the issue at the moment, and you know it. Right now we need to start home or we will be flying at night and these stupid birds refuse to take us."

"So you are feeling trapped—we've been kidnapped and now we are trapped by stupid birds. Does that make us stupid for letting them trap us?" Lettie teases.

"All right, so I'm feeling trapped by very smart birds!" Ruston sighs and takes a different approach. "Lettie, you must understand, it's difficult to take care of you when I have absolutely no control of the situation. I want to leave while it's light enough to see what's in the air around us." For a moment he clenches his fists, a deep frown shaping a crease in his usually cheerful brow. Taking a deep breath he adds, "I want you and the boys safe."

"Ruston, I happen to know Jason is right, Bert won't take us until it's safe. The sawtooths can't see at night so they don't fly at night. Bert is waiting for dark to take us home when it is safe," Lettie has a smug little smile on her face and she hopes to tease Ruston out of his miff.

"How do you know this?"

"I asked Hunter."

"Ahhhhh!" Ruston throws up his hands in utter surrender, "I give up."

"Good ..."

"No, it's not good. Being kidnapped by a flock of giant chickens is not my idea of anything good."

For some unknown reason this seems to tickle Lettie's funny bone and she laughs.

"Lettie, this really isn't funny," Ruston doesn't understand.

Lettie sighs and apologizes, "I'm sorry—let's explore and see if we can find Hunter. He's here somewhere."

Somewhere turns out to be quite an understatement. The cave and all its tunnels and side rooms make looking for Hunter a serious undertaking. During their search Jason guides them to what he and Hunter call the back door.

"Dad, let's light some kind of a torch so we can see. Queenie took Hunter and me and we couldn't see a thing for a ways, but it's not that far."

With a little flint and steel, dried leaves and some ingenuity Ruston makes several torches. Topper is curious and wants to help so when all is ready he and Jason take Lettie and Ruston to the back door. The tunnel out the east side of the huge main room is large enough to drive a nice sized semi through. The floor climbs steadily and makes several turns that no semi could ever manage, and then opens into another large room with big stone pockets around the edges. Light gleams through several holes in the ceiling and through a long slit that runs ceiling to floor.

Intrigued, Ruston steps out through the slit into the sun and finds himself in a deep narrow crevice in the stone landscape. As to size, it is comparable to an alleyway between sky-scrapers, only here the floor is sandy and crowded with scrubby bushes. A honey bee zips by Ruston's nose suggesting a hive not too far away and a game trail passes in front of the opening and wanders in and out and around the bushes and boulders leading of to the right and the left. On either side, walls of stone rise toward the sky and soak up the sunshine. They are even warm to the touch. Looking round him, Ruston starts down the game trail and Topper pops his head out of the back door and clucks a warning to him, but he doesn't understand and curiosity pulls him on. Walking down the trail a little ways he then starts to climb a steep tumble of rocks. As he climbs he wonders how far he is from the holes in the ceiling of the cavern's main room and an idea begins to take shape. He can hear Topper's call and wonders what his problem might be, but keeps on climbing. After a bit of a scramble he is out on top and feels sure he must be well above the sky-top's cavern, and the holes in the ceiling should be somewhere near. Amid a tangle of bushes he finds the two holes and with a little work he manages to clear the bushes away enough to see down inside.

Just as he's about to go back down to where he'd left Lettie and Jason a shadow passes over him and he turns to see Bert standing several feet away and it's obvious he's quite cross. Bert's clicks and clacks tell Ruston he has offended the great bird for some reason.

"Bert, I'm sorry. Am I not supposed to be up here?"

Bert's firm nod tells him this is quite correct, and hoping to appease the situation he explains, "Bert, Lettie and I want to help you get rid of all the sawtooths and I was just looking around hoping to understand how we might accomplish this."

While Bert does not understand all Ruston has said he understands he wants to get rid of the sawtooths. He raises his head in surprise and forgets his anger at Ruston's mistake.

"Are you on guard up here?" Ruston wants to know and Bert nods. "Do the sawtooths fly over very often?" Bert shakes his head and nods it adding a variety of clicks and rrrrs. "Is that not very often?" This time Bert nods without the confusion. "And you keep watch and stay out of sight?" A definite nod follows with a shhhhhh that is unmistakable in its meaning. "When the sawtooths see you or any of the sky-tops flying about, do they follow?"

Yes, yes, yes, they do, is the unmistakable answer.

As Ruston walks back through the passage toward the main cave, he and Jason do some serious searching and an idea grows in Ruston's mind.

"Are there any other ways of getting in or out of here," Ruston asks Topper once they are back in the main cavern and he learns there are several large rooms, rooms large enough for a group of sky-tops to be comfortable. People sized tunnels connect various bubbles in the stone and make interesting possibilities. There are two other exits, one of which opens out into the canyon and drops straight down at least two hundred feet. Not a nice drop. This exit is small, too small for even Queenie, but a number of bubble-like pockets make a variety of rooms leading to the hole. The other exit is down a narrow tunnel and ends a long ways up the canyon in a pile of massive rocks. It is even smaller than the first. It is human size and of no value to the sky-tops except for the circulation of air.

"So there are only two usable entrances or exits for the sky-tops," Ruston smiles with satisfaction, "I think I've found a way to trap the sawtooths. It'll work! It'll work, and it's safe," Ruston tells Lettie once he, Jason and Topper return from their wanderings. "Imagine being chased by a sawtooth and ducking in here to the main cave—the sky-top would then ..." He stops and never finishes because he can see Queenie and she can find Hunter for them.

Sure enough, Queenie knows right where Hunter is and leads Ruston and Lettie back into a corner where it is rather dark and shadowy. A great nest of leaves and twigs fills a large area against the wall and on top of the nest sits a soft gray blue sky-top who watches them with interest. Queenie points into the nest and makes some sounds and the big sky-top moves back one of her wings and there beneath the wing, is the little blue sky-top that wanted to keep their picnic basket, a very black baby about the size of the blue one, and Hunter. All three are sound asleep.

Ruston feels a small smile swelling from somewhere deep inside. He rubs the top of his head much the same way Hunter does when he's figuring something out and makes his hair stand on end, just like Hunter. "Well, we've been finding him in sky-top nests for over a year now, so I guess the fact he's now in a strange nest with two babies about his size shouldn't surprise me," Ruston shakes his head as he and Lettie decide to let Hunter finish his nap.

The shadows are long and deep, with very dim light in the cave, when Hunter wanders out to find his family. He is covered with leaves and small sticks, he looks as though he's been hibernating—which indeed he has—and as though he is not quite yet fully awake. The two baby sky-tops follow him, each wanting to be close and it makes walking a little difficult for the sleepy Hunter.

He shuffles toward his family and stops in front of his father. For a moment he studies the situation trying to decide what to say. It's getting dark and soon the cave will really be black. Right now his family is gathered in what light is left under one of the big holes. Taking a deep breath he announces, "I have a plan."

"A plan?" his father questions and Lettie almost chokes on things she knows she hadn't better say, *Oh, be careful Hunter—ask your father—don't tell him.*

"Yes, a plan. You know Bert is always gone. Well, he's coming here to take care of Mrs. Bert and his babies—these two." He turns and looks at the two little sky-tops. "You see Mrs. Bert wants to come and live with us and her babies want to come and live with us, but they can't because the babies can't fly yet. So I told Mrs. Bert...," Hunter pauses a moment to consider then adds, "I think we should call her Patience, its gonna take a lot of patience to put up with these two.

"Oh yeah, I forgot what I was saying about the plan." Hunter gives his head a good rub and continues, "I told Patience the babies could be strapped into the passenger harnesses and fly home with us. She's getting ready to go now. I put Topper's saddle on her and she's as bad as

Queenie—she loves it. It's good we brought the big saddles today, because they will hold three. Jase and I can ride with one baby and you and Mom can take the other one up with you on Race or Bert, whichever he thinks is best."

For some reason Ruston looks a little helpless—his face is actually changing colors as he stands there with his mouth open. But Hunter doesn't notice. He's missed the whole impact of his announcement, and confidently finishes outlining his plan, "Bert says we may go as soon as the sun is down. Then it is safe, you see Dad, the sawtooths can't see at night. So we need to get ready to go while we still have a little light." He pauses, looking up at the hole in the roof above them, "It looks as though we ought to hurry, I think this place is about to be really dark," then turning to go, he adds, "I'll go get Patience, so we can get these babies up." Without a backward glance he heads off into the rapidly gathering darkness.

Ruston almost chokes with strange sounding emotion, you might say he snorts, or chokes or strangles, whatever, he has a little problem right this minute. A gurgle of laughter behind him causes him to turn and glare at his wife. "Don't you dare laugh!" he orders.

"Oh Ruston, if only you could see your face," Lettie laughs and Jason has to look the other way, because he is having the greatest difficulty not dissolving into laughter and that would not be a good thing at all.

"You two are impossible," Ruston growls at them.

"I can't help it," Lettie sputters with mirth.

Ruston glares at them, "You were right Lettie, I'm trapped. I've been kidnapped by a flock of giant chickens, and now I'm trapped with a pack of hyenas."

This only makes Lettie's and Jason's laughter more or perhaps better, depending upon whose side you happen to be on. So it is when a few minutes later Hunter appears astride a very lovely sky-top—if you can ever declare a sky-top lovely—with an excited blue baby strapped behind him, that Ruston looks up at his son and does his best to appreciate the absurdity of the situation. Shaking his head, he wonders if any father in the history of all mankind has had to deal with anything quite like Hunter and his sky-tops. These thoughts and a few others help him admit, with a weary smile, that it's been a rather trying day.

183

In all fairness to Ruston, he has a right to be more than a little perturbed. Fathers, good fathers that is, feel a great responsibility to take care of their family and to keep them safe. So it is only natural whenever circumstances jeopardize the father's position as chief protector there is apt to be trouble. Hunter in his young innocence hasn't thought of his father, he's only thought of himself and the sky-tops. This is sadly out of order.

However, because Ruston is a kind and compassionate father, one who seeks to avoid contention of any kind, there is hope for this stressful situation when the little black sky-top scurries around his mother and stops a moment to study the new situation. His mother is carrying Hunter and his sister. The puzzled excitement of the little black sky-top is touching and Ruston, seeing the little bird, feels a soft smile steal across his face. The little sky-top seems to be gathering his courage. Reaching his long beak out, he bobs his head in tiny jerks then takes a timid step closer. When Ruston offers several little clicking sounds, just like Hunter, the little fellow perks up his head and tipping it to one side gives Ruston a very serious stare with many little nods.

"What did I just tell him?" Ruston asks Hunter, who watches from Patience's back.

"You told him, *things are happy.*" Do it again with a little humming sigh at the end and he should come up to you."

Ruston gives the clicks and the little hum a try and sure enough, the little fellow steps right up to him. "What does the little sigh mean?"

"When they make that sound it means lots of things. Mainly it means you are a friend, or something or somebody they really like. So you told him you like him and want to be his friend—and that you are happy."

The little sky-top moves closer to Ruston and wraps his long neck around him then rubs his head on Ruston's shoulder.

Hunter is delighted, "He's picked you as his favorite. He's giving you a hug. Our big sky-tops used to try that until I told them they were too big." Hunter's merriment makes him sputter as he finishes, "So you've been hugged by a sky-top."

Lettie has watched this process and moves close to Ruston and his little friend. She gives a little click, click with a soft humming sigh and is so pleased to receive a hug from the little creature.

184

As Ruston saddles Race for the homeward flight, he has many thoughts fleeting through his mind. His smile grows into a chuckle. Glancing toward where Hunter waits with Jason and Patience, he can hear their conversation and shakes his head. *This is absolutely ridiculous—the sounds are gibberish—they can't possibly mean anything.* His mind argues, *But, they do! They must ...* Taking a deep breath he squares his shoulders and finishes strapping the saddle into place and decides, *So now I'm going to take language lessons from my eleven year old son or continue to be out maneuvered and managed by this pack of chickens,* and this thought finally makes him laugh.

It is now quite dark and time to go. A spirit of adventure and pure delight fills their souls as Ruston helps Lettie into the saddle in front of their small black passenger. There is no doubt as to Bert's and Mrs. Bert's, or Patience's, feelings—they are thrilled. As Ruston watches Bert, he can't help but understand his joy—after tonight he will no longer have to fly back and forth to care for his family. Bert is almost comical as he checks his children's harness not once or twice, but three times. He wants to be sure they are on tight and Ruston wants to tease the giant bird, while at the same time, he understands his anxiety.

At least twenty sky-tops gather close to bid the Lynn's and Bert's family farewell. They are ready to fly and the excitement is infectious. A constant hum of clicks and purrs surround them as they start through the tunnel leading out.

"Dad," Ruston hears Hunter calling and turns toward him. "Dad, Bert is going to lead us with several sky-tops. We are to fly in the middle and Blinky and a few of his friends will follow behind. If anything goes wrong we are to go home fast."

"This is the plan?"

"Pretty good, huh?"

"This is an excellent plan," Ruston answers with a slight shake to his head—his own plan taking shape as they head out through the dark tunnel. *If sawtooths can't see in the dark we'll have to give them a little light to encourage them to come on through into the main cavern..*

"Isn't this just great, Dad?" Hunter's cheerful voice echoes off the walls close around them.

Lettie is glad to hear Ruston's soft chuckle and understands his feelings when he turns toward her and says with a very straight face, but clowning voice, "There are times I feel I have lost absolutely all control and this happens to be one of them." With these words he gives one of those big forced toothy grins and continues, "Sweetheart, I suggest we follow Hunter's plan."

"Do we have a choice?" Lettie asks.

"Somehow, I don't think so."

As Race steps out into the sky and the wind catches beneath his great wings their little black passenger lets out a delighted whistle and Lettie hopes he won't hurt her with his excited wings. For a moment Ruston looks back at the hidden entrance and imagines sawtooths landing there.

Yes, I must perfect this plan.

Chapter 15

HUNTER'S DREAM

Life around Lynn Farm isn't what you'd call normal these days. First Grandpa's sky-top spurs are in demand by a number of the sky-tops from Bert's sky-top cavern community and Ruston has told them only the sky-tops that were willing to help fly the mail may have spurs and a helmet. This is more than a little awkward. How do you tell creatures the size of very tall elephants "no," or to be patient? Even more difficult is to figure out what to do with ten more sky-tops all wanting to fly with the mail? Also the Lynn family budget is challenged with the new circumstances. Family budgets are difficult enough without adding the cost of pig feed for dinosaurs and then even more when you add the expense of fighting armor for these giants. It has taken a number of stressful days to work out these complications.

The situation at this point is first, Patience, this is what everyone calls Mrs. Bert, and her babies, Princess and Scamp, must learn the Lynn Farm rules. There is a bit of a problem in this quarter. The first and foremost is baby sky-tops are not allowed inside the house. It doesn't matter how small they are or the fact they are just Hunter size and fit easily wherever he goes—they may not come inside—period! They may not hide in closets and hope Lettie won't find them, and they may not help Ruston in his shop or at any other time for that matter and his tools are sacred. The second most important thing for them to learn is pig feed is given only twice a day. That's just the way it is. Patience will be the size of a mammoth flying hippopotamus very soon if she ever learns how to open the feed crib door.

The situation currently also includes changes in Samuel's life. The lovely gray sky-top Samuel calls Wings, and has wanted so long has moved in, however because of a slight misunderstanding with Patience he has moved into Samuel's barn. While Wings is quite happy, the small barn is more than full of sky-top, and the milk cow has dried up and moved out—but Samuel is thrilled. It seems Patience is territorial and

187

the Lynn barn is now her barn. It's a wonder Race managed to maintain his bed and the right to remain there.

As to the size of the Lynn barn—it is no longer large—the very large barn seems to have shrunk. Size is relative and when an extremely large barn is filled with six or more sky-tops it becomes small in a hurry, especially if one of the sky-tops happens to be mad. Yet, the barn has survived the ruckus, and so did Samuel's sky-top. However, at one point this was questionable.

Patience's territorial temper is not the only little bump in the road around Lynn Farm. It seems understanding and speaking the sky-top language is paramount in restoring peace and order to simple day to day living. Hunter and Topper are teaching regular classes in sky-top language. They are somewhat comical in their approach, but manage to be excellent teachers and this time has proven to make a difference in the Lynn's survival skills. As a matter of interest the word "no" is a quick growl followed by a sharp cluck. The cluck is similar to the sound you might make to ask a horse to move forward. A growling cluck all at the same time, which is not very easy to accomplish, but the sky-tops manage it easily enough, is a really strong "no" and Ruston has used it a great deal lately.

Patience is a very nice sky-top, she is quite intelligent and wants to learn, yet she's never had to follow people rules before and it has taken more than a little adjusting. We may assume she hadn't expected her life to change quite so dramatically with her move from the cavern. Moving is stressful, especially to mothers and when you disrupt their way of doing things you can expect flashes of temper, even from really nice mothers. Because of all these changes and complications, Hunter and Queenie have spent hours working with Patience as well as Princess and Scamp, hoping to create a peaceful working unity as quickly as possible.

As to other circumstances, it was a near catastrophe when Samuel saddled Wings and climbed aboard the first time. The bird was willing and delighted and took off with his passenger. All was well and wonderful until they disappeared over the far horizon and weren't seen again until after dark. Samuel learned an important lesson in that day's venture. He learned all about controlling a willing yet green broke sky-top while traveling faster than a fast train through the clouds. He learned such experiences can be most unnerving.

Papa is in about the same situation. Blink moved into Papa's big barn, and so did Patches, one of Blink's buddies. While Papa is most pleased, he's having no more luck with his situation than is Samuel. Grandma has insisted Papa stay on the ground with his new sky-top, Patches, until they understand one another. Clicks, churps, and whistles are not easy to interpret. Although Blink is a great help with his limited understanding, it's not enough. So Papa comes to Hunter's classes with the hope he will be able to speak fluent sky-top sometime in the next century.

In the midst of this difficult time of adjustment there is a current of excitement. Papa and Blinky, along with Patches, have been back and forth several times, and together with Ruston and Samuel, a great map has been drawn of the sky-top cavern. Two trips back to the cave have been made and the map is now rather accurate in its detail. It is time to set their trap and put "Project Sawtooth" into action.

So it is Samuel, Papa, Jason, and Ruston and five armed sky-tops loaded with all the necessary equipment take to the sky and head for the sky-top cavern. As the great birds fade into the distance, Patience calls her farewell with long singing cries while the babies along with Topper and Queenie are content to watch with silent interest. After a moment Patience heaves a huge sigh then hurries her small children off toward the farthest south pasture where she enjoys spending her days.

Hunter stands beside his mother and wonders why he hadn't been permitted to go with them. Dexter pushes against him wanting attention, but Hunter doesn't even notice. His mind is filled with complaints, *After all, Jason is only a few years older. It simply isn't fair.*

"Mom, when will Dad let me go too?"

"You and I will go when the time comes to trap the sawtooths," Lettie answers.

"I thought you'd be too scared."

"Sometimes staying here and not knowing is more frightening than seeing and being in the middle of scary things." Lettie sighs and sadness seems to wrap heavy arms around her. "I don't like what we are about to do, but I honestly don't see we have a choice. Life's like that. We have to take giant steps into the dark sometimes. And that's what we're doing."

"Don't you want to get rid of the sawtooths?" Hunter speaks with some force as he seeks to understand.

"Oh, yes, I want very much to be rid of the sawtooths, but I don't want to fight them ever again. Anytime you take on a project like your father's 'Project Sawtooth,' there is considerable danger involved, and I'm not ready for any of us to die."

"So what do we do, they'll get us if we don't go ahead with Dad's plan," Hunter reminds her.

"That's right. I know we can't sit here and wait. If the sawtooths ever discovered things like pig feed or our sheep and pigs and our comfortable barn, who knows what might happen. No, there comes a time to declare war, and that's what this is."

"War?"

"Yes, war. When one people, nation, or creature endangers the homes, families, lives, and freedom of another, sooner or later there will be war. Your father fought in one war for our freedom and this is really no different."

"Freedom? Mom, the sawtooths don't want to be king and rule over us or make us slaves like the war Dad fought against King Loudon."

"No, but they rob us of our peace, our security, our safety, and each of those are a part of freedom. As parents or as just good people, we must make sure we protect our families and our homes. This is no different. We fought King Loudon for the right to rule ourselves, for the right to live here without his troops watching us and taking our children, crops, and livestock from us. We fight the sawtooths for the right to fly in the air over us without fear. So we will take the fight to them rather than wait for them to fight us here at home where so many defenseless people could be killed."

"Are you okay, Mom?" Hunter asks as he watches slow tears run down her lovely face.

"Yes, I'm fine. I married a soldier, I cared for the soldiers in the hospitals during the war with Loudon and I vowed then I wanted a fighter for a husband. I don't like men who sit back and hope someone will do something. So like it or not—I will fight beside him now."

"Why are you crying?"

"I know what we have to do—I know what I must do, and I will not back up a single step—but I don't have to like it."

"I think I understand," Hunter sighs and keeps a steady hand on Dexter's big head. "So this is a war? And Dad, Papa, Samuel, and you, me, and Jason are going to fight it all by ourselves. That's a rather lop-sided war."

"Its okay, your father doesn't want to involve the valley people unless we have to. He and Papa will know what needs to be done. And Hunter, don't forget the sky-tops. They are incredible, and as we make more helmets and spurs for them our forces become stronger and stronger. When all is ready we will go, and we will decide how many we need to help us. There are several from town who have said they want to help. So we will wait and see. "

Both watch as the sky-tops become tiny specks in the sky then finally vanish. A gentle breeze stirs the air and a wild squawking from the hen house provides a distraction as both turn and wonder what could possibly make the hens make so much noise. Dexter listens a moment then runs to the hen house and around to the side where he can see inside. If there's a fox or a snake in the hen house, Dexter will let them know, but he is silent and the hens settle down.

"I know what we need to do today," Lettie gives Hunter a fiendish smile, "Let's go shopping! We haven't gone to town just for fun in a long time." Lettie takes off her apron and gives Hunter a little pat, "Go saddle Topper and let's go somewhere."

Once in the air Lettie and Hunter plan their day's activities. This is to be an extra special day for just the two of them. As a part of their little celebration Lettie hands Hunter a fist full of coins with the instructions to invest them wisely. As they touch down in the village square their minds are filled with what they might find to take home with them.

"Remember, I want you to invest the money I've given you in something that will still be of worth tomorrow, and the next day, and the next," Lettie's eyes sparkle as she watches Hunter's expression. Then giving him a rub on the top of his head, she plants a kiss on his forehead and turns him loose with his assignment. Minutes later she is lost in a world all her own amid bolts of colorful fabric and her mind fills with images of all the lovely things she might make.

Hunter's mind runs along a different track. *Something that will be of worth tomorrow, and the next day and the next, well, it can't be candy.* His mouth waters as he looks at the shop counter lined with jars of sweets. Wandering up and down the narrow isles of the dry goods store he touches, sniffs, ponders, and wishes. *An investment means something that will be better in the future.* Two more trips up and down the isles in the dry goods store without seeing anything he would call a sound investment, he stops to reconsider. He wonders what his friend, old Mr. Hopkins would choose and this gives him an idea. With a little grin he heads out the door and with a hop and a skip, he steps into a nice jog and heads down the street. With a "Hello there," to Mrs. Stevens, and a high-five for Earl Jones, he rounds a corner thinking, *A book—a book can make a difference in the future—it will be good today, tomorrow and even next year. Mom'll be really proud of me.*

Stopping in front of the local newspaper office, he sighs a contented sigh. *Books—I will pick a book.* Hunter loves books and Mr. Hopkin's bookstore is really a side room off his newspaper office. Many of the books are used, but that's okay. If somebody else liked them enough to make them used, then they must be worth reading. With this kind of reasoning, Hunter always looks at the used books first.

Heavenly contentment sweeps over and around him as he steps into the quiet room and sees the walls of books. This is a very special place—it even smells nice and booky with all the paper and ink. Minutes pass and Hunter has made a little pile of books and is in the process of choosing when several people enter the newspaper office. They are quite noisy and interrupt Hunter's peaceful contemplation. Glancing through the door into the main office he sees the huge Arnald Dixon.

It has been days since Hunter has thought of Chat Dixon or his injured hands. He seems to have managed to put these thoughts behind him. A funny little feeling now creeps over him as he watches Chat's huge father and his foreman. A third figure moves toward the counter and Hunter's heart skips a little beat—yes, it's Chat.

This is a strange moment for Hunter, because he is more curious than he is afraid or mad. The anger seems to have faded away, and he cranes his neck wanting to get a good look at Chat. It's been weeks and weeks since their battle and the last time he'd seen him, his face had been covered in blood and he'd been about half crazy with anger.

He's thinner—no—yes, he is—he doesn't look near so mean, and he's standing sort-a funny. Hunter's mind is busy. Chat fidgets while his father talks to someone behind the counter. He can hear Chat's father and understands he wants to put some kind of an ad in the paper. He wants it big. *That figures—Dixon always has to have everything bigger.*

Chat turns away from his father and wanders toward the book room. He stops in the doorway and sees Hunter, and their eyes meet. Hunter is curious and wonders what Chat might be thinking. He doesn't look at all like the Chat he remembered—no, not at all. He is thinner and his eyes are all sunk in like he might hurt or be sick. Hunter wonders what had happened to make Chat look the way he does. The Chat standing in the doorway doesn't look like the same Chat that was going to poke his eyes out, or the one who haunts his dreams.

The two boys stare at one another for an uncomfortable minute or so and Hunter for some unexplainable reason gives a timid little smile and says, "It's good to see you Chat." Even stranger, these simple words make Hunter feel a wonderful feeling inside, and he knows he meant what he said.

A flicker of hope flickers across Chat's pale face, and he opens his mouth to speak, but nothing comes out. He tries again and his father bellows, "Come Chat, you don't want a book, those are for silly women. Come, boy!" He orders, and Chat obediently turns to go. He glances back over his shoulder and sees Hunter still watching him. Then they are gone, and Hunter turns and watches as they pass the window where Chat's eyes meet his again.

For a long time Hunter sits in the quiet room wondering over his own feelings, and the fact he had told Chat it was good to see him again. Then with a little grin, he realizes it was good to see him, and to have this step over with. There had been no threat in Chat's expression—only what was it, he had seen? Puzzlement pesters him for an answer as Mr. Hopkin's clerk comes in with a pile of books and sets them on a side table.

"That was Dixons who was just in here. Did ya see them?" Thompson, the clerk, asks and Hunter nods. "He wants to have a big archery contest in the valley. He wants to make it a big event and have people come in from all over. He says the winners will represent our valley in the big Lakeland Harvest Festival. The entry fees will pay their way and he wants the news paper to print a whole page and make him posters for all the neighboring towns." Master Thompson is full of important gossip as he continues. "You know what I think?"

Hunter hasn't the foggiest idea—but of one thing Hunter is certain and that is the whole town has no idea how his older brother or his dad can shoot. A little smile turns up the corners of his mouth as he imagines a contest. *Cool*!

"I think our big bragging Master Dixon is worried about that kid of his. Did you see him? He looks terrible. Did you know here some weeks back Chat came home all beat to smithereens. He didn't even know where his horse was. He'd been riding some green broke colt and something must have gone wrong. His face was beat up somethin' fierce," Master. Thompson pauses and scratches his bald head while peering over his half moon glasses. "Funny thing, that pal of his they call Dorf, got hurt the same day. Dixon says he thinks Dorf tried to help Chat and made things worse, and both of 'em got tromped. Dorf's folks said your pa found 'im and took 'im to Doc's. What do you know about it?"

Hunter isn't ready for this and his eyes about pop out of his head as he stutters, "This is all news to me," and grabbing up two books he asks, "How much for these two?"

This shuts Master Thompson down for a minute, and then as Hunter heads for the door he calls him back and leans over the counter in a confidential manner and almost whispers, "Dixon has had Chat in some nut house over in Riverside. They have some kind of witch doctor there to straighten people's minds out."

Hunter's head fairly spins with questions he wants to ask, but doesn't dare so he stands rooted to the spot as Master Thompson continues. "Chat's been about half crazy since the accident. He doesn't remember what happened and his dad has done everything he can think of trying to get Chat to talk to him. The kid has just shut up. He doesn't talk to anybody. So Dixon took him to this mental place. Somebody said he tried to run away so they locked him up. He just got home a day or two ago. He looks bad, don't he?"

"Doesn't he?" Hunter whispers.

"What's that, son, ya gotta speak up, I don't hear as well as I used ta."

As Hunter escapes out the door he races down the street to find his mom. He is to meet her in the café for lunch and is so glad to find her there waiting.

"Who was there?" Lettie can't believe what she thinks she's just heard.

"Chat—Chat was there, I saw Chat!" As the story comes tumbling out, Lettie places a gentle hand over Hunter's mouth several times to remind him to whisper. They scarcely taste their lunch as they consider the magnitude of what Hunter has learned.

That night Hunter dreams about Chat, only this time it's not a scary dream, but rather one filled with sadness. Everything is sort of fuzzy and sometimes even a little tipped to one side or the other. A boy crawls through the shadows, he cries soft cries of misery, there is blood and Hunter feels pain. Trying to see more, he strains to see the boy's face. The face is pale and filled with fear. Then the boy collapses and rests before crawling on. It seems a long time passes and then the boy stands and faces another much larger figure, and Hunter senses anger although he cannot hear the words, and the figures drift and slip in and out of focus. For a time the boy is taller and stronger as he follows the big figure through a maze of confusing events, but always cowers when the big figure turns toward him as if in confrontation. Several figures surround the boy and he runs, and runs, and cries, and runs again—then there is a cage—a terrible cage and the boy begins to shrink. His shrunken body becomes a mere shell and the cage opens and the big figure takes him out, and they walk into the sunshine where Hunter sees the boy's face and recognizes Chat. Hunter doesn't see anymore—he awakens and sits up in bed.

During the long dark hours of the night, Hunter sits in a splash of moonlight hugging Dexter. At first Dexter is awake and helpful as he listens, then he sleeps and Hunter speaks in soft whispers, "If only Dad would come home, Dext, I need to tell him about Chat. I want to tell him about my dream." But Ruston doesn't come home the next day or the next. Lettie has to remind Hunter again and again that it will be later in the week before the men get back.

Hunter is not very content with the situation, but since there is little he can do about it, he decides to make a flying harness for Dexter with his new leather working tools. Figuring how to design the harness has been a bit of a problem because Dexter doesn't have long legs to go down in stirrups like a person. He doesn't have hands to hang on with either for that matter. After many hours of fitting and refitting, Hunter decides the harness is ready for a test run and saddles Topper. With a push and a mighty shove Dexter is in the passenger seat at the back of the saddle. Topper keeps getting his big beak in the way and Hunter tries to be patient, he knows Topper just wants to help. He clicks and clucks with all kinds of advice which neither, Hunter or Dexter pay any attention to. Getting Dexter strapped on is one thing, and taking off and having Dexter remain strapped on proves to be quite another, so it is with three bounding leaps Dexter slips and falls to one side all while making rather strange noises.

"Opps......." After three tries, in exasperation Hunter goes into the barn and rummages through their pack saddles, panniers, and equipment. Finding what he wants he drags a large pannier out toward where Topper waits.

"Balance," Hunter mutters. "Dexter has to be in the middle not off to one side. Hummmm....." thoughts of how this might be arranged muddle through Hunter's mind along with images of a cat carrier he saw once. *Why not?* Giving the top of his head a serious rub he knows he must start all over with his flying dog harness.

During the wee hours of the night an impressive sky-top patrol slides silently out of the sky and lands in the Lynn Farm courtyard. Hunter is sound asleep and doesn't move. Dexter raises a lazy head and listens, then with a big sigh closes his eyes and goes back to sleep. All is very well.

The next morning there is much to be done and Hunter must wait with patience until his father has time to listen. Not just sort of listen, but really listen, and Hunter knows there is a big difference. When the time comes and Ruston is able to listen to Hunter's story, he is both relieved and upset with what Hunter shares.

"How do you feel about Chat now?" Ruston asks.

"Dad, just looking at him made me sad. Something is wrong, really wrong."

"I agree. But I feel better—I was so sure Chat would come and apologize and we'd have the opportunity to help him with his father. If Arnald really did send him to some mental hospital it explains why Chat hasn't come. It makes me sick inside to think of what he has been through." Ruston pauses and studies Hunter's serious face. "Are you ready to help Chat?" Hunter's gentle nod makes Ruston's heart swell with tender love for Hunter as well as for Chat. "How do you feel about going with me to see Chat just as soon as we've finished "Project Sawtooth?"

"I'd like that very much—just you and me."

"Have you been praying for Chat?"

"I do all the time. I don't want to see him crawling in my dreams any more. I want him to stand up and smile at me so I can know he's all right. That's what I want."

"Then we have a plan?"

"Project Chat," Hunter grins and with a high five, Ruston gives his son a little hug then asks, "Have you packed your bedroll and all your camping things? We will leave just as soon as it's dark."

Good listeners are essential in the peaceful workings of every family situation and Ruston's undivided attention, plus his willingness to assume the weight of the Chat situation lifts Hunter's spirits back to their usual unrestrained heights. Project Chat is no longer of paramount importance, and Hunter rushes to the barn to saddle Topper and load his things.

Chapter 16

CHAT

Later that night the as the Lynns fly through the silent starry night toward Bert's Cavern, Hunter has a moment of sadness. Dexter wanted so much to go with them. Hunter can still see him standing beside Grandma in the courtyard as they made their running leaps into the sky. With a little sigh he promises himself, *Someday, Dexter will fly with me.*

As they dip down into the canyon they tip and slide between the shadowy walls and as the canyon widens the birds do not dip and swerve to land on the shelf below. Instead they make a graceful swoop and sail over the top of the cliff and land on the south side, near the holes in the main part of the cave's roof. On this side, massive weathered stones give the appearance of having been stacked by a giant from ages past. The stones up here aren't little stones. The one Ruston chose to use as a home base or a base camp for Project Sawtooth is about fifty feet tall and perhaps a half a mile around—it would cover Glendale. This huge rock is one of many piled on top of each other. On the side facing the holes in the roof of the cave below, the mighty rock has a gaping overhang—a huge curving lip sticks out at the base and opens into a space underneath. The opening is about twelve feet from ground to ceiling at the front edge and tapers into a nice pocket of about eight to nine feet at the back. This area is just right for Lynns and too small for the big sky-tops. The outer edge of the overhang permits the sky-tops to be back out of sight and not in the way of the Lynn's camp. The situation is quite nice. It is dry, out of the wind and rain and out of sight of flying predators. It is only a few running feet from the largest of the two holes allowing for a place of retreat for those working around the hole during Project Sawtooth.

"Welcome to base camp," Ruston cheerily announces. "Lettie, take the lantern and go check out our headquarters while I unload. Everything is all set and I think you will be quite comfortable."

Within a very few minutes, Lettie has a nice fire going and a kettle of stew warming over the flames. A glowing lantern illuminates the shelter's dark corners, making their home away from home better than expected. Once all the saddles and supplies are in under the shelter and bedrolls tucked into the back along the steeply sloped walls, all is well for the night.

With the cavern map spread out on a stone slab serving as a table, Ruston bends over the map and explains the details of the trap.

"Bert has chosen four of the fastest sky-tops to fly over the sawtooth community and attract attention, and then lead them in noisy alarm back to the cavern and into the trap. The plan is for all the sawtooths to give chase, but we can't be sure they all will." Ruston pauses and looks at his family's serious faces before continuing, "The sky-tops are to lead the sawtooths into the cave. The tunnel entrance has lanterns strategically placed along the top of the walls. The lamps are hidden and only the light is visible making the tunnel inviting to the night blind sawtooths. We hope the sawtooths will follow the sky-tops all the way into the cave and once inside barricade one will go down blocking their retreat back out. The sky-tops will duck out the back way through the totally dark tunnel and once all the sky-tops are out, barricade two will go down and whoever is to let this barricade down will have to make their way to the second back up barricade, put it down and then go on out the back door in the dark. This is the tricky place."

Lettie picks up the plan and taps the small hole on the map with her finger and continues, "When we know the barricades are down and that the sawtooths are trapped, we will begin setting the piles of trees and wood in the center of the cave on fire. I will take care of the flaming arrows and Jason will shot them through the hole and turn the cavern into a giant smoke-filled oven. As soon as the fires are burning we will cover the holes—it's very effective and quite simple." Lettie looks up at her husband and is pleased. "Ruston, I'm impressed. It's actually much safer for us than I'd expected."

While Ruston and Lettie discuss every possibility, Hunter listens and isn't very pleased. No, not at all. He is to stay in under the base camp shelter with Queenie while Jason and his mother light the fires. *That's not fair! Jason lights the fires, Dad and Papa put down the front barricade, and Samuel puts the back one down, and I'm stuck under a rock!* Hunter looks as though he might explode, *Fine and dandy!* It's enough to make a very nice fellow mad. He'd like to say so, but manages to keep his feelings down to a low grumble.

The next morning Ruston and Lettie are still going over every step and the dangers surrounding the project, and as Lettie places a pile of hot cakes before them, Hunter hears her say, "I'd feel better if Samuel had someone down in the back tunnel with him. Couldn't we get someone to help? I know we can manage as we are if all goes well, but we must be prepared for something to go wrong."

Ruston sits back as Lettie hands him a steaming mug of hot chocolate. Taking a swallow he savors the taste then suggests, "Samuel and Dad will make the mail run today and won't be back here until tonight, so there's time to send a message back and ask the Spalding brothers to come. They've said several times they want to help. They'd like to fly the mail or do anything to be involved, and I don't mind asking them. How do you feel?"

Lettie places a stack of pancakes in front of Jason and answers, "Race could take the message, your mother is there and can get it to the Spaldings. We'd better send several armed sky-tops, just in case," she pauses and continues, "....we need to be very careful. And I don't think you have near enough lamp oil. We don't know how long the lamps will have to burn in the front tunnel and you want to be sure the fire in the cavern springs up fast. I say we send for more lamp oil, and the Spaldings."

A little later Race and two volunteer sky-tops complete with spurs and helmets, take to the air headed for Lynn Farm with a note for Spaldings to come and to bring lamp oil.

***

At this same time Chat Dixon rides at a slow pace toward Lynn Farm. Twice he has turned back only to stop and ponder before turning around again. With a slow plodding walk he makes his way toward Lynn Farm. He wants desperately to talk again with Ruston as he had on the terrible day of the fight. He wants to leave his home and never see his father again, but what he wants most is to be near Ruston. You see, there are many different ways of starving, and love and approval are almost as vital as food, water, and air. For a brief few minutes Chat had been in Bert's saddle with Ruston's arms around him showing him how to guide and work with the magnificent sky-top. Right now every part of him starves for that feeling again. No matter how hard he tries, he cannot please his father, and he cannot forget Ruston and the tenderness he'd felt as they'd talked. He hungers for a little praise. Ruston told him most dads weren't like his father and that he didn't have to "make" people do what he wanted them to do. He had explained that you can't force people to respect you. Down deep inside Chat's heart, there is a fierce desire to start over and become the Chat, Ruston said he could be. But he doesn't know how. He can still hear Ruston's words, *You must come and apologize to Hunter for what you have done, then we will start all over, and I will help you.*

He remembers Hunter's little smile and his words, *It's good to see you again, Chat.* Hunter will never know how much his kind words helped Chat find the courage he needed to make a try at starting over and becoming the man Ruston had suggested he could become. Father-to-son traditions are difficult to change, and Chat is about to make a break and be free from his past. For him, this is far more difficult than a bloody fist fight. His heart pounds and his mouth is dry as he sees the Lynn Farm buildings up ahead.

He reins to a stop at the turn off into Lynn Farm and looks down the pleasant road where he can see the majestic barn above the tall trees. *It's always so peaceful here. Why did I not understand before? Why did I think beating up Hunter would make me feel better?* Chat's mind has so many questions. Taking a deep breath, he tries to gather his courage.

Several mother geese on the far side of the stream splash and make a fuss over a tiny fish and he watches the mothers and their goslings a few minutes. When they settle down all is still and quiet. Not a sky-top is in sight—it's rather eerie to have the big place be so quiet. Riding on down the farm lane into the courtyard his horse's hoofs make loud clopping sounds and disturb the peaceful silence. Stepping down from his saddle he loops his reins over the tie rail in front of the house and walks toward the door then knocks—there is no answer.

Standing alone in front of the house he wonders where everyone is. Then he crosses the courtyard and opens the barn door and calls. Stepping inside he looks around and is surprised to find every stall empty. With a sigh and a heavy heart he walks back to his horse and is about to step into the saddle when a sudden wild squawking from the hen house makes him turn in time to see Grandma step out through the door, loaded with a basket of eggs over one arm, and a chicken held snugly in the other.

"Greetings, I thought I heard someone call," she is a bit out of breath as she hurries toward him while holding the rather distraught chicken. Smiling she explains, "Dinner."

Chat begins to relax, he can't help himself, this lady is certainly no threat and besides she's really cute. She's not old as in old, but she's not young either. Wispy gray brown hair floats around her happy face and as she hurries toward him, her steps have a lively bounce. Her heavy dark blue skirt and very white apron have stems of straw and a few feathers clinging to them, there's even a soft fluffy feather in her hair. He finds himself smiling as he reaches to take the heavy basket of eggs.

"I understand somebody from town will pick up the eggs sometime today. Do you know anything about that?" she asks as she motions him to follow her into the house—chicken and all.

"Forgive me, Mum, I don't," Chat is very careful to be extra polite as they enter the Lynn's big keeping room and head for the kitchen.

"Well, that's too bad. I don't know who's going to come for them," She smiles at him while trying to push the hair out of her eyes and asks, "What can I do for you, young man?"

"I came to see Master Lynn, and Hunter," Chat answers.

"Well, you missed them both. I'm taking care of things for a few days. You see, I'm Ruston's mother and he needed someone to help while they are gone." She places the chicken under a tub on the counter and takes the eggs from Chat's hands then seeing his surprised face, she explains, "Oh, the chicken will be fine right there, she can wait. She's certainly isn't in any hurry to hop into my pot." Her eyes glitter with humor as she peeks under the tub. "Now, maybe I can help you in some way?"

Before Chat has a chance to comment, Race and his two companions drop into the courtyard with their booming voices calling for attention. Less than a minute later with note in hand, Grandma whispers, "Oh, dear me," while Chat inches closer, hoping for a glimpse at the note.

"Oh, dear, dear me," Grandma exclaims again. "Do you know the Spalding brothers?" When Chat nods, she continues, "I'm supposed to get word to them that Ruston needs them and five gallons of lamp oil. My stars, that's a lot of lamp-oil, still, Ruston knows what he needs." Grandma looks up from the note and studies the boy before her, "How old are you?" she asks.

"Fifteen."

"Are you busy today?"

Surprised, Chat answers, "No, Mum."

"Would your parents mind if you ran a few errands for me .... It shouldn't take too long. Have you ever ridden a sky-top?"

Again surprised, he answers the affirmative.

"Excellent, it seems you are not here by chance, you see I need your help because, Samuel and my husband won't be back from the mail run until later this evening, and that will be too late. We need to find Spaldings and get the lamp oil to Ruston before they get back." Noticing Chat's puzzled expression she explains further, "Ruston and Papa are building a trap for the sawtooths and he needs two good men to help. He's asked me to get word to the Spaldings that they are needed. I'm to tell them to go with Race and to bring five gallons of lamp oil with them." With a little frown she looks closer at Chat, "Do you know what I'm talking about?"

"Not really ... I know it was a sawtooth that Jason killed, and I heard one attacked Samuel not too long ago. I know they have teeth and are quite different from the sky-tops." Chat pauses staring at the wicked looking spikes sticking out of Race's helmet and his gleaming spurs. "Is that why the sky-tops look like they are going to war?" Chat is fascinated with the weapons and their underlying meaning.

"That is exactly why the weapons. Ruston doesn't let anyone fly around alone anymore. The sawtooths are dangerous and have attacked some of our sky-tops. So we have escorts with weapons now," Grandma points to the two volunteer sky-tops then adds, "Although I don't know these two fellows—do you?"

"No, I don't, but I've always wanted a sky-top and if I had one of my own I'd call him Ruffas," Chat grins as he enjoys sharing his dream with this little lady.

"Good, then pick one and call him Ruffas until you know his real name," Grandma doesn't miss the excited gleam in Chat's rather pale face. "What do you want to call the other one?" Grandma asks and enjoys Chat's reaction.

"Scooter,"

"Why Scooter?"

"I dun-no, it just popped into my head," Chat smiles and feels weight lifting from his shoulders with every passing minute.

Grandma then places a small hand on his arm and asks, "Will you do me and Ruston a serious favor, please? I want you to find Spaldings and tell them they are needed and stop by the hardware store in Glendale and pick up the lamp oil. Ruston has an account. It shouldn't be a problem."

Chat is pleased to be of help and with a few final instructions, he turns toward his horse and Grandma stops him, "Oh, you must fly. It will be much faster. You've flown before, haven't you?"

Joy and wonder flutter into Chat's eyes as he answers, "Yes, Mum, I have. Ruston taught me."

"Then take Race, he understands perfectly well and will take you wherever you need to go." She pauses considering the situation. "Your parents aren't going to mind are they—do you mind?"

"No, no, I love to fly—I want to help Master Ruston. I came to ask for a job. I want to work for him."

"Perfect, so let's get you up and on your way. I will put you to work myself," she smiles and is pleased with the solution to her problem.

However, there is a rather large obstacle standing in the way of Grandma's simple solution and the large obstacle is none other than Race. You see he knows exactly who Chat is, and the grief he has caused the Lynn family. Now he understands he is to carry a Lynn enemy—right at the moment he doesn't think so. So as Chat steps toward him he stands several feet taller as he raises his big head and neck his very tallest and looks down at the boy and growls. Frankly, Chat doesn't blame him and steps back wondering what to do—like run, for instance. A growling sky-top can be more than a little worrisome.

"Race, what has gotten into you?" Grandma's voice is quite firm and reprimanding. "This nice young man has offered to help, and you act as though you don't want him to touch you." Grandma walks up to Race and gives him a swat on the side of his leg—because that's all she can reach. "Where are your manners? Here you are trying to help Ruston and Bert, and you are picky when someone offers to help and do what Ruston needs to have done." Race gives a surprised chirp and lowers his proud head and looks at Grandma as she continues, "Everyday there are surprises and we have to change our plans. Today is like that. You want to choose your rider, well today we don't have a choice. Do you want to get the Spaldings and the lamp oil for Ruston?" Race blinks and nods his head. "Right, we all do. This nice young man has said he will get what Ruston needs. Papa and Samuel are gone. I can't leave—I don't know Spaldings and the chores here aren't finished. If you are to do what Ruston has asked you to do then you must work with this young man ....," Grandma's words trail off as she turns to look at Chat and asks, "By the way what is your name?"

As Chat rather blurts out his name, Grandma never flinches as she turns back to Race and finishes, "You are to fly for Chat, just as you would for Jason. Do you understand?"

Yes, he does. He may not like it, but he does understand. And so he puts his head down and steps up to Chat, who braces himself but doesn't step back and run. With the sky-top's face right up next to his, Chat hears a deep grumbling sound followed by a series of clicks and a few grrrrrrs which ends with a quick jerking nod. It would be nice to know what he said

Grandma watches this performance with a funny little wrinkle in her forehead, just like Hunter has when he's thinking. She knows she's heard Chat's name before and wonders, just wonders...... then choosing to be positive she says, "Thank you, Race," and pats the side of his neck. "Take good care of him now, just as you would Jason. I'm counting on you. He's a nice boy and he's doing us a big favor." For a moment Grandma stands with hands on her hips looking from Race to Chat, and a delightful little sparkle comes into her eyes and she smiles a funny little smile as she says, "I somehow have the feeling this errand today is very important, so do it well."

Race eyes Chat a moment and Chat is sure a decision is about to be made and steps forward and touches the big bird's long neck, while a myriad of thoughts crowd his worried mind. Deep clouds of regret and sadness envelope him for a moment as he considers the possibility of Race's refusing to take him up. Gently he strokes the leathery neck and whispers, "I won't let you or Ruston down. Give me a chance to try."

Race squawks a funny sound and reaches his proud head around and touches the boy's shoulder and makes a big sigh before sinking to the ground for Chat to step into the saddle.

Moments later Chat stands in the stirrups as Race makes a running leap into the air. This is a monumental moment for Chat. After weeks of suffering he feels free and needed. He wants to shout for joy as he feels the powerful wings beneath him lift them from the ground. Looking back he sees Grandma standing watching with a hand shielding the sun from her eyes. Taking a deep breath he thinks of Hunter and wants to make a "Hunter Yell," but doesn't, and wonders if he's too old for foolish shouting. So instead he waves and shouts, "Thank you," feeling better than he has felt in a long time.

The two wild sky-tops glide easily beside him and he is fascinated with their beauty and the ease with which they slip through the air. Wingtip to wingtip they fly and occasionally the birds click and cluck back and forth, and Chat wishes he could understand. For a moment he sits in heavenly silence enjoying the cool wind on his face, and every motion beneath him. A very few minutes later they slip out of the sky at the Spalding home and find Al with a broken leg and learn that Mel is in town doing something for Doc Hanlin. In the hopes Ruston would call for him, Mel had packed before he left, so with Mel's things loaded on Scooter they bound into the air and head for town.

Ruston needs two good men ... two good men ... Two, and Mel is only one, Chat's thoughts bump around in his mind. With a slight detour they land again, this time in front of his home. He's rather sure there will be no one at home and hopes he will be able to do what he intends to do and have no one see him. *Yes, yes, yes, I'm alone! Everyone is off doing other things.* He slides to the ground and invites the birds into their almost large enough barn and shovels out feed for each bird and is delighted with their enthusiastic gobbling.

Leaving the birds in the barn he hurries to the house and throws together a duffle bag full of clothes, and bedding. He scrawls a quick note to his father, and stands for a moment looking at the note he's just written. It's the first words his father's will have had from him since he'd come home with Ruston and Bert. What will his father think he wonders? How will his father feel? A flicker of sadness creeps over him as he places his note where his father will be sure to see it, then hurries out to the sky-tops.

A few minutes later they are back in the air and Chat has a smug smile on his face. Ruston now will have two good men. Oh, how he hopes Ruston is pleased.

Town and lamp-oil are the next stop and as he looks down on the busy little street he sees people pointing up at him and remembers how he has longed to land in town just the way Jason and Hunter do. This is a special moment for him.

If the truth is to be known, landing in the street in front of the hardware store is excellent medicine for young Chat. The thrill of the flight and the trust granted to him by Ruston's mother has brought color to his pale cheeks. He's forgotten he hasn't uttered a word in weeks and once on the ground, seeing the startled respect in the faces he sees gathered around him gives him a new kind of confidence. As he steps down from Race's back he remembers Ruston's words, *you gain respect by setting a good example and by serving, never by force.* Ruston needs help, his mother needs help—Chat rejoices as he realizes he's serving them in what he does. Standing a little taller, he breathes the words, "I will not let them down." Then, doing his best to copy Ruston in his every move, he cares for the sky-tops, hoping to set the right example.

Sky-tops with spurs and helmets are new to most of the town's population and Race and his friends are nothing short of spectacular. Their spiked helmets gleam in the brilliant sun and their spurs with their knife edges cause everyone's eyes to bulge.

"Chat, what are you doin' with Jason's sky-top and why the armed guards?" a friendly voice asks, and Chat looks around to see who's asking.

"I'm running some errands for Master Lynn's mother. She's here for a few days and sent me to town to find the Spaldings and to pick up some lamp-oil." Giving Race a firm pat he moves off through the crowd and adds, "And the armed guard is just that. The sawtooths are on the prowl and Master Lynn won't let anyone fly alone anymore." He repeats Grandma's words.

Chat and the sky-tops have created quite a stir in the pleasant little community. We must remember the whole town has been a-chatter about Chat and his mental illness. Everyone's been told he hasn't said a word in weeks. Now here he is riding Race, Jason's sky-top, and asking after Spaldings just as if he was as normal as can be.

"He must be working for Ruston." Oh, how tongues can wag.

Now they learn sawtooths are on the prowl, and the Lynn sky-tops are dressed for mortal combat and last but not least, Chat is supposed to be crazy and sick in the head, but he surely doesn't look crazy. At this moment he looks as cool and efficient as Jason. Just look at him working with three armed sky-tops and doing errands all by himself. Ruston wouldn't trust just anybody with his sky-tops.

While the town gossips, Chat purchases the lamp-oil and a bushel of apples. He's very wise in his purchases and odd as it may seem, the apples are an excellent insurance policy. He hopes to secure a positive relationship with the birds. We can call it bribery or a peace offering, whichever, for both are appropriate.

A small crowd gathers and watches as Chat shares his apples. "Gulp—slurp," the apples are gone and the big sky-tops smile and beg for more. No one has a clue, two of the sky-tops are carrying saddles for the first time and have never ever had an apple before. As Race slurps his juicy apples he decides Chat may be all right after all—still he'll keep a close eye on him, just in case.

So it is off to Doc Hanlin's to find Mel, who is ready and wants to go right this minute. Too bad for Al, he'll have to wait and help next time. Mel keeps a steady stream of small talk going as he adjusts his harness and pats Scooter, all the while not knowing Scooter is totally new to this situation. But Race clacks a constant flow of instructions and Scooter clicks and is careful to do exactly as Race tells him. Mel's enthusiasm has an interesting effect on the situation. Chat feels his spirits lift and lift again. This man hadn't challenged or asked him why he was riding Jason's sky-top. He's just glad to be going. He seems totally ignorant of the fact Chat was supposed to be crazy and his big hearty voice is most welcome.

Doc Hanlin steps out a moment and seeing Chat on Jason's sky-top is more than a little surprised as he asks, "What's up, Chat?" and is pleased to hear Chat answer with absolute sanity.

"Master Lynn needs a couple of good men to help with his sawtooth trap and I was sent to pick up the Spaldings and run an errand at the hardware store." Chat swells with pride as he speaks and Doc Hanlin wonders what has happened in the past few days to create such a miracle. *Just what I thought, not a thing wrong with this boy.*

Scratching his head, he ruffles his white hair and mutters to himself, "So Ruston is going to do it, and Lettie is going to let him." He chuckles in pleased approval. "So he needs a couple of men and Al is out," he speaks a little louder, then he asks, "Mel, how are you with the flying?"

"Taint nothing like flyin'," Mel answers as he finishes tying down his things. "I go every time Master Ruston asks me—I'll go anytime-anywhere." He grins and heaves a happy sigh. No need to ask how pleased he is to be going.

"Chat, give me a few minutes, I think I'll just leave a note for my missus and come along with you. Ruston'll be glad to see us. You bet he will. I've been thinking about his trap for as long as he has and I wouldn't miss this for anything."

Doc is good to his word and in very little time his duffel is loaded and asks, "Son, where do you want me? I'd as soon ride with you if it's permissible. I don't recognize these other two sky-tops and I've never ridden alone."

So it is, a boy and two good men take to the sky and head for the sky-top cavern and Project Sawtooth.

Chapter 17

THE TRAP

The evening shadows grow long and dark as the sun's light fades from violent reds and oranges, into burgundies, plums, and soft purples. It is as if a velvety deep blue cloak has settled over the landscape. Everything is so still, even the night chirpers are reverent as the evening turns to night, and the first stars appear. Hunter stands looking over the canyon watching the changing shadows and light. He munches a tasty brownie and there is a wee bit of chocolate dripping down his chin and when he tries to wipe it off, it smears leaving a chocolaty streak. As he licks his fingers a strange sound hums from somewhere and he jumps wondering which way to run.

"It's okay, Son," Ruston speaks softly as he steps out of the shadows and joins him. "The bats living in the cave make the strange sound. Listen, you can hear them—they are close now. In a few seconds they will come swooping out of the big hole right in front of us."

Ruston places a reassuring hand on Hunter's shoulder and whispers, "Shhhhhhhh ....," as a shifting cloud of bats spew from the cave's depths. They swarm in a wreathing black mass before slipping over the edge of the cliff and disappearing into the canyon's dark depths.

"Man, that's creepy—do they come out every night?" Hunter asks.

"Every night that I've been here," Ruston answers. "They sleep all day hanging from the walls in some remote part of the cave. Your grandfather and I have looked for where they stay during the day and haven't found it yet."

"Where do they go at night, I mean?"

"They have to eat, so every night they go down into the forest where there is a lush banquet waiting for their tiny stomachs."

"What do they eat?" Hunter is a little concerned and wants to understand.

"They eat all kinds of little insects. If I knew how I'd invite a few to come live in our barn. They would help keep the mosquito and fly population down."

Hunter considers his father's idea and isn't sure he likes it. All those little creatures were more than a little spooky. "I don't think I'd like to be in the forest with them swooping all around," he comments. "So they only come out to eat at night, just like the sky-tops?"

"That's right, only I hope after tomorrow the sky-tops will be able to come and go at any time, day or night and not have to worry about being safe," Ruston pauses as he and Hunter turn back toward the shelter beneath the rocks. All is so dark and peaceful. Pausing, they stop at the large hole and peer into its depths. It's quiet now, the bats are gone and all is still. Ruston studies his son and with a gentle finger wipes the chocolate from his chin. He's rather serious, but Hunter doesn't notice.

"I was really proud of you this afternoon. Could you tell Chat was afraid of how we would accept him?" Ruston watches Hunter's expression in the pale moon light.

"Dad, you didn't see him the other day in the newspaper office. He looks a hundred times better than he did when I saw him then. He might have been scared of us, but he wasn't near as scared of us as he was of his dad when I saw them together in the news paper office." Hunter looks up into his father's face hoping he will understand.

"I'm afraid you may be right," he pauses with a deep sigh then adds, "Regardless, you and Jason are real troopers to accept him and I'm proud of you both—but I need to ask if you've forgiven him?"

"You told me forgiveness is complete when you've forgotten all about it. Well, I haven't forgotten Chat, but I'm not mad at him anymore—I just feel sorry for him. And I have forgotten all about our fight except when somebody brings it up. Of course I remember then. Is that good enough?"

"What about your dreams at night when Chat would come to poke your eyes out?" Ruston hopes all this is past.

"I only dream now about Chat crawling and running and it makes me want to help him. I don't like those dreams either." Hunter considers a moment then continues, "I don't know if my forgiveness is right, but there's no mean spot inside me anymore."

Ruston gives Hunter a tender squeeze around his shoulders and tells him, "Then, you've passed the test."

A soft melody floats toward them as Hunter returns his father's hug. The evening air sighs with a heavenly violin lullaby and they turn to join the rest of their family.

"Jason likes your violin," Hunter smiles a little smile.

"Yes, I don't blame him—I need to get a better one for him," Ruston gives Hunter's shoulder another little squeeze as they disappear into the dark shadows of their base camp.

The gentle notes take a sudden turn as Jason steps up the beat into a lively jig that gives the night a festive feeling and Hunter bounces a little skip. "You need to play for us Dad, I feel like dancing."

"Let's dance to Jason's music first. How will he learn if we don't let him play?"

"Right, but it's more fun when Jason dances too. He's so cool."

Jason sees them coming and with a few quick notes, a foot stomping melody beckons. Hunter gives a delighted yell and grabs his mom, and with a whoop and a holler the stomping begins. Laughter, singing, and a whole lot of silliness fill the stone shelter on top of the sky-top cavern. The fire blazes giving a red warm glow to the walls and creates dancing shadows.

Where is Chat? He's right in the middle of them. To look at him you'd never guess there had ever been a problem. When Race touched down on top of the sky-top's cave earlier that afternoon, Ruston had scarcely believed his eyes, and when the boy slid to the ground he was right there. Before either of them had a chance to think about what they said or did, Ruston had bundled Chat into his powerful arms and hugged him in a crushing embrace. With deep emotion he managed to say, "I'm so glad you've come."

In wondrous relief, Chat had stammered, "I came to apologize, I need to tell Hunter I'm sorry."

Hunter and Jason were there too and heard Chat's words, so as Chat and Ruston stepped apart, Hunter grabbed Chat with a bear hug exclaiming, "Its okay, you're forgiven." Ruston then pulled both boys to him and whirled them around just the way he had when Jason and Hunter were little. With one arm around Chat, Ruston held him close as Jason stepped forward with an outstretched hand of friendship. Pulling

Jason to him, Ruston held the boys together for a moment while Doc and Mel watched with silent knowing smiles.

The relief felt at this moment is beyond our understanding. Forgiveness is a beautiful thing, and until it is complete there can be no lasting joy, or real peace. Lettie had watched from the shade of their rock shelter wiping stubborn tears from her eyes. Mel had looked over at Doc and whispered, "I'd a not missed this for anything," and Doc had nodded in agreement.

To help ease through those first awkward minutes, Ruston had insisted Jason take everyone on a tour and explain the sawtooth trap. Now there is a tender little glimmer of a smile on Ruston's face as he watches Hunter cavort around and dance with his mother. Doc Hanlin cuts in and swings Lettie around and they clap and stomp and Jason fiddles away. With a whirl, Lettie grabs Chat as she goes by and Hunter and Old Doc cavort together. Mel is content to sit to one side, but he's stomping and clapping as the others whirl in every direction. With a gleeful whoop, Ruston steps in and steals his wife. He is so proud of his family's acceptance of Chat and their willingness to befriend him. The relief felt by all is beyond description. Yes, Hunter has passed the test.

A warm swelling fills Ruston's soul as he dances with his family in the remote setting. *Hunter has overcome the mean and mad streak he's had in his heart for Chat and has actually experienced some compassion.* Ruston contemplates the changes he recognizes in his sons and knows, *Jason and Hunter are both better, stronger young men because of the whole situation.* He knows the possibility of growth without adversity is all but impossible. *The boys have gained considerable strength of character because of this.*

Imagine Chat's determined fear as he contemplated what the Lynns might do upon seeing him arrive riding Race. Would they accept him? Would Ruston permit him to stay—would he teach him as he had said he would, once he apologized? Imagine his feelings as Ruston took him into his arms. If ever there had been a way to erase the feelings of being unwanted, rejected or hated, Ruston had chosen the most effective. Words sometimes can't express quite what Ruston's embrace expressed so easily.

After the shock and the relief of those first moments had passed, a whole new vista of hope and opportunity opened before Chat and he hesitated, wondering if he was to be truly included. At first he'd been unsure and almost afraid to take part. So it is as he dances and enjoys a

213

physical release—through a good stomping hoedown—that his heart fills with gratitude, excitement and a certain amount of wonder as well as genuine relief. This family's unconditional acceptance of his apology and their happiness at just being together is an unbelievable experience for him.

In the few hours since his arrival he'd been hugged, told he was wanted, complimented, and accepted into their circle. Now they are dancing and singing and carrying on, and more than anything, he wants to make a "Hunter Yell." When Ruston suggests Jason dance and he fiddle, Chat is amazed to hear the music this man, who flies sky-tops, builds bridges, and is able to stop a bad fight without so much as raising his voice or seemingly to lift a finger, is able to create. For a moment he watches Ruston and his precious violin. With a little shout Jason grabs him and spins him around and the stomping becomes livelier. Growing more and more adventurous, Chat tries some of the ridiculous steps Hunter and Jason are cutting round him—he doesn't want to think about what his father would say if he could see him now. When Jason turns a flip right in rhythm and comes up stomping with a delightful clicking rhythm between his heels and toes, he decides he doesn't care what his father might think. *This is so cool.* With a grand right and left they weave in and out and around in an unorganized maze. Glancing toward Ruston as he fiddles, *Man, he can make that thing talk.*

A warm feeling fills his heart and soul as he remembers, Ruston had hugged him! His father never hugged him, never told him he loved him, never noticed him except to find fault. His father gave orders that only a fool would disobey.

At this point, years of pent up emotions are finding a happy release as Chat dances and steps to the lively melody of Ruston's fiddle. From time to time, Lettie tosses one of them a rich chocolate cookie. It looks a bit like a reward for fancy dancing. Tossing one to Mel, who sits watching, she motions him to the floor and he shakes his head with a comical grin.

When Blinky and Wings slip out of the sky in front of Home Base the shelter glows with welcome light, smells of home cooking, and sounds like a dance hall. Papa and Samuel hope there is a little food left and time for them to dance a step or two. A little while later Ruston shuts the party down and bedrolls are spread over their dance floor near the fire.

Early the next morning Hunter raises a sleepy head and wonders what time it is. A deep roll of thunder vibrates deep and rich around him, and looking out under the edge of their shelter he sees rain and more rain. Sheets of it envelope the landscape and gives the morning a cold dismal feel. Studying the various bed rolls he finds Jason, his mother, and Chat. For a moment his eyes linger on Chat's sleeping form, *He doesn't look like a mean bad person at all. No, and last night he'd been pretty cool.* With a little sigh, Hunter is glad Chat had come. Then with a little smile he rolls out from under his warm covers and staggers out close to the edge of the shelter; he wants to watch the storm.

It's a wet soggy morning.

***

At this very moment many long miles away, Arnald Dixon has just found Chat's note and is in a bellowing rage. His housekeeper flees the premises hoping for serious distance between herself and her boss. She doesn't want to be blamed for Chat's disappearance. Her tender heart pounds as she runs round the barn, past the tool shed and on into the orchard where she plops down on an old stump and tries to calm herself. After a moment her breathing eases and she tucks her wispy gray hair back into her bun, all while hoping no one has seen her escape. She'd seen Chat's note and knew Master Dixon would be in a terrible temper. She should have left then, but she hadn't. Now she fears his temper and waits to see what her boss will do?

We must remember Arnald Dixon has not heard his son speak one word since the day he'd attacked Hunter, and when he read Chat's very brief message stating only—"I have gone to help Master Lynn and I don't know when I will be back. Chat"—Dixon explodes in an adult temper tantrum.

Rather than give Dixon some degree of comfort, the note infuriates him. His color has gone from white to a deep smoldering red, with blotches of purple—if it's possible for one human being to send steams of smoke into the atmosphere, then Arnald Dixon steams with fury at this moment. Chat is at Lynn's and he intends to put a stop to this at once. While his alarmed housekeeper watches from the trees he saddles his fastest horse, and whipping it into a startled run, he bolts down the country road heading for Lynn Farm.

Grandma Lynn is no dummy—she had a glimmer of what was afoot when she realized who the pleasant young man was with the tired eyes and reluctant smile. So when Arnald Dixon's lathered horse gallops into the quiet courtyard she has a fiendish little grin on her pleasant face. She has wondered if this man would come and if he came, what he would be like.

As Dixon's horse comes to a trembling stop in front of her, she is shocked at the livid temper she recognizes in Dixon and finds herself backing up, and glad to have Dexter beside her with his teeth bared. Dixon hurls rude questions from his horse's back and Grandma politely answers.

"No, Chat isn't here—he went with Doc Hanlin and Mel Spalding to help Ruston. And no, I don't know exactly where they are or when they will be back."

Grandma stands with her hands resting on her hips and watches him fume.

"How can you send a boy off and not know where he's going?" he challenges.

"I didn't send him off, he asked if he might go and said he'd told you where he was, and Doc and I thought it an excellent idea," Grandma explains.

"Where have they gone?" Dixon asks again, his voice vicious as he steps down from his saddle and moves toward her with clenched fists, and Dexter steps between them snarling with his hair standing up on end.

Breathing a silent prayer, Grandma steps back and answers, "Master Dixon, the sawtooths are a serious threat to all here in the valley, and Ruston has found their nesting grounds. He plans to trap them and cannot possibly hope to accomplish this alone. He sent a note asking me to send the Spaldings to him, and Chat happened to be here when Race arrived with the note. Chat said he wanted to help and went to find Spaldings for me. I needed the help ... why shouldn't I let him go?"

The look on Dixon's face is a mixture of disbelief, confusion, and anger as he interrupts, "He was here, he came HERE, and he talked to you?"

"How else would he have known I needed some help? He was most polite, he came to see Ruston and when he learned I needed help he was most willing."

"He talked to you!"

"Of course he did—why shouldn't he?"

Dixon isn't given the opportunity to answer as Scamp and Princess bolt into the courtyard heading straight for Grandma. Their wings whip about and the large-little birds make a terrible fuss as they crowd close and beg to be petted. Grandma is very happy to have their company and is even more pleased when Patience rounds the end of the barn and joins them. Patience doesn't need to growl and snap to make a person stand back and be respectful. Size tends to be intimidating, and right now Grandma needs to be a little more intimidating, and since she isn't physically capable, she is most happy to have Patience fill this need for her. Feeling properly fortified, she calls Dexter to her and gives him a gentle pat, "It's okay big fellow—Master Dixon isn't a problem." Then standing a little taller, she introduces the birds to Dixon, who can't believe what he hears.

"Master Dixon, this is Patience and these are her two youngest, Princess, and Scamp." When Patience nods her head and gives a series of clucks as if to say, "Nice to meet you." Dixon backs away from the giant bird and almost trips over the rough cobble stones wondering over the mental condition of this woman.

"Now, as to Chat and where he is, although I can't tell you, Patience knows exactly where he is and can take you to him if you like. All I can tell you is they went to a cave in the mountains northeast of here and won't be back for several days."

"Several days! That's kidnapping, I'll have you arrested." He steps toward her raising his fists and Patience acts instantly. With a quick nip she has Dixon off the ground dangling in her beak. Dexter lunges and snaps at his feet while Dixon franticly kicks and yells obscenities. Scamp is quick to act and pulls on one leg, and Princess sets up a terrible screeching racket.

"Careful, Patience, you mustn't hurt him.....be gentle, don't squeeze," Grandma lays a firm hand on Patience's leg and has to bite her lip to restrain a bubble of laughter that threatens to get the better of her. "Set him down now nice and slow and if he moves you may pick him up again—and Dexter you behave yourself." Although Patience doesn't understand every word, she's gotten the idea and lowers Dixon to the ground while keeping a firm hold of the back of his shirt. Grandma makes a quick lunge and grabs a hold of Scamp and tries to cool his savage little temper. He hisses and strikes at Dixon in an alarming manner while Princess screeches and bounces about and looks like a very excited mad swan—a rather large blue swan. Imagine being pecked to death by an infant sky-top.

"Much better, thank you Patience, easy now children, stay back Dexter," Grandma does her best to soothe the situation, "This man has a very rude way about him and I wonder what we should do with him. He's apt to be a real nuisance." She studies him a moment or two and decides he doesn't look so good. He looks as though he has lost a bit of his bravado and might be willing to be nice about the circumstance now. His color isn't beet red any more, it's changed to white-white with red splotches and the arrogant posture is most definitely been reduced to a nicer level of submission.

Oh, Grandma, be careful. You are going to laugh and that wouldn't be nice at all, she gives herself very good advice.

"I think we can get along much better now if you can manage to restrain your temper. I am most happy you are here and would like very much to be of assistance." Grandma backs up to square one and starts all over as if nothing of a negative nature had happened.

Taking a deep breath Dixon tries to pull himself together then asks, "How do I get to this cave? Just tell me and I will go and bring my son home."

"There, that is much better. Politeness is better than anger any day of the week. Anger can get you into all kinds of trouble." Grandma gives a pleasant little smile while shaking her head and continues, "The last time Chat was here he was angry and I think he learned it was a painful waste of time." Grandmother has no idea Chat's father hasn't the foggiest idea what she refers to.

"Chat came here and was angry?" Dixon pulls against Patience's restraining hold and tries to be calm.

"Oh, not yesterday—he was fine then. It must be over two months now since he came with that Dorf friend of his, you know that big fellow, anyway they had a terrible fight with my grandsons up by the cliff."

Dixon's temper causes spasms that make him sort of jump and twitch. He makes a little frantic jump toward Grandma and Patience snaps him from the ground again. Things aren't going at all well for Arnald Dixon. Patience's beak runs over his left shoulder across his chest and down under his right arm. His chin is against Patience's shiny black beak and he fully understands the power resting easily within her great jaws and twitches with uncontrolled nerves. There is a great battle going on inside of him. Part of him wants to fight and scream terrible things, and another part of him knows if he does, Patience might decide to snap him in two—not a nice thought! While his legs dangle in the air he battles between fear, anger, and the desire to relax and be pleasant to this most unusual lady. It is with relief he sees Grandma motion for him to be lowered. People who have hair trigger tempers have a serious problem. While one part of him wants to strangle Grandma, the other part of him wants to understand what she has just told him. It's sort of a conflict of interests. So it takes him a second or two to get himself under control and able to speak in a gentlemanly manner. "What fight?" he finally manages to sputter.

"Well, I can't hope to see how you could have missed it, unless you were gone for several weeks. All four boys had black eyes, lumps all over their heads and bodies, and poor little Hunter's hands were a bloody mess. Remember, or are you too busy being rude to nice folks to notice when your boy comes home with a purple face and welts all over his body?"

With a funny jerk, Dixon calmly asks, "Please tell me more about this fight, indeed I thought he'd been thrown from his horse."

"Master Dixon," Grandma has a gentle little spark in her green eyes, "horses don't usually walk around on people's faces and that boy of yours got hit hard in the head several times. His nose was smashed, his lip split and both eyes were near swollen shut by the time he left here."

When Dixon makes no comment and just stands there looking rather perplexed and strange, Grandma continues. "It seems he was mad at Hunter for some fool reason and came with Dorf to beat him up. He followed him up to the cliff and when Hunter was alone went after him, only he hadn't counted on Hunter being difficult. So in the middle of their battle, Hunter's big dog came to the rescue—this one right here—then Jason showed up and he and Hunter had your boys about whipped by the time Ruston got there. It was ugly, Master Dixon, and Ruston was going to come straight to you, but Chat talked him out of it and said he wanted to tell you himself. He did not want Ruston to talk to you. Chat was supposed to report back to Ruston as soon as he'd done whatever Ruston had asked him to do." Grandma pauses and studies the large frustrated man standing before her and decides he might be a handsome man if he could manage a pleasant expression.

Pride is ugly, many times as ugly as the expressions of anger or hate. The look of frustrated submission she sees is many times more appealing physically as well as spiritually. She takes a deep breath and moves Patience a little to one side. Then asks, "What is it you do to Chat that would make him afraid to tell you about what happened here?"

When Dixon doesn't answer, Grandma can see he has come to his senses. He no longer twitches and his face isn't all blotchy, and his fists are no longer clenched. He looks as though she has just hit him in the pit of his stomach, not once but several times. The awful angry light has gone out of his eyes.

The two of them stand together in the morning sunshine and Grandma finds it in her heart to feel sorry for this big brute of a man. In the silence, Arnald Dixon manages to relax and after taking several deep breaths his arms hang limp—he looks totally beaten. Raising his eyes to Grandma's he asks, "How may I go to my son?"

"Sir, there is only one way I know of and that is for a sky-top to take you." When Dixon turns and looks at Patience, Grandma interrupts his thoughts, "Yes, she could take you, but I don't think it wise to send you off alone with her. You haven't made the best impression and no telling what she might do."

Dixon gives Patience a more serious look with his brows knit close together his thoughts bumping from one extreme to the other.

"I'll tell you what we need to do," Grandma decides, "I will take you to Chat myself, providing Patience is willing and these children promise not to get into trouble. I'd better shut them in a stall and make sure they can't get out." Grandma is positive as she dusts off her apron with a funny little gesture she makes when she's made a decision. It almost looks as though she's washing her hands of the situation. "Yes, this will work splendidly. I'll go and put some food together and you must go on into the barn and put your horse in a stall and give him a nice rub down. You may help yourself to the feed and grooming equipment."

Only a little time later Patience makes her run for take off and Dixon hangs on for dear life while wondering if it's too late to change his mind. He wants to cry and curse all at the same time. His hands feel as though they might rip the strapping right out of the saddle. Every running stride is pure torture to his poor bouncing body—yet the little lady in front of him hasn't even quit talking! *How can she talk at a time like this?* Then all of a sudden things are still. The huge wings whip and

220

surge and seem to cover an acre of land with each sweep and they rise. Looking down, he watches the farm buildings grow smaller and smaller. The heavenly air is cool and gives his frenzied mind refreshing relief. The joyous freedom felt while floating effortlessly upon gentle currents of air is beyond description. Patience's wing span is enormous and her carriage light upon the air. Unbelief is followed with awe and divine appreciation for the experience, and Arnald Dixon has a spark of sincere, reverent appreciation. Relief floods over him as he settles down into the comfortable sheep skin saddle and begins to ponder what he has learned about his son from the little lady sitting in front of him.

***

While this strange pair fly through lovely sunshine to find Chat, the clouds lift and the sun begins to peek through and warm the steaming landscape over the camp at Bert's cave. It is time to set the trap and Hunter is told he and Queenie are to retreat to a safe place underneath the base camp shelter.

"Is everyone in place?" Ruston shouts down into the cave and hears the muffled answers of his father and Samuel from the depths below.

"Everyone's ready. All except for you," Lettie gives him a rather serious smile.

"You know what you and the boys are to do?" Ruston looks at his wife and sees the hint of worry in her eyes.

"I do. Everything is set. Chat and Jason are at the far hole, with Doc. They have the arrows and the lamp oil, the lanterns are lit in the tunnel, and I have the pot of coals to light the arrows with me."

"Hunter and Queenie are under the rock shelf and know they are to stay out of sight?"

"Yes, they are there and know they are to stay there. We are all ready—we've checked our countdown list several times. Now go, and Ruston take care of yourself. Remember, I don't want a life without you."

"I love you Lettie, and I will come back. God willing we will win this conflict."

Topper swoops down from his look-out position and clacks a warning and Hunter shouts to his father, "The sawtooths are coming and Bert's leading them."

"Give the alarm ..." Ruston shouts over his shoulder as he leaps into Race's saddle. No time for flying, they literally drop from the top over the edge and duck into the main entrance below. "You there, Dad?" he shouts up into the hidden cavity at the top of the cave's opening and hears his father's answer.

"I'm here—you'd best hurry. I've got one of those feelings we haven't much time."

"Careful of your shadow, Dad, we don't want to scare them. I'll be right up." Ruston is pleased, the lanterns light the passage with just enough light. Stepping from Race's back into a crack in the wall he tells Race to go on through and to wait for Samuel behind the last barricade. Race hesitates a moment watching Ruston climb up onto the high crevice before trotting on through to find Samuel and Mel.

The trap is set. The minutes of waiting seem long, and Hunter is impatient. He wants to go out and look up at the sky—he wants to see; he also wants to shoot a few fire arrows with Jason and Chat. From where he sits, he can't even see them crouched next to the far hole. He knows they have little cover—and that's not good. Hunter understands their position offers a clear shot at the oil soaked targets, and that's why they have to be there.

Hunter has a little wrinkle in his forehead as he thinks about the front barricade going down, and the fact he won't see it or know when his mother has handed Jason the first fire arrow. He won't get to see Jason's shot or the huge piles of firewood begin to burn. *Jason and Chat are going to have all the fun.* Hunter wishes he could see over the brush and the mounds of endless rock. *I can't see anything from here!*

Topper searches the sky from a partially covered position at the front of their rock shelter and with a startled little cry he trots in under the cover. Turning around he gives Hunter a few clicks before reaching his head and neck back out from under the rim and watches the sky again. Queenie hesitates then snakes her long head and neck out with her brother. Hunter wants to see what they see, it's frustrating to have to hide and not see anything at all.

A distant call comes, a shriek and Hunter recognizes Bert's big voice. They are almost here. Again a call and Hunter can't stand it and runs out of his cover and looks back over the canyon. Queenie grabs him and drags him behind some sheltering bushes, very near the large hole—there's no time to make it back in under the stone shelter. Bert and the sky-tops are coming in fast and behind them, not too far back are .... are way too many sawtooths. *How will we ever stop so many?*

Hunter's heart pounds and he's afraid he might scream and covers his mouth, and closes his eyes. *Get a grip,* he tells himself and tries to look again as the first of the sawtooths dip down toward the entrance after Bert and the other sky-tops. A sawtooth's scream makes Hunter jump and want to run. They are so close. They swirl round in the canyon way too close to where he and Queenie hide. They are a literal mass of whipping wings filling the canyon in front of the cave entrance. Hunter watches with frozen fascination and can see the sawtooths' powerful jaws and their deadly teeth as they dart back and forth vying for a turn to land through the narrow opening. There are fewer of them circling in the canyon now and he can hear the commotion coming from the cave beneath him. He knows they have to be down there—some of them are anyway. Their noise is awful. Screeches and shrieks echo up through the large hole and he wonders if any of them are in the main cave yet.

His curiosity gets the better of him and he begins working his way through the bushes toward the near hole. He scoots and crawls to the brush covered opening then leans over the edge and peers down inside. Queenie makes frightened little soft cries as she takes a hold of his shirt and crouches over him. It's not as easy for her to hide as it is for Hunter and their situation is not good. She cowers in the bushes trying to be inconspicuous while Hunter stares down into the hole where he can see a number of sawtooths milling about in the big cave. For the moment they seem more interested in the cave than in the handful of sky tops standing in a far back corner. Most of the sky tops have gone on out through the dark back tunnel past the second barricade. As Hunter strains to see, he watches two sawtooths circle round the fire wood and stand near the waterfall. After a little pause they dip their fierce noses into the pool. For a moment Hunter has a glimpse of Bert and the others and wonders why they don't move out into the tunnel. The second barricade won't go down until Bert goes through, this is the signal. *Why doesn't Bert go on out?* Hunter wonders then decides, *Bert must be waiting for the other sky-tops to go out—he won't go out until they are safe.* Leaning farther into the hole he searches the dark interior to see if there are any more sky-tops besides those at the back door with Bert. Queenie whines and pulls on his shirt, but Hunter doesn't notice. He sees two young stupid sky-tops in a dark corner watching the sawtooths. He wants to shout at them, *get out of there you idiots,* but nobody has to remind him to be quiet. Right now his heart isn't near quiet enough to suit him. It bangs against his ribs and he places a hand over his chest hoping to slow it down.

The minutes pass and sawtooths keep coming into the main part of the cave. There are so many of them, if there are many more, it's going to be crowded down there.

A sawtooth stops right under the hole and looks up into the light and Hunter shrinks back. For an awful moment their eyes meet and he is very glad the hole is very deep. The sawtooth bellows a horrid challenge just as a huge sawtooth explodes into the cave and screams with a deafening roar. The other sawtooths gather around him and echo his fearsome roars. The ground trembles with the sound, and Hunter covers his ears and is glad to see the sky-tops hurrying out the back door. The monstrous sawtooth looks around him while snapping and screeching a steady awful sound, then sees Bert, who waits for the last of the sky-tops to get out, and charges.

"Go Bert, run," Hunter screams, but no one hears him.

Bert shoves the other sky-tops ahead of him and they disappear into the dark hole with the sawtooths coming fast. They leap the piles of dry fire wood and with very little room for error, Mel swings his huge ax and the barricade crashes into place. "They're safe," Hunter whispers to Queenie while his heart pounds and he hears another booming crash that tells him the front barricade is down. *The sawtooths are trapped! We've done it!*

The fierce creatures slam into the barricade snapping and shredding bits of bark and splinters from the logs, and Hunter is afraid the barricade won't hold. A flaming arrow hits the pile of wood in the center of the cave and the flames sputter then spew into life. Flames dart along the oily paths. Several more fire arrows light the wood farther back in the cave. An arrow sinks deep into a sawtooth and it turns shrieking a piercing cry, another arrow, and another, Jason's and Chat's arrows rain down upon them. The big sawtooth that started the charge, his neck and back are now a pin cushion of arrows, turns and snaps not knowing from where the arrows have come. Looking across the tangle of brush hiding him, Hunter can see Jason and Chat with their bows. Then sees his mother hand Jason another fire arrow and wave her hands as if telling Jason something.

Down below, behind the back barricade Samuel and Mel listen to the sawtooths trapped on the opposite side. Again and again the wall of logs jerk and crash against the beams and the ropes holding them in place. Peering through a crack, Samuel sees a sawtooth bite a vicious portion of a log and is glad to see an arrow sink deep into the creature's neck. Samuel drops down next to Mel and shouts over the noise, "The fire's started. It's going to be an inferno down here pretty quick." He pauses with an excited smile, "So, let's get out of here."

"Come on, Mel," Samuel shouts over the deafening noise. A sudden crash booms through the tunnel and they look to make sure the barricade has held. "Let's get the second barricade down and see if anybody else needs help."

Up on top everyone is relieved to know there are no sky-tops in the main part of the cave. They all made it out. A little color has come back into Lettie's face and she even has a tiny smile.

Hunter can't help himself and runs to his mom and gives her a hug, "We did it, Mom, we did it."

"Yes, we have, but Hunter, it's not over yet. What if the barricades were to break?" seeing the look on Hunter's face, she gives him a little squeeze. "Now we have to hold them and pray the cave is hot enough."

"The front barricade is taking a terrible beating, better put another arrow into that dry woodpile near it," Doc shouts. "I hate to think what would happen if it went down."

Chat is quick and sends a flaming arrow into the pile of wood and grins as Doc says, "Well done."

"We're about to have company," Doc waves as Race, with Samuel and Mel, skims the ground toward them. He lands light and easy, then drops to his knees as Mel slides to the ground.

"I've brought you some help," Samuel shouts above the noise, "I'm going on down to bring Rus and Papa back up," and is on his way the instant Mel is on the ground.

"Samuel says you'll need help covering the holes," Mel speaks as he takes up a tarp and carries it toward the smoke filled opening. Then glancing down into the inferno, he tries to see and leans closer, "Oh, my stars—how many of them are down there?"

"We've been wondering ourselves, it's hard to get a count with them all running around like they are," Lettie waves the smoke from her face as she speaks.

"You can see the heat is getting to them, look, some are in the water." Mel considers then adds, "The smoke will finish them if they manage to endure the heat. So let's cover this baby up."

"Jason, a couple more arrows into the sawtooth at the front barricade," Doc suggests. "He's slowly tearing the thing apart. Pepper him good and see if you can move him, then let's close 'er up." Doc takes the end of Mel's tarp and starts spreading it out.

Seconds later Race touches down next to them with Ruston, Papa and Samuel.

"Has anyone seen Bert?" Ruston asks.

"He and that sky-top, Patches and several we don't know are all down at the back door with the young armed sky-tops. Looked to me as though they's havin' some kinda argument. Bert's mad about somthin' He'll be up in a few minutes, I'd imagine," Mel answers as he and Doc prepare to close off the hole.

"We'd best be watching—two of the sawtooths got away. We waited as long as we dared to put the barricade down, but they wouldn't go into the tunnel. They're out here with us somewhere." Ruston comments as he sees Bert flying toward them.

"Mat, I want to go after the ones that got away. They've seen us and I'm sure they will be back. They may have gone for help. Do you want to go with me?"

Samuel doesn't bother to answer. Wings and Blinky are right on Bert's heels and as they touch down, Samuel heads for Wing's saddle with a wild grin. Ruston turns to look at his wife and gives her final instructions, "... so when the tarps are tied down get back in under the shelter and make sure our sky-tops are out of sight here with you." Ruston pauses to look at his smoke blackened friends then gives them a triumphant smile, "You all are awesome! Hold tight it's not quite time to celebrate. Samuel and I will be back before you know it."

Lettie steps toward him with an outstretched hand, and Papa hurries to Blinky and steps into his saddle. Ruston blows Lettie a kiss and shouts to his father.

"Dad, you need to stay here and take care of things."

"You mean, and miss all the fun?" Grandpa has a distinct twinkle in his eyes and with a challenging grin he turns Blinky around for take off.

"Dad, this is not going to be a party. It's not your responsibility."

"No Son, it is my responsibility. Whenever there is a problem that threatens any part of my family, the problem is my responsibility to deal with." When Ruston starts to argue, Grandpa Lynn raises a warning finger, "So it is together we will end this conflict, and together we will defend our family."

The sky-tops fidget and bounce, wanting to take to the air, "I know you're impatient." Grandpa speaks as he gives Blink a firm pat on the neck. "Now, let's go up and make sure not one sawtooth gets away." Raising an eyebrow he looks at his son, so very much like himself in every respect, and gives him a challenging smile.

Ruston sighs and returns his father's smile, "It is together then?"

"Together," Papa answers.

"Together!" they shout as they simultaneously leap into the air with Samuel and Wings right behind them.

Chapter 18

THE BATTLE

Hunter watches his father and Papa disappear overhead and looks at Topper and wonders if he might dare. No one is the least interested in what he's up to and he whispers to Topper who clicks and agrees.

While Hunter wrestles with his decision, Chat stands to one side watching Grandpa Lynn and Ruston disappear in the distance, their relationship interests him—it's so different. Even under the stress of the situation each had been thinking of the other. Their love evident in all he's seen in the brief hours since his arrival. With a painful twinge he considers the men he might call heroes. Always he has thought heroes as being the men who slashed through the enemy with bloody swords, incredible shooting, and riding big powerful horses. A slow realization creeps over him as he realizes his imaginary heroes are as nothing when compared to this quiet pair of men. *Maybe, caring is what makes men into heroes*, for a moment he wonders. *Maybe, heroes become heroes because they have something to fight for?*

Trying to shake himself free of his thoughts he picks up a tarp and drags it toward the largest hole. Seeing him, Hunter's mind is diverted and he hurries to help, and together they try to stretch the tarp over the large opening. The heat and smoke billowing up out of the hole is immense and most painful to their eyes. They can barely see. They cough and choke all while trying to move out of the smoke's path and still get the tarp into place.

Seeing their difficulty, Jason grabs one end of the tarp and starts to pull it over the hole, when a horrible scream erupts from the cave beneath them. A sawtooth suddenly makes a frantic leap up through the hole, his fierce head reaches out toward them snapping in wild furry. Hunter falls and rolls backwards out of the way, and Jason manages to shove Chat to one side, while grabbing for his bow—but his quiver is empty.

"Get my arrows!" Jason bellows at Hunter who takes off at a run.

The sawtooth slips back into the hole then leaps again, this time its claws are right under his chest and he braces himself, trying to force his way through the opening.

"Grab that rope Chat, and rope him," Jason shouts above the roar. "We need to hold his head still."

Chat has roped many of his father's calves and prides himself in being very good, but calves and steers don't lunge and strike with razor teeth.

"Hold on, Chat, stay back and get the rope over his head," Jason shouts as Queenie bounds to his side. "Get back Queenie, stay out of the way!"

The savage sawtooth roars with rage, his deadly fangs raking the air around him as Chat waits for the right moment. "Don't let him get it in his mouth, he'll cut it in two," Jason stands off to one side wishing Hunter would hurry with his arrows.

With trembling hands Chat swings the loop round and round and for a moment stares at the thrashing body of the immense creature. It looks more like a flying reptile than any bird he's ever seen. Its huge clawed feet grip the rock and it gains a foot or two as he strains against the too small opening.

Taking the end of Chat's rope Jason shouts over the deafening shrieks, "Throw it over his head—NOW!"

Chat makes his throw and it's good.

"Hang on—we can't let it go slack. Hold him," Jason screams and the two boys throw themselves against the thrashing rope. With mighty lunges the sawtooth snaps and wreathes trying to force his way out, yanking his captors in every direction. Topper takes the end of the rope and sets his weight against the sawtooth. "Hold him Top," Jason shouts as he and Chat turn loose. "Chat, lets get another rope on him."

Chat swings a second rope over the thrashing sawtooth's head and both boys take up the slack and lean their weight against the violent pulls. The sawtooth increases his efforts and makes it a few inches farther through the opening.

"Queenie, come hold this one for us," Jason shouts and Queenie hurries to take the rope.

"What will we do if he makes it out?" Chat shouts above the roar.

"There's no way for him to make it through, his wings are holding him. I think they'd break before he'd make it out." Jason pauses with a little grin and chuckles, "At least he's blocking the smoke."

Chat gives Jason a funny look and is amazed at how this little punk kid can enjoy and even laugh at a time like this.

The sawtooth wreaths and tries to catch the rope in his teeth and Topper growls giving the rope a terrible jerk, and Queenie almost looses her grip as she braces on the opposite side.

"Chat, go get your bow. Go on, hurry, we've got him." Jason shouts in his excitement and places a hand against Topper hoping he can hold the sawtooth steady.

Chat sprints the short distance to his bow and arrows and brings them to Jason. "No, you shoot him, he's yours," Jason points at the sawtooth.

An excited grin spreads across Chat's determined face as he realizes what he is about to do. He shoots one, two arrows into its neck and still the creature has hardly weakened.

"Shoot into his open mouth, wait for him—don't hurry. You want it deep in his throat where it will hit the base of his brain."

Hunter's shrill yell reaches them, but they are too busy to notice as he races toward them with Jason's arrows. Lettie is right on his heels with Mel and Doc a little ways behind.

Taking one look at the situation Lettie grabs up Jason's bow and takes the arrows from Hunter's hands and gets set.

"Stop, Lettie! Don't you shoot!" Doc is there in time to take Lettie's arm and bring the bow down. "The boys need to do this alone. Don't spoil it for them. Get your bow set and cover them if you like, but try not to let them see you." Lettie turns to look at him, disbelief in her frightened eyes. "If we help, we ruin their victory. They've got him tied, they are out of his striking range—now cover them. They've almost won, let them finish this themselves."

As Lettie watches, the sawtooth begins to slip back into the hole, then finding footing in the roots around the edge, he surges up again, his head swinging about trying to reach the arrows in his neck, his screams deafening. Chat draws his bow and stands steady waiting.

"Now," Jason screams, and the arrow flies.

"I did it," Chat shouts as he watches the sawtooth jerk then collapse and slide back dragging Queenie and Topper with it.

Hunter gives an ear splitting yell, and bounces in a victory dance as the sawtooth takes a last struggling breath still clinging to the lip of the hole.

"Let go, we can't hold him," Jason shouts at Topper and Queenie.

As the sawtooth slips back through the hole, the smoke pours out and together the boys, with Mel's help, grab the tarp and shut the smoke back inside. The heat is awful. Taking a glance into the cavern's depth it is as though they look into the burning horrors of hell.

"Run boys, we've been seen," Mel yells above the excitement.

Jason is the farthest out and can hear the heavy whipping sounds of huge wings in the air as he makes a dive for the shelter right on Chat's heels. "Mom, you've got my arrows," he yells as he runs under the welcome cover. Less than a second later the head and shoulders of a sawtooth reaches under their retreat. Two more follow the first and their razor teeth grind and snap at the air around them.

Race, Topper, and Queenie are backed as far under the cover as their bodies will permit and are out of reach, but just barely.

Jason has his bow and stands waiting for a shot while Chat and Mel hurry to join him. From outside their shelter they can hear Ruston's voice over the roars of the sawtooths, Bert's battle cry sounds as the nearest sawtooth shudders going to it's knees, then turns from the shelter and whirls with blood streaming from the wounds in it's back.

"In the mouth, if you can," Jason shouts. One sawtooth goes down under their arrows and the third takes to the air. Rushing out to the side, well away from the still thrashing sawtooth, Jason looks up in time to see three sawtooths in the air diving and swooping around Blinky and Bert, his father and grandfather lost amid the great heaving wings. As he watches, Wings makes a dive at the body of one of the sawtooths, his deadly blades forward and ready. As he hits the blades sink deep and the two birds tumble together as they fall. Jason marvels as he watches—Wings is so agile. He seems to purposefully stay barely out of reach, teasing and tormenting the sawtooths. Jason watches as Bert and his father dive after the battling pair while Blinky and Papa circle and dodge amid two sawtooths vying for a better position.

"I can't stand it," Jason watches with his fists clenched, his body rigid with emotion, "They need help, there's too many of them, I'm going up," he shouts as he runs for Race. Chat whirls and bolts after him, and both boys hit Race's saddle at the same time. In a matter of seconds they are strapped on and moving.

"I hope you don't mind my going with you?" Chat asks after Race plunges into the air.

"The more the merrier," Jason gives Chat a devilish grin and adds, "We are much safer with two of us up here—Hunter and I learned that last time."

"Last time?"

"Yeah, we had one heck of a time of it. You watch our back side. They'll sneak right up on us if they can. You'd better tie you arrows down. When we roll upside down we don't want to lose them."

As they climb neither of them hear Lettie's scream, "Noooooo." She's tackled Hunter and is holding him down.

As Race gets closer to the battling birds, Chat keeps remembering Jason's comment about flying upside down and considers what he has done. Out of sheer impulse he is about to do something no sane man would do. Yet, here he is flying into combat with flying dinosaurs that have teeth—lots of very sharp teeth. He watches Jason leaning into the flight pressing Race for more speed with his eyes riveted upon his grandfather. *He's crazy—I'm crazy—he's doing this because he loves his dad and grandfather, why am I doing this?* Chat's mind is a whirl. *Why am I doing this?* Then, with slow realization he understands. *I'm doing this because it's right. They need my help, our help, and I'm not going to let them down. They are my friends and no real friend would stay down on the ground and watch.* Ruston had told him great men become great because they do what is right and what needs to be done, regardless of the consequences.

This realization is pure joy to his starved soul. You don't become great by beating up little kids, you don't become great by going to the gaming dens, or swearing, or cheating people. You don't become great by always being first, or biggest, or best. No, a hero is a hero because he defends all that is right and good. *No, no! Dad has it all wrong.* His soul screams with new understanding.

I'm doing this because its right and Jason and I might make a difference. I have friends now, real friends. Not just big bully friends. These people are different. Thoughts of courage and heroes fill his mind as they close on the sawtooths.

"They haven't seen us yet, Race. Go up over them—we've got to take one out. Blinky can't do anything while dodging the two of them."

Seeing them, one of the sawtooths turns and Race dives into him with his beak blade whipping. The sawtooth meets the blade head on as Race slashes then spins in the air stabbing forward with his spurs. The boys hurl backwards slamming into their harness and Race turns and rolls out of the way.

"Get an arrow ready Chat, put it under his wing in that little hollow if you can. Aim for the heart through that spot." Jason shouts while holding his bow ready and Chat clambers to recover from the shock of the turn's momentum. *How can Jason even think about placing an arrow?* he wonders, but isn't given much time to think as Race hurls his body into the sawtooth a second time, this time his spurs find their mark while his beak blade slashes at the head and neck.

"Let him go, Race, Blinky needs us quick." With a roll and a quick climb they are beside Blinky, who is too close to a whirling snapping sawtooth and is barely making it out of the way.

Those on the ground watch in spellbound horror as Grandpa shouts, "Keep that other one out of the way. Rake into his wings, I'll take care of this one." His words drift down to them and they watch Blinky as he makes a quick climb as if running then does what looks like an end over end and comes back into the chasing sawtooth, raking and slashing. The two fighting creatures roll and tumble, while Blink stabs with his beak blade then rolls away, giving Jason a good shot at the sawtooth's unprotected underside and the sawtooth falters. Race makes a leap through the air at the second sawtooth and lands, spurs first, on the sawtooth's back.

"Take him down Race," Jason shouts.

Looking back Jason can see his father and Bert darting back and forth doing their best to keep the other sawtooths off their back.

Moments later Ruston shouts, "Look out, Dad," as sawtooth dives at Blinky from above. Blink does an incredible roll with a mighty whip of his wings and the sawtooth misses and Grandpa pats his harness and shouts, "Good job, Son, fantastic harness." One sawtooth has blood running down his side in several places and seems to be weakening.

As Race forces the badly injured sawtooth to the ground he continues to stab and rip into the body and Jason sees the huge wings beneath them go limp and barely flutter as they fall.

"Don't worry about him, Race, he's done for. Let's get the big one following Bert." Making a fast turn, Race hurls himself forward to help Bert as another sawtooth circles up from below and shrieks as he charges toward the conflict.

"Look there," Chat grabs Jason's shoulder and points toward the sawtooth climbing beneath them.

"Where are they coming from?" Jason whispers through his teeth. "Dad said only two didn't go into the cave."

"This one makes five." Chat leans toward Jason and asks, "Where are the other sky-tops—the ones your dad gave the helmets and spurs to this morning, there should be at least six more of them up here with us?" Jason stands in his stirrups leaning off to one side watching.

Meanwhile from the ground Lettie sees the same sawtooth climbing toward the battle and whispers, "Where are they coming from—and where are the other armed sky-tops?"

With a frantic look around she runs for Topper, and yells, "Queenie, take care of Hunter." With a wild scramble she is up in Topper's saddle and he is already running. Hunter runs after them, but it's no use, he isn't fast enough and must be content to watch as his mother and Topper make the climb above them to where the battle rages.

The little group gathered on the ground watch with disbelief. Hunter is the only one able to relate to the battle, he alone knows what it feels like to roll and tumble in the sky barely missing a sawtooth's savage teeth and then to force the creature to the ground. He's done it and he cheers and screams and leaps about giving the impression of fighting an invisible battle there on the ground.

Doc Hanlin and Mel turn and look at the child, who looks as though he would charge bare handed into battle for his brother and his parents. Hunter warns and directs the battle all by himself, and both men feel something deep within themselves stir as they recognize the fearless love that binds this incredible family. Their hearts miss a beat as they see Race charge into a sawtooth, rake it with his spurs and then go end over end. They can hear Jason's and Chat's yells and marvel with startled realization, *they are cheering!*

"Those boys are incredible!" Doc can't help himself and yells for them with Hunter.

234

Samuel's voice barely reaches them and they hear him shout, "Hold him, boys, I'll take his wings off." Race sinks his spurs in the back and they hear the boys cheer again. They can scarcely bear to watch as Wings rakes the bird's wings and are relieved to see Race push free. They hear the echoes of Ruston's voice as he warns his father, and they see Lettie and Topper drop out of the sky and smash into a sawtooth's back moments before the sawtooth would have reached Bert.

The fighting birds separate and circle giving the impression of wrestlers circling for a take down. They shift and adjust their positions seeking for an advantage. Bert makes a sudden climb as if to get away and then with a quick roll comes around over the biggest sawtooth and all in the same motion drops, sinking spurs ripping and tearing then shoves himself away, pushing the wounded sawtooth, who turns on them and Ruston fires, a miss. Rolling again, Bert just misses the claws of another sawtooth and they can hear Grandpa's shouts. As Bert levels, Race makes a sudden dive and sinks his spurs into its back.

"We've got him now Dad, cover us," Jason shouts as they begin to fall with the wounded bird.

"Ruston, I'll cover Jason, you go give Dad some help," Lettie calls out to him.

Surprised, Ruston gives a quick look around and sees Lettie and Topper flying toward Jason as he and Chat take the sawtooth down. *Will I ever have control of this family?* His mind screams as he and Bert turn toward where Blinky and Wings battle for positions against one vicious sawtooth. For a moment Ruston watches Wings and Samuel, *They are insane—They fly too close.* Wings is a holey terror, slash, hit and get away.

Two sawtooths are headed straight for Race, and Lettie screams a warning and Bert makes a quick shift and dives, the speed incredible, smashing into one sawtooth with his spurs and raking the other with his beak blade. The screams are terrifying. Blinky manages to make it there with them, and Papa fires into the second sawtooth's soft belly as he rolls away, his arrow disappearing into the fleshy underside. Blinky makes a sharp turn and levels out, and Papa fires again making a nice hit. Two more wounded.

A strange noise keeps bothering Hunter and he decides he wants to know where it comes from. Moving to the lip of the canyon, he listens. *It's coming from down there somewhere.* For a moment he stares down toward the cave's main opening and the sound comes again. It rumbles beneath him, there is a pause then comes again, a deep rumbled banging—it sounds like logs banging together against the stone walls. Looking back where Mel and Doc are watching the fight he wonders if he should ask them to come and listen. When it comes again there is a banging crash followed by a roar and seconds later a sawtooth lunges out of the cave hurling himself into the air, then seeing the fight above him propels himself toward the fight.

The barricade, it's the barricade—it's come down and Dad's net didn't work!

"The barricade, the barricade it's down!" he screams as he runs. "Hurry Queenie, we have to stop the sawtooths from getting out!" Grabbing up an ax he thrusts it into a saddle bag and ties it to Queenie's saddle. Yelling at Mel and Doc, he tells them of the problem and without giving them a chance to argue, he and Queenie whirl around and head for the rim. As Doc shouts for him to wait and let one of them go down, Hunter yells back, "Queenie is too little to carry you and I know how to bring the net down, I helped Dad set it in placeeee….." And over the rim they go down into the cave with the sawtooths. Seconds later two sawtooths explode out into the air and rise from the canyon headed toward the battling sky-tops.

Down below, Queenie is mere seconds ahead of the sawtooths and she hears them coming through the tunnel in time to duck into one of the dark pockets near the cave mouth. Hunter flattens himself against Queenie's neck and together they peer out into the opening where daylight streams across the floor. The sawtooths bellow as they come out through the tunnel and Hunter is sure they will be seen and glad to feel Queenie scoot deeper into the depths of their hole. The fact sawtooths cannot see in the dark is most comforting. As the huge creatures leap into the air Hunter is down and running toward the smoke filled tunnel, with his bow and quiver over his back and the ax held tight in one hand, he scrambles up the side of the tunnel wall toward the shelf where the lanterns still burn.

"Queenie, they can't reach me up here. Go back up on top where you are safe," without looking back he disappears into the depths of the tall crevice running along the top of the tunnel.

Heavy moaning sounds vibrate from the tunnel and Queenie does a little dance of indecision. Listening she can hear Hunter's running steps—she doesn't like this at all. She bounces and whirls, one moment she wants to plunge off into the canyon and go back up on top the next she wants to help Hunter.

At this same moment four of the sky-tops that had been given the spurs and helmets early that morning slide out of the sky exhausted, battered and bleeding. They land trembling with their eyes on the skies over them where Bert and Ruston force a sawtooth to the ground. Bert slashes with his beak blade at the back of the sawtooth's head and Ruston sees the wings fail and they begin to fall.

"Let him go Bert, let's get the one that's after Dad." As they turn Ruston sees Topper and yells for Lettie to go back down. Moments later he and Bert lock with a sawtooth and fail to see another fast moving flying reptile coming up on their back-side. With a glance back, Ruston is barely in time to see Topper crash into the sawtooth and force it to turn. As it turns, Bert whirls and slashes into a wing as it whips by and severs the entire end. The bird shudders, and starts to fall. Topper does a roll over and rips into the other wing and the creature goes down with Topper right after it. Ruston watches a moment fully appreciating his wife. *That was too close!* He takes a deep breath as he watches Race join Topper in pursuit and knows the sawtooth they follow hasn't long to live.

The two sawtooths that have just passed Queenie and Hunter, climb steadily toward where Race follows Topper to the ground. In a matter of seconds they manage to trap Race between them. One makes a dive at Race who whips a quick slash with his beak-blade and severs the end of the sawtooth's nose.

"Get set, Chat we're going down and over," Jason warns, his voice echoing down the canyon as Race dives and rolls slashing the nearest sawtooth's wings then rights himself and rolls, spurs first, into the other one.

"Did that wing get you?" Jason shouts back.

"Not so's you'd notice," Chat yells while setting an arrow in place.

Grandpa and Blinky are closing in and Grandpa fires arrow after arrow into the two sawtooths. Both carry wounds now and draw back for a better position. Wings and Samuel make a dive at the nearest one, the one with the severed nose, and Wings' spurs penetrates the creature between the shoulder blades. With both feet on the sawtooth's back he rides it stabbing at every wing stroke, and then they fall and he lifts off into the air screeching his victory. Wings and Samuel do a roll back that almost looks like an end over end. Somehow Samuel comes up still with his arrow set and ready; they are right under a startled sawtooth who snaps as they go by, ripping into Wings' side and Samuel fires into the soft under-section of the sawtooth and it shudders and tries to move out of reach.

"Get out of the way," Ruston screams and Wings and Race slice the sky with their great wings and drop just as Bert runs his spurs deep into the back of the sawtooth, then stands on him, stabbing as they fall.

Swooping back toward base camp, Jason can see Mel and Doc franticly waving and shouting at them. "Chat, look—something's wrong down there. Look at them! Hang on—let's go see... and that's Patience with them—she's not supposed to be here."

Grabbing Jason's shoulder, Chat points, "Over there—look—those are the other sky-tops, where have they been?" As they swoop closer, they are able to see more clearly, "Oh, my stars, one of them's about ripped to pieces—look at him!" As they glide down they hear Mel's voice, "The front barricade is down, and Hunter's down there trying to fix it!"

Swooping up and over, Race drops onto the cave opening and disappears into the lamp lit tunnel.

Chapter 19

THE FRONT BARRICADE

The narrow tunnel vibrates with the deafening sounds of raging conflict. In the midst of the screaming bellows, Jason and Chat can hear Hunter's shrill voice. Rounding the last bend in the dimly lit tunnel they find a tangled mass of logs and netting barely holding a raving sawtooth. He snaps and wreaths trying to rid himself of the impossible layers of logs and netting. Queenie has one end of the netting and is braced for all she's worth against it. She shrieks and growls terrible sounds while yanking back on the net with all her strength. She can't quite hold him and as the sawtooth lunges he gains a few inches, then jerking Queenie off balance he manages to gain about a foot.

"Hang on Queenie, I've got to get one in his mouth, it's the only way." Hunter stands in front of the sawtooth with his small bow waiting for a shot.

Hunter doesn't know Race, with Jason and Chat, are right behind him. With panicky determination he holds his position. "Hold him still, I can't shoot like Jase does. He's gotta be still." Hunter screams and Queenie pulls harder against the netting—then Jason is there beside him, with Chat not far behind.

"Man, am I glad to see you!" Hunter gives his brother a quick glance and explains, "My arrows only make this fellow mad. See, he can't open his mouth big enough for a shot into his throat—the net is too tight over his nose."

"Under his throat in the soft spot right up at the very top," Chat yells as he lets an arrow fly. The sawtooth lunges as the arrow sinks deep, then thrashes toward them dragging Queenie with him.

"Good shot," Jason shouts and sends another arrow into the base of the sawtooth's throat.

"One more lunge like that and he's out'a there," Hunter screams over the roar.

"He's not going anywhere, I'm going to cut one of the ropes and let his head through. Chat, you be ready to put an arrow into the back of his throat—Queenie the moment his head comes through, you get back out of the way. Drop the net and get behind us—understand?" Queenie gives a little nod and Jason sets his arrow and asks, "Ready?"

"I'm set," Chat answers, and none of them realize Ruston and Arnald Dixon have come through the tunnel and are standing behind them. Ruston's bow is drawn and ready. The big powerful, Arnald Dixon stands weak and shaking as he stares—appalled at what he sees.

Jason's arrows zip through the air, slicing the taunt netting on the lunging sawtooth. When its head comes through, Queenie drops the snarl of netting and runs. As the sawtooth bellows with rage and lunges forward, Chat and Jason both shoot with beautifully aimed arrows into the terrifying mouth and throat.

"Get back! He's falling!" Hunter screams and turning, he runs right into Arnald Dixon, who scoops him up into his powerful arms and this, to Hunter is as bad as running right into a sawtooth. He's already distraught with frazzled nerves. He's been screaming and filled with adrenalin, pent up emotion, and anger. Add these to his sleepless nights with their terrible dreams, and everything explodes into a horrific crescendo. Hunter attacks with bare fists, feet, and claws. It is as if a savage wild cat has jumped right in the middle of Arnald Dixon.

"You can't be here! Go back—go away, we don't want you here, Chat doesn't want you here—he's happy when you are gone. You are a terrible, terrible man." These are some of the nicer things Hunter has to say as Dixon does his best to restrain the violent attack. While Ruston and Jason make sure the sawtooth is dead and check what is left of the barricade, Chat stands in shocked silence watching Hunter's dramatic display of hostility.

"Hunter!" a little late, Ruston's voice penetrates his son's hysterical tirade as he rushes to Dixon's rescue and snatches his son's small body away, "What has gotten into you?" For a moment Ruston keeps a restraining hand on his passionate son then asks, "Hunter, I can't believe you would do such a thing—what could have possessed you? I think you owe Master Dixon an apology."

Hunter's body heaves with seething anger, with his fists clenched he answers through bared teeth, "Dad, he treats Chat and everybody else like dirt, he thinks because he's rich he can push everybody around, and the whole town hates him. He told Chat to beat me up because I wouldn't let him ride on Topper with me. He told Chat if he was a man he'd beat me up because I'd beaten him, fair and square in our race. Then he sent Chat to that awful place and they locked him up because he wouldn't talk." Holding up a fist he shakes it at Arnald Dixon, "Chat told me about that place and no father ever has a right to do that. It's because of him I have nightmares." Hunter points at Dixon, his eye glaring, "it's because of him I see Chat crawling and trying to escape from HIM. He is the monster in my dreams." The words are yelled as loud as he can yell them. His face is contorted and he shakes with pent up rage. "He's not a fit father, I want Chat to stay with us, Jason and I would like him for a brother."

Hunter finishes and bursts into tears and Ruston pulls him into his arms. Silence surrounds them as Hunter sobs, "He can't have Chat, he can't take him home—I like Chat the way he is." His plea is muffled into Ruston's shoulder, but heard by all.

"Things are going to work out. Son, you have to believe they will. Arnald Dixon is a good man, he just doesn't know how to raise a boy. The fact he's here says he really does love Chat. Now you must apologize to him for you were quite awful—then we will all give Master Dixon a second chance." Ruston gives Hunter a firm pat on the back and turns him around to face his antagonist.

Hunter stares down at his feet, not wanting to look up. The lamps over the edge of the tunnel flicker, soon they will run out of oil and it will be difficult to see. Hunter doesn't want to look at Dixon, he doesn't want to apologize, what he wants is to plant a fist into the big man's face, but somehow he knows it wouldn't do any good. Except for maybe making him feel better for a second or two, then he'd probably feel really bad. With a sigh he decides he doesn't want to have to face that kind of consequence. Looking up he studies Arnald Dixon and notices he doesn't look near as mean and bad as he'd remembered him. Taking a few steps toward him he notices there are tears glistening on his cheeks. Extending his hand he sighs and manages to say, "Master Dixon, my father says I have to apologize for what I just did," Hunter sniffs and wipes his dirty shirt sleeve across his blackened and tear-smeared face. "I guess I really am sorry—I was pretty horrible and I don't like it when I disappoint my father." As Dixon takes Hunter's small hand, Hunter continues, "but I'd like to ask you to not be mean to Chat anymore. You can't tell him to beat people up. We hate that and it makes us hate you and Chat, and besides Chat's cool. Will you promise me you won't do that anymore—I don't want any more nightmares."

In spellbound surprise, Ruston and the others watch the drama before them. Hunter in his youthful innocence has managed to tell Master Dixon all the things Chat, Jason, and Ruston have wanted to say and he's done it in a manner no one else could have managed.

It is a heavy moment as Chat watches with great tears running down his face. He wants to hear his father's words, he wants to have his father love him, and be like Ruston Lynn. His young heart wonders, *is it possible?* He wants his father to promise Hunter he will make those changes, but is afraid to hear what his father will say.

After what seems a very long minute, Arnald Dixon shakes his big bullish head as if for a loss for words. Then looking down at his small opponent he answers through his tears,

"I promise to do as you ask. Today, I've learned of a number of mistakes I've made." He wipes his tears away and looks up at Ruston, "I thought I was teaching Chat to be a powerful leader of men. I didn't want him to do boyish things. Somehow, I got it all wrong." Shaking his big head he looks off into the dark space around him and explains, as much to himself as to those standing in numbed silence near him, "When Chat's mother died I never thought about what Chat needed. All I could see or understand was my loss—I was mad at the world. I was bitter toward everything, and I hated the men around me who had their wives, and were not alone. Chat has suffered because of my grief and anger." He stops with a choked sob. Tears run down his big face and with a tender whisper he finishes, "You told me you want Chat for a brother, will you come and teach me what a father is supposed to be like? I'm going to need some help."

"Yes!" Hunter shouts and yanks up and down on Dixon's hand "You bet I will, an' my Dad'll help too."

Suddenly Chat is there, and as Dixon crushes his son to him in the dark smoky tunnel, there are many tears of joy as father and son prepare for a new beginning.

Chapter 20

DEXTER FLIES

"Hold still Scamp, this is going to be so cool," Scamp and Princess arch their long necks over their backs as they watch Hunter wrestle with the double tree. "Now you two have to be really careful and do exactly what I tell you. We don't want to mess up Mom's buggy, she'd be pretty upset." Hunter pauses a moment to think about what his mom might say if she knew what he was doing, and a momentary flicker of warning crosses his mind. Giving his head a serious rub he reconsiders.

All of the other sky-tops are gone—some are flying the mail while the rest of them are back at the sky-top cave cleaning up the mess. It is a really bad mess, and frankly Hunter is glad to be left out of the activity. The sawtooths are all gone, every last one of them, thanks to Project Sawtooth. As for the six wayward sky-tops that hadn't been there to help when they'd been needed, they'd gone back to the nesting grounds to destroy any sawtooths that hadn't been caught in the cave. They thought they were tough enough to whip them all by themselves. That was because they had spurs and helmets. They'd won, but in the winning one of them had been killed, two were still too weak to fly while the three remaining are all battered and stitched up. It's a wonder any of them lived to tell about it. Doc Hanlin had had a time of it, with Jason, Hunter, and Chat cleaning up wounds, and Ruston helping with the stitching, it had been quite an ordeal. Bert and Blink had taken a few armed sky-tops back to the nesting ground and made sure the work was finished. Lettie told Hunter he didn't need to know the details, because they weren't pretty. All he needed to know was Project Sawtooth had been a success. As far as success goes, Project Chat had been a success as well.

The six wild sky-tops had thought they were invincible because they had spurs and helmets and this prideful thinking had gotten them into real trouble. *Confidence is a good thing, but it will never replace being wise or using good judgment, you have to think and act smart,*

Hunter can still hear his father's words. A sky-top had died because he hadn't used good judgment, and another one may never fly again. *They didn't think things out first—like Dad says, if you can't live with the worst, don't do it!* Hunter smiles a little smile as he remembers the advise. *Nope, they hadn't thought it all out first.*

These and other thoughts flit through Hunter's mind as he looks again at Scamp and Princess, who are now harnessed to his mother's traveling buggy. *What a kick!* He wants to drive into town. His mother is off at some neighbors and he's alone with Scamp, Princess, and Dexter. *Why not drive Scamp and Princess into town? What can possibly go wrong?* Giving a pleasant little nod he climbs up into the buggy seat and wishes he had reins. *Maybe this isn't such a good idea—I have no way of controlling these two.* He climbs back down and finds some lengths of old light weight rope and insisting the birds take the rope in their mouths he runs the lines back to the driver's seat and climbs in—things feel much better. Calling Dexter to jump up with him, he gives a little cluck and off they go. A gentle circle around the courtyard then out to the farm road.

Very carefully the small birds walk and chatter and clack back and forth to each other and then back to Hunter, who sits proudly guiding his handsome team. The buggy is light and pulls easily along the smooth dusty road, perhaps too easily. With a grin Hunter suggests they trot and oh, what a merry time it is. A long gentle hill is a bit of a problem because the birds are small and the hill makes them work, and this is not at all a part of their plan. A slight argument begins and Hunter is at a loss as to how to solve it. He doesn't want to pick up the buggy whip, which rests in its usual place, you don't spank a baby sky-top especially when you are smaller than the baby sky-top. When the buggy comes to a stop, both birds demand they be unharnessed and Hunter refuses, telling them they must take the buggy and him home. They stand in the middle of the hill bouncing and fussing and Hunter is ready to use the buggy whip when Dexter bounces out and proceeds to herd them just the way he would stubborn sheep or a cow. He nips, growls and snaps, and Hunter picks up his awkward reins and pulls them around.

"Now go home, and quit fussing, it's down hill, it'll be easy," Hunter shouts over the ruckus.

Yes, it's down hill and will be easier, but Hunter didn't rig any kind of breechen or strap to keep the buggy from running over the sky-tops, and there are no brakes! Sky-tops don't have a rear end like a horse and the usual strapping is totally unsatisfactory for a bird. Thus it is Scamp and Princess feeling the lack of weight begin to hurry toward home and Hunter bounces along behind and as the speed increases he tries to slow them down. When the baby birds try to slow down the now fast moving buggy runs right up against their tails giving them an understandable fright and they try to out run the buggy chasing them. Now they are moving at terrible speed and Hunter hangs on with genuine anxiety, while Dexter runs beside them barking and trying to get them stopped, but only makes things worse.

The turn into Lynn Farm is up ahead and they are moving way too fast to make the turn and not roll the buggy over. Hunter braces himself, pulling to keep them straight on the road.

"Go straight! Don't turn!" He yells and Dexter runs up front snapping and snarling and they swerve. Somehow Dexter gets them straight again and they run on by and it isn't until the next hill that Hunter is able to get them stopped.

This time he gets out and carefully unharnesses the two sky-tops, all while wondering how he's going to get the buggy home. Scamp and Princess are of no help what-so-ever. The moment they are harness-free they bolt, literally, for home leaving him to push the buggy out of the road all by himself. Piling the harness in the back of the buggy he then pushes it into the bushes where he carefully hides it before beginning his slow walk home—so much for a pleasant drive to town. Dexter gives moral support, but at pushing buggies out of roads and hiding them in the bushes he is rather worthless.

So it is Hunter doesn't make it home for almost an hour, and by the time he does, his good humor has about had it. Scamp and Princess are nowhere to be found and this makes him very nervous. Those two have a genuine talent for getting into trouble and he has been left in charge. *Things are not going at all well.* With a buggy to get home, two sky-top babies to find, and a garden patch to turn over and prepare for planting, he figures it's a bad, bad day. And whose fault is it? It's best not to point this out to Hunter—not at the moment anyway.

Tromping into the large barn he stands in front of a line of stalls wishing he didn't have to try and harness a team to the buggy all by himself. He knows how to harness the donkey cart, but a full set of harness on a team? *I don't think so. Man, I'm apt to get into more trouble.* As he leads the donkey out of the lower pasture he sees rimming the sky a familiar pair of wings, *It's Queenie, she'll help me!*

"No, Queenie, you don't understand—I want to get the buggy back here in its place before Mom gets home. We don't find the babies first! They aren't anywhere around here so they are off in one of the far pastures and will be fine until we get back."

A series of firm clicks tells Hunter, Queenie will find her little brother and sister first and then bring the buggy home, and off she goes. But it's not so bad because within the next few minutes Scamp and Princess march in front of their big sister into the center courtyard.

Moving a lightweight traveling buggy with three sky-tops should be an easy process—that is providing the sky-tops are getting along—but Scamp and Princess refuse to help and Queenie will not just move the buggy and leave well enough alone. Hunter and Dexter are on the point of going back for the donkey when Topper joins the party and thinks the whole thing is very funny.

"Will you quit laughing and help me," Hunter raises his voice at Topper who doesn't seem to pay any attention. It's quite a sky-top gathering in the middle of the road when Farmer Owen happens to come along and stops, wanting to know if Hunter needs some help. Topper is still laughing and Queenie is at the point of doing bodily harm to her younger siblings.

"Hunter, you mean to tell me the babies ran off with your mother's buggy?" Farmer Owen is incredulous and Hunter doesn't want to explain and yells, "Topper, PLEASE help me take the buggy home."

At this point compassion for his young master motivates Topper and he picks up the rope Hunter has drawn through the ring on the end of the tongue and moves the buggy a few feet. It works beautifully and with a little click and a chirp he trots off with the light carriage bouncing easily behind his great strides. Both babies bolt after Topper with Queenie making a racket close on their heels, thus leaving Hunter stranded in the middle of the road with Farmer Owen who is about to burst his suspenders laughing in delighted snorts.

Hunter wants to say, *It's not the least funny,* but manages to restrain himself.

"You seem to have lost your ride, young man, hop aboard and we'll see if we can keep up with that big sky-top of yours," he chuckles as he speaks. "I'd like to have seen those babies sneak off with your mom's buggy. That'd be a story to tell. What could they have wanted to do with it anyway?" Hunter is quiet; he has no intention of giving him any facts. Right now he's very glad he's the only one who can speak sky-top well enough for anyone to understand what really happened. It's true the babies ran off with the buggy, no one needs to know he had harnessed them and tried to drive them to town. He decides he will keep that a secret, and right now he hopes Topper will be careful as he makes the tight turn off of the farm road.

With the buggy back in place and the harness neatly arranged on the proper hooks in the barn, and the babies with Queenie in the south pasture, it is time to tackle the new garden plot his mother wants turned over for planting. Gathering up the necessary tools, Hunter thinks maybe he should have pressed to go and clean up the sky-top cavern. The day would undoubtedly have gone better. Today hasn't gone very well and he can't imagine the work at the cave being as bad as what he's just been through. *Still moving all those sawtooths out of the cave is a big horrible project, and Bert wants the cave clean. Bert's as bad as Mom about wanting things just right. Yah, and Dad wants the sky-tops happy so they won't all try and come here to live.* Hunter wrinkles up his nose and rubs the top of his head thinking, *I guess it would be gross to live with the dead sawtooths—yuck— and the mess the fire made was rather bad too.* He pauses in his thoughts, remembering what the cave had looked like when they'd opened it up.

It was nice of Dixon, Ugg! I can't call him that, Dad says it's not polite, Hunter stops in his progress toward the garden plot and corrects himself. *It was nice of Master Dixon to send a crew of his men to help with the clean up. Dad was really pleased.* Plodding on toward the allotted area, he plops the tools down and selects a nice round nosed shovel. *Dixon may be all right after all.* Hunter considers, completely forgetting his resolve to not call him Dixon. *School this fall will be so cool. Jason and I won't have to eat on the school steps, we won't have to stay close to the teachers until one of the sky-tops comes to pick us up, we can walk down the street and not have to worry.* He takes a deep breath savoring the thoughts. *The archery contest is going to be awsome too. Nobody knows how Jase or Dad can shoot. Chat might have a clue, but he's working with Jason and the two of them are really something. I wonder if Dad's right about there being a team archery contest at the Lakeland Fall Festival. Dad thinks we need to be a team, an' I wonder who Dad will pick as the fourth?* Hunter's mind goes off the deep end as he wonders. *I could shoot with them if they'd move the target up close—really close.* He gives this a thought and with a little laugh and a shrug he knows the team will be his father, Jason and Chat, and who knows who the fourth will be. It's nice to know his dad wants Chat to shoot with them. For a brief second the image of the figure he'd painted on the old target wavers in his mind and he remembers the arrows he'd viciously shot into the imagined Chat. *Things can really change. Dad tried to tell me we had to be nice even when we didn't want to be if we were going to make Dixons change.* He sighs wondering over the miracle.

Dexter interrupts his thoughts and trots toward him hoping for a rub. As Dexter's big wet nose pushes his hand into action, Hunter studies the stretch of grass he's to turn into a garden plot before everyone gets home. "Ug!" With a little shrug he attacks the sod and works down a straight even line turning over the rich earth.

Dexter watches and thumps his tail, *This might prove to be interesting.* Another line of turned over soil and Hunter's well into the project when Topper comes hunting for him. He watches the project a few minutes, then clacks a question.

"I have to get this done before Mom gets back. I think she was trying to keep me out of trouble, you know giving me something worthwhile to do."

Topper clacks and clucks with a grrrr and chirp or two and steps up beside Hunter hoping to distract him.

"No Top, we can't go flying until this ground is all torn up and soft. Mom wants to plant something here. You know how we plow and work the soil so we can plant your feed—you know, the pig feed you like so well." Hunter huffs and puffs all while working the shovel and trying to explain and Topper clucks a serious question, and Hunter looks up with a delighted grin. In a matter of seconds he outlines the area to be turned over and Topper gives a pleasant nod and with his great big feet he rakes along one side ripping the grass and the soft earth, his big toes are better than a plow. Getting the idea he goes to work scratching just like a mammoth chicken. He scratches and rips; he rakes with his beak and digs in with his great toes. He clacks as he scrapes and scratches, and the torn up area gets bigger and bigger. Hunter goes to work pulling the grass and the weeds out and Topper follows his example and pulls the weeds and grass out with his beak while his big feet chew up the dirt.

Dexter watches the two of them for a few minutes then strolls over to an area where Topper has ripped the earth to shreds and sniffs. With a little sniff here and there he finds a nice spot and begins to dig. He digs and digs and moves to a new spot. Everything smells so exciting when it is freshly turned over for his sensitive nose to sniff.

"Topper, we have to have the edges straight—I know Mom, she doesn't like anything ratty looking and this garden plot is a ratty shaped mess," Hunter studies their work and begins working his shovel to even up the edges. "If we want to make Mom really happy we will have the soil all crumbly and soft, so we gotta work on it a little more."

With Dexter digging, and Hunter, and Topper crumbling the fresh earth, the garden plot is transformed into something worthy of Lettie's praise in little more than an hour, and Hunter stands back with his hands on his hips looking at their work. "You're really something Top—that would've taken me the rest of the day. I might not have even gotten finished today. We've done really good work."

Topper clacks out a question and nods as Hunter gives him an affectionate pat.

"Let's do it—I have an idea of how I can strap Dexter on so he can go with us. He'd like that."

A little later Topper steps out of the barn carrying Hunter and Dexter, and this time Dexter looks as though he will stay securely in place. Hunter has put a horse halter on Dexter's front end around his head and neck, with his front legs through the back part of the halter. The throat latch is buckled around his body. A second halter holds Dexter's rear end, and his tail now sticks out where a horse's nose is supposed to be. All this is tied together and attached to the saddle's safety harness. The whole inventive harness contraption even looks rather nice, and Hunter is so pleased. Dexter now sits proud and tight behind his little master. He's secure in the rumble seat ready to fly.

A few running strides and Dexter is still there leaning into the wind, his big tongue slobbering at Hunter's ear. As the ride becomes smooth and they rise on the air currents, Dexter gives an excited little yip and Hunter reaches back and gives him a hug.

"You won't fall off now, I think we could roll and dive and everything and you'd still be there," looking back Hunter studies his harness and is very pleased. Dexter's behind is held firmly down against the sheepskin saddle and his big paws are dug into the soft fleece. He leans forward with his ears flying back, while his whole body quivers with excitement. He's wanted to do this for so long. Hunter is glad he will no longer have to be left behind.

Banking a graceful turn, Hunter leans back in his seat and they circle over the neighbor's house and he wonders how much longer his mother will stay and visit. *They'll talk 'till it's dark,* he decides and smiles as they glide over the place where her buggy had been hidden only a few hours ago. *I really need to think things out better before I do them. I should have known the breeching was important—otherwise horses wouldn't have to have them. Dhhh. Sometimes I do the dumbest things.* Smiling contently to himself, he looks back and gives Dexter a hug and can see his big tail going, thump, thump, thump against the back of their saddle.

"Dext, we've had a wonderful summer, and I did a few things right. I didn't let Chat whip me—an' I learned how to tame an enemy." This thought makes Hunter laugh a delighted laugh. "You know Dext, Dad was right when he said we have to be really nice and forgive and lift if we are going to get along with people. It really worked." He ponders a moment, a question filling his young mind, "I'd like to think I've become a real man," he pauses then asks, "Do you think I'm a real man yet, Dexter?"

As Hunter turns back to look, Dexter licks him right across the face and shakes his big head. Topper glances back making a funny sound, then gives his head a very negative shake. "You two aren't very encouraging." For a moment they rise on a heavenly air current and Hunter decides, "You're right, I'm not a real man yet, but I will be. One of these days I'll be just like my dad—I'll be a real man."

***

ABOUT THE AUTHOR

CaMary Wynne was born in Stillwater, Oklahoma, and grew up astride a horse with a paintbrush in one hand, and a pallet in the other. She never has been able to decide whether she'd rather ride or paint. After graduation from Monticello College and Preparatory School, she completed her education at Oklahoma State University where she met and married her husband, Lee Wynne. The couple is unique in their lifestyle in that their lives are rooted in training International Sport Horses and riders. Their horse-related enterprises have taken them all over the United States, Canada, and parts of Europe—giving them a broad spectrum of experience to work from—as well as a list of accomplishments within the Hunting, Jumping, and Dressage horse world. While Lee juggles business and a variety of investments, CaMary paints and writes with numerous publications to her credit. *Three Too Many* being her first novel, soon to be a major motion picture, with The *Women of Value* being the best known of her works. *Hunter and the Sky-Tops*, was written to go with a painting created for an imaginative grandson. He wanted a portrait of himself with a dinosaur. The painting created such a sensation there needed to be a story to go with it, and so *Hunter and the Sky-Tops* was written about a very real little boy.

The Wynnes have two children of their own, Russell T. Wynne and Thea W. Boden, and 17 "adopted" children. Most of their adopted children were teenagers having difficulties of one kind or another with life in general and needed a home. The Wynne's large combined family is now scattered, but the bonds remain. Their son, Russell, and daughter, Thea, have blessed their lives with nine delightful grandchildren. The Wynnes make their home in Grand Junction, Colorado.

ALSO BY CAMARY WYNNE

Three Too Many
A light western adventure and romance about the Pony Express
Gwyder Studio & Desert Moon Pictures

Women of Value—Their Works and Their Values
Eve, Ruth, Esther, Mary, Joan of Arc, Sacajawea,
Florence Nightingale, and Eliza R. Snow
Cedar Fort & Gwyder Studio

Captain Moroni - A Man of Faith
Gwyder Studio

Oklahoma Prairie Plowed Under
The Story of the Berry Brothers In Indian Territory
Co-authored with Camelia U. Berry
T.N. Berry Publication

Line Upon Line – The Keys of Social Success
The whys and wherefores of modern manners
Randal Book & Gwyder Studio